The *Pacific Affair*

A CHARLES LANGHAM NOVEL

The Pacific Affair

By Gary Paul Stephenson

LANG
BOOK PUBLISHING

BOOK PUBLISHING

langbookpublishing.com

Cover design by Blair McLean

National Library of New Zealand Cataloguing-in-Publication Data
Lang Book Publishing 2016

ISBN 978-0-9941290-3-1 – Paperback
ISBN 978-0-9941290-6-2 – Hard Cover
eISBN 978-0-9941290-4-8 – eBook
eISBN 978-0-9941290-7-9 – ePub

Published in New Zealand
A catalogue record for this book is available from the National Library of New Zealand.
Kei te pātengi raraunga o Te Puna Mātauranga o Aotearoa te whakarārangi
o tēnei pukapuka.

This book is dedicated to my wife, Davina, for her patience and love and everyone suffering from Multiple Sclerosis.

Table of Contents

Chapter One

The United Nations Meeting

Charles Langham stood at the lectern, looking at the large circle of United Nations members facing him behind their long, curved conference tables in the imposing hall. The lights were dimmed and the screen behind bright with images from his presentation. He was a formidable figure in an impeccable casual Saville Row blue suit that was tailored to fit his six-foot slim frame, slightly greying hair, deep brown eyes and clean-shaven face. His crisp white shirt open at the collar gave him a relaxed, cool look. Except for his wedding ring and watch, he shunned jewellery. He intended to come across more casual than formal to avoid looking overbearing to this politically motivated group. He also wanted the presentation to be the main focus.

'So, in summary, I will say this.' He leant forward with both hands gripping the lectern. 'You have seen the evidence throughout my presentation, irrefutable proof with photographs, videos and scientific reports showing the damage to our world and its people. We have extinction rates that are rising exponentially with 50 per cent of the world species forecast to die out in less than 100 years. Food gluts in western countries, while children die of famine in others. Rainforests, to which we owe our every breath, are cut down for palm oil and soy plantations which we do not need.'

He took a breath and looked around the hall. 'Ladies and gentlemen, whilst my company buys back palm oil plantations, mines, and large farms and returns them to the rainforest, planting millions of trees, and sets up aid in famine-stricken countries to help them grow their own food and develop species protection centres, world governments need to do more – must do more.'

Charles spread his arms wide as though to draw in the entire room. 'To legislate against the extinction of our flora and fauna, to legislate against fossil fuels, to drive out the corruption and greed that are endemic in our world governments where some rulers and politicians live in magnificent luxury whilst their populations starve!'

Some angry voices rose from the audience. Charles banged both his hands on the lectern – 'Remember! ... Remember! If you want to!' He let his raised voice stem the noise from the floor. 'Remember the world conference on poverty where members of this august group and their teams arrived in their private jets, stayed in five-star hotels and ate very expensive gourmet foods whilst hidden from the poverty around them by specially erected barriers.' He turned and raised one arm to accentuate the slide show that had just started showing pictures from the conference. 'Many of you were there, of course, in the name of ending world poverty. Christ, what was spent on that conference could have fed all the kids in that town for a year!'

The roar of voices once again rose from the delegates, many now standing. He raised his voice to get the attention of the room. 'So, I challenge the United Nations and the world leaders, here and now, to do something to stop this madness. You know my demands. You have one week to consult your governments. Talk amongst yourselves, and get back to me, or action will be taken until you do so.'

Charles picked up his papers from the lectern and looked at the stunned Secretary General. 'Mr Secretary General, I thank you for giving me the opportunity of presenting to you today. I will be on my yacht, waiting in anticipation.' Without as much as a sideways glance, he stepped away from the podium and walked towards the double doors at the front of the hall, escorted on either side by his two bodyguards who looked like Secret Service agents in their black two-piece suits, white shirts and black ties. Their ear pieces were visible only by the coiled wire that tucked into their collars. The noise from the delegates rose to a crescendo as they started talking amongst each other, some waving their arms.

Kim Lee Hoon, Secretary General of the United Nations, banged his gavel to try to restore order. 'Ladies and gentlemen, please, let's have some order. We need to discuss this in a mature and formal way, ladies and gentlemen, please.'

Charles looked at the room. 'Let's get to the yacht. I've had enough of this,' Charles said to his large bodyguards who stood near him menacingly. 'Get Max on the radio, and make sure the car's outside.'

One of the guards touched his ear and spoke into his sleeve microphone. 'Max, we're on our way. Get the car ready.' A few seconds later, he said, 'Okay, see you in a moment.' The guard glanced across at Charles Langham as they went through the doors. 'Car is out front, ready and waiting, sir, but Max says so are loads of TV crews and reporters on the steps, waiting for you.'

Charles Langham sighed heavily. *What do they want?* Charles thought. 'Well, we don't stop till we get to the car, okay?' Charles said as he put on his dark sunglasses.

'Right, boss,' they replied and edged closer to him as they went through the doors to the outside terrace leading to the steps which were crammed full of journalists, photographers, TV crews and state police. He could see the car at the base of the marble steps with Max waiting by the rear door dressed in a double-breasted black suit, a chauffeur's hat covering his short cropped black hair, his dark eyes hiding a ruthless past. Camera flashes and shouted questions from journalists and TV reporters made for a surreal scene. Ignoring it all, the three men descended the steps towards the silver Mercedes, Charles between the bodyguards. Before getting into the car, Charles Langham turned to the encircling crowd and quickly said, masking his face, 'Go to my company website, and you will see a statement and video of the information I presented to the United Nations today.' He got into the car, with one guard getting into the front beside Max and the senior guard getting into the back after Charles.

Charles sat back in the luxurious seat and pressed a button, and the seat reclined; pressing another button, he turned on the massage feature. *They are not going to do anything, he thought. They have all the information and evidence, and they know what they need to do, but they won't. They are gutless politicians.* He could not understand the reaction of the United Nation; surely, they should be concerned about the welfare of the planet, but they seemed to show the smallest amount of understanding that was appropriate and expected, and what were they doing, arguing it about amongst themselves? *We are going to have to force their hand.* That was the last resort. Although he had planned and built the necessary equipment to take action, using the very latest cutting-edge technology his company could develop, he had hoped, in vain, that he would not need to use it.

'Max, back to the yacht, and make sure all the cars are fuelled up and loaded on board, and while you are at it, check the helicopter. I want it ready to collect Anne.'

'Sure thing, boss,' Max replied over his shoulder. 'The Range Rover and Aston are both on board and fuelled, the bird is 100 per cent, just this one to top up. Are we leaving soon?'

'Yes, we're leaving very soon, but keep that to yourself for the moment,' replied Charles quietly.

'Hey, boss, have I got time to see this girl I met this morning? She is a real beauty, boss. You'd like her,' Charles and the guards laughed.

'Max, every time we are in port for more than a day, you meet a beauty!' said one of the guards.

'Unfortunately, once this thing is refuelled, I want you on board, getting the garage ready for sea, and I'm pretty sure the captain will have enough for you to do. Sorry, Max,' said Charles.

Without another word, Max closed the dark-glass partition and drove off. The car swung into the port and stopped at the security gate. Max showed the pass and carried on to the super yachts' berth.

'I'll drop you off and go top the car up,' said Max as he brought the car to a stop beside the super yacht. 'You're sure I can't go and see her, boss?' Max asked as he held the door open and Charles alighted from the car.

'Max, next time we're in port, you can, but I need you and the rest of the crew on board, ready to go.' Charles and the two bodyguards boarded the super yacht through the lower starboard gangway next to the open garage door through which the Aston Martin Vanquish and Range Rover could be seen.

The super yacht was a 185-metre sleek piece of design based on a sketch by Charles himself who also oversaw every step of the final design and build by the Italian shipyard that built her. With eight decks, she had everything on board suited to living life at sea, including a sophisticated communication and surveillance system, cinema, a galley more suited to a five-star hotel, on-board armaments, video conferencing, a seven-metre swimming pool next to the spa pool, Pétanque course, and a fully stocked wine cellar. Powered by four Rolls Royce engines, totalling 75,000 horsepower, her range of 10,000 nautical miles gave her true cruising abilities. Water-jet propulsion ensured shallow water capabilities, whilst sea water desalination, extensive galley stores, tool room and solar panels complimented the self-sufficiency that Charles wanted to achieve. With a full-time crew of thirty-two plus Max and the bodyguards who doubled as deck hands and waiters, she was a busy ship, but the size and space meant it was always quiet. Charles made his way up to the bridge to find the captain, first officer and the technical officer checking the vast array of dials and display screens.

'Are we in good shape?' he asked the captain, an intensely serious, tall, well-built man dressed impeccably in white slacks and a white shirt with epaulettes on the shoulders.

'Yes, we are fully provisioned and ready to roll as soon as you give the word. All the crew are on board except Max, of course,' said John Whitcome, the captain. John had been head hunted by Charles many years before to help him buy his first super yacht and recruit the crew to man her. They had flown from Florida to Monaco to Dubai to New Zealand in search of the right vessel. John had overseen the refurbishment and upgrade, and carried out all the interviews except for Martin Deeks, whom John had known and wanted as technical officer. Charles had left the design and fitting out of the bridge of *Sundancer* solely in John's hands, who had, in turn, left the engine choice with Mr Langham and Martin Deeks. The building of *Sundancer*, and the interaction that the three had, had brought them closer together. But when on the bridge, formality was the order of the day for John. He looked at Martin Deeks, the technical officer. 'Engineering has just reported everything shipshape, as was to be expected,' the captain advised, showing his finger was on the pulse of the ship, a habit from his Navy days. 'The fuel tanks are full, fresh water is topped up, and the spare fuel for the helicopter has been replenished as requested by Max.' He smiled.

'Good,' replied Charles. 'We will be leaving tonight. Tell the chef I will have my dinner on the sea-view deck at 6.30 pm.'

As he turned to leave, the captain asked, 'If you don't mind me asking, did the presentation go down well?'

'Not good, really. I think there are some there who truly understand and see the need for change, but politics raises its head and muddles their thoughts with...' He sighed and sat in the technical officer's sumptuous leather chair and continued, 'If they admit to their superiors that change is needed, their careers, salaries, expense accounts and pensions could be in jeopardy. The public will not like the changes to their lifestyle and tax raises; and therefore, they will lose votes. It's all about power and holding on to power. Real needs come second.' It felt good to get that off his chest. The captain was an astute person and one whom Charles saw as his second-in-command in the organisation.

'So we carry on with the plan, I assume,' the captain responded. 'Darn shame that politics has to come into everything. If only they could see past their lousy careers.'

'Join me for dinner, and we'll discuss our next move. I also need to get Anne out of the Amazon HQ,' Charles said as he stood up and left the bridge.

'Mr Langham, call on line 1. Mr Langham, call on line 1,' chimed one of the handsets on the helm. Charles stepped back in to the bridge, picked up the handset and pressed the one button.

'Charles Langham,' he said into the mouthpiece. 'Hello, Ambassador.' Then after a brief pause, 'Yes, that would be convenient. Why don't you join me for dinner at 6.30 pm? I'm dinning alone.' He smiled at the captain as he listened intently. 'They would be welcome, of course. I will see you all then, goodbye.' He replaced the handset and looked at the captain and technical officer. 'Interesting. The British ambassador wants to meet and, apparently, so do the New Zealand and Australian ambassadors. He indicated that the UN is split into three over the issues, those who want change, those who don't, and those who don't know what to do! So a stalemate in any vote there might be.' He grinned at the captain.

'Better make the chef aware that dinner is now for five people, and better lay on a good wine from the cellar and Remy Martin. I've had dinner with the British ambassador before, and he likes his cognac.'

The captain picked up his handset, then paused. 'I'll get the preparation for sea completed by six pm to avoid any questions from the visitors. Also, do you want the 747 on its way to the Amazon HQ? She's currently in Washington DC.'

'Yes, do that. I'll put a call through to Anne and let her know it's on its way. I will be in the library.' Charles left the bridge.

'Martin, go to all stations and get the sea preparations speeded up, and keep an eye on Max. You know what he's like.' He sat in his leather captain's chair, leaned back and pressed a button on the handset. 'Hi, chef. Dinner for five at 6.30 pm. All the trimmings. We've got UN ambassadors coming. Best wine, Colombian coffee and cognac on the sea-view deck. Okay, thanks.' He pressed another button, and after a short wait, 'Keith, John here. Charles wants the 747 on its way to Amazon HQ. It will ultimately rendezvous with us, so they will need some meals on board for the crew and Mrs Langham.' He listened while Keith spoke. 'Not sure on rendezvous location at this time. We can work that out as soon as we know the departure time from Amazon HQ.' He listened, deep in thought. 'I will leave that to you. We depart at midnight, and I get the impression that we will be at full noise until we are out of US territorial waters. Then we will cut back to twenty-one knots cruising.' He listened whilst Keith spoke from the company's Kermadec underwater headquarters in the Pacific Ocean North of New Zealand, then replied, 'Yes, we are headed your way. I will send our route later on. Bye for now.' He replaced the handset and looked at the large navigation screen and started planning the super yachts course.

Charles entered the library, situated on the same deck as the bridge on the sea-view deck, just behind the formal dining room. The room had expansive windows and shelves lined with books. Suede-lined ceiling with recessed LED lighting and a deep-pile rose-wool carpet gave the room a warm cosy feel. Two cherrywood desks and a large display screen recessed into the wall at one end of the room, and a high-back three-piece settee and armchairs to one side faced the display screen and cherrywood table in the centre. A keypad and mouse were recessed into each desk and table next to pop-up display screens. Charles removed his suit jacket and hung it on the back of a chair and sat down. He leaned on the desk and tapped at the keyboard whilst pressing an intercom button. 'Galley here,' said a voice over the speakers as the display screen tilted up from the deck, showing the face of a galley steward.

'Send some coffee and a cognac to the library, please,' Charles replied and let go the button. The display screen came alive, and his wife's face appeared on the screen, her hair ruffled. 'Hi, darling, good to see you,' she said.

'Hi, love,' he replied, touching the screen. 'It's been too long. The past two weeks have dragged by. The 747 will be on its way soon to pick you up. We're working on the rendezvous point now, so not long till we're together.' *She's gorgeous*, he thought. Her black hair had a tint of grey, and her hazel eyes showed a deep warmth and love; she never wore make-up – she did not need to. He could see she was in the open-plan office with people busy in the background.

'I can't wait,' Anne replied. 'Been busy here with the local Akuntsu tribes on the reforestation of the new sector. I should have time to go through the new area you've just purchased, before I leave.'

'That's not a bad area. The owners advised that they had only cut roadways and an area for the offices. The rest should be pristine forest, but not sure they can be trusted.'

'Unusual, but useful. Less work for the tribes. Don't want to overload them. They have well over a year of work ahead of them as it is.'

Max entered the library with a silver tray. 'Your cognac, boss,' he said as he put the cognac on the desk. 'Oh, hi, Mrs Langham. How you doing?' he said as he leant over Charles.

'Hi, Max, I'm fine, thank you, and how are you?' Anne replied, smiling. Max was one of her favourite people in the organisation. She liked his cheeky charm which was always present, no matter what the situation.

'Oh, I'm very good. Keeping busy as usual,' Max saluted the screen. 'Well, back to my duties. See you soon, Mrs Langham.' Max left the library.

Anne smiled on the screen. 'He doesn't change, does he? Still as smiley and as cheeky as ever.'

'He has got a heart of gold. I'm honestly not sure what I would do without him. He's part of the furniture and knows his way around places that I would rather not know about!' Charles agreed. 'So you get ready for the 747, and give me a call when you are in the air. Keith or John will contact the pilot and agree the rendezvous point.' In his heart, Charles wanted to fly to the Amazon HQ tonight, but that was off the cards, and he would now have to wait another twenty-four to thirty-six hours before he could see his wife again. 'I'll tell you more, but I have three ambassadors coming tonight – British, Aussie and Kiwi.'

'Okay, darling. I'd best get back to sorting the Akuntsu tribe out and briefing the team here before the plane arrives, and I still need to pack.'

'All right. Bye for now, and see you soon. Love you.'

'Love you,' Anne said and blew a kiss on the screen just before her image disappeared.

Charles picked up the cognac, moved to the settee and stretched out. The steward arrived with fresh coffee and placed it on the table beside the settee. Charles took in the aroma of the cognac and coffee and closed his eyes. *So much to do*, he thought. *I need to get more people on side to spread the word wider than just politicians. Greenpeace would jump on board, as had Sea Sheppard earlier. It's not really World Wildlife Funds usual area, but they might come on board in a small way. Every little helps,* he pondered. He remembered how far they had come since he first decided that throwing aid into famine areas did not resolve the problem. The people had to learn the skills to manage on their own in a sustainable way. He had decided to send specialist teams into those areas to teach the people how to help themselves how to dig wells and pump water. How to irrigate the land and how to sow crops and plant trees. His specialist teams stayed until the people had been taught how to maintain the equipment, do crop rotation, and manage by themselves. Only after a deep appraisal and a review with Charles himself did a team withdraw. He was deeply satisfied with how the morale of the people improved. With the great result of the first project, Charles had rested the team for a month before they were sent to their next famine relief project. Other charities jumped in to help, and soon there were four teams working full-time, keeping his luxurious A380 busy carrying freight.

Then Sea Sheppard came knocking on his door. John Houston, a big bull of a man with a large scraggy beard, baggy trousers, a tee shirt that had seen better days, and a denim jacket. 'Mr Langham, we desperately need more help to save the whales in the Southern Ocean. We have been trying for years but need to do more than we can resource ourselves.' He moved to the edge of the chair and placed both hands on the edge of the immaculately polished desk, looking intently at Charles. 'I appeal to you for help. Hundreds of whales will be slaughtered in the next season if we don't intervene. We need stronger, faster boats that can find the whaling fleets and effectively get between them and the whales, creating a shield.' He sat back in the large visitor's chair, almost filling it. 'You've no doubt seen it on the news, those dreadful scenes, so there's not much more I can say.'

With his fingers entwined and his chin resting on his hands, Charles thought for a moment. 'When does the next season start? How long have we got?'

'Just seven months,' John replied.

'I think we can adapt a boat design we've got, and we have a new tracking isotope that may help in tracking the whales and their meat if slaughtered. The isotope will tell us when the whale was killed – good evidence for you to use. But, and this is a big one for me.' Charles stood up, 'There can be no more aggressive actions. Everything must be done peacefully if you want our help and involvement.' He sat on the edge of the desk. 'So how does that sit with you?'

'If that's what it takes to get your organisation involved, you are on.' He looked intently at Charles. 'My people will agree if it helps to save the whales.'

Charles picked up his phone and dialled. 'Keith, I am sending someone to meet you.' He looked at John. 'His name is John Houston of Sea Sheppard. I have agreed to support their next "Save the whale" campaign. I think we can adapt the V20 design. Anyway, discuss it with him, and keep me advised.'

He hung up and called his secretary on the intercom. 'Please take Mr Houston to see Keith; he is expected,' he said when she entered the office.

'Thank you very much. You don't know what this means to Sea Sheppard,' John said as he vigorously shook Charles by the hand with his huge and calloused fist.

Charles opened his eyes after recalling how far he had come. In the intervening years, they had moved from being an onshore local operation to building a secret deep-sea HQ and working worldwide. Charles finished his cognac and looked at his watch. He had just time enough for a shower before dinner. He picked up his jacket, walked over to the glass lift and went down to his cabin where he showered and changed. At 6.15 pm Charles, dressed in a timeless three-piece dark-blue suit, entered the sea-view dining room to discuss the table layout with the steward. The room was dominated by a large polished cherrywood table and twelve chairs which sat centred on a Persian rug surrounded by parquet flooring. The table was laid with silver cutlery and cruets, cut crystal glasses, and fresh flowers in a cut crystal vase as the centre piece. The walls were cream with large floor-to-ceiling windows. LED lights, recessed in the ceiling and at floor level, could be controlled to give just the right amount of light and colour. A large display screen was recessed into the wall at one end.

Charles lifted each bottle of wine and checked the labels; New Zealand Chambourcin and a New Zealand Pinot Gris might upset the Australian ambassador. 'The wine is wrong. There are some good South African wines in the cellar.'

The steward picked up the bottles and left the room. Charles checked the menu. *Good selection of meat and fish. The chef has done a good job. Should please all tastes.* He went over to the entertainment console, dialled up the music menu and selected some quiet background music. He changed the lighting colour and the air-conditioning setting and, once satisfied, descended to the main deck. The evening was warm with a gentle breeze. A large dark sedan pulled up beside the super yacht, and Charles saw Max, dressed in a black suit with white tie, descending the boarding ramp to welcome the three men as they got out of the car and escorted them to the ramp. Charles entered the rear lounge and went to the electronics console and opened the glass dividers so the lounge opened directly onto the vast rear deck with its swimming pool, spa pool, outside galley, bar, barbecue, pétanque court, and teak tables and chairs. He turned on the deck lights, pool lights, mast lights, and the underwater hull lights. As he pressed more buttons, music came on and the lounge lights changed colour. The lift bell chimed, and Max guided the three men into the lounge and introduced each to Charles in turn before going to the bar to put a bowl of nuts, coasters, and menus on a silver tray and returning to Charles and the three ambassadors. 'Excuse me, gentlemen,' he said formally with a dip of his head. 'Where would you like to sit, boss?'

'Just over there.' Charles pointed to one of the teak tables just outside on the deck. 'Might as well make the best of the good weather. It's a lovely evening.' Max placed the coasters, menus and bowl of nuts on the table. Charles led the three men to the table and sat down. After Max had taken their drink and meal orders, Charles spoke, 'Well, gentlemen, I would like to officially welcome you to *Sundancer*. You are actually the first guests we have had on board since her launch four months ago.' He clasped his hands beneath his chin. 'I would like to give you a quick tour, but we have some sensitive areas below deck, so I can only show you what you see here and what you will see on our way to the dining room.' He paused while Max served the drinks. 'Thanks, Max. Now, gentlemen, shall we open the conversation on why you are here and asked for this meeting?'

The British ambassador, in a three-piece striped suit and college tie, spoke first. 'Well, Mr Langham, may I say that this is a very impressive vessel, almost a small town on the water.'

'Thank you,' Charles said with a slight nod of his head. 'She is my main residence, and most of the crew live on board full-time.'

'How large is she?' asked the Australian ambassador.

'She's 185 metres long and is mostly self-sustainable,' Charles answered.

'To business, I think.' The British ambassador crossed his legs and rested his chin in his hands, his bald patch showing amongst his grey hair. 'My government is very concerned about the state of the world as portrayed in your presentation which, if memory serves me well, is a collage of many things you and other environmental scientists have been saying for the past two to three years.' He paused. 'Please let me continue,' he said as Charles leaned forward. 'Needless to say, we have been campaigning for change amongst World leaders and have many initiatives under way, and my colleagues from New Zealand and Australia have and are doing the same.' Both the New Zealand and Australian ambassadors nodded in agreement. 'After your presentation, as instructed by my prime minister, I called him and spelt out in concise terms your presentation and the immediate reaction from the UN. He was duly gravely concerned and advised that I contact you and open a dialogue on what we, as in the broader sense of we, can do and achieve together.' He opened his hands. 'So here we are.' He lifted his glass from the table and took a long drink.

'I see. Well, I think we can discuss this fully over dinner and coffee,' Charles said amicably.

'Not forgetting your veiled or not-so-veiled threat,' the Australian ambassador said as a reminder to the group.

Charles smiled and raised his glass. 'Please, my demands, not threats.'

Max joined them from the lounge. 'The chef says he is ready when you are.'

'Good timing, Max. Gentlemen, if you would like to follow me, we will take the lift to the sea-view dining room, which is four decks up.' Charles pushed his chair back and stood up and led them to the lift where they ascended to the sea-view deck.

The ambassadors walked around the sea-view dining room in amazement at the sheer luxury and simplicity of the fitting, taking a great interest in the large number of oil paintings. The New Zealand ambassador peered through the solid wooden door into the library and whistled beneath his breath.

'That's the library, my favourite room on the yacht,' Charles said as he came up to the ambassador.

'And that's a pretty large helicopter for a private individual to own,' the ambassador said, looking through the glass wall that led to the helipad.

'Yes, the Bell 525 Relentless modified specifically for our use and to extend its range,' Charles explained. 'For convenience, we can service and refuel her on board, which is a first for any super yacht.'

Charles returned to the table and saw the captain being introduced to the ambassadors by Max as they took their seats. A dumb waiter chimed, and the steward retrieved the silver trays whilst Max serviced the wine.

'So, Mr Langham, may I ask how many crew you have on board?' asked the Australian ambassador.

'We have thirty-two full-time crew, but many have dual roles. For instance, Max is my chauffeur, pilot, and personal assistant. He can pilot this yacht with ease, but we have the captain who actually does that.' He tasted his wine. 'We have a range of over 10,000 nautical miles, and should anything happen, we have a workshop on board, so other than fuel and food, we are totally self-contained.' Charles let Max serve his main course of steamed sea bass. 'Gentlemen, forgive me if I start to talk business. Quite simply, I cannot see why world governments cannot do more for the welfare of the planet and its people. If my organisation can affect the reforestation of tens of thousands of acres of rainforest with the help of the indigenous peoples, why cannot the world governments?' He took a bite of his sea bass. 'My organisation has sent teams into famine-stricken areas not only with food but also with the equipment and personnel to help teach and educate the local populations on how to access water, irrigate crops, do crop rotation, and how to maintain and repair the equipment.' He paused and sipped his wine. 'Yes, it's time consuming, but at the end of the day, the local people become self-reliant.' He took another drink of his wine. 'But you know all this and more, so my question is, quite simply, if we can do it, why can't you?'

'It's about getting agreement across country politics as to what projects come first, who does what, where the money comes from, who is in charge, and who validates the work, going through diplomatic channels,' said the British ambassador.

'You see, that's what I cannot understand.' Charles sat back in his chair, glass of wine in hand. 'That sort of crap does not stop me or my organisation. We just get on and do. People are dying, CO_2 levels are increasing and species are dying out, while people play politics and grandstand to keep their power by looking good in front of their own electorates!'

'Well, it's not quite like that. We cannot work in another country without their permission, and I can say for one the British taxpayer would not like us spending money, which is very tight at the moment, on a reforestation project abroad whilst they want a new high-speed rail link.'

'But there is also a lot you can do in your own country that you don't,' Charles interjected. 'So tell me what your three countries can do to help or work with my organisation.'

'If we know what projects you have lined up next, with a detailed outline and budget, we can talk to our respective prime ministers who can then make a decision together on how we can either undertake the project ourselves or support you,' said the New Zealand ambassador whilst looking at the Australian and British ambassadors in turn.

'Once they have got agreements from their ministers and cabinets, of course,' said the British ambassador, frowning.

'We have four projects in the pipeline. Supporting Sea Sheppard. Controversial I know. We have more reforestation work in the Amazon and more famine relief and support in Africa. Drug elimination in Mexico and Brazil is something we have been asked to look into.' He leant back to let Max clear his plate. 'Thank you, Max. Tell the chef that was divine.'

'Could you explain the scope of those projects so we know a little bit more?' asked the Australian ambassador.

'Yes, of course,' replied Charles. 'First, Sea Sheppard, as you are no doubt aware, tries to save whales from the so-called scientific whale hunt by getting between the harpoons and the whales. Well, we are looking at upgrading the boats we supplied to them a few years ago and more up-to-date electronics to do the job. In Indonesia, we undertake lot of reforestation work by buying palm oil plantations and replanting them with native flora and fauna. In the Amazon, we replant what the soya and lumber industry takes, again with native plant and trees. In both cases, we hand the land back to the local tribes with the caveat that the native flora and fauna must remain protected.'

'And the local governments are okay with your activities?' asked the British ambassador.

'Very much so. The Indonesian and local Brazilian governments are very happy as we provide jobs and education for the local people and also assist in developing the self-reliance of the people. We also help them promote ecotourism.' He smiled. 'I am not sure what Japan will say if they found out we were supporting Sea Sheppard though.' He raised his glass with a smile. 'Time will tell.'

'Your famine programmes are well known, but drug elimination must be something new?'

'Yes, indeed,' replied Charles, 'And we have much more investigative work to do, but elimination of the plantations and cartels would be our aim, by whatever means we find is the best approach.'

'Sounds like it could be borderline legally, which could get you into hot water with the Mexican or Brazilian authorities?' asked the British ambassador, looking very serious.

'It could indeed, but whatever we decide is the best approach, we will conduct talks with the local authorities, but I do know that the Mexican and Brazilian governments are open to all ideas,' Charles responded casually.

'This is all well and good,' chirped the Australian ambassador, 'but what about your threat to the United Nations?' he asked.

'If the UN and world governments do nothing, then we will have to shake them to the core to get something done, and we are prepared and ready to do so.' Charles stood up. 'Coffee, gentlemen?' he asked.

'But what are you threatening?' asked the Australian ambassador.

'Time will tell. I will not divulge that at this time,' Charles said in a clipped tone.

Max handed out coffee in porcelain cups and saucers, Charles's favourite freshly ground Columbian coffee, while the steward served a selection of cheese and crackers on matching plates.

'Max, cognac for all,' said Charles.

Max poured Remy Martin for each person, served at the perfect temperature. The three ambassadors followed Charles into the library. 'Gentlemen, please do not get me wrong. My motives are clear. The world needs attention on a global scale to stop rising ice melts, millions from dying and mass extinctions. Governments are sitting on their hands, playing blind man's buff.' He drained his coffee and picked up his cognac and swirled it around the glass. 'Talk to your prime ministers, and while you are at it, tell them to talk to their counterparts, as from my point of view, the time for talking is over.' He drained his cognac.

'I see,' said the British Ambassador dourly. 'I understand where you're coming from, but diplomacy has its place in all this. We cannot just go charging off on our own.'

'Diplomacy is what has let these issues get to the poor state they are in. The Kyoto agreement took too many years to negotiate and then floundered,' Charles said in repute. 'We have not got another twenty years to negotiate another agreement with so many compromises that its effect is useless.'

'I think we can all agree on that, but our governments have diplomatic channels to go through,' said the British ambassador. 'We will discuss it together and talk to our respective prime ministers, but I will personally let you know their response.' He put his hand out and shook Charles's hand. 'I support your stand on the environment and hope we can get some governmental support.'

'Thank you, and thank you all for coming.' He shook hands with the Australian and New Zealand ambassadors. 'Max will show you to the jetty where your car is waiting.'

As the Group followed Max, Charles went to the bar and poured himself another larger cognac and looked at the captain. 'John, we leave at midnight. Prepare the crew and yacht. I want full power too till we get to international waters, then back off to cruising.' Charles returned to his cabin and changed from his suit to tee shirt and slacks, then made his way to the library and picked up a book and relaxed.

At midnight, Charles made his way to the bridge where Max was heading with a tray of freshly brewed Colombian coffee. The deck crew reported lines clear, and the captain touched the small joystick and guided the yacht away from the dock. The bridge was quiet and dimly lit with just a few recessed LED ceiling lights that had been dimmed and the glow from instruments and group of large display screens lighting the space.

'Radar is all clear, looks good for a power run,' the captain said to Charles, whilst concentrating on the Infrared camera screen.

'Port authority notified we're leaving?' asked Charles.

'Called them just before you came in. Did not want to give them too much of a warning. Thought a fait accompli would be the order of the day.'

'Good thinking,' said Charles.

Max poured coffee for the group of men on the bridge and one large one for himself. Besides Charles and the captain, there were the technical officer and first officer. The captain and first officer sat in their chairs, side by side. The technical officer sat in his bridge chair to one side. Charles and Max stood to the side. The captain had given up trying to pass his chair to Charles. The yacht quickly picked up speed as it left the harbour for the clearer waters of the Atlantic Ocean. Charles watched as the speed slowly increased to thirty-three knots. The captain smiled as he nudged the throttles forward, watching as the four tachometers showed increasing revolutions as the super yacht hit forty-two knots.

The run was smooth and uneventful, so the captain, with Charles's approval, picked up a handset and told the deck and cabin crews to stand down for the night.

'We are now in International waters,' stated the first Officer.

'You good?' the captain called over to Martin, the technical officer.

'All in the green,' he replied, scanning his instruments.

The captain balanced the revolutions of the four engines as he eased them back to cruising speed.

'Turn south, deploy stabilisers. First Officer has the bridge,' commanded the captain as he rose from his chair. 'Not much to do now except enjoy the cruise.' He looked over at Max. 'Is there any more coffee?'

'You can refill mine while you are at it, and the others as well,' said Charles, passing his mug to Max.

'One tour of the decks, then I think I will call it a night,' said the captain, then to Martin, 'Let your number two take the night duty. You need the rest after today.'

'Okay, Captain, I could do with some shut-eye,' replied Martin as he picked up the intercom.

'Well, I will leave you all to it. Goodnight, gentlemen, and avoid bad weather, please,' Charles said and left the bridge.

Chapter Two

Amazon Rainforest HQ

Anne awoke to a busy day ahead and, after a shower, chose a flower-pattern skirt, white blouse and flat shoes. She was not one for make-up, jewellery or flashy clothes. Her style was free and easy with a who-cares-what-people-think attitude. Her slim frame and dark hair with a hint of grey gave her a homely look. She headed to the kitchen where the chef was preparing breakfast for her team of workers. She grabbed a cup of tea and sat with the other three who were chatting at the table, enjoying the air conditioning.

'Morning, guys,' she said as she sat down. After the normal morning pleasantries, she continued, 'Today, I need to check on the progress of Site 2, then go on to the new site which is just a short drive further on.'

'Is the Akuntsu tribal chief coming with us? I assume his tribal lands cover the new area?' asked Mark, the team's driver and maintenance expert.

'I spoke to him on the radio last night, and he will be joining his people at Site 2 today and will come with us to the new site. He was quite excited at having two sites.' She smiled. 'Apparently, it puts them above the other tribe in importance in this region as they will have the largest tract of land.' She remembered something. 'Oh yes, I nearly forgot, the local federal representative is coming with us.'

'No worries,' Jo commented. Jo was the team's second-in-command after Anne and an expert off-road driver who always had a relaxed, laid-back style and always dressed in the same chino and tee shirt combination. The chef served up a typical British cooked breakfast, and the group was quiet while they concentrated on eating, knowing they might not eat again till nightfall.

The compound, which was home to Anne and her five staff and four security guards, was surrounded by a four-metre-high wire fence beyond which was lush virgin rainforest. The compound covered one acre and housed an L-shaped wooden building which, in one leg, contained the en-suite bedrooms, kitchen and dining hall and, in the other leg, contained the offices and technology centre. The roof was covered with solar panels. The centre of the compound was marked out as a helipad, and in the furthest corner was a tall wind turbine at the very top of which sat a satellite dish. When the team finished their work, the compound was to be turned over the local tribe to serve as an ecotourist centre.

Anne greeted the federal representative, Jorge Silvia, whom she had met on many previous occasions. He was a small man in a shabby suit, his tie an inch below the collar, with a ready smile and particularly amiable towards Anne whom he saw as a big help to his local popularity by aiding the local tribes to thrive in these very difficult economic times which exasperated their loss of tribal traditions and lands.

'Anne, it is so nice to see you again.' He clasped her hand between his. 'And you bring such good news with this new area that can be saved.'

'Hello, Jorge.' Anne smiled. 'Regretfully, we have not got long today as I must leave early this afternoon.'

'Oh, what a shame, but never mind. I am sure we can conclude our business in our normal expedient manner.' He smiled graciously.

'So am I,' replied Anne. 'Shall we?' She opened the door to the lead Land Rover and climbed in first with Jorge following. Jo joined Mark in the front. Two heavily armed security guards in safari suits climbed into the second Land Rover.

The ride was uncomfortable on the badly rutted single-track road that wound its way through dark forest and dense brush with Mark concentrating on the track upfront to avoid the deepest of ruts. It took them just over an hour to get to Site 2 by which time everyone was ready to stretch their legs and sooth aching body parts.

'I would have thought this was Site 1,' Jorge commented. 'It looks nothing like the Site 2 I saw on my last visit. It's so lush and green, and just look at those saplings, Anne. They are marvellous! I congratulate you and your people.' He strode off on his own, deeper into the site.

'One happy camper,' Jo said to Anne. 'Shouldn't be a problem getting his okay for the new site.'

'Nope,' replied Anne. 'Ah, there's the chief.' She pointed into the distance and waved at the chief who stood out with his colourful robe and feather headdress. Walking towards the chief, Anne spoke to Jo, 'We need to set up the same system here as we set up at Site 1 to monitor the progress of insect and mammal reintroduction. Can you organise that while I am away?'

'Of course, I will see to it,' replied Jo. 'It would be great if we have the same level of repopulation as Site 1. That was a really unexpected result.'

'The diversity was a brilliant result, but we still do not know how it went so well. It was against all the predictions made.'

'True, but let's not look a gift horse in the mouth. There is no reason to assume a different result. Site 1 is not that far away and has the same native species of both insects and plants,' explained Jo, wiping the sweat from his face and neck with a handkerchief.

They reached the chief, and Anne bowed in recognition of his standing. 'Chief, you've met Jorge Silvia,' Anne said, introducing the federal representative.

'Yes, some time ago though,' replied the chief as he and Jorge shook hands.

'So how are things going, Chief?' asked Anne.

'Wonderful! Look around. All the plants and saplings have been taken, and my people tell me we have a good number of different wildlife. There is still a lot of work to do.'

'There's about five hectares on the northeast boundary still requiring a lot of work,' Jo explained. 'The saplings are due in a few days. All the equipment is in place ready, and the drilling rigs are already working.'

'Our people?' queried Anne.

'No, we have trained the Akuntsu tribal people on the rigs, and they are using them,' answered Jo.

'Okay, let's get to the new site then,' Anne said as she looked at her watch.

Mark drove them to the new site, which at first looked like

the result of a tornado. Tree trunks littered the ground alongside empty oil drums, broken equipment and an old shipping container.

'Jeeps!' exclaimed Anne. 'First, a few trucks to take away all this rubbish, then you can start work!' She looked at Jo and the chief.

'It's not as bad as it looks.' Jo shrugged. 'Two truckloads should do it. We can use the container to store our gear, and the trunks can be cut to make a fence of sorts.' He looked at Anne. 'At least the deforestation is limited to this work area and the track into the forest,' he continued, trying to cheer her up.

'Let's drive down the track and check that assumption,' Anne replied, concerned that more damage had been done.

They all got back into the Land Rover and Mark carefully negotiated the track for fifteen minutes before they all concurred that the rest of the forest was untouched. Mark did a six-point turn to get back to the clearing.

Standing beside the Land Rover, the chief put a hand on Anne's shoulder. 'The majority of the forest has not been touched. Your husband purchased at a good time.' He looked at Jorge. 'It is good, yes?'

Jorge wiped his forehead with a grubby handkerchief. 'I agree with the chief. It is good that your husband purchased before more destruction took place. The wildlife has been spared as well as the trees. You may continue your work here, and I will recommend as such to my superiors.'

'Thank you, Jorge,' Anne said and shook his hand.

A shot rang out and pinged as it hit the armoured Land Rover. In an instance, one of the security guards ran to Anne and pulled her down and led her behind the Land Rover as more shots rang out. 'You two follow me!' he shouted to the chief and Jorge, opening the rear door. 'Get in and stay down, please!' he said, shouting at them.

His counterpart lay on the ground behind a tree trunk and opened fire with a burst from his sub-machine gun at the treeline 400 yards away.

Mark grabbed his rifle and took up position at the rear of the Land Rover. 'Can you see anything?' he shouted.

'Just the occasional muzzle flash. I would say at least three of them,' said the guard by the tree.

Jo pulled his handgun from his shoulder holster and lay flat beside the vehicles.

The second guard took up position near the front of the Land Rover and rested his machine gun on the bonnet.

Mark looked through his scope and waited until he could see a muzzle flash. *Come on*, he thought, *just fire, then I can get you.* When Mark saw the muzzle flash from the shooter's rifle, he took careful aim and fired off a series of shots in quick succession, the first directly at the muzzle flash, the others to the left and right. The guards let loose with machine gunfire and broke cover and, with their SAS training kicking in, made their way to the shooter's location, keeping low and weaving through the undergrowth, dropping flat, laying down a barrage of shots, then on the run again till they reached the tree line. Mark and Jo kept a volley of covering fire going. The guards entered the trees at a run and soon found the shooters: three Latin Americans, two dead from multiple gunshot wounds and the third mortally wounded. Mark and Jo arrived at a run and found the two guards tending to the surviving shooter. 'Has he said anything?' asked Jo.

'Mumbled something about losing his job and were trying to

scare us off so they could get their jobs back. They need their jobs to support their families and now they have nothing,' said one of the guards.

'He's dead,' the second guard said, standing up and looking down at the shooter. 'What a waste of life!' He grabbed his gun and, with the other guard, walked back to the Land Rovers.

Jo checked the bodies for anything that would identify them; he found two wallets and some papers. He then stood up and walked back to Anne through the treeline into the clearing and explained the situation.

Mark and one of the guards scouted the area nearby before walking back to the vehicles.

'That logging company was given money to pay directly to its employees. Three years pay, ample compensation, and with training to help them find work.' Anne was furious and looked at Jorge. 'It would appear they kept the money for themselves.'

'It would appear so.' Jorge looked at his feet. 'I am ashamed that they would do such a thing.' He stared at the ground, shaking his head. 'I will brief my superiors, but you should not let this interfere with your good work. You are good people.' He continued, 'My superiors will support your continuing to work here.' He raised both arms in despair. 'I am sure they will sort the company out.'

Jo handed Jorge the papers and wallet. 'I found these on them. Might help to locate their families and return the bodies to them.'

Anne looked at the chief. 'We will need to provide some security for your people when they work on this site.' Then turning to Jo, she asked, 'We can do that?'

'I think that's very sensible, and yes, we can,' Jo replied.

'We would be eternally grateful.' The chief brought his hands together as if in prayer. 'My people are easily frightened. They do not like outsiders. You know how long it took them to trust you and your people.'

'Eh, excuse me, but I would be much happier if you would sit in the safety of the car,' said one of the guards.

'Good point,' said Mark.

'I believe we have concluded business here, and I have a helicopter to catch,' said Anne, checking her watch. She knew the departure time was up to her, but she did not want to delay any longer than she had to.

Once in the Land Rovers, they headed back to Site 2 and dropped the chief off before returning to the compound. Anne and Jorge discussed the situation, and Jorge reluctantly agreed to leave the investigation into the shooting for Charles to sort out. Jo cringed; he knew what that meant: no more logging company. He pitied the directors and what else they would face besides bankruptcy. When they arrived at the compound, a sleek helicopter was sitting on the helipad. The two security guards drove directly to their office and met their two colleagues who came outside to greet them. Anne bade goodbye to Jorge and went to her bedroom to collect her things, while Jo spoke to the pilot.

'Jo, you are now in command here,' Anne said when Jo came to take her bags to the helicopter. 'We need to increase security here and at the reforestation sites. We cannot be too careful.'

'You think there's more to this than just the unemployed looking for revenge?' Jo queried.

'Yes, it's something Jorge said on the way back.' She looked thoughtful and frowned. 'I think the logging company might be behind the shooting.'

'Grab the money, and try and force the land back,' Jo said thoughtfully. 'Have your cake and eat it too.'

'Precisely,' replied Anne. 'I'll talk to Charles. But in the meantime, be very careful and increase surveillance and security patrols.'

'That goes without saying,' Jo said, looking over at the four security guards. 'I think a plan is already being developed.' He watched as Anne climbed into the helicopter. 'Have a good trip.'

'You know I hate these things,' Anne said with a grimace on her face.

Jo laughed. 'You've been saying that for years. You know they are safe.'

One of the guards came running over with an overnight bag. 'I've briefed them on what to do,' he said as he stowed his bag. 'We have another two members coming back on this bird to beef up the team.'

'That's quick thinking and action.' Anne smiled at him as he climbed into the helicopter and then turned back to Jo. 'I'll call you once I'm on *Sundancer*. Take care.'

Jo closed and locked the door and stood back as the Bell 525 Relentless rotors wound up to speed. He shielded his eyes from the dust and went over to the security team and watched the helicopter disappear into the distance. 'Will a team of five give us enough cover?' he asked the lead guard.

'I think so – three in the field to cover the work area and two back here.' He wiped some dust from his eyes. 'We will keep the electric fence on at all times and activate the movement alarm on the night-vision cameras,' he explained.

'Okay,' Jo said as he started for his office and passed his rifle to the guard. 'Have this thoroughly cleaned, and get it back to me, please.' He pointed to one of the Land Rovers. 'And get the paint chip from the bullet hits touched up.'

Forty-five minutes later, they started their descent to the private-jet zone at Brazil international airport. Anne could see the company 747-8i sitting outside the Private Jet Terminal.

'Captain says he is ready for immediate take-off,' the pilot said into his microphone. 'And he has the rendezvous point from Keith.' He deftly landed the helicopter craft next to the 747 stairs so Anne and the security guard could go straight on board. Two men in company security uniforms walked over and climbed on board the helicopter and said a perfunctory hello to the pilot while they strapped themselves in and donned headphones, and the pilot took off, heading back to the compound.

The 747 was palatial inside even for the crew who had the top level all to themselves with bedrooms, shower, toilet, lounge, television screens and bar. The main deck was business and luxury in cream and beige leather and rich dark woods, the colour scheme chosen by Anne to induce a sense of calm. The nose, normally used for first class, was the master bedroom with en-suite. The business class area was taken over with a private lounge and private office. The vast economy area housed the galley, cinema and conference room with two guest bedrooms with en-suites at the rear.

Anne was welcomed on board by the chief steward, Andrew Mulligan, his uniform of dark-blue trousers and white shirt clearly newly pressed. 'Hello, Mrs Langham, nice to have you aboard again.' His smile was genuine and friendly.

'Thank you, Andrew. I'll be glad when I am back on board *Sundancer*, though.'

'Hi, Andrew,' said the security guard, handing the luggage to a steward who wore the same uniform as the chief steward. 'I'm Mrs Langham's personal bodyguard. Mike is the name.'

'Nice to meet you, Mike.' He shook hands. 'Now, if you would both be seated and buckle up, we will start our taxi run for take-off.'

Anne and Mike went forward to the private lounge and even before they were seated in their large reclining seats, they could feel the giant airplane start to taxi.

'I did not know you were my personal bodyguard,' Anne said to Mike.

'Orders from the boss came through while we were away from the compound. I am to see you safely back to *Sundancer*.'

'Cabin crew to take-off positions, please,' the captain announced.

Anne buckled her seat belt and picked up the remote control, and the BBC World News appeared on the large LCD screen on the wall in front of the seats.

Anne felt the enormous thrust of the plane as it sped down the runway, pushing her into the back of her deep leather seat, then the slight lightness as it left the ground behind and started its crawl into the blue skies above. There was a slight thud as the wheels retracted. The plane was surprisingly quiet due to the extra sound insulation fitted during its build. Three bell dings sounded, and the chief steward came to Anne and Mike. 'A drink, Mrs Langham?' he asked.

'Andrew, please call me Anne. I've told you before.' She smiled. 'I'll have a glass of red wine. Mike, anything for you?'

'Just a mineral water with lime, please,' he replied. Mike

never drank on duty. He was driven by the pride of his profession and duty to guard Mrs Langham until she was safely on board *Sundancer*; only then would he relax, as nothing could touch them on board a yacht with such sophisticated protection systems.

Anne watched the news while she relaxed with her drink. 'Ladies and gentlemen, we are now in level flight, so please feel free to walk around.' The announcement was a relief to Anne who wanted to have a shower and get changed. She unbuckled her seat belt and went forward to the private quarters and had a shower and changed into a loose-fitting blouse and blue wool skirt. Feeling refreshed, she went upstairs and pressed the intercom button to the flight deck. 'Captain, Anne here. May I enter?' The door clicked, and she entered the realm of the captain.

'Hi, Captain.' She then turned to the copilot. 'Hello, Peter, when do we land?' she asked, standing between the two seats, the cockpit slightly dim except for the bank of lights from the displays and button tabs.

'We have clear weather all the way and should touchdown in seven hours,' the captain advised.

'Well, that gives me time to catch up on some paperwork.' Anne chuckled. 'Either of you guys want a coffee? I'm going to ask Andrew to put a fresh brew on.'

'Thought you'd never ask,' answered the captain, keeping his eyes on the instruments, scanning them automatically.

'Great,' answered Peter.

'Coming up,' Anne said as she left the cockpit, closed the door and went downstairs to find Andrew. He was in the extensive galley, preparing dinner with George, the steward. She organised the coffee and told George to bring hers to the private office where she would also have dinner.

Sitting at the cherrywood desk, she switched her laptop on and started to make notes about the future needs to fulfil the regeneration of the new site. *I might as well write a report on the shooting*, she thought, *while it's fresh in my mind*. The leather chair felt comfortable and relaxing as she typed on the laptop. She tried to think of the mentality of those who had died and those potentially behind the shooting. There was a knock on the door, and George entered quietly with a fresh pot of coffee; he poured a cup without a word and left as quietly as he entered, knowing that it was best to be invisible when either of the Langham's were working. Anne lifted the cup and tasted the warm liquid. She felt the invigorating liquid awaken and relax her. The office was quiet with just the gentle background of the engines as she continued to work. The walls covered in suede with a deep wool carpet gave it a warmth that she appreciated. Anne looked at the console on the desk to the right of the laptop and pressed one of the many buttons. The wall-mounted display came on, and she chose the BBC World News. After a few minutes, she thought of changing the channel to the flight plan world map but then decided to listen to some music. *Change the channel to music*, she thought and then looked at the list of albums; *which one? Ah, Steve Harley & Cockney Rebel. Long time since I listened to that*. She pressed another button, and the music played.

After spending some time working, she stretched her neck and arms and heard a tap at the door. Andrew entered with a dinner tray. Anne moved her laptop to one side and let Andrew place the silver tray on the desk. 'Pate to start, then veal steak, jacket potato and fresh vegetables, and a lemon and lime sorbet to finish with fresh coffee,' he said, removing the lids and laying the cutlery and napkin out.

'Just in time. I think I was about to fall asleep,' Anne replied. Andrew collected the old coffee things and left the room. She dimmed the lights, slightly clasped her hands in front of her, elbows resting on the table, and then started to eat. The past weeks were catching up now that the day-to-day pressure was off. After dinner, she ran her fingers through her hair and poured another coffee from the jug. She sat back and cradled the cup, staring at the laptop's bright screen, reading what she had already entered. *I am tired*, she thought and drained the cup. *No good pushing myself. I might as well get some sleep.* And she closed the laptop's lid, stood up, pressed a button on the console to stop the music, and headed for the bedroom to sleep.

Chapter Three

The Houses of Power

The president's advisors sat in the Oval Office. The president, Mike Read, leaned forward and put his briefing papers on the coffee table. 'Who the hell is this guy? And how come I've never heard of him before?' he asked of his White House team seated around the coffee table.

'He is very secretive and likes to keep under the radar,' the secretary of state advised. 'His publicists operate in reverse by keeping his name and pictures of his family out of the media rather than in it. His company's structure makes it almost impossible for us to work out what companies he owns.'

'So what do we know about him?' demanded the president, an edge to his voice as his patience started to be tested.

The Secret Service chief removed his glasses and rubbed the bridge of his nose. 'He is believed to be a New Zealander who made his fortune early in life. Later, he re-established his corporation around conservation, but initially shunned the green movement. His investment portfolio is believed to have changed in the same vein.' He replaced his glasses and glanced at the papers on his lap. 'He is a billionaire, a few times over, owns Sundancer, one of the world's largest super yachts, built under heavy security with all the workers carefully vetted and signed up under a strict secrecy clause. He has an extensive fleet of aircraft, Boeing 747-8i, Airbus A380, a Learjet, and a few of the very latest Bell 525 Relentless Helicopters. Married to Anne, children unknown, he is thought to live on the yacht rather than own any land-based residence. That's about all we know.'

'Well, contact your New Zealand counterparts and see what they know about this guy, about his corporation,' the president said, before rounding on the Secretary of State. 'So what does he want?'

The secretary of state shifted in his chair. 'A wholesale reform of all our policies.' He chuckled. 'I quote from his UN presentation.' He raised a sheet of paper to eye level. ''To legislate against the extinction of our flora and fauna, to legislate against fossil fuels, to drive out the corruption and greed that are endemic in world governments.' He flapped the paper in the air. 'Or in simple terms, devastate our economy. It's laughable really, like a spoilt child throwing his weight around.'

'And the level of his threat, what is he capable of doing?'

The defence chief, Clive Harris, replied, 'Mr President, who knows? We believe Mr Langham owns several very highly technological electronic companies which could be capable of a threat, but we cannot confirm.'

'But we don't know – is that what you are saying?' queried the president. 'Get on to the New Zealand Premier and find out about him.' The president sat back, exasperated by the lack of information his top team could provide. Finally, after some thought, he said, 'Do we know where he is now or where his wife is?'

'His yacht left US waters last night, actually around midnight, and headed south, so we assume it is heading back to New Zealand. His wife left Brazil late today by air, heading south, so we can assume they will be meeting at some point.' The secretary of state opened his arms. 'But that's all we know. Personally, I do not see him as a threat to our national security. He has shown no terrorist tendencies or affiliations nor does he have access to weapons of mass destruction.' He leant forward in his chair. 'Yes, I know, Mr President that he made a veiled threat to the UN, but that's all it is.'

'Gentlemen, I am not happy. We do not know enough about this man or his threat.' He walked behind the presidential desk and slammed his clenched fist onto the desk as he sat down. 'Find something – good, bad, indifferent – but find something. Meeting over.' As they filed out, the president said to his chief of staff, 'Ryan O'Hare, you stay here.'

After they all left, the president stood up and walked to a bureau where he poured himself a Jack Daniels and another for the chief of staff. 'Ryan O'Hare, we have a problem here, and I need you to find out the truth.' He took a drink. 'Get together with the director of the FBI, get a small task force together, but keep it low key. In the meantime, I am going to put a call into Charles Langham and assess the situation myself.'

'Call him direct, a risky move but could be very worthwhile.' Ryan O'Hare thought the president was taking this into his own hands as he had a tendency to do. 'Do you want me to join the conversation or listen in?'

'No, I think I will make it a personal call, see if we can find some common ground.'

The chief of staff put his empty glass on the table. 'Okay, I'll go and work on setting up the task force.'

Alone in his office, the president wondered if everyone was jumping to conclusions to a problem that did not exist.

He picked up the phone. 'Get me Mr Charles Langham,' he said. 'I understand he is on his yacht *Sundancer*.' He replaced the handset heavily. With a huge budget deficit, Detroit declaring bankruptcy, cuts in defence spending, the last thing he needed was another crisis, draining more money that he did not have. The senate would not agree to an increase in defence spending or more money going to the CIA or FBI; all they wanted was cutbacks. Only six days before, he had managed to avoid another fiscal cliff after ten days of stalemate and the government being shut down. He had never met Charles Langham, only heard titbits about him, so he had no idea what tack to take on the phone call. *Just be honest and open*, he decided, *and take it as it comes*. He poured himself a Jack Daniels, took off his jacket and loosened his tie.

Chapter Four

Undersea

The beams of light cut through the gloom as the divers set up the last two laser targeting probes on the acoustic generation device, checking angles and distances again proving challenging. Bruce checked his dive computer as he watched a shark swim by. He then connected a cable to the device and switched on a tablet computer in a waterproof membrane. 'Setting up the configuration tests,' he said to Adam and started tapping away on the tablet. After sometime, he checked his dive watch again. *This has been the most difficult to set up*, he thought, *but it should have been no more difficult than the others.* He checked the tablet: all lights were green. 'We are all green, Adam. Let's get back to the submersible.' He disconnected the cable and joined Adam as they swam back to their submersible and entered the dive tube, closing the hatch behind them, and waited while the water was pumped out. Taking off their masks, they entered the cabin and removed their dive gear and dried their hair and hands.

'Well, that's the last one. Time to call the mother ship. Let's go home.' Bruce moved towards the port helm seat. A small stout man with a trim beard, Bruce was in charge of the installation of the device, ensuring it was properly orientated and the target lasers at the precise angle and distance. Adam, his counterpart, was the submersible pilot and had accompanied Bruce on all the installation missions. Bruce picked up the microphone. *'Deep Sea to Launch One, Deep Sea to Launch One,* testing device, standby for recovery, over.'

The reply came through the VHF speaker, '*Launch One* to *Deep Sea, Launch One* to *Deep Sea,* ETA fifteen minutes will have moon pool doors open, ready for your recovery, decompression chamber all set up.'

Adam sat in the pilot's seat and started the electric engine of the submersible and lifted her off the bottom for the ascent to the mother ship. *After spending so long at such depth, we have a five-hour decompression,* he thought. *Time to lie back, eat a nice meal and relax before heading back to base.* He eased the nose gently upwards and watched their scope for the mother ship. 'You really think the boss will use these things?' he asked Bruce.

'Yes, he will,' replied Adam as he ran a final system test on the acoustic device, 'but only as a last resort.' He stretched. 'We're buggered if nothing happens, so someone has to rattle some sense into the brains of our so-called world leaders, and the boss is the man to do that, and if they don't listen and do something, he will use them.' He checked the computer screens. 'All system testing positive. So we are clear to dock with *Launch One.*'

'Not the whole lot in one go though, surely?'

'No, he will use one. If no reaction, then two and so on.'

'But people will die. That won't bode well with him or Mrs Langham.'

'No one will die. Timing, modelling and calculations have

worked it out, but there will be a lot of damage.'

They sat quietly for a while, and Adam did some retesting of the system.

'There she is,' said Adam as he guided the submersible towards the brightness of the moon pool beneath *Launch One*. Adam brought her to a stationery position in the moon pool and altered the buoyancy until she broke the surface. Two divers jumped on board and attached two large sling hooks, and the submersible was raised out of the water as the two moon pool doors closed. The crane eased the submersible rearwards and lowered her into a cradle. The hatch was opened by one of the divers as the other diver connected hoses and cables. Adam and Bruce climbed out and made their way directly towards the decompression chamber where a nurse was waiting for them.

'In you go, gentlemen. Dinner is on the table. Have a good rest. You have four hours,' she said.

'Thanks,' said Bruce. 'Can I book a wake-up alarm call?' he asked as he climbed into the chamber.

Adam laughed. 'Always the joker. Thanks, Jean. See you in five,' he said as he followed Bruce into the chamber. The door closed behind them as they made their way towards the dinner waiting for them on the table. There was no wine but orange juice and mineral water. They felt *Launch One* power up and turn away from the coast of New York on a southeasterly heading.

The captain of *Launch One* was happy to be finally under way after spending six hours loitering just off the coast of America, trying to look like a private yacht lazily cruising around for no reason other than enjoying a cruise. Although *Launch One* looked like an average small super yacht at eighty-seven metres, below decks was totally different and would not pass muster. He picked up the private communications phone and called James Young, the undersea operations manager at the Kermadec base. 'James, its David aboard *Launch One*. Mission complete. *Deep Sea* is aboard. We are heading home.'

'Very good,' replied James. 'I will let Charles know. Congratulate the teams on the successful mission. Talk soon.'

Charles will be ecstatic, thought James. *It's taken four months to deploy the systems after years of development and testing, and we still met the target date.* James sat 200 metres below sea level in the Kermadec headquarters of World Earth, with a hooded window, looking out into the wonders of the ocean deep. One hundred and forty people lived, worked and played in the headquarters building, five smaller pods linked to a larger central pod. Wool carpeting, lined walls and paintings gave the centre a feeling of warmth and homeliness. Access was either through deep-sea subs or through an elongated tunnel that opened on to a remote island. Each pod was equipped with watertight doors that automatically opened and closed to allow access. Power was generated by tidal movement and thermal and solar energy; barring some foods, they were self-sufficient. James was happy to spend his time down here where he finally had a true purpose in life, saving the planet after spending years rolling from one useless job to another, brushes with the law, and being rejected by his family after drugs became a part of his life. He was saved by the drug rehabilitation programme run by the Langham Trust, and Charles offered him a job if he cleaned his act up. Down here, he could not access drugs, but neither had he the wish to. His girlfriend, the therapist who guided him through his rehabilitation, was down in the undersea city, making sure everyone was psychologically unaffected by being below the sea for months at a time.

James started his video screen mounted to the rear of his desk and tapped the call button on the touchscreen, then tapped Charles Langham name, then tapped *Sundancer*.

Charles was in the main-deck lounge with the captain and Max, discussing the rendezvous with the 747-8i over coffee when the display screen chimed and James's face appeared on the screen recessed in the wall. Charles pressed the accept button. 'Good day, James, how are things?' Charles said.

'Brilliant, Mr Langham. I also have good news. The mission has been successful. All devices deployed and successfully tested,' James said, guarding his language carefully.

'That is good news. May I correctly assume that *Deep Sea* and *Launch One* are both on their way back to you?' Charles asked.

'That is correct. They are heading our way at full speed,' James replied.

Charles's handset rang. 'James, I have another call. Thanks for the information. We'll talk later.'

Max grabbed the handset and answered, 'Mr Langham's phone. Who may I say is calling?'

Charles cut the call to James and looked at Max who said, 'It's the US president.' Charles took the handset, sat back and crossed his legs. 'Good morning, Mr President,' Charles said. 'And to what do I owe the pleasure of this call?'

'Mr Langham, I am calling to simply have an honest conversation with you following your address to the UN the other day,' Mike Read, the US president, said.

'Okay, that's fine, but please do call me Charles.'

'Okay, Charles, you can call me Mike. Now what are you expecting the UN and, therefore, the US to do?'

'It's quite simple, Mike. The earth and its people are on a knife edge of survival, and the politicians of the world are turning a blind eye to it.' Charles stood up and walked on to the open deck. 'CO_2 levels, as you know, are increasing, and that is due to rainforest destruction and automobiles. People in the third world are dying through famine, whilst other western countries throw excess food away.' Charles carried on, 'So world leaders need to get their acts together and get something done before it's too late rather than ignoring the issues.'

'That's not quite true, Charles. We are doing a lot to overcome these issues,' the president said bluntly.

'Let me reiterate,' interrupted Charles. 'Prime rainforest is being levelled at an increasing rate to produce hardwood for the US market, soy and palm oils. The US, in particular, is delaying the reduction in fossil fuel use in cars.' Charles drained his coffee and walked back into the lounge and passed his mug to Max for a refill. 'My teams are working with famine-stricken peoples in many parts of Africa and India.'

'But, Charles, not everything can be fixed as quickly or as easily as you make out.'

'Mr President, sorry to interrupt you again, but that's a wildly untrue statement, and I can prove it as well. Take a look at the reforestation work we have done, and take a darn good look at our famine-relief rebuild efforts, and you will see the truth. It takes a determined effort and the ability to ignore the lobbyists and political bluster that drives politics. Mr President, I know that you have the power, so why do you not use it?' Charles said calmly.

'We have many demands on our budgets and have to balance what we do for the American people and peoples from other countries.' The president's tone of voice was sharp as a knife.

Charles laughed and smiled at Max and John. 'Mr President, I am a private citizen who cares and is worried for the future of our planet, and quite rightly, I demand that the world leaders do something. If I can as a private citizen, the world powers should be able to for bloody sake. What is your biggest budget expenditure – military equipment, which says a lot about your priorities!'

'I think it would be useful if we can meet and discuss this face to face,' the president said, trying to cool himself down to deal with this man, who did not seem to buckle under the weight of talking to the US president.

'Somehow, I don't think that will happen, Mr President. I know you will not come to my yacht, and I certainly will not set foot on an American vessel. You see my sources tell me that your people have contacted the New Zealand prime minister to check up on me. I know that the US ambassador to the UN has fully briefed you, so what would be gained, except maybe my rendition to somewhere unknown. The trouble is you do not see further than your own advisors and the lobbyists for the oil companies. Please talk to your climate scientists and your humanitarian people, then get back in touch with me without a hidden agenda and then we can meet. Goodbye, Mr Read.' Charles pressed the off button.

'You just cut off the president of the United States?' asked the captain.

'So what? He's just another politician. It will be interesting to see what happens. In the meantime, go to full surveillance and fire up the scanning sonar and long-distance radar.' Charles thought for a moment about what actions the US president or his advisor would take, knowing how gun happy they could be. They would start analysing all communication for words that could be linked to Charles or his organisation. Undoubtedly, if they had made contact with the New Zealand prime minister, then they would try and find any of their installations. *We need to button everything down and use the highest level of encryption for all communication.* 'Max, send a message to all our location heads on the company frequency. With immediate effect, full security and defence protocols are in operation, and get some fresh coffee.'

'Okay, boss,' said Max and left the room and headed to the elevator to go down to the secure communications room.

'John, get this yacht to the same level and get the surveillance team on duty round the clock.'

'Aye, sir,' The captain picked up his hat and walked forward towards the bridge. Charles called up James's name on the screen and tapped the connect button. James's face appeared on the screen. 'Sorry about that, James. We had a call from the US president.'

'That's fine. So where were we?'

'Before we get back to that, I have Max sending out a full security and defence protocol to all locations. You will be receiving the same, so button everything down. No one leaves the base. That means this call is on full encryption on my count – one, two, three.' Charles pressed a button on the keypad.

'What's the buzz?'

'The US president is checking on us, so I want to be very careful and not take any chances,' Charles explained.

'Okay, that's fine. Now, what I originally called to advise was that all the devices are in place and fully tested. So all you have to do is give the word and advise which locations. *Launch One* is steaming to us at full speed. She is a day's sailing behind you. The submarine *Jupiter* is on its way to rendezvous with you and is two days away from your location. The submarine *Mercury* is in the Pacific South East of Tasmania and on route to us.' He paused. 'That's about it.'

'A good quick round-up as usual, James. Thank you. Do we have any other vessel that needs recalling?' *James Young always has everything in control and at his fingertips*, Charles thought. Charles had seen something worthwhile in James in the rehabilitation programme and had offered him a low-key position. James soon proved more useful and talented and rose through the ranks quickly and was admired by his superiors and colleagues alike. James could not believe it when Charles offered him the operations manager position at the newly built Kermadec base; it was a dream come true and a heavy responsibility.

'No, everything else is securely docked, and all aircraft are at their bases except Mrs Langham's 747-8i which should be touching down in a few hours.'

'Max is due to take off in just under one hour to pick Anne up,' Charles said.

'Ah, I have just got the protocol from Max,' James said. 'May I suggest that the 747 refuels and heads to Tonga once Mrs Langham is disembarked.'

'Good idea, pretty neutral ground,' Charles agreed.

'Sir, may I suggest that they land and refuel in Auckland, then head on to Tonga,' Max interrupted as he entered the lounge with a tray of fresh coffee. 'That way, they will not have to refuel at Tonga where the fuel quality is not as good.' He put the tray down.

'Good idea, Max. Tell them when you meet up,' James said. 'Well, I had better get back to work.'

'Before you go, upload the UN presentation to Duke Warren, YouTube and send it to all the news networks, Greenpeace, the works and keep up the good work.' Charles cut the connection.

Max picked up the Thermos from the tray. 'I'll be off to get Mrs Langham,' he said and headed for the lift to go to the sea-view deck and the helipad. Once on board, the rotors started to wind up, and Charles poured himself a coffee and watched from the deck as the helicopter lifted from the helipad four decks above and rapidly disappeared into the distance. *Soon Anne will be back on board*, he thought and, tapping the side of the yacht, made his way down the gangway and headed up to the bridge, enjoying the wind in his face as it swept away his thoughts.

All was quiet on the bridge; the captain and first officer were seated in their chairs, deep in conversation, pointing at the radar screens, and Martin Deeks, the technical officer, was seated in his chair, concentrating on his tablet computer.

'Everything okay?' asked Charles to no one in particular.

'*Sundancer* is running perfectly. Just keeping an eye on a radar contact', replied the captain, 'that seems to be following our track.'

'*Launch One* is too far behind us. Can't be them,' said the first officer.

'Doubt it's anything to worry about, but keep an eye on it,' Charles suggested and left the bridge for the library where he picked a book, went down to the main deck, stretched out on a lounger and started to read. The call to the president ran through his mind. Did he go too far and push the president a little too hard? Should he have spent more time explaining his ideas and searching for a more mutual area for an agreement? Anne was usually good to have in these conversations, taking the heat out of both sides. *It might be worthwhile discussing the call with Anne when she gets back, and see if there's any point in calling the president back in a more relaxed way. Maybe by video so they can have the benefit of seeing facial expressions that can say a lot more than words can.* He attempted to clear his mind and concentrate on the book.

Chapter Five

The Reverse Threat

The distinctive helicopter sound attracted Charles's attention. He put his book down, stretched, picked the book up and headed back up to the helipad. He was pleased to see two crew members already there with fire-fighting equipment, a strict requirement that Max had and one that Charles did not question. Max brought the helicopter to a gentle landing, quickly cutting the engine while the two crew members put their fire-fighting equipment down and went to the straps to secure the helicopter's landing gear to the deck. Charles ducked under the still-turning rotors, opened the door and greeted Anne with a long kiss. 'Hi, darling,' she said. 'It's great to be home.' He helped her down, while Max sat clicking switches and turning knobs. 'Thanks, Max,' she said.

'Anytime, Mrs Langham,' Max replied. 'Once I've secured this bird, I'll bring your lunches to the library.'

Charles poured Anne a coffee. 'So tell me what happened at the base, then I'll tell you about the chat I had with the US president that did not go as well as it should have.'

Anne gave a detailed account of the status of all three sites. She advised how well the Akuntsu tribe were coping and went into a complete description of the shooting and passed over copies of the contents of the wallets. Charles was angry, quickly coming to the conclusion that the logging company that sold the land was definitely behind the shooting, and discussed what he intended to do to them. They discussed the security arrangement that Anne had put in place with Mark. Charles could not offer any improvement over what had been put in place and was pleased. Max came in with lunch, a fresh cheese salad with bread that was baked on board, fresh fruit and a bottle of New Zealand Pinot Noir. Over lunch, they discussed the call to the president and agreed that the best way forward was to video-call him after lunch. When Max came to collect the tray, Charles asked him to pop into the surveillance suite and get the communication officer to connect them to the US president by video phone and put the call through to the library and bring a fresh pot of coffee.

The video screen came to life. 'Mr Langham, I have the US president on the line,' the communications offer on the screen advised.

'Thank you. Put him through,' said Charles. The president's face appeared on the screen.

'Good afternoon, Mr President. Hopefully, you can see us as clearly as we can see you,' Charles said with a smile on his face.

'Yes, I can thank you. I did not expect to hear from you, Mr Langham, and I am certainly not used to being cut-off!' Mike Read, the US president, replied; he had his suit jacket off and necktie loose.

'I apologise for that unreservedly,' Charles said with a slight nod. 'May I introduce my wife, Anne?'

'Hi, Mr President,' Anne announced herself cheerfully. The president nodded.

'I thought it advisable to call you back to discuss in a more informal way, preferably face to face, the issues we discussed in the earlier call that did not go very well. Also for that reason, I have Anne present to keep things cooler and calmer,' Charles explained.

'That sounds fine,' Mike Read replied.

'Okay, Mike, so first, maybe I should give you a full explanation where I am coming from. The earth, as we all know, faces some very serious issues that need to be resolved, and I am of the opinion, like many fine and respected scientists, that they need to be resolved very urgently and that the governments of this world are not moving quickly enough and bureaucracy is holding back all attempts. So I see the need to get under the skin of the world's government to get things done.' He paused. 'You see, many of the problems, if not resolved now, will cause irreparable damage, and some of them will cause the commencement of an irreversible decline in world ecology. I have five world leaders who, so far, are behind my organisation, and I am sure more will join in our efforts.' Charles leant back in his chair and waited, while Max placed the fresh pot of coffee on the table and poured two mugs. 'I am sorry that we cannot share this fresh coffee with you, Mike.'

Mike chuckled. 'That's okay. So tell me, what do you expect me to do?'

'Help us to stop the destruction of the rainforests in Indonesia and the Amazon, and prioritise the development of electric vehicles by US manufacturers. Tesla is a great example, Toyota and Honda hybrids, even Mercedes Benz have made an electric super car, but

US manufacturers concentrate on petrol engines as there are no incentives for them to do anything else. It may even help Detroit end famine. Just look at the amount of food that the US throws out each day. It could feed millions,' Charles explained slowly.

'Okay, okay, I get that. I do understand what you are saying, but how can the US do these things? How can I get the senate to agree when they want money spent on their constituents, and we have just averted a major final meltdown?' the president said, almost shouting.

'But that's not all. I'm afraid we have species decline at the fastest rate ever with 50 per cent estimated to be extinct in the next 100 years,' Charles continued. 'But to answer your question, easy, they won't have constituents if they do nothing. New Orleans, for example.' Charles paused as Anne touched his arm and frowned. 'Take the millions from the billions spent on defence and put some in electric-vehicle R&D, send teams into famine-stricken areas to help them develop their own crops and farms alongside our teams, spend money on reforestation, and teach US citizens recycling.'

'If I reduce defence spending, the senate will want that money spent on local issues, or saved and not spent at all,' the president said. 'But no one will want defence spending cut, so it's a rhetorical answer.'

'The issue I assume is that many of the senate have vested interests in suppliers to the military and, therefore, will lose money if military spending is cut.'

'Be careful what you say, Charles. You are on shaky ground.'

'But investment in electric-vehicle research and development will increase jobs in Detroit, which needs the work,' said Charles.

Anne cut in, 'And that will spill over on to defence programmes, surely.'

'That's true, but a lot of US citizens will fight the move away from oil,' the president said.

'You will need a massive campaign on the effects of continued petrol use, deforestation and species loss, and we can help with all that,' Charles said.

'My advisors will have a lot to say about this and so will the senate. What I will say is that I understand the issues – I truly do – but I am not sure what the American public will accept as the consequences of any actions, especially if Europe, China and the former Soviet republics do nothing.'

'Mike, we cannot play the waiting game. You need to convince the American public and take action. You cannot do anything on the basis of other countries doing nothing. That's suicidal,' Charles countered.

'And if nothing is done by us, then what?'

'Two things. First, America will fall way behind on the electric-vehicle technology and lose more jobs. Being the world's largest consumer, you will be blamed for the loss of rainforests, so publicly, worldwide, you could be ostracised. We will take action and show the American people the consequences of their inaction, what nature can do in the future,' Charles said.

'You will attack the USA?' the president exclaimed.

'I did not say that, but nature will, yes, and we may precipitate nature's response,' Charles said calmly, sipping his coffee.

'You know you have just threatened the United States, and I cannot ignore that fact and will do whatever it takes to protect the United States.' The words were said very precisely.

'We haven't threatened the United States,' Charles replied calmly.

'You have just said you will precipitate nature's response, Charles,' the president said harshly.

'Hardly, Mike. The biggest threat is from nature precipitated by human activity.'

'But if we do nothing, you threaten the United States,' said the US president in exasperation.

'I have not said that. But you know it makes sense to take the actions necessary to save the earth.'

'You know what would happen to me if the American people found out that I knew America was threatened and took no action,' the US president said. 'I cannot ignore the threat and must take action to defend America.' He stood up and walked away from the camera.

The defence chief came into view. 'I've never heard so much baloney, Mr President. The USS *Resolution* and USS *Eisenhower* have been deployed.'

Charles shook his head. 'Mike, I do not understand the relevance of deploying an aircraft carrier and a nuclear submarine. We are not your threat. But please note, however, that I took the precaution of recording this exchange, and it may be uploaded to the news agencies at the end of the call, so I advise you recall your forces and not take action against an unarmed private yacht,' Charles said quietly.

'Charles, I will not recall our forces. I have a scheduled meeting with my staff starting now. I suggest we carry on this conversation later, if we must.'

'They cut the link,' said the communications officer as his face appeared on the screen.

'Okay, thanks,' Charles said and shut off the video screen.

'He has spoken to his White House team already and made his decisions,' Anne said thoughtfully. 'He is being swayed by the Secretary of State, the defence secretary and the lobby groups and is more worried about votes and his time in office than what happens in the future when he is out of office.'

Charles pressed a key on the keypad. 'Max, Captain and Technical Officer, to the library, please.'

'What's the status of the *Sundancer*, gentlemen?' Charles asked as he motioned for them to sit as they entered the library.

'The vessel on radar is still following our track. Nothing else is showing,' the captain advised. 'Same speed and heading, matching us, course change for course change.'

'All shipshape on the technical side, boss,' said Martin Deeks, the technical officer.

'What I want to do is change our course. How far off the coast are we?' Charles interlaced his fingers, thinking.

'Around 250 miles,' replied the captain.

'Make it 150 and increase speed to 28 knots. I want the surveillance on twenty-four hours and load the rear torpedo tubes. Make sure all guns and missiles are armed and ready with their deck doors clear,' Charles said. '*Jupiter* is on her way to us. She has the EMP system, and she will shadow us all the way home as added security.'

'Max, send the video of the conference to the news agencies, just in case,' Anne said.

'Are we going to war, boss?' Max asked.

'No, Max, I am just getting prepared. Make sure the helicopter armaments are ready.'

'Sure thing, boss,' Max replied. 'I will get the deck crew to take the covers off her so she's ready for action.'

'So what's the threat then, sir?' asked the captain with a serious face.

'Just something the US president said,' Charles replied.

'You mean the secretary of defence statement that we were the threat,' cut in Anne. 'So we need to be careful and take whatever preventative action we can to protect ourselves if need be.'

'In any case, *Jupiter*'s EMP system would disable any US aircraft carrier or sub with one shot,' Max said, rubbing his hands gleefully.

'That's all, gentlemen,' Charles said, dismissing the three crew members.

'Why don't people understand?' Charles said in exasperation.

'They do,' Anne said in a calming voice, leaning forward and resting her hands on his knees. 'But they have not got your drive or passion for nature. The people need more educating, and then they can rally on the politicians and get behind us. Let's talk to Greenpeace and the World Wildlife Fund and see what we can do.'

'We can put a conference call in to them later.' He looked at the clocks on the wall that showed different times across the world. 'Sea Sheppard should be in on the call, but I don't think we can wait for the outcome of any actions they take. By the time they do anything, and it ripples through the public in enough numbers...' he let the sentence hang there.

'But at least they can agree to any action we take and provide publicity before and after,' Anne countered. 'Let's forget all that for the moment. I need a swim,' Anne said. 'Come on,' she said and grabbed Charles's hand. 'And you need to unwind.' She pulled him out of his seat.

They walked down the three flights of deep wool-carpeted stairs to the main deck and stepped through the pair of trifolding doors that opened the main lounge onto the deck. The huge deck was laid with teak and with the seven-metre swimming pool and spa pool sunken slightly within it. Both could be closed off by sliding doors for larger dance parties or an extra helipad. A fully equipped galley, barbecue and bar were on the port side and changing rooms with showers on the starboard side. Anne was the first out in a black bikini and went to the bar and waited while the steward poured two gin and tonics. Charles came out and dived straight into the pool, did one length and then swam to the bar end where Anne was walking down the tiled steps that led into the shallower end. 'You were right. I needed a swim to clear the old brain matter,' Charles said, taking the gin and tonic Anne offered and sat on the steps.

'You need to get away from things occasionally, you know, or you'll drive yourself crazy,' Anne said.

'I know, but it's not easy with people dying, defenceless animals being wiped out and the earth's future in jeopardy,' Charles replied.

'Forget it for the rest of the day. Just relax. I've told Max to tell the crew we are on vacation for the rest of the day, so we won't be interrupted.' Anne smiled. 'I need some quality time with you as well, you know?'

Charles finished his drink and swam to the other end of the pool. Anne put her drink down and swam towards him. 'I think I need to do a few lengths,' she said. 'I am out of condition.'

'Come on then,' said Charles, before sinking into the water and kicking off from the side. After a few lengths, he swam to the shallow end and walked up the steps to the bar where the steward refreshed the drinks, wandered over to the spa pool, put the drinks down and sank into the gently bubbling water. 'Come in here. It is glorious,' he called to Anne who was gently swimming lengths, doing the breaststroke. Anne left the pool and stepped into the spa pool. Max came over to them dressed in black shorts and a white tee shirt. 'The chef thought you would like to know what he can offer for dinner tonight. His recommendations are the grilled Barramundi, which he says is an excellent choice, and the scotch fillet, both to be cooked on the main deck BBQ.'

'The Barramundi for me,' said Anne. 'Darling, what will you have?'

'I think I'll plump for the Barramundi as well, with a bottle of Pinot Gris, and I think we'll eat here,' said Charles.

Max nodded slightly. 'The chef bet me you would choose the scotch fillet, so that's great, boss. He owes me now.' Max said with a cheeky grin and left to see the chef. Charles and Anne left the spa pool and lay down on the teak wooden loungers upholstered in a soft white canvas.

Charles watched as a steward quietly set up the teak dining table with silver cutlery, cruets, crystal glasses and cotton serviette, and the assistant chef prepared the main deck galley. He felt the yacht change course slightly. *Okay, we are now within 150 miles off the coast, so back on the southerly course. The Panama Canal, of course!* The revelation came to him suddenly. He had always sailed around Cape Horn which had become a habit. But the Panama Canal would offer a level of protection if needed. He picked up the handset that was on the small table between him and Anne. 'I think we should go through the Panama Canal,' he said to Anne.

'It will cut down the journey time and provide some protection if we need it.'

'Sounds like a good idea,' said Anne without opening her eyes.

Charles tapped a button on the handset. 'Captain, head for the Panama Canal and contact *Jupiter* and let them know our course change. If they can change course and arrive at the same time as us, they are to do so.' He listened to the captain and then said, 'Okay, that's great.'

'The vessel following our track is still right on us, changed course shortly after we did. *Jupiter* is just four hours from our position,' he said, looking over at Anne.

'Ah-ha, so all's good. Now close your eyes and rest,' she said quietly.

Not much more I can do, he thought. *Jupiter closing fast, Panama Canal's a good choice. Everything's under control. So Anne's right. Might as well close my eyes for a while.*

Charles sat at the dining table. He had showered and changed into an orange polo shirt and white shorts, his hair still damp. Anne sat opposite, wearing a light-blue blouse and matching shorts. The early evening was wonderful, the sky just darkening as the sun set in a cloudless sky with a slight breeze. The super yacht lights came on, bathing the area in a warm colour hue. The entrée of pate was being cleared by the steward, whilst Max was pouring them another glass of Pinot Gris. 'Where's Abbey, by the way?' Anne asked.

'Ah, now, she's with the chef. She's been running around him all day. I think she's adopted him,' said Max.

'Bring her up before you serve the main course, will you?' Anne said to the steward.

'Yes, Mrs Langham,' said the steward, turning towards the stairs to go down to the galley.

Charles pressed a few buttons on the table's corner and scrolled through the list of films displayed on the extra-large video screen, then chose the James Bond film *Thunderball*. The steward returned with a boisterous Border collie at his feet and went to the deck galley to get the main course.

'Abbey,' said Anne loudly with a broad grin and bent down to ruffle the dog's ears as its front paws landed on her lap. 'Oh, how much I've missed you.' The Border collie was overexcited at seeing Anne, nearly as much as Anne was excited to see the dog.

Chapter Six

The Chase

Charles awoke to the knock on the polished curved wood door of the master suite. He swung the quilt back, put on his woollen robe and checked the clock beside his bed: 5 am. He wondered what the issue could be as he padded over the deep white wool carpet to the door, keeping as quiet as he could so as not to awaken Anne. He opened the door to find the captain standing there, immaculate in a white shirt and crisp blue shorts.

'Sorry to wake you this early in the morning, but the target that's been following us has closed in enough for our long-range vision camera to obtain clean imaging. It's an American aircraft carrier, the USS *Eisenhower*, and we can see that there are aircraft being brought up to the flight deck, and the activity on deck has been increasing,' the captain reported.

'Where is *Jupiter*, and have we turned towards the canal?' asked Charles.

'*Jupiter* is by our side, and we are a few hours from the canal yet, but on track, and they are aware of our passage.'

'Okay, I do not like the sound of the activity on the US vessel, so I think we should get *Jupiter* to fire the EMP at the aircraft carrier and then shadow our tail,' Charles said.

'Okay, sir, I will set that in motion.'

'And increase our speed to maximum immediately,' Charles said. 'I'll get dressed and come up to the bridge. Better get some fresh coffee up there. No, thinking about it, meet me in the surveillance room, then we'll go to the bridge.'

'Aye, sir, will be done.' The captain turned and headed for the surveillance room via the galley to organise the coffee.

Charles quietly closed the door and crept over to the wardrobe, opened the door, walked in, and changed into slacks, tee shirt and deck shoes. He combed his hair in the full-length mirror and rubbed his chin; a shave would have to wait. He walked quietly to his bedside table and put his watch on and left the suite with Anne still asleep in the custom-built king-sized bed. The suite stretched nearly the full width of the vessel, with huge picture windows on one side. A door that led to the stern bathing platform was on the wall opposite the bed, and on one side of the cabin, a large section of the wall could be lowered to become a large private balcony.

In the surveillance room, it was dark and quiet except for the hum of electronics and the glow of many display screens. The room was large and cool, thanks to the power of air conditioning. Three walls were full with electronics from floor to ceiling, and two operators sat on sliding chairs in front of a bank of display screens, radio speakers and keyboards. 'Hi, guys, any word from the aircraft carrier?' Charles asked.

'No, only a lot of mechanical sounds and no other tracks. We've been keeping a lookout for any submarine, but nothing has shown,' said one of the operators.

'Show me what's going on board,' Charles requested.

'That screen there, sir,' the second operator said and pointed to a large display on the right-hand side of the wall.

'Those are Super Hornets. They carry 20-mm guns and air-to-air and air-to-surface missiles,' the captain said, leaning over Charles's shoulder.

'Patch me through to the captain of *Jupiter*,' Charles asked the operator who immediately contacted *Jupiter* and passed a headset to Charles.

Charles put the headset on. 'Captain, target the aircraft carrier with the EMP – one shot, low power level and small cone. Make sure we are out of the EMP range,' Charles said. 'Yes, do it immediately.' He continued and then removed the headset. 'Captain, let's go to the bridge. Bring this baby up to full speed.'

'Yes, sir,' said the captain enthusiastically and started on his way along the gangway to the lift.

Charles grabbed the door jamb. 'Guys, good job. Keep me advised on all changes. If I am not in the library, then find me,' Charles said as he left to catch up with the captain.

Max was waiting on the bridge with the coffee where the only light was from the bank of displays and a reading light over the first officer's shoulder. Before Max could say anything, the captain said, 'First Officer, make full revolutions on all four engines, please, steady on this heading.'

The first officer leaned slightly forward in his deep seat and gripped the four throttle levers and edged them forward to the notch, then, keeping a close eye on the four revolution gauges on the large display screen, adjusted each lever to match the revolutions across all four engines. 'Full speed reached, Captain,' said the first officer. 'Engine revs are matched at full.'

Max poured coffee and handed mugs around. 'John, let's check the chart plotter,' Charles said to the captain, using his first name to ease the tension. 'Overlay the radar, please,' he said as they looked at the 20-inch Raymarine display screen. 'Okay, so that's our position. The US vessel is here, and we are headed here, yes?'

'Side Scan, does it show *Jupiter*?' Charles asked.

'No, sir,' said the first officer. 'She has just manoeuvred and is out of range.'

'Now, we could play a bit of cat and mouse. If we cut through between the Dominican Republic and Puerto Rico,' the captain suggested, pointing at the screen, 'we can offload you there to Jupiter and then meet up at Niue. What do you think?'

'No, I'm staying on board *Sundancer*. *Jupiter* will leave us before we enter the canal and head south and join in the Pacific,' Charles said.

'*Mercury* is on her way to meet us as we leave the canal?' asked the captain, smiling.

'You got it,' said Charles.

On board *Jupiter*, the captain, Mike Holdsworth turned the submarine and headed away from *Sundancer* to line up on the aircraft carrier. He spoke to his second officer, 'Tell the EMP crew to get ready for a low-power firing, small cone of attack, distance 1,200 metres.'

'Dive Officer, make periscope depth,' he called and waited by the periscope. *I hope Mr Langham knows what the bloody hell he's doing*, he thought. *Firing on an American vessel is not exactly a sane thing to do. But a low-power EMP will not disable the entire ship, just the more vulnerable system, radio, radar, sonar, display screens, navigation systems, satellite feeds and winch controls. The nuclear power plant will be unaffected, so maybe it's a good tactic as Sundancer is too far away to be blamed for that sort of attack.*

The dive officer called periscope depth, and Mike raised the periscope slowly, only just breaking the surface. He checked the bearings and distance. 'Steady, steady, fire EMP, down scope.'

'EMP fired,' called the second officer.

'Make our depth 200 feet and head back to *Sundancer*,' he said clearly. 'Call *Sundancer* and say the big fish has been caught.'

The super yacht's internal communications handset rang out. 'Bridge,' said the first officer, picking up the handset and listening carefully. 'Sir, *Jupiter* has fired the EMP, and the aircraft carrier has gone quiet. She is still under way. Surveillance says they can see the airplane elevators have stopped and lots of people are running around.' He put the handset down.

'Martin, get hold of James Young and have *Mercury* head towards the Pacific end of the Panama Canal to meet up with us,' Charles said.

Martin picked up a handset and tapped a few keys to connect with James at the Kermadec base.

Charles walked over to the camera display and looked at the aircraft carrier. He could see the white breakers at the hugely flared bows dying down. On the deck, he could clearly see an elevator stuck three quarters of the way up and crew moving all over the deck. Two men stood on the bridge deck arm, looking down and pointing to men, obviously shouting commands.

Charles looked at the captain and smiled. 'We can return to normal operations. Tell the boys in the surveillance room, one-man duty roster for now. Bring us back to cruising speed. I'll be in my cabin. I need a shave,' Charles said, rubbing his jaw, as he left the bridge and made his way to his cabin, stopping at the galley on the way to get the chef to organise a full English breakfast for three by the pool and breakfast for Abbey.

Alex Boyed, commanding officer of USS *Eisenhower*, bellowed at his XO, 'What do you mean most electrical systems have gone down?' He was in his large command chair on the bridge.

The XO, Steve Henson, removed his cap. 'We have a blackout on most electrical systems, communications and navigation. Christ, we can't even move the jets around. Engineering department is all over it, the IT teams are concerned about data programs, and we're at a loss as to what caused it.'

'And the reactor?' asked Alex, rubbing his eyes.

'Stable and unaffected. We still have power and propulsion. The navigator and his quartermasters have gone back to paper charts for now and are advising the officer of the deck on position and course.'

'What a mess! I don't suppose we can contact Fleet Command either?' asked the commanding officer.

'No, all communications are down,' advised Steve Hanson. 'There is *Sundancer*. We could always try to contact them and ask them to contact command. She's the closest vessel to us.'

'The lion asks the prey for help. Ironic, don't you think?' replied Alex, 'Do so, signal flare.'

Charles was on deck with Anne, having breakfast at the teak table, when they saw the signal flare. Max was with them, enjoying the occasional breakfast he had with Mr and Mrs Langham. Abbey was beside Anne, with her muzzle in a silver bowl, enjoying some chopped steak and egg. Charles pressed a button on the table's keypad. 'Captain, the American vessel has signalled for help. Launch one of our tenders. Use the leeward port side open tender, not the rib. Max will be our envoy. Bring the commanding officer back here. I am sure he will want to use our radio,' Charles said, cutting into the last piece of bacon.

'Okay, bringing *Sundancer* to a halt,' the captain replied. Max had just finished his breakfast. He downed a quick coffee refill and said, 'See you shortly with the yank.' Max pushed back his chair to leave.

'Max, on your way down to the tender, ensure we close up security. They see only what we want them to see,' Charles said.

'Sure thing, boss,' Max replied and headed to the lift.

Charles pressed another button and spoke, his voice echoing all over the ship. 'We are about to have visitors. Secure all sections. We must look like any normal super yacht.' He pressed the button again.

'Now the fun starts,' Anne said and smiled, cutting her egg, with Abbey looking at her with woeful eyes.

Max entered the port-side boat hanger and went over to the control console. He switched on the panel's safety switch and pressed one button. A large section of the hull folded upwards. Two of the shore-crew team climbed into the tender that sat beside an eight-metre rib. Max followed them. One of the shore crew sat in the helm seat, opened a panel cover and pressed a button. The sled the launch was sitting on moved out of the hanger and angled till most of the hull was in the water. He started the engines and pressed another button that released the bow catch and then closed the panel's cover. The thirty-foot launch backed away from *Sundancer* and turned towards the American vessel. The helmsman turned on his Raymarine Radar and GPS units and brought the boat rapidly onto the plane and sped towards the American vessel. Two American sailors waited by the gangway that had been lowered and took the mooring line as Max jumped onto the gangway and made his way to the top.

'Permission to come on board. I am Max from the super yacht *Sundancer*,' he said at the top to two well-dressed officers who had two ratings standing with him.

'Permission granted. I am Alex Boyed, commanding officer of USS *Eisenhower*, and this is my XO, Steve Henson.' They all shook hands.

'You sent out a distress signal. How can we help you?' asked Max.

'We have had a major electrical failure and have no radio or guidance systems and must contact Fleet Command,' explained Boyed.

'No worries,' said Max. 'You can use our radio to contact your Fleet Command.'

'XO Hanson will be returning with you to your vessel and will be accompanied by these two ratings,' the commanding officer said. 'I trust you have no objections?'

'Can't see any reason why there would be, so shall we go?' Max replied and headed for the gangway.

'This is a tender?' Hanson said in disbelief at the opulence of the extensive leather seating, polished wood, galley, bar and entertainment system and the helm electronics. 'This must be worth a few millions?'

'As far as I know, about a million and a half, and we have two of them, but hold your breath,' Max said. 'You haven't seen the mother ship yet.' Turning to the helmsman, he said, 'Off we go then.' The helmsman powered up both engine and glided the tender on the plane across the choppy sea back to *Sundancer* where he skilfully lined it up with the sled till the bow attached to the automatic retrieval device. He turned off the engines, opened the panel on the dash and pressed a button, causing the boat to move up the sled whilst the sled tilted and was drawn back into the hanger in a smooth orchestrated action. Max disembarked and went over the control console and closed the hanger door. 'This way, please,' Max said to the three Americans, leaving the two shore crew to hose the salt water off the polished hull of the tender. Max carefully led the Americans through the ship's luxuriously appointed gangways, passed the sweeping staircase to the glass lift and up to the main deck where Anne and Charles sat at one of the teak tables with fresh coffee and a jug of iced lime cordial on a silver tray. Abbey went racing over to see them, her tail wagging vigorously. 'Abbey, come here,' she called. 'Sorry about that, but she loves meeting people,' she said to the three visitors. 'I'm Anne,' she greeted them. 'And this is my husband, Charles.'

'Steve Hanson. I'm the XO of the USS *Eisenhower.*' He shook hands with Anne and Charles. 'That's some tender you've got, and this is some vessel,' he remarked, looking around.

'We're pretty proud of her, and we live on board, so she is our home,' Charles said. 'She was very carefully designed to fit in with our lifestyle and philosophies. For instance, she is made of as much recycled material as possible, although you would not notice.' He paused, then continued, 'Can I offer you a coffee, water or lime cordial?'

'Coffee would be great, thanks,' Hanson replied.

'Anne's already taking good care of your crew members,' Max said as he poured Hanson his coffee.

'Now, how can we be of help to the American Navy?' Charles asked. 'I thought those things were floating cities?' asked Charles.

'It is a bit embarrassing, and we do not know exactly what happened, but we have lost most of our electrical systems,' Hanson explained. 'Which means we have no communication to CINCPAC Fleet, and navigation is back to paper systems.'

'Well, feel free to use our radio to contact them,' Charles said. 'Have a seat while you drink your coffee, then we will go up to our bridge and see what we can do. Your two ratings can stay here. I am sure that Anne and Abbey will keep them occupied.'

'That'll be great,' he said to Charles, then turned to the two ratings. 'When I go to the bridge, you two stay here, and for heaven's sake, do not break anything,' he said with a very serious face and a raised finger.

'Were you on an exercise of travelling to a new destination?' Charles asked the XO. 'Or are you not at liberty to say?'

'We were on a mission, and as you say, I am not at liberty to explain any further,' the XO said with a smile.

Charles stood as the XO put his empty coffee cup down. 'This way,' Charles said to the XO. They walked into the cavernous main lounge and headed forward towards the lift. 'We go up four levels to the sea-view deck where the bridge is,' Charles explained as he pressed a button on the lift panel.

When the lift reached the sea-view deck, it opened on to the gangway between the dining room and bridge; Charles turned and opened the bridge door to be greeted by the captain.

Charles did the introductions. 'XO Steve Hanson, this is the captain of *Sundancer*, John Whitcome,' he said. 'XO Hanson needs to use our radio to contact CINCPAC Fleet.'

'No problem, XO, here's our radio. Help yourself,' said Whitcome. 'You can use this chair,' he said, pointing to the first officer's chair.

'Thanks.' XO Hanson sat down and looked at the radio controls. Martin Deeks, the technical officer, came over to him and helped the XO operate the radio. The XO placed the headset on his head, adjusted the microphone and tuned into the frequency he required.

Charles and John left the bridge, leaving XO Hanson, the first officer and technical officer on the bridge. 'We seem to have had the desired effect and the bonus of being the Good Samaritan,' John said.

'He said they have lost all navigational capabilities and are back to paper systems,' Charles advised.

'Well, we can guide them safely to Manzanillo International Terminal, which is on our route to Panama, if they want,' John suggested.

'We'll ask their XO when he's finished,' Charles agreed.

XO Steve Hanson came out of the bridge and walked over to join Charles and John. 'That's some bridge you have there, a phenomenal electronics and computer set-up. Looks like you can run the ship single-handedly and moor it as well,' he said.

'Thanks, and yes, you can,' agreed John. 'How did the call go?' he asked.

'CINCPAC cannot believe what they heard. They say nothing showed on their sensor. They reckon Washington will go ballistic, but they have ships on route but days away,' Steve said.

'John suggested that we could act as your navigation system if you follow us to the Port at Panama, where you can moor up. All we would need to know is how much water you draw,' Charles offered. 'Shall we go and sit down?' They followed Charles through the dining room into the library and sat down in the armchairs.

'I'm a little lost for words. This ship is bigger and more opulent than I first thought.' He shook his head. 'Anyway, I had better call my commanding officer and get his agreement,' Steve said and lifted a two-way radio from his belt. 'Sir, XO here. I have been on to CINCPAC Fleet and explained the situation, and *Sundancer* has offered to guide us into Manzanillo International Terminal, acting as our navigation system.'

'That's very thoughtful and also a good idea. Set it up, and thank the owner and captain,' Alex Boyed, commanding officer of the *Eisenhower*, said. 'We will talk about the CINCPAC Fleet call when you get back here.' He cut the connection.

The XO turned the handset off and replaced it on his belt. 'Well, you heard that. We accept your kind offer of assistance,' the XO said.

'That's good. I will leave you with John to organise things, and when you are ready to return to your ship, he will get Max to run you back.' Charles extended his hand. 'If I don't see you before you leave, it's been nice meeting you.' He shook hands and left the library.

Chapter Seven

Leaders Are Blind, One Flees

The president stormed into the White House Situation Room, and the hum of conversation instantly died, and the officials around the table shifted in their seats or fiddled with their papers and pens, desperately trying to avoid eye contact with the president. The screens around the walls showed location maps and satellite images of the stricken aircraft carrier.

The president pointed to one of the displays of the aircraft carrier. 'What the hell is going on?' the president shouted. 'You had better have a bloody good explanation,' he demanded of the defence secretary.

'The USS *Eisenhower*, commanded by Alex Boyed, has suffered a major electrical failure, the cause of which is so far unknown,' the defence secretary explained, silently wishing that he could be doing this on the phone rather than in the White House Situation Room where the president had called all his advisors.

'Is it not obvious that this unknown failure was caused by this boat *Sundancer*? I assume it was the only boat in the vicinity?' the president asked in a sarcastic but controlled tone.

'I think we should strike the *Sundancer* now while it's in open and very deep water,' William Paige, the president's military advisor, proffered.

'Unthinkable', the secretary of state cut in, 'and unlawful. Too many people are aware of its exact position. It's a stealthy yacht, but the Panama officials know it's there and, no doubt, so do all Langham's lawyers. This guy is way too clever for us to try that sort of illegal action.' He paused and looked directly at the president. 'Don't forget that the presentation he gave at the UN is all over the Internet plus your video conversation with him, Mr President.'

'So will someone tell me what happened to one of our so-called invincible aircraft carriers?' the president asked in a more controlled manner.

'Mr President,' the national security advisor, Helen Stark, said. 'At this time, we do not have a direct known causal effect of the failure. We can, I believe, rule out external forces, as, with the exception of the super yacht, there were no other vessels, submarines or aircraft detected by the USS *Eisenhower*.' She paused and looked over at the defence secretary. 'Our satellites picked up no external activity or radio waves of any kind.'

'Mr President, I concur with Helen. Whatever our views are of Mr Langham, we have no evidence of his involvement other than his offer to assist our vessel. I would suggest that we wait until the commanding officer completes his investigation and reports to us with his findings,' the secretary of state said. 'We have a team of investigators on their way to Panama.'

The president cut off all further discussion with a wave of his hand. 'We have one of our most modern vessels disabled and vulnerable, and we do not know why, which is wholly unacceptable. Get me some answers in twenty-four hours.' He grabbed his folder and left the room.

'So what now?' Helen asked of the others around the table.

'Pray we find an answer in twenty-four hours,' William Paige said, rubbing his eyes with both hands.

'And get more vessels into the area to protect the USS *Eisenhower*?' Helen questioned.

'Already under way, Helen. I redirected the Fourth Fleet to Panama,' Gregory Adam, chief of naval command, advised.

Duke Warren sat in front of the president's desk in the Oval Office in an antique armchair.

'So, Duke, do you believe what this Langham guy said in his presentation? You were at the UN meeting, weren't you?' the president asked.

'Yes, I do, Mr President,' Duke answered. 'And I have seen a copy of your video call with him.' Duke crossed his legs and dusted some lint from his knee. 'He is very sincere and has the science to back him up, plus the backing of many of the top scientists around the globe.'

'Even you now admit that climate change is not advancing as fast as you predicted,' the president, Mike Read, countered.

'That's clutching at straws, Mr President, and you know it. He is talking about a lot more than just climate change.' Duke leant forward. 'He is talking about extinctions, famine, habitat destruction, deforestation, CO_2 levels that contribute to climate change, all of which affect mankind and all of which are interlinked.' He gestured for the president to not interrupt. 'Take extinctions. Biodiversity keeps mankind alive. Without biodiversity, the planet will slowly die and us with it – even the smallest of creatures has its part to play in us being alive.'

'But you are talking tens, if not hundreds, of years from now,' the president's chief of staff, O'Hare, commented.

'Ryan, that's true, but it's our future, your children's future,' Duke replied with exasperation in his voice.

'Our budgets are at breaking point, coping with the here and now, Duke, and you know that. I have a budget meeting, starting in a few minutes. That's going to be difficult enough without asking to spend more money on an event years in the future.'

'I am aware of that, Mr President,' Duke agreed. 'But you also have your deputy assistant energy and climate change representative at that meeting who will be clamouring for aid.'

'Well, you had better support me, Duke. Do not stir up any more climate debates, or there will be consequences, and no, the deputy assistant will not be asking for more aid.' The president glared at Duke.

'You've put pressure on her!' Duke exclaimed.

'Yes, I understand she likes her salary and benefits, and you would be wise to follow suit.'

'Yes, Mr President.' Duke stood and left the Oval Office and headed for his office downtown. *There is money for votes but not for our future and/or our children's future*, he thought. *I need to contact this Langham guy and speak to him now. The world leaders do not see the urgency of what's facing them.* Duke had contacted some of the world's top scientists on seeing the UN presentation, and they had all agreed the urgency would multiply exponentially each year that no action was taken. This Langham guy seemed to be a key element in forcing world leaders into action. He entered his office and went to his desk and sat down. *I will be going behind the back of the president of the United States, but what choice do I have?* He picked up the phone and dialled.

Charles sat with Anne, with Abbey at their feet, watching Max play table tennis with one of the ratings when the captain came on to the deck with XO John Hanson. 'We're finished, so Max can return them to their carrier,' John Whitcome said, as the ratings came smartly to attention at the sight of their XO.

Anne got up from her teak chair and went over to the ratings and the XO. 'It's been nice meeting you. Have a safe journey,' she said with meaning. Charles got up and stood at Anne's side. 'Same here,' he said to them all.

Max put the table tennis bat on the table and placed the ball in the holder by the net. 'Follow me, gentlemen, your tender awaits.' Max saluted cheekily and led them into the lounge towards the lift.

'Mr Langham, with the USS *Eisenhower* following, Martin has suggested we run on the two outer engines only, which I have approved,' the captain said.

'Sounds sensible. Anne and I will be on the star deck with Abbey. Let the chef know we will have lunch there.'

Charles held Anne's hand, and they walked through the lounge with the captain who had Abbey at his side. In the lift, Abbey barked; she always did bark in the lift, although they never knew why. The captain tickled her behind the ear, but she still barked. They all got out on the sea-view deck, the captain going forward to the bridge. Charles and Anne paused at the base of a circular staircase, while Charles pressed a button that opened the sealed hatch at the top of the staircase, just in time for Abbey to go straight through on to the uppermost outside deck called the star deck. Charles and Anne climbed the staircase onto the deck. The star deck was the highest deck on board, and at its centre was the main electronics mast. The circular space was covered by a matching circular tinted-glass roof that curved downwards at the edges with very narrow supports from the central spa. The area was protected from the wind created by the boat's speed with a tinted-glass windbreak at the front. The rear area was fitted out for the ultimate in relaxation, with sumptuous lounger chairs, tables, bar, a large display screen and spa pool. Lights twinkled from the glass roof supports. Abbey jumped up onto one of the loungers and lay down. 'Well, she's sorted!' Anne said and laughed.

'Typical,' Charles said and ruffled Abbey's head as he walked past and sat on a lounger by Anne. 'Up here is like a sanctuary, quiet and away from it all.'

The display screen lit up, and a familiar face appeared. 'You spoke too soon,' said Anne, laughing.

'I wonder what Duke wants.' He pressed the accept button on the keypad built into the lounger.

'Hi, Duke, and to what do we owe this pleasure?' Charles said.

'Err, not something I can talk about over the open airways, Charles,' Duke said very guardedly.

'Right, I think I understand. Not sure, but I think I do. Why don't you take a few days off and join us for a holiday?' suggested Charles.

'That sounds like an offer I could not ignore,' Duke said.

'Hold the line a second,' Charles said and called up Max's number.

The screen remained blank when Max answered. 'Yes, boss?'

'Max, where is the Learjet and its pilot?' asked Charles.

'Both are in Newark on standby as usual, boss,' Max replied. 'I'm on my way back to *Sundancer* now.'

'Good. Contact the pilot and tell him to get ready to head to Panama with a guy called Duke.'

'Sure thing, boss,' Max replied.

Charles pressed a button on his chair's keypad, and Duke's face reappeared. 'Duke, make your way to Newark where our Learjet will be waiting for you.'

'Thanks, Charles. See you soon.'

Charles cut the connection and called up the captain. 'John, contact Keith and get him to submit a flight plan to Enrique Adolfo Jiménez Airport for the Learjet in Newark,' he said and then ended the call.

'Well, maybe now we can relax.' He looked across at Anne and held her hand. 'I do so love you,' he said.

'I love you too.' Anne smiled. 'Sounds like Duke has got himself into a dangerous situation.'

'Yes, I think this president is a nasty piece of work. I have heard rumours that some people have disappeared or had fatal accidents, and I don't think he wants to become another statistic.'

'I wonder how Cathy and Chris are getting along,' Anne asked. 'Are they still on Niue?'

'Yes, we will pick them up as soon as we get in helicopter range. They should have some good stories on the corals and rainforest they have been exploring and measuring.'

'I think Keith gave them too easy an assignment,' Anne chuckled.

'It's valuable work that needed to be done. The samples they collect are important to the whole area and pacific ecosystem.' Charles said, lying back and closing his eyes. 'Wake me up when lunch arrives.'

The captain's face appeared on the display screen. Anne accepted the call. 'Sorry to disturb you, Mrs Langham. We are just entering into the canal now.'

'Thank you, John,' Anne replied. 'Oh, is our lunch ready?' she asked as an afterthought.

'I will check with the chef and hurry him up, Mrs Langham,' the captain advised. The screen changed to a plot of their course entering the canal.

A few minutes later, Max and a steward appeared with two trays and laid the lunch out on the table, placing a silver bowl on the deck that got the undivided attention of Abbey.

'Hmm, smells good,' said Charles, stretching. 'Where are we?'

'We are just entering the canal, boss,' Max advised. 'And Duke is on the Learjet, heading this way. As soon as he touches down, I'll pop over in the helicopter and pick him up.'

'Very good, Max. Thanks,' Charles said and put a selection of salad and cheeses on his plate as Max and the steward left. Charles stood up and saw the USS *Eisenhower* being guided by a team of tugs to the container terminal. The entrance to the canal was full of cargo ships and tankers waiting to pass through, although *Sundancer* seemed to be jumping the queue. Just eight to ten hours and back in the Pacific, home territory, and under the protection of the whole organisation. He walked slowly around the circular space, enjoying the view. Some background music started. *Anne playing some of her favourite pieces*, he thought. Abbey nudged his leg, and he gave her a piece of beef. He grabbed some more food and sat down beside Anne again. 'Nice spread. No wonder the crew like being on board,' Charles said as he lay back and slowly finished his plate and glass of wine. Abbey tucked herself at the base of Anne's lounger. 'You are aware that the chef also cooks her food.' Anne tickled Abbey with her toes.

'So tell me, Duke, what's going on?' asked Charles, who was dressed casually for dinner in a white shirt and slacks in the main lounge with the doors closed against the biting insects that were buzzing around the super yacht. A steward hovered around, serving quietly from a silver platter. Anne, resplendent in a flowing white blouse and dark-blue skirt, sat next to Duke, who was thankful for the opportunity to shower and change into slacks and a polo shirt before dinner. Duke chose to sit opposite Charles. Max had joined them for dinner – not an unusual occurrence when guests were dining with Charles and Anne.

'We have problems looming and a fight on our hands with the United States. I do not believe that Mike Read will acquiesce to the environmental demands that you made to the United Nations. He is against being backed into a corner and is as dangerous as a rat in that situation.' Duke dabbed his lips with his napkin. 'His chief of staff is up for a fight and has dispatched more of the Fourth Fleet to Panama.' He leant back as the steward removed his soup bowl. 'That was great, by the way,' he said. 'I have been warned by the president not to make waves on climate issues, or I am out of a job, and I know what that means in the short- and long-term.' He rested an arm on the table and held his wine glass. 'The Secret Service is now all over me – personal life, financial, the lot.'

'You're safe with us,' said Anne. 'Where we are going, nothing can touch us.'

'Surely Mike is listening to his scientific advisors?' queried Charles, looking at Duke.

'He has gagged them. It's tantamount to a bribe. If they so much as squeak, they are fired. Even the deputy assistant, Energy and Climate, dare not say a word if she wants her position, salary and benefits.' He sighed. *A bad day for the US and the world, and my career is finished*, he thought.

'So if he won't listen to reason, he will have to be made to see the ill of his ways,' Charles advised in a low voice. 'And we can do that.'

'How can you? If he will not listen to his closest advisors, he sure as hell won't listen to you,' Duke remarked coldly.

'Trust me, Duke; we can make him see sense, and all the other politicians as well. You'll see soon enough.' Charles smiled at Anne. 'We were prepared for this eventuality. Ah, the main course,' he changed the subject, as the steward served the main course.

Max was the first to see the subtle change in the super yachts attitude. 'The captain's just deployed the stabilisers, and we're picking up speed,' he remarked to Charles. 'So *Mercury* will be with us soon enough.'

'*Mercury*? What's that?' Duke questioned.

'*Mercury* is one of our submarines,' Max answered with a rueful smile. 'In the Atlantic, our submarine *Jupiter* shadowed us for protection. She's now heading for the Pacific at flank speed the long way around. *Launch One* enters the Panama Canal at 10.30 am tomorrow. We have quite a fleet, you know?' He toasted Duke with his wine glass. 'Welcome to our organisation. You are in for a few surprises.'

Anne looked questionably at Charles. He looked back, and

although no words passed their lips, a great deal of conversation took place with their eyes, and an agreement was reached.

'Duke, you're at a loose end, your job in the White House is over, and you are more or less ostracised from the United States. Why don't you join us?' Charles asked, with sincerity in his face and voice. 'You're a great lobbyist, and you know the subject, plus you have the advantage of knowing a lot of scientific advisors that we do not have access to.' He took a sip of his wine, while Duke sat deep in thought. 'I believe you will be mind blown when you see the technical ability, resources and facilities we have.'

Duke sat deep in thought, playing with his meal; the size of the super yacht and its luxurious fittings had already blown his mind. Now he learned that they had two submarines; undoubtedly that was not the end of it. *This yacht*, he looked around him, *is fully electronic. I suppose the 747-8i is the same. The electronics and luxury on the Learjet were phenomenal. I could do worse. As soon as I open my mouth, the Secret Service will start their intrusive review and bend the facts, and I will be finished.* 'So what am I joining?' Duke asked.

'Max, tell Duke a bit about *Sundancer* and her capabilities,' Anne said. 'That would be a good starting point.'

'Torpedo tubes fore and aft, full surveillance facility to rival anything the US has, missile launchers hidden beneath disguised deck hatches, top speed forty-two knots.' He smiled. 'Shall I continue?'

'I am not bloody surprised! But the XO of the *Eisenhower* reported nothing out of the ordinary when he was on board.' Duke put his knife and fork down. 'So everything is carefully disguised, but how did they not track the submarine? The US had their own in the vicinity, the USS *Resolution*, one of the latest hunter class.'

'Duke, we are very careful – we have to be,' Charles explained. 'We also have an underwater facility, housing over 140 people. In fact, we're heading there now.'

The steward cleared the table, while Max poured everyone a coffee.

'Unbelievable!' exclaimed Duke, looking rather shocked. 'Okay, count me in. I believe I can achieve more working within your organisation than from the outside.'

'Welcome on board.' Charles smiled at Duke. 'With your help, I think we can achieve our aims. It will take a lot of work, most of which we have completed, but I will leave the full briefing till the morning.' He looked at his watch. 'It's too late tonight.' He touched a keypad, and a large display screen rose from a rosewood cabinet. He pressed another keypad, and the screen lit up with a display of the super yachts position, direction and speed. '*Mercury* should be just off our port beam.' Charles pressed another couple of buttons. The rear deck lights came on, the swimming pool and spa pool both lit up, and the display screen changed to a world map with red dots. 'Those red dots show the position of our assets,' he explained to Duke. 'Aircraft, boats, submarines, submersibles, buildings and our deep-sea HQ.' He took a drink of his coffee. 'The buildings are mainly in famine and reforestation areas. All our technical development is carried out at either our deep-sea HQ or contracted out under the utmost secrecy.' He stood up and slowly walked around the table. 'All our assets, like *Sundancer*, are very well protected; we have, what you could call, I suppose, our own well-armed secret service.' He put his hands on the back of Anne's chair. 'We look after all our staff like they are members of our own family.'

The captain's face appeared on the display screen. Max leant over the table and pressed the keypad to accept the call. 'Apologies for the interruption. We are now in the Pacific, heading to Niue, and *Mercury* is five nautical miles off our port beam. I am standing the crew down to night watch.'

'Thank you, Captain,' said Max and retracted the display screen.

'Well, if you don't mind, I think I will call it a night,' Duke said. 'Max, would you be kind enough to show me to my cabin and save me from getting lost?'

'By all means. Follow me,' Max said and led Duke forward towards the lift as he said goodnight to Charles and Anne.

Chapter Eight

The Pacific

A knock on the door woke Charles and Anne, and a steward entered their stateroom with a trolley. 'The captain thought you would like breakfast on your balcony as it's such a beautiful day and calm seas.' He moved the trolley over to the starboard wall and pressed a button on the wall keypad. A large section of the wall lowered to form a balcony, side rails automatically lifted into position. He moved a table and two chairs on to the balcony and laid out the breakfast. 'Breakfast is ready for you,' he said and left the cabin. Anne got up and put on a white cotton robe. Charles swung his legs out and put on a pair of shorts and joined Anne on the balcony. The super yacht was moving swiftly through the water, and the sea was a wonderful deep blue against an azure sky with just a few wispy clouds here and there. Anne served the cooked breakfast of poached eggs, bacon, hash browns, and tomato on the plates, while Charles poured the Earl Grey tea. 'Where do you think we are?' Anne asked.

'I think we should be off Niue tonight,' Charles replied.

'Are you going to brief Duke today?'

'Yes, I will show him the surveillance room, then let him talk to Keith and James at the base for a while. After that, I will explain our plan of attack.'

'I think I'll take Abbey for a run around the deck a few times and then a swim in the pool to burn off some of her energy.'

'A lot of barking to come, then. Better warn the crew!' Charles said and laughed.

Charles buttered some wholemeal toast and dipped it in the poached egg. 'Perfectly cooked,' he remarked.

In the distance, a dark shape appeared amidst a swirl of white water. At first, Anne thought it was a whale, then the shape of a conning tower appeared followed by the hull of a large black submarine. The black conning tower was accentuated by the blue-and-yellow logo of their company. 'It's the *Mercury*!' exclaimed Anne as she watched members of the crew leave the interior of the submarine and stand on the deck. It kept up the same pace as the *Sundancer*, and Charles knew that the captains would be talking to each other. He could envisage that the captain of the *Mercury* was just giving the crew some air time and would be diving again in twenty or so minutes. Charles drained his cup of tea and wiped his mouth with a napkin. 'If you don't mind, darling, I'm going to have a shave and get dressed.' He walked around the table and kissed Anne. 'I'll join you,' she said.

Charles and Anne left their stateroom and headed along the wide corridor, with its deep wool carpets and warm lighting, for the main deck. There were pictures on the inside wall and windows on the external walls. They decided to forgo the lift and went to the central atrium and took the wide curving stairs. Anne went off to look for Abbey and take her for a run, while Charles went to find Duke and Max.

Duke was sitting, reading the news on the Internet, and stood to greet Charles. 'Duke, good morning. Are you ready to start your induction?'

'Morning. Yes, I'm ready, still not totally sure what I've got myself into,' he replied.

'Okay, follow me,' Charles said and led Duke to the lift and went up to the sea-view deck. 'This deck we call the sea-view deck. It houses the formal dining room, which is here.' He opened the door and led Duke into the dining room and carried on through and opened the next door. 'And this is the library, my favourite room, and as you can see through the glass wall, that's the helicopter.' He pointed to a staircase. 'Up there is Anne and my private area. Come this way, and I'll show you the bridge and introduce you to the senior crew.'

The bridge was its usual peaceful self. All three of the captain chairs were occupied, and Charles introduced Duke to the captain, John Whitcome, the technical officer, Martin Deeks, and Max who occupied the first officer's chair. 'I see *Mercury* is alongside,' Charles said to the captain.

'She'll be diving in a few minutes. With nothing on the radar, it seemed a good time to let the crew stretch their legs and get some fresh air,' the captain explained. 'But we do have the US *Pacific Fleet* on the move. Some of the vessels have just left Pearl Harbour. Our ETA Niue is around ten tonight.'

'Well, okay, Duke. Max, let's go to the surveillance room,' Charles said as he left the bridge with them in tow. They got into the lift, and Max pressed the button for deck two. They walked along another plush corridor towards the aft of the super yacht and entered the large surveillance room.

'This is our input from the outside world. Everything comes through here – radio communications, video calls, Internet, TV signals, satellite feeds, sonar, and radar. Every screen on the bridge is duplicated here and can also be controlled from here. They also intercept certain signals,' Charles explained. 'So these two guys are very important to our safety on board.'

'Quite a set-up for a private yacht,' Duke said, rubbing his chin, taking in the display screens, servers, and other high-tech equipment. The room had one large long window. 'Must get fuzzy eyes in here after a while?'

'The guys work in shifts, and normally, only one would be on duty at a time, but as soon as any heightened activity starts, they double up,' explained Charles. 'What is the news on the United States *Pacific Fleet*?' Charles asked.

One of the operatives turned in his chair. 'One destroyer and a single aircraft carrier left Pearl about three hours ago and are heading southwest at present.'

'Okay, keep an eye on them for now.'

'These guys also control the armaments,' Max commented to Duke.

'Now you've got me,' said Duke, looking shocked and taking a step backwards.

'Torpedo tubes, ship-to-air missiles, we are pretty well covered. Okay, now the conference room for a video call to the Kermadec base. Please connect us,' Charles said to one of the communications officers.

Charles led them to the cabin next door. 'Max, organise some coffee, please,' he said as he entered the cabin and sat at the oblong table. Max picked up a handset and called the galley to organise the coffee.

The large display lit up and showed Keith Pritchard and James Young. 'Good morning, gentlemen,' said Charles. 'I would like to introduce you to our newest recruit, Duke Warren. Duke, the old guy on the left is Keith Pritchard. He is my worldwide operations manager, and the young gun is James Young, the operations manager for the Kermadec base.'

Duke nodded in recognition at each introduction.

'So let me explain how this works. James is in charge of all Kermadec base operations and reports to both Keith and me directly. Keith coordinates all activities worldwide – be it ships, subs, airplanes, personnel, terrestrial operations, undersea operations, the works. Even Anne keeps him up to date when she is in the field as it's important that nothing is left to chance.'

'A pretty tight ship all round,' Duke commented as Max poured a coffee.

'So Keith, where are *Jupiter* and *Launch One*?' Charles asked.

'*Jupiter* is heading north at full speed to intercept with you and *Mercury*. *Launch One* will arrive Tonga the day after tomorrow, and both the Learjet and 747-8i are in Tonga as we speak, refuelled and in their hangers,' Keith reported casually. 'The A380 is still unloading and will take off tomorrow.'

'James, the undersea sonic installations, what's their status?' Charles asked.

'All systems are tested and ready, with control further refined to a five percentage point capability, which we are pretty happy about,' James reported with a smile.

'That's not bad, so please explain for Duke's benefit how these work and their purpose,' Charles requested, sitting back so that James could direct his reply to Duke.

'Well, we needed a way of gently at first forcing the hand of those governments that do not, or do not want to, understand the issues facing the planet environmentally and refuse to take action. At various strategic locations around the world, we have, fitted to the seabed, very special autonomously powered units.' He showed a picture on the screen of a box-like structure with a large cone shape on the front, flanked by four tubes, one at each corner. 'These tube-like appendages are lasers which have been aimed at a specified distance from the unit. When the lasers are fired, they heat the water to beyond boiling point and that creates an elasticity film a few microns thick over a massive controlled area. This cone shape then directs an intense sound pressure wave to that area and, in effect, pushes the area forward.' He paused.

'Carry on,' said Charles.

'When we fire the unit, the sound wave can be controlled to within five percentage points of power. This causes a pressure wave to hit the area targeted, which will cause a tsunami of the chosen varying intensity towards the target,' James finished.

Duke looked at Charles with his mouth slight agape.

Keith leant forward, his facing nearly filling the screen. 'Duke, I know what you are thinking, and you do not have to worry. The tests we have done and the computer models show that at the times that have been chosen at each location and taking into account tides, only property will be damaged. There will be no loss of life.' Sincerity filled his face. 'That was one of Charles's criteria for the project.'

'Well, I don't know what to say,' Duke commented, scratching his ear.

'Show the virtual tour of the base, please,' Charles asked the guys on the display screen. The screen image changed to show an external view of the base from live underwater cameras. The main circular pod built into the side of the sloping face of the island could be seen with its myriad of hooded windows. As the camera panned, windowless tubes could be seen that linked each of the five smaller circular buildings with the same hooded-style windows. The view switched to another camera that showed a different style of building slightly further away from the rest. It was more of an elongated shape than the other buildings, and beneath it hung two submersible vehicles. This building had a longer linking tube supported on angled legs with a large bulge midway along the tube. The view switched to another camera which showed another tube from the main building disappearing into a rock face. Duke sat watching the display screen with a bewildered look on his face. The view switched to the inside, showing a busy manned laboratory, then an even busier electronics development laboratory, tool room with a few technicians using CNC equipment, an accommodation module, large canteen, games room, then back to the activity of the control room. James and Keith reappeared.

'You're joking, of course. It's a film set,' Duke said.

'No, it's as real as we are, as you'll see for yourself when you arrive,' explained Keith.

'How do we get in?' Duke asked.

'Either by submersible or you can walk in via the tunnel from Curtis Island,' Keith replied.

'The walk in sounds preferable,' said Duke.

'Okay, guys, thanks. I think that covers enough for today,' Charles said to Keith and James who bade their farewells to Duke and Max.

'Max, can you give Duke the ship's tour? Then meet us for lunch on the main deck.'

'Sure thing, boss,' Max said and guided Duke from the room.

Charles sat with Anne and Abbey on a large deep settee in the main lounge when Max and Duke entered. 'Enjoyed the tour, Duke?' Charles asked, but before Duke could reply, Max said, 'Excuse me, boss.' then went over and turned on the large display screen. Max lifted a handset and said, 'Run it now.' He sat down in a matching armchair and turned to Charles and Anne. 'You had better watch this.'

The BBC television news ran with a story on riots taking place in Washington, London, Paris, Munich, and Tokyo. The rioters were seen displaying placards, demanding governments to take action to save the planet. The leader of the Washington riots, standing on the steps of the Washington memorial, was saying, 'Our government is supposed to work for us, not that we should work for it. We demand that they take action now to do whatever is necessary to reverse the destruction of the rainforests, which are the lungs of the earth, phase out fossil fuel use, stop wasting money on their war machine, and help the poor and starving of the world. World peace and unity – it can be achieved. It just takes guts, and it seems we have politicians who are gutless!'

The news report then changed to the lawns of the White House where the president stood in front of a lectern, his chief of staff at his side and Secret Service team on the edge, eyes searching. 'These riots, these riots that are taking place right here in the United States,' his finger stabbed at the lectern. 'And in many other countries around the world have been orchestrated by one person. That person is spreading untruths and lies. The United States is doing more than any other country to engender world peace and progress environmental change. We are investing heavily in alternate fuels.' He looked around at the reporters. 'The person who has deliberately lied and perpetrated these dangerous riots will be found. The might of the United States will bring him to justice.' He raised his hand to quell any questions. 'He has directly threatened the United States, its people, and me personally, which we will not let go unpunished. Thank you.' He turned and walked back into the White House.

Max switched the TV off, and it disappeared back into its cabinet. Charles stood up and walked on to the deck, his mind spinning. Why was the president talking such lies and nonsense? Everyone knew that the US was not doing a damned thing about world peace; it was common knowledge that they were building more aircraft carriers and enlarging their nuclear arsenal. *Investing in alternates to fossil fuels, that's a joke! Oil production has recently reached peak levels in the United States. Okay, he wants to play tough. Well, I can play tough and from a stronger position.* Anne came to his side and entwined an arm through his. 'What game is Mike playing?' she asked.

'A rough game as he is obviously uncomfortable on his back foot,' Charles said as he wandered back into the lounge. 'Max, find out where the United States *Pacific Fleet* is now, speed and heading.'

Duke leant forward and said, 'So do we have a game plan?'

Charles's mind had been going over the next steps: What will the president do next? Which other world leaders would side with the president? Who would baulk at the idea? He had to get Anne and the children to safety, and Duke, of course. The Kermadec HQ was the safest place, unknown to anyone outside the organisation; from there he could orchestrate his actions and communicate easily and safely with those he needed to.

Max returned to the lounge. 'Around 2,000 kilometres northeast of Nassau and headed clearly in our direction. Oh, and the captain is on his way.'

They all sat around the teak table on the deck. 'So this is what I want to do,' Charles said emphatically. 'Any objections, suggestions, or ideas, now is the time to shout.' He looked at the captain. 'How are we for fuel?'

'Fine. We filled up in Panama and have been cruising on just two engines since then.'

'Okay, go to full power on all four engines. Keep on track for Niue. We will slow down but not stop, so work out with Max on when he leaves, when he needs to be back on board. *Mercury* is to stay ten kilometres off our stern at all times. We then steam full power to Curtis Island. After dropping us off by submersible, *Sundancer* will continue to Auckland, shadowed by *Mercury*.' Charles paused as a steward laid the table and another served the lunch, and he chose his selection from the tray. '*Mercury* will head for Kermadec once *Sundancer* is safely moored in Auckland. Any questions?' Charles looked at Max. 'Max, I only want a skeleton crew left on board *Sundancer* in Auckland, so organise with the first officer and captain as to who will stay on board and who will transfer to *Mercury* and when,' Charles said.

'Boss, I have an idea. What if...' Max said, deep in thought. 'You'll have to bear with me as I'm still formulating this in my mind. *Sundancer* does not go to Auckland but, from Curtis Island, heads along the Tonga ridge doing, eh, soundings, marine research. She can have the research pennant flying. She can still dock in Nuku'alofa well before the US fleet and be protected by both submarines.'

'Okay, I'll go for that. Non-essential crew can disembark by helicopter on to Curtis Island, and once she's docked in Tonga, we can put the shore security crew on board and bring the rest back on board *Mercury*.'

The captain stood up. 'Well, as I have quite a bit to do, so if you don't mind, I'll take my lunch to the bridge and get started.' He chose a selection from the tray the steward held and left for the bridge.

'That's fine, John. If anything changes or comes up, I'll shout,' Charles agreed.

'This is sounding more like a military campaign than I like,' said Duke with a worried look on his face.

'It's about protecting those you love, your assets, and the only planet we have, Duke,' said Anne quietly, touching his arm.

'I know, but it's certainly heating up,' Duke said. 'Warships are on their way, being hunted down by the United States government.' He looked at the sky. 'For all we know, we are on camera at this very moment.'

'It will not get that far, and besides, *Sundancer* is capable of forty-two knots, is fully armed, and once we are in the Kermadec

HQ, we are totally safe,' Charles said reassuringly. He could feel the increase in speed as the two other engines came online, matched the revolutions of the others, and then wound up to full speed. The bow-up attitude that became evident as the yacht increased speed levelled off as the stabilisers and trim tabs automatically adjusted to the boat's new attitude. *I think I need to lead the play on this*, he thought. *Jupiter* can protect our backs from the encroaching fleet and disarm them, using the EMP and a first tame strike to Washington harbour to ward off the president.

'Max, what's your take on Mike's speech?' Anne asked.

Max thought for a moment while he chewed on a sandwich. 'I've a feeling he is under pressure from lobby groups, the oil barons, and the senators who have fortunes invested in armament companies and logging companies, all of whom would lose their fortunes if the president carried through with what Charles had suggested, and lest we forget, his own wealth is mainly from the contracts he and his cronies got from the Gulf War, so he has a lot to lose personally.'

'Fine, I agree with all that, but how far will he go, Duke?' Charles asked.

'To save what he has, all the way,' Duke said, then paused. 'Think about what he has to lose,' he continued, ticking off each of his fingers one by one. 'His position, his wealth, most of his senators, his standing in the world, and his future.'

'Max, have *Jupiter* head to intercept the *Pacific Fleet*, hold position, and be ready to hit the United States fleet with another EMP pulse burst.'

Max refilled his plate and left the lounge via the lift to head towards the bridge.

Mike Read, the US president, walked – or, to be more accurate, stormed – into the Oval Office with his chief of staff and security advisor in tow. 'Sir, I don't think the public will go for your version of the story,' the chief of staff, Ryan O'Hare, said as he sat down on the settee.

'Well, I don't give a damn,' President Mike Read snapped back. 'Get my PR advisor in here now. It's their job to make people believe the truth, and don't forget that what I say is always the truth. Get me the defence chief now!' He sat on the corner of his desk. 'I want this guy Langham crushed, publicly and physically.' A tall, silver-haired man in a grey striped suit entered. 'Ah, Clive! Just the man. Please sit.' He gestured to the settee where Ryan O'Hare was seated. 'Now tell me how many ships have left Pearl looking for this yacht, eh, *Sundancer*, and what's the news on the *Eisenhower*?'

The defence chief sat down and unbuttoned his jacket as he did. 'Well, the effect on the *Eisenhower* was the same as one would expect from an electromagnetic impulse, similar to that of a nuclear explosion or solar flare, none of which have occurred. She will be out of action for months. We have one aircraft carrier, the USS *Ronald Reagan*, and one missile cruiser, the *Port Royal*, heading southwest.'

'That's all we have sent out of the entire Fourth Fleet!' the president exclaimed. 'What about aircraft?' the president asked, his voice rising.

'We have an AWAC airborne out of Kadena, Japan.'

'Japan! What the hell's use is that? We must have something closer!' The president stood up and walked to his chair behind his desk.

'That's the closest, Mr President,' Clive said uncomfortably. 'The USS *Ronald Reagan* carries a short range AWAC.'

'Send more of the Fourth Fleet, get them down there fast, and sink that yacht!' the president commanded. 'I'll sign the order. Ryan, get it drawn up and bring it to me today.'

As Harris and O'Hare both stood, Ryan said, 'It's an unwise move, if I may say so, Mr President. Neither the senate nor the White House legal team will sign on such an order.'

The president turned to O'Hare. 'When I want your advice, I will ask for it. Now get out of here, and do as I have ordered.'

The president sat at his desk, and the two men left. Deep in thought, he did not notice his personal secretary enter the office until he heard a muffled cough. He looked up. 'The public relations advisor is outside, Mr President.' The secretary had stayed by the door to the office, having been made aware of the president's mood by the departing chiefs.

'Well, send her in,' he glared as he stood up and walked around the immense desk.

The public relations officer entered and sat on the settee as directed by Mike Read. 'You know why you are here?' he asked.

'Yes, sir, I do,' she said confidently, smoothing her black skirt. 'My team has been keeping up with all the briefings and media reports.'

'So you will agree that they are all biased against me.'

'Not you personally.' She chose her next words very carefully and precisely. 'The stance of the government as a whole is not in line with public opinion on the complex issues that have been raised to the forefront of media attention.' She clasped her hands in her lap.

'Well, I want you to reverse that situation,' the president said quietly, using all his best self-control and guile. 'Draw the media's attention away to more important issues – our defence, economic policy successes, and the unprovoked attack on the USS *Eisenhower*.' He smiled congenially. 'You can do that, can't you?'

'We will do our utmost, Mr President,' she replied with a small smile. 'We can guide the media, but we do not control them.'

'Well, do what you can,' the president said and stood up, bringing the meeting to a close. 'I am counting on you. You can achieve great heights in my administration if you play your cards right.'

There's the silent threat, she thought as she stood and left the Oval Office. *Fail, and I am out of a job. Success will mean that I will be vilified by the public and out of a job anyway when he loses power. I need to talk to Ryan and get his advice, or Charles Langham, yes, that's a good idea. I will call him when I get home, but first, I need to see Ryan and find out what's going on.* She knocked on Ryan O'Hare's door and entered to find him sitting behind his desk with Clive Harris, the defence chief, sitting in an armchair in front. 'Come in,' Ryan said. 'Have a seat, and join our little enclave.'

Chapter Nine

Game Plan

Charles sat in the library with Anne, Duke and Max in front of the large display screen which showed Mike Holdsworth, the captain of *Jupiter*, and both Keith Pritchard and James Young in the Kermadec deep-sea HQ. 'Gentlemen, we are bringing the game plan forward. Mike, I want you to close in on the approaching United States fleet, and as soon as you are in range, fire an EMP burst to disable them. Keith, I want to hit Washington – low level, no loss of life at all, a warning shot across the bow, if you like, and, so as to make sure it's not mistaken for a freak weather pattern, New York at the same time.' He waited while James and Keith had a quick discussion which he could not hear.

Mike was the first to break the silence. 'Do you want us to take out just the lead vessel or a wider pulse to impact more of the fleet?'

'As many as you can, Mike. Stay in stealth mode, and dive deep after the pulse.' Charles smiled. 'I don't need to tell you how to suck eggs, but as soon as the pulse is fired, head straight to Kermadec base, and keep deep all the way.'

'Okay, we're on to it. Out,' Mike cut off communication, and the screen filled with Keith and James who now spoke.

'Coordinated energy pulse will take us an hour to programme and model. Tides state suggests firing time would be 3.30 am,' James said and looked over at Keith.

'Charles,' Keith said, 'we will need maximum publicity for the waves at that time. I will send out a release to all media, world leaders and our friends at Greenpeace.'

'I would send the computer model with the release,' Duke suggested, 'Especially to the TV networks. They will love to use it for sure in their bulletins.'

'Call me as soon as the computer modelling is complete,' Charles requested, rubbing his palm across his lower lip. 'Once the press release is drafted, send me a copy.' Keith and James nodded in agreement as the call was terminated.

'I think I'll get some fresh air with Abbey on deck,' Anne said and kissed Charles on the cheek as she left. Max also excused himself to see the captain on the bridge, leaving Charles and Duke both deep in thought.

Charles was not sure if he was pulling the trigger too early. Should he wait a bit longer? It was a bit like being in a match race: Pull the trigger too early, and your opponent can hook around you as you need to slow down and get their bow into the circle first, forcing you to tack away and lose ground. But if you pulled the trigger too late, well, you lose. He tried to think of any potential retaliation from other countries and came up blank. America was the only country showing an aggressive stance; all others were either in favour of change or playing the neutral game, preferring to wait and see what other countries would do, before committing themselves. Public support was growing by the day around the world with mainly peaceful protests and calls for referendum in many countries with overwhelming numbers signing petitions. The social media networks were full of admiration for Charles Langham and his organisation, from every country spanning the world. Public figures and celebrities from every arena were full of praise and pledged support to the cause. Still, the president's actions were a might excessive.

Max came into the library. 'Sorry, boss, another news update according to the surveillance team,' he said as he turned on the display. 'Coffee is on its way as well. Thought you both looked like you could do with some.' He sat down as the camera crossed to a pretty news reporter in a beige trouser suit standing outside the United Nations building. 'Kim Lee Hoon, the Secretary General of the United Nations, has called on the United States to recall its fleet to Pearl Harbour amid mounting rhetoric from the president of the United States to take military action against the private yacht owned by Charles Langham. Earlier this week, Charles Langham called upon the United Nations to do more to cease the destruction of rainforests, reduce fossil fuel use, stop the increasing rate of extinctions, and end world famine. The United Nations has yet to respond to his demands and, according to our investigations, will be doing in the next few days. Public support for Charles Langham's demands are increasing daily across the world and putting pressure on world leaders to take action. The United States has laid the blame for the crippling of its aircraft carrier, the USS *Eisenhower*, directly at Charles Langham, although they have not stated how it was done nor provided any direct evidence. No word has been heard from Mr Langham since his presentation to the United Nations. He is, however, believed to be in the Pacific. Mary Prior, BBC World News, outside the United Nations building.'

Max leant forward and switched the display off.

'Duke, can you make a few calls?' Charles asked as he put his coffee cup on the table. 'You know the Chinese premier quite well, the Japanese prime minister and the Russian, I think. I will call Kim Lee Hoon, the Brits, Kiwis and Aussies, and the president of the European Union.'

'Our aim is to do what?' asked Duke, a frown creasing his forehead.

'The old lobbying game. Find out where they stand and what's stopping them from agreeing to change things. You know the old game.'

'Okay, I need a phone, a desk, a pad and the Internet,' Duke said. 'This will be fun, I think.' The frown on his face turned to a grin.

'Use that desk over there,' Charles said, pointing to one of the desk on the port side. 'When you pick up the phone, ask the surveillance team for a direct line, and they will set it up and call you back.'

Duke refilled his coffee cup and walked over to the desk, turned on the built-in computer, picked up the phone and spoke to a member of the surveillance team.

The *Sundancer's* captain, John Whitcome, popped his head around the door. 'Max, we are at your departure point. Cathy and Chris are already at the pick-up point.'

'Okay, I'm on my way,' Max said and drained his coffee; he then got up and cheerily said, 'See you soon, guys.' He walked towards the rear of the library, opened the glass door of the left side of the glass wall, closed it behind him, climbed on board the helicopter and flicked a few switches, and the flight deck displays lit up. He typed the pick-up coordinates into the navigation touchscreen, pulled on his helmet, and attached his throat microphone. Max started the engine and watched through the glass canopy as the rotors slowly started to turn. He saw the two crew members appear and unlock the helicopter's landing gear from the deck and disappear as quickly as they arrived. The rotors started to pick up speed, slowly at first, then faster and faster until he was ready to lift the burgundy-coloured helicopter slowly from the deck, moving towards the yachts stern. Max turned the Bell 525 to starboard and pushed her up to 280 kilometres per hour. This was the bit he loved: flying over the sea at high speed. He scanned the display with a trained eye, checking that everything was reading as it should. All he had to do was track to the rendezvous point on the navigation display. Forty-five minutes later, he slowed the Bell 525 and scanned the ground below, eased the helicopter to port and saw the landing area amongst the trees. He hovered and slowly lowered the Bell 525 to the ground. He saw Cathy and Chris running from the trees, keeping low, each with a backpack slung over one shoulder. He typed in the coordinates where he was due to rendezvous with *Sundancer*. Once the children were on board, Max motioned for them to put headphones on and strap in. The rotors increased in speed, and Max lifted the helicopter into a fast rolling turn, heading back out to sea. 'You kids all right?' Max said into his throat microphone.

'Fine, Max, just tired. Had a busy time – enjoyable but busy – and could do with a sleep,' Cathy replied.

'Sleep? I thought you kids were supposed to be full of get-up-and-go,' Max retorted with a grin on his face.

'Yeah, yeah, yeah,' groaned Chris. 'We've just been hiking for six hours to get here and spent last night securing everything.'

'And copying all the data to backup drives,' chipped in Cathy.

'Well, may I suggest that you recline those comfy seats and relax for fifty minutes,' Max said and left them to relax whilst he concentrated on flying the Bell 525 back to *Sundancer*.

Charles could hear Duke talking on the phone. *Well, here goes*, he thought, refilling his coffee and picking up his phone to dial the number for Kim Lee Hoon, the Secretary General of the United Nations. This was the first of many long conversations he and Duke were to have.

Duke stretched his arms above his head. 'Well, that's it. All done,' he said and stood up and walked over to Charles who had just finished his last call.

'And just in time, I think I hear the helicopter returning,' replied Charles. He stood up and walked over to the glass wall and opened the door and walked onto the helipad and looked to starboard. Duke stood at his side, and they watched as the helicopter came closer. 'Better go inside. While she lands, this glass wall is hardened.' He tapped the glass wall as he walked inside and closed the door. They watched as Max came alongside and lowered the Bell 525 to line up with the deck and expertly matched the forward speed of the yacht. He carefully held the position and slowly eased the Bell 525 over the deck and moved forward to hover above the helipad before gently lowering her onto the helipad and cutting power. The rotors slowed, and two crew members appeared and locked the landing gear to the deck; one disappeared, while the other connected a reinforced hose to the fuel tank and started to refill the tank. Anne quickly entered the library with Abbey at her heels. She watched as Max climbed out of the cockpit and opened the first rear door. Cathy and Chris climbed down the step and headed for the glass door to the library. Abbey started barking, with her tail swishing this way and that. Max went over to the crew member and started giving him instructions on how much fuel would be needed and to clean the windscreen before covering the Bell 525 with its weather cover.

Before anyone could get near Chris and Cathy as they entered the library, Abbey was all over them, dancing from one to the other, tail swishing from side to side, and making little whimpering noises. Anne managed to get to them and hugged them both with a kiss on the cheek. 'I'm so happy to see you both.' Tears filled her eyes. 'It's been so long. Look at you both.' She stepped back, still holding their hands. 'Chris, I swear you are taller, but you've lost weight, and Cathy, well, you're almost as tall as me, and by the looks of your faces, you've been getting a bit too much sun.'

'Mum, you never change,' Chris said and laughed.

'And you never will,' said Cathy, joining the laughter.

'I think you two would love a shower before dinner,' Charles said as he hugged Cathy, then Chris. 'You know where your cabins are, and Cathy, I think Abbey will be your constant companion.'

'Thanks, Dad,' Cathy said as she headed with Chris to the lift with Abbey in tow.

'I'm going to call Jo at the Amazon HQ and get an update. Make sure everything's okay,' Anne said to Charles as she sat at one of the desks and placed a video call to Jo.

Max came into the library, having supervised the refuelling and covering of the Bell 525. 'Well, we are all back together again,' he said happily. 'I miss those kids when they are away.'

'We all do for sure. Good flight?' questioned Charles.

'No problems at all. She's the best helicopter we've had – handles like a dream. The fly-by-wire system is so responsive, and *Sundancer* was exactly where the captain said she would be.'

'Now for round two,' Duke said.

'We had better share notes on those phone calls,' Charles replied. 'Max, freshen up, get yourself a drink, then join us.'

'Thanks, boss, I could sure do with a few minutes,' Max replied and went to the lift to go to his cabin.

Charles and Duke gathered their notes from the desks they had been using and sat down in the settee.

'Let's make this easy,' Charles said. 'Who is an ally, who is not, and who is on the fence?'

'Okay, I'll start. All are allies – Japan unreservedly, Russia okay, but we must keep them up to date and no big moves without talking first. China, okay, but they need a lot of time. They say they have a lot of catching up to do but are willing to work with us if we are willing to help them.'

'Brilliant,' said Charles. 'Just the news I wanted to hear. So from my calls, a mixed bag: Kiwis, Aussies and Brits are okay. European Union not so, as it wants to negotiate on everything at the next European Union conference and take a vote. Kim Lee Hoon is very worried about the US president's stance and thinks he may have had a breakdown of some sort!'

'He could be right there,' Duke commented. 'But what are his feelings on the rest of the United Nations?'

'From the conversations he's had, he thinks more in favour than not but requests that we take a slower, more diplomatic approach.'

'So we seem to have pretty good support,' Duke said.

'Yes, I think so. After dinner, we will link in with Kermadec and have a conference call. For now, I am going for a swim, shower and get changed,' Charles said. 'You have free-run of the yacht, you know, Duke. On the next deck down is a sauna, fitness studio, two spa pools and a lap pool. Help yourself.'

'I know,' Duke said sheepishly. 'It just takes a bit of getting used to.'

'Charles,' called Anne. 'Come here, darling. Jo has some brilliant news.'

Charles got up from the settee and went over to Anne, standing behind her and placing both hands on her shoulders. 'Hi, Jo, what's the news?'

Intrigued, Duke heaved himself from the comfortable settee and joined them.

'Jorge was here this morning to let us know that the Brazilian government has declared all the rainforest a national park, and those areas inhabited by indigenous peoples are now designated areas of significant importance within the national park,' Jo continued smiling broadly. 'All mining and lumber is to cease immediately. Felling a tree becomes a crime punishable by a minimum of five years imprisonment.'

'Did he tell you what caused the change of thought?'

'Public opinion. Jorge explained that many of its own government officials lobbied for the change on a groundswell of public opinion.' Jo advised.

'That's brilliant news, Jo. Offer our full support to Jorge and the government. We will help in any way we can.'

'Sure thing, boss,' Jo said.

Charles and Duke returned to the settee, leaving Anne and Jo to chat away.

Chapter Ten

The Movie

After dinner in the main deck dining room, Charles suggested they all retire to the main deck lounge for coffee and liqueurs. The lights were low with a hint of blue, and in the background, low music played. Charles had invited Max, Duke and the captain, John Whitcome, to join them for dinner to celebrate the return of the two children and decreed no business talk during the dinner. Abbey had sat by Cathy all through dinner and now trotted beside her as they moved forward to the lounge that was open to the main deck.

They settled in the lounge on the large curved settee, with the display screen rising up from its cabinet in front of them. A steward poured Columbian coffee, whilst another sorted out the liqueurs from behind the bar.

'So before we start, the most important point is our ETA at Curtis Island, Captain?'

'Ten tomorrow morning,' the captain replied, sipping his coffee. 'We made good time using the flying pick-up at Niue.'

'And our fuel situation?' asked Charles.

'Fuel is not an issue. We can refuel at Kermadec. I've already organised for the guys to release the refuelling pontoon on our arrival. I had James refill their tanks while we were in Panama, as a precaution.'

'Organised as always, John,' said Charles and lifted his Cognac glass in a toast to John.

'But how long will *Sundancer* be a sitting duck while she refuels?' asked Cathy with a concerned look on her face.

'Not as long as you think. The Kermadec system is similar to the system they use in Formula One racing. A thousand litres will take sixteen minutes, and don't forget we have four tanks filling at the same time, so that's 4,000 litres in those sixteen minutes,' explained John.

'Until we arrive at Kermadec, there's really nothing we can do, is there?' queried Anne.

'True,' agreed Duke. 'We know which governments are on our side. We also know the position of the United States Navy.' He sipped his Southern Comfort and looked at Charles. 'But we have not had the report back on the computer modelling.'

Charles pressed a few buttons on the table keypad, and the display screen came to life, and they saw Keith move into position next to James on the screen. 'Hi, guys, how is the modelling coming along?' Charles asked.

'Hi, all,' James said. 'It's finished, and we needed to reset the timings. This is what we have.' The screen turned to a simulation of a tsunami hitting New York from a satellite view. The words 'Simulation One' appeared along the bottom. The wave entered the city by just over a kilometre. The screen reset, and the words 'Simulation Two' appeared as a new simulation ran. The wave hit the edge of the city and stopped without flowing into the city. The display cleared, and James reappeared. 'So you see,' said James. 'In Sim One, there is major damage, and there is bound to be some loss of life, but in Sim Two, only material damage.'

'Sim Two it is, then. Which is when?' asked Charles.

'Simulation Two shows 3.40 am tomorrow, New York time. Our simulation shows that Washington will be affected in the same way,' James said, looking down and referring to the notes on his desk.

Keith quickly came back into view. 'Err, I just heard from Mike aboard *Jupiter*. He has hit the fleet with an EMP pulse and is now diving deep and heading to Kermadec at top speed,' he said between pants of breath.

'Did he get a result before diving?' asked Duke.

'Yes, he reported the three lead ships hit and disabled.'

'Okay, I think that's it for the night then,' Charles said, motioning to the bar steward for a refill.

'Might as well watch a movie,' suggested Chris.

'Good idea,' Cathy said.

'Well, see you in the morning,' Charles said to Keith and James, and the screen retracted into its cabinet.

'So where do we watch a movie?' asked Duke.

'In the cinema, of course, on the next deck up!' Cathy said and laughed.

'I just don't believe this.' Duke sighed as he stood up and followed the others to the deeply carpeted spiral staircase to the next deck. The cinema was twenty metres long and the full width of the deck, with a 2.5-metre-high ceiling. The twelve large recliner style armchairs, which had electronically controlled backrest, lumbar support and leg rests, mimicked the cinemas of old. The armchairs were covered in dark-red upholstery and were in banks of four, each on a higher tier. Max sat down and, using the controls on his armchair, closed the window blinds, dimmed the lights, reclined his backrest and extended his footrest. Cathy stood by a control panel and selected the movie *Fear Is the Key* and sat down. A steward circulated, taking drink orders as the movie titles started to roll as the lights slowly dimmed. Anne smiled and looked at Charles when she heard Duke quietly say to himself, 'Unbelievable! Bloody unbelievable!'

'Oh, by the way, everyone is to have their bags packed before breakfast,' Charles announced.

Eleven

The Oval Office

Mike Read sat in the Oval Office, his head resting in his hands, elbows on the desk. He sighed heavily. The latest report sat before him, and he could not help but stare at it in disbelief. Another three of their most technologically advanced ships disabled suddenly and without apparent reason. No power, no guidance systems, on-board aircraft useless – three floating hulks of useless iron. Puzzlingly, the same fault as the USS *Eisenhower* had suffered. He pushed his chair back, stood up, removed his jacket and necktie and stretched. *How is Charles Langham doing this? And if it's not him, then who is it?* He drained his china coffee cup and placed it on its saucer. He buzzed his secretary. 'Get William Paige, Ryan O'Hare, Helen Stark and Clive Harris in here now.' He sat behind his desk, swung his feet up onto the desk and rubbed his face. He picked up the report. Not one of the captains reported any ships in the vicinity. Sonar was clear, which ruled out submarine attacks, and there was no aircraft in the area. *Surely it's not the Chinese or a satellite attack? Who would have that sort of technology? Certainly not a private individual, so it must be a foreign power, but who and why?*

The intercom buzzed. 'They are all here, Mr President,' his secretary's voice said.

'Well, send them in, please,' the president said as the Oval Office door opened, and the four entered. He motioned for them to sit in the comfortable chairs in the centre of the room. As he came round from his desk and sat in the main armchair, he asked, 'Have you all read the report?' They all nodded in agreement as they sat down. 'So what are your thoughts?' he asked, looking at each in turn.

'Mr President, we had no intelligence of any impending attack and have not picked up any indicators following the disabling of the fleet, nor has anyone taken responsibility,' Helen Stark, the national security advisor, said.

'Which leaves us where?' the president questioned, raising both hands in the air.

'Exactly back at square one, following the USS *Eisenhower* event,' William Paige, the president's military advisor, said. 'Mr President, it seems to me that there is more to this than any coincidence. Two of our state-of-the-art aircraft carriers are disabled in the same manner by an unknown force or technology that even we do not have access to. That is a major concern. We need to understand exactly what has occurred and how before we can take any action, politically, militarily or defensively. Stalemate.'

'I will not have the United States in a stalemate position when we could be attacked again,' the president stated.

'Mr President, whilst I agree with your sentiment, there is very little we can do until we isolate the cause and those responsible,' Clive Harris, the defence chief, interjected.

'Mr President, whoever is responsible has technology way

beyond our capabilities, and there are only a few countries that can finance that kind of research and keep it secret from our intelligence gathering.' Ryan O'Hare postulated. 'Either North Korea or China.'

'We have no indications that either North Korea or China had any collateral in the vicinity of either attacks,' Helen Stark said. 'Our feelers indicate that they are as surprised as we are about the events.'

'How far away is the rest of the fleet?' asked the president.

'A couple of hours at most, plus we have our top scientific advisors flying across from the USS *Eisenhower* to run further tests and comparisons,' Clive Harris advised.

'Mr President, I would suggest that we raise our alert level during this situation,' William Paige said with grave concern.

'Yes, I think that would be wise. Go to Defcon One,' agreed the president.

'And, Mr President, you should leave for Camp David with the First Lady,' Ryan O'Hare suggested.

'I know, I know, we will leave tonight, but let's keep things under wraps for now to avoid any panic setting in.' The president thought carefully. 'And we need a carefully worded press release before news gets out about the disabled vessels. Let's say it is part of our planning-and-testing exercise to test operational stress management and various rescue modes.' He stood up. 'I have to tell you that I am not happy about this situation or the state of our knowledge and understanding.' He tapped the back of the settee. 'With one of the biggest intelligence operations in the world, I would have expected more.' He raised his voice, 'And I do expect more. Get back to work, and get answers.'

They all stood, gathered their papers, and left the Oval Office, whilst the president returned to his desk. *With all the billions we spend on intelligence gathering by the latest technology and the world's largest and most powerful computer, incredibly we know nothing.* He rested his arms on the desk. *It has to be one of the three – North Korea, China or Charles Langham. But why? What's their reason? North Korea would do anything to harm the US, so nothing new there. China's relationship has chilled of late but nothing near bad enough to cause this sort of reaction. Charles Langham, surely he cannot possess the technology to undertake such an attack – technology that even the United States itself does not have. And would a private individual attack a nation like the United States? Unlikely,* he thought, *but not beyond a megalomaniac's reach. So is Charles Langham a megalomaniac? A philanthropist, yes, but how far is that away from being or becoming a megalomaniac?* Seeing a dead end at every turn, he leant back in his chair and rested his feet on the corner of the desk. *Why on my watch?* He sighed. *Why on my watch?* He closed his eyes. He opened his eyes wide. *Of course, that's it! I will bring in the president's special intelligence force and get them to uncover what's going on.*

He picked up the blue phone on his desk and dialled. 'Thomas, come to my office at 6.30 pm tonight. I have a job for you and your team.' He replaced the handset. He had an hour before Thomas arrived. *Might as well find the First Lady and get ready for Camp David while I'm waiting,* he thought and stood up and left the Oval Office, telling his secretary he would be in his private quarters if required. Only the sitting president and those before him knew of the president's private special intelligence force, a mix between a private army of Navy SEALs and the CIA; they were a formidable force of just eight men, the best chosen from the best and reporting to only one man, the commander-in-chief, the president himself. The force was well funded with its own long-range aircraft, latest equipment and operated out of a private secluded base in Texas. Their use was defined in a Charter handed down by the departing president and signed by the incoming president. The Charter stated clearly that the special intelligence force was only to be used in exceptional circumstances to protect the United States or the incumbent president, where and only when all other means had proved incapable of doing so.

The president sat opposite Thomas in the Oval Office. Thomas was a bull of a man, having dark but clean features, shortly cut black hair swept back neatly, piercing blue eyes and muscles bulging beneath a tailored black suit. 'Thomas, I have a mission for your team. It is stated very easily but may require the use of every skill in your arsenal to carry out.'

'Yes, Mr President, we are ready. I assume it is something to do with this man Charles Langham who has been causing you some, shall we say, concerns of late,' Thomas replied, his voice low and hoarse.

'Correct. I need him to be quiet and advised to cease his activities which are embarrassing to the peoples of the United States.'

'Do you want him permanently silenced, sir?'

'I supposed that depends on you and your team and what you come up against.'

'You choose your words very carefully. Are you fearful this office may not be safe for free speech?'

'That could well be the case,' the president said quietly.

Thomas slowly stood up. 'I understand, Mr President. I will report through our normal channels with regular updates. Goodnight, sir.' He inclined his head and, with measured steps, left the Oval Office.

The president smiled to himself. That should take care of Mr High-and-Mighty Langham. Nobody can win against an onslaught from the president's special intelligence force, either on the cyber intelligence front or against direct offensive. He sighed visibly as he relaxed. *All I have to do is act as though nothing has changed and let the team take care of business. The team is dispensable, and I have deniable liability, just some rogue activist group working on their own.*

Thomas left the White House and got into his black SUV. He removed his tiepin and plugged it into a small silver electronic box. A red light started to flash, and the unit downloaded a video recording of the conversation he had just had with the president. *That's our insurance policy*, he thought and smiled to himself. *I'm just too smart to lose my entire team to some self-serving politician.*

Chapter Twelve

Kermadec

The captain slowed the super yacht and said, 'Martin, tell Kermadec to release the refuelling platform.' John watched carefully until the first officer pointed to the refuelling platform emerging slowly from the sea. The platform was six metres square and rose one metre above the waves. The captain, using the small joystick, deftly brought the super yacht beside the platform until Martin Deeks, the technical officer, said, 'That will do fine, Captain, hold her there.'

The captain said to the first officer, 'Set thrusters to position holding.' Martin Deeks went on to the bridge arm and watched as his team lowered a large side hatch and walked on the platform with mooring lines. Once they secured the platform, they carried out four large reinforced hose lines which they connected to four pump housings on the platform. The pumping of fuel could commence. 'We are pumping fuel, Captain,' Martin Deeks advised.

'Shut down engines one, two and three,' the captain ordered, and the first officer leant forward and shut them down.

'I'm going to the engine room,' Martin Deeks said as he left the bridge and took the lift down to the engine-room floor. The engine-room chief greeted Martin, and together, they checked over the refuelling system and pumps. A broil of water in the distance signalled the arrival of *Mercury* as she broke the surface a few metres away from the refuelling platform and slowly came alongside. Two crew members exited the submarine and threw mooring lines to the members of *Sundancer's* crew who were on the platform, waiting for the submarine. Two more disturbances of water and two submersibles broke the surface.

'Lower the midship hatch,' commanded the captain, and the first officer pressed a button on one of the many switch panels in front of him. The super yacht became a hive of activity with the crewman walking quickly to the midship hatch to secure the two submersibles.

On the main deck, the group consisting of Charles, Anne, Cathy, Chris, Duke and Max was just finishing a leisurely full English breakfast around one of the teak tables, with Abbey at Cathy's feet, eating from her bowl. Max stood up and was at the deck rail with a mug of coffee, giving a running commentary of the activity taking place on the starboard side of the super yacht.

'So, Duke, you will soon see our headquarters,' Anne said. 'Are you packed and ready?'

'I have not even unpacked, in all honesty,' Duke replied. 'Haven't had the chance.'

'Submersibles and *Mercury* are on the surface,' said Max, walking back to the table.

'Why *Mercury*?' asked Duke, standing up and patting this stomach.

'The crew will use *Mercury* to get to the HQ, then *Mercury* will follow *Sundancer* to Nuku'alofa and bring all our people back except for the security team taking care of the boats and planes,' explained Charles. 'Enjoying your breakfast?'

'Will the food be this good down there?' Duke questioned.

'Yep, it's the exact standard,' Charles answered.

'Hope you have a tailor. I might need my waist band expanded at this rate.' Duke patted his stomach again.

Cathy and Chris had walked to the stern and opened a locker by the Pétanque area which consisted of hard sand in a shallow three-inch-deep trench in the deck, three feet six inches wide and twelve feet long. Along the sides were recessed lights for night playing. Cathy threw the Cochonnet, and Chris lined up his first shot.

Martin Deeks left the engine room and walked down the long carpeted central gangway, the walls lined with mirrors and painting. He turned towards the lift and took it to the bridge level. He advised the captain and first officer how the refuelling was progressing. The captain's display screen changed to show James Young. 'The submersibles and *Mercury* are ready to transport,' he informed.

'Thanks, James, we will start to disembark shortly,' the captain replied. Then turning to Martin, he said, 'Round up the crew who are disembarking here, and while you are at it, tell Charles and his guests.'

'Right,' said Martin. 'I'll tell Charles first so they can ensure their luggage is ready to go on *Mercury*.' He patted the door jamb and took the lift back to the main deck level.

He walked through the main lounge and could see the Langham's on deck, sitting around one of the teak tables, and Cathy and Chris playing Pétanque in the distance on the far side of the pool. He went over to Charles. 'Excuse me, sir, the submersibles are ready for you, and *Mercury* is ready to take your luggage.'

'Thank you, Martin,' he said. Then he turned towards Cathy and Chris. 'Cathy, Chris, come over here, please.' Turning to Max and Duke, he said, 'Are you guys packed?'

Duke replied, 'Yes, my case is in my cabin, ready.'

'Mine is just outside my door,' Max replied.

Cathy and Chris came over at a trot, with Abbey barking in tow.

'Are your bags packed?' Charles asked them when they stopped.

'Yes, all ready,' they replied together.

'Bags are ready,' Charles said to Martin. 'Abbey will go on *Mercury*. There will be more space for her there than on one of the submersibles.'

'I'll start the loading now with the disembarking crew and baggage,' Martin said and turned on his heels.

'I'll go with Abbey,' Cathy said. 'She will be frightened on the submarine by herself.'

Charles smiled at Cathy. 'You can go with Abbey. Okay, everyone follow me.' He led the party to the main wide stairwell down to the engine-room level, along the carpeted gangway to the midship's hatch. 'I'll take Cathy and Abbey to the *Mercury* while you board the submersibles,' said Charles and left the group in the hands of the submersible crews. The engine room housed the four main engines, generators, desalination plant, pumps and toilet macerator, and cleansing equipment. It was a pristine environment that Martin proudly stated was clean enough to cook in. He took Cathy and Abbey on to the pumping platform, and they carefully stepped on board *Mercury* with the helping hand of a crew member. Cathy climbed down the hatch followed by a crew member carrying Abbey whose tail was wagging wildly. Charles climbed through the hatch and followed them down the ladder into the control centre of the submarine. After making sure Cathy and Abbey were okay, he spoke briefly to the captain about the plans to drop some of *Sundancer's* crew off at the HQ, follow *Sundancer* to Nuku'alofa, and return to the HQ with the crew of *Sundancer*. The *Mercury* captain advised that he had heard from Mike, captain of the *Jupiter* that they were making good progress and heading straight for Nuku'alofa to pick up the crews of *Launch One*, the Learjet and 747-8i before heading for HQ.

Charles bade farewell to the captain, kissed Cathy on the cheek and said he would see her within the hour, and shook paws with Abbey. He climbed up the ladder and made his way back on board *Sundancer* and walked towards the submersibles which were moored in tandem. The others had already boarded, and Charles stepped on board the second which Anne had boarded. He looked at the faces of the five crewmen who were already on board and sat next to Anne. The submersibles were primarily used as transport to and from the subsea headquarters and, if required, as emergency evacuation vessels. Some researchers used them in the local vicinity to the Kermadec Islands but never to venture into the Kermadec trench which reached depths of 32,000 feet. The subsea headquarters lay at 300 feet below the surface, and the submersibles were designed to reach depths of 800 feet. The interior layout left little room for comfort, with two seats in the cockpit with one large circular thick glass window and four smaller circular windows, one to each side, one above and one below. Behind the cockpit were four rows of double seats, either side of a narrow aisle. The seats were canvas and easily removable to house experiments or cargo. The copilot closed the hatch, and they started their descent towards the submersible docking station. Charles could just make out the first submersible in front of them through the thick circular main window.

'There's the HQ,' said the pilot. 'Slightly off our port bow, should be docking within ten minutes.' Everyone, including Charles and Anne, peered forward, trying to see the deep-sea HQ. 'We will hold back until the first submersible has docked and is secured. We will then move in and dock. *Mercury* is expecting to dock fifteen minutes later.'

'Has *Mercury* submerged yet?' asked Charles.

'I'll just check for you,' the copilot said and touched his throat microphone. '*Mercury*, your status, please?' he asked. He listened for a reply, then turned to Charles, looking over his shoulder. 'They have just closed their hatch and are moving away from the refuelling platform.'

'Thanks,' said Charles and sat back in his canvas seat and held Anne's hand. 'I see Chris went with Max and Duke.'

'He wanted to talk to Max about a deep-sea dive. He and Cathy want to see some of the unusual fish species around the island and possibly take one of these down to its maximum depth and see what they can find,' Anne said. 'You know what those two are like.'

'They had better talk to James. We may have a researcher on to the same subject who they can tie in with,' Charles suggested.

A few minutes later, the copilot announced, 'We are positioning for docking. If you watch this display here, you can see our docking alignment.' He pointed to a display on the roof between the copilot and pilot seats. The display showed a video of the docking target points with four red circles showing the docking stubs of the submersible. Once aligned, the pilot vented the submersible so that it rose, and everyone heard the thud and loud clicks as the submersible locked and secured itself to the pod. They heard a pump start. 'That's the water being evacuated from the docking collar. As soon as it stops, we can open the hatch and enter the HQ,' the copilot explained. 'For those who have not been here before, please be aware that when moving around the habitat, the next door or hatch will only open after you have secured the door or hatch you have just passed through. This is a safety precaution to ensure that each pod remains secure and watertight in its own right in the event of a disaster.'

The sound of the pump stopped, and an indicator lamp on the cockpit control console lit up green. The copilot stood up in a crouched position and manoeuvred his way around his seat, and standing fully upright, he raised his arms above his head and turned the circle handle above his head and pushed the hatch open. He climbed up the short ladder and swung down onto the airlock chambers floor. He could see the passengers from the first submersible gathering around the pod's exit hatch. He helped Anne and Charles disembark the submersible and left the rest of the crew to sort themselves out. The pilot powered down all the submersible systems and climbed out of the hatch.

The copilot leant over and closed and secured the submersibles hatch, while the pilot went over to the pod's exit hatch and swung the circular handle and pulled two levers down. 'This way, everyone. As soon as we clear the docking pad, *Mercury* will be docking,' he said and watched as everyone filed through the hatch. Charles was the last through the hatch and swung it closed behind him and turned the circular handle and pulled the two large levers down. The light above the door went from green to red and was also signalled on *Mercury*, letting the captain know that he could safely dock. The pilot of the first submersible pushed up two levers and turned the circular handle of the hatch at the other end of the long connecting tunnel. As soon as everyone was clear of the tunnel, he swung the hatch closed and reversed the procedure. 'This is the most tedious dual-hatch system, owing to the pod being the docking station for two submersibles and two submarines.' He smiled broadly.

'Okay, please gather around, and I'll give you a brief orientation of the station,' he said, looking around. 'We are now in the circular corridor that runs around the main and largest pod. The floor above is the command centre, with conference rooms, open plan offices, media centre, some technical laboratories and a restaurant. The floor below houses research laboratories and smaller meeting rooms, and the floor below that houses life support systems and the tools room. All around this corridor, you will find further hatches leading to other pods, which are accommodation pods, recreation pods, a café, restaurant, cinema and a fitness room. On this floor, the inner wall of the corridor, are five hatches, which lead to different laboratories, the restaurant, recreation areas, offices and studio.'

To the amazement of those new to the habitat, the floors were covered by deep wool carpet. The walls lined in suede-like material with recessed lighting in the grey metallic grilled ceilings. The design gave an atmosphere of quietness of a luxury liner, which was the intention. He glanced back to the docking pod they had just left. 'The docking pod is also an escape pod, so in the case of an emergency, that is where we assemble. But for now, we will go up to the command centre and link you up with your section heads. This way, please.'

Keith Pritchard and James Young both stood up when Charles and Anne entered the command centre and greeted them both warmly. 'It's good to see you face-to-face again. It's been a long while,' Keith said.

'Chris, you've certainly grown,' James said. 'And I am glad you are here, as I could do with your help around here.'

'I'm all yours,' said Chris. 'Anything I can do?'

'Follow me,' James said and led Chris over to the booth he used which housed two large displays, two laptops, printers and two comfortable-looking swivel chairs.

Charles watched as the submersible pilots matched the assembled crew to their supervisors, who in turn, allocated them sleeping quarters and showed them to their workstations. The *Mercury* captain entered the control room with the rest of *Sundancer*'s crew, Cathy and an excitable Abbey, who did not know who to jump up to next. Her excitability certainly brought a smile to everyone's face. The captain came over to Keith and Charles. 'All the luggage is outside the accommodation pods, so I'll round up my maintenance crew and, over lunch, take them through that work list you sent me, Keith.'

'Who will be commanding *Mercury*?' Charles asked.

'Lisa,' replied the captain. 'She's been my 2IC for the last few months.'

'Thanks. We will be in the conference room for a little while,' said Keith, knowing that Charles deplored long-talk meetings and preferred snappy get-it-done meetings.

Charles sat around the cherrywood conference table with Anne, Max, Keith, Duke, Cathy and James. The room had hooded windows and, like the rest of the deep-sea habitat, had daylight lighting recessed into the ceiling that came on when body heat was sensed. A large display screen took up one wall at the end of the conference table, and a conference phone sat in the table's centre. 'Okay, guys, before we start, what's the latest with *Sundancer* and *Jupiter*?'

'The refuelling platform has been retracted, and *Sundancer* is now picking up speed for a high-speed run, with *Mercury* staying 500 yards off her port beam at a depth of 200 feet. *Jupiter* has just passed Niue and is staying deep. Mike's intent is to refuel using the platform before diving and docking. Lisa will be doing the same on her return,' Keith explained.

'Boss, I have arranged for *Sundancer's* name to be covered with another and her silhouette altered while she is steaming to Nuku'alofa,' Max said. 'I thought it might be worthwhile, and the security team have everything in hand for when she arrives.'

'Neat idea, Max, what other security arrangements have been made?' Charles asked Max.

'Well, the helipad side and rear panels will be lifted and secured into position and so will the funnel surrounds, which will, along with the main deck curving side extension panels, provide *Sundancer* with a different silhouette. *Launch One* and *Sundancer* will have all doors leading below deck locked and secured. Gangways will be withdrawn into their hull recesses. Access to decks above main level will also be secured. Closed-circuit TV, underwater surveillance and protection systems activated, and on-board armed security guards on twenty-four-hour rotation,' explained Max.

'Good. Now what about here?' Charles said, pointing to the table. 'We have 140 people, plus another 15 who arrived today, and 18 still to come – that's a lot of people to look after.'

'Well, space is not an issue. Design parameters allow for 200 in total. Water and air are not an issue either. I would suggest that the chef takes a provisions stock check and emails the team on *Launch One* a list of what he wants so they can get the stuff before *Mercury* arrives,' Keith said.

'Max, see to that with the chef,' Charles said to Max and then turned back to the others. 'And security?'

'Full surveillance is in operation. We have activated the sound and echo sensors at ten-kilometre radius. We can go a further ten kilometres if required. Radar is active and so is the radio listening post. The nets are ready to deploy to protect from torpedo and depth charges,' James said.

'Okay, so all is well. Now what's the latest on the new channels, James?'

'The same rhetoric from the United States, but that's to be expected. The European Union has just had a highly heated debate with the French leading the charge that any changes would severely affect their farmers, but this follows riots, processions and blockades from French farmers in Paris.'

'So nothing new there,' he said and looked at the group around the table. 'I think I need to make a video about the consequences of taking no action and explain what we have to do and how long we have to do it before irrevocable damage is done.' He looked at Duke. 'And you can add your own comments.'

'Sure, no problem. Would be a pleasure,' Duke confirmed.

'James, have you got the time and consequence of no-action

world model that we can include?'

'Yes, it can be used on its own or as a backdrop or forefront to you speaking,' James replied.

'Let's set that up for, say, one hour's time. We still have the New York and Washington tests on schedule?'

'Yep, 3.45, New York time. Nice gentle wave that should leave some water on the roads,' Keith reported.

'Right, that's all then,' Charles said, dismissing the team from the conference room. 'James,' he said as James got up to leave with the others. 'Duke and I will meet you in the media room in thirty minutes, and Max, once you have spoken to the chef, come to the media room. Duke and I are going there now.'

'Right, boss,' Max replied.

'This way, Duke. We have some note writing to do.' Charles pushed his cherrywood armchair back and stood up and led Duke out of the conference room and next door into the media room. Duke blew a whistle. 'I've seen worse at many a TV station,' he said as he took in the large video-mixing desk, large display screens, digital television camera and microphones, sound cones on the walls, and a stainless steel, glass-topped coffee table with two matching chairs that sat in a corner with tablet personal computers on each in front of a curved blue screen backdrop. Charles sat on one of the chairs, and Duke followed suit. 'Mind you, I should be used to this by now.'

'That's all right, Duke. As the old saying goes, you ain't seen nothing yet! But we need to be able to make high-quality presentations on our scientific and technological finding, so it gets a lot of use by the team down here. Believe it or not, it has paid for itself a few times over already,' Charles replied. 'Now our script – our target audience is the general public and scientists, but also the world governments who are more interested in the here-and-now rather than the planet's future.'

'Well, I suppose we need to lay the facts out clearly enough that the average man in the street can understand the serious nature of each issue in its own right, then the impact of the whole,' Duke postulated.

'Correct, so let's start by listing each item and its impact with video-showing the issue in all its glory, then we show the projected outcome in its disaster state, and then bring them all together, showing the full impact on planet earth, its animals, plants and people, and shame the world governments for letting things get to the state they are in and the why,' said Charles.

'I can do that bit. I've already been there and know it from the insider,' Duke stated with confidence and turned on a tablet.

'You start on that, and I will start on the lead in.'

Charles sat back with the other tablet and started to think about what to write. He listed each item in turn as a bullet list, then expanded each bullet into a set of notes. At the end of the bullet list, he typed two words, *World Impact*, and wrote a few lines that encompassed all the bullet points into a global event, and the words *Duke takes over here*.

James and Max entered, and Charles looked at his watch and thought, *it's that time already? How fast time goes when you get engrossed in things! Am I ready for this? What the hell! They can do retakes until we get it perfect.* He handed the tablet to James and held out his hand for Duke to pass his over. 'Download to your desk, camera and auto cue. It shows the running order and rough script. I'll talk to you through it as we will need video tie-ins.'

After twenty minutes, they were ready to roll, and Charles and Duke sat in their chairs, with Max behind the camera and James at the mixing desk. Charles looked at James who gave the thumbs up, then at Max who said, 'Take One.'

Charles started talking. 'Ladies and gentlemen, for those who do not know me, my name is Charles Langham, and with me is Duke Warren who, I am sure, you will almost certainly know. The reason I am speaking to you today is that we have spoken to world leaders about issues that affect your future and the future of your children, but to no avail. They seem more interested in the here-and-now which, I suppose, reflects the length of the electoral terms in office. Pressure needs to be brought to bear on these world leaders to take action, and that can only be by the population as a whole.' He could see in the video that the image had changed from a brilliant picture of the world from space to the United Nations building.

'The air we breathe is given to us by the planet from the plankton in our seas and rainforests, both of which are at grave threat. Rainforests are depleted by destruction from lumber and mining for gold, palm oil and soy plantations.' The video changed from lush rainforest with forest mammals to the desecration of a barren land. 'Regretfully, this also removes the habitat of some of the world's most endangered species. The seas are being destroyed by pollution and warming which also increases desalination by the melting of the ice sheets.' The video changed from a bountiful ocean of fishes and colourful corals to the barren landscape of dead coral.

'Of course, this leads to a reduction in fish stocks and reduces a huge food source. The result of this lack of oxygen unbalances the carbon dioxide in the atmosphere, thereby increasing global warming – a vicious cycle. We are destroying the habitats of the world's most precious species and also killing for so-called medicinal purpose. We now have extinction rates that are rising exponentially with 50 per cent of the world's species forecast to die out less than 100 years. The impact of this on human life is devastating and cannot be underrated.' More videos changed to show orang-utan orphans and dead rhinoceros with their horns removed.

'The stupidity of the world's current system is simply that in the Western World, more food is thrown away that can easily feed all the starving in the African and Indian continents, and we do have the technology to help those famine-stricken nations to grow food on a sustainable level. But we do nothing but throw food away and ignore the dying.' The video showed waste food, then famine-stricken people. 'And to cap it all, whilst we have the ability to easily move away from fossil fuels, we continue to burn oil and coal and pump the carbon dioxide and other poisonous gases into the atmosphere, further destroying our air, rainforests and seas, when instead we can use electric cars, hydro-power stations, wave machines, solar and geothermal.' The video went through a sequence of clips showing towers pumping out clouds of dark smoke, car exhaust pipes, acid rain affects and two geothermal stations.

'I recall the G8 leaders meeting on world poverty with eight-course dinners with starving people less than half a kilometre away. Now my company buys back rainforests from lumber, mining and palm oil companies and replants them. We actively assist famine-stricken people to sustainably grow their own food and install irrigation systems. I ask a simple question – why do the governments of the world do so little to address these issues? Over to you, Duke.'

Max smoothly swung the camera over to Duke who straight away said, 'Ladies and gentlemen, what you have just heard is the tip of the iceberg. The effects on the world, our one and only home, is the piece of the iceberg that is hidden.' Without glancing at his notes, he continued, 'We are, without doubt, on the precipice of an irrevocable change that we must take immediate action to forestall. This is not scaremongering. On the contrary, the top scientific brains from every country around the world concur with the data and forecast outcomes as outlined originally in *An Inconvenient Truth*. Well, this research and the finding and details outlined by Charles Langham have taken it to the next level. Man has lost his connection with the earth and connected with an ever-increasing zeal to globalisation and materialism with an ever-growing population that is stripping the earth off its resources and those ecosystems that we depend on for our very lives.' Duke watched the video play snippets from his previous presentations and end with an overlay of the current scientific forecast. 'Please, for the sake of your lives and that of your children and grandchildren, contact your local government officials and demand that they take action now, and please visit our website, and sign the petition which will be sent to all world leaders.'

The camera swung back to Charles. 'At 3.45 Eastern Standard Time, the cities of New York and Washington DC will both suffer a tsunami.' Charles saw the video showing a tsunami devastating a coastline and winced internally. 'Both the tsunamis will only cause minor damage.' He paused for effect. 'They are, however, designed to remind our leaders of what will become more of the norm, flooded coastline, pastures destroyed by salt water, cities made unliveable, the very tip of the iceberg of things to come if we do not change.' He paused, then continued, 'With that, we bid you goodnight.' The video changed to show the website address with the earth pictured from space as the backdrop.

'James, let's see it from start to finish on the display, please,' Charles asked. James ran the full recording so that they could see the video backdrops playing whilst Charles and Duke were speaking.

'Brilliant,' said Duke. 'Not too heavy but certainly heavy enough impact. Don't you think so, Charles?'

'Yes, I'm happy with it,' he said and looked at James. 'Get it out to every network news station immediately with the heading: 'Tsunami to hit New York and Washington DC'. That should get their attention.' With that, he looked at his watch and said, 'And just in time for lunch, and I'm starving.' and left the room.

Chapter Thirteen

Fury at the Oval Office

The US president sat in the Oval Office of the White House and replaced the telephone receiver. 'That was the French president. He wants to know why I am winding everyone up over this Charles Langham business,' he said to Ryan O'Hare, his chief of staff, William Paige, his military advisor, Clive Harris, the defence chief, and Helen Stark, the national security advisor. 'Before that I had the British prime minister, before him Kim Lee Hoon, the Secretary General of the United Nations, and Fu Yong, the Chinese premier, all demanding we recall our *Pacific Fleet*, which they see as a blatant act of aggression.'

There was a knock on the door, and the president's secretary entered. 'Mr President, I am sorry to interrupt, but your public relations advisor has insisted that you watch the ABC news that's on in a few minutes.' He walked over to the TV and turned it on, changing the channel to the ABC news, and left the office.

The president and his team watched in silence as the ABC news anchorman introduced the next item. 'News just in: a tsunami is due to hit New York and Washington DC at 3.45 Eastern Standard Time. This is from our reporter on the ground in New York.' The news programme switched to a female reporter in a beige trouser suit.

'All news agencies around the globe have received a video entitled *Tsunami to hit New York and Washington DC* from Charles Langham and Duke Warren. The video explains in detail the issues that both Mr Langham and Mr Warren have been championing for some time now.' The reporter was replaced by the video which played for its full length. The president shifted uncomfortably in his seat. At the end of the video, the reporter returned to the screen. 'Our teams will be covering both events live, and as soon as we receive a reaction from the White House, we will bring it to you.'

The president got up and paced the office. 'So tell me, has he got the technological capability of doing that?' he demanded from those in his office.

The advisors looked at each other. 'Mr President, we just do not know,' William Paige stated.

Helen Stark agreed. 'No, Mr President, and we know that none of our allies have that sort of the ability either, nor have we picked up any intelligence that China or Russia might have that sort of technical ability.'

'So tell me, can he do this?' the president stood behind his desk chair, hands firmly gripping the backrest, his face grim.

'To be honest, Mr President, I do not think any of us can say for sure,' Ryan O'Hare stated guardedly.

'Then why say it on TV on a worldwide basis?'

'Ask him?' suggested Helen Stark. 'Call him and ask him why he threatens the United States so openly which will only garner opposition against him.'

The president swung his desk chair around and, sitting down, picked up a handset. 'Get me Charles Langham,' he said and then replaced the handset.

Charles sat in the command centre, looking at the display screens and out of the windows on to the depths of the ocean beyond. 'Sir, we have a call from the president of the United States for you,' James said, with a slightly startled tinge to his voice.

'Put it through to my headset, James,' Charles said, picking up a radio headset and placing it on his head. 'Mr President, Charles Langham here. How are you, sir?' Charles said with a jovial voice.

'Well, as you would imagine, Mr Langham, concerned about the safety of my citizens and very concerned about the actions of your terrorist group,' the president said through gritted teeth.

'Oh, come now, Mr President, terrorists cause destruction and, by the very word *terror*, do not advertise the fact. On the contrary, we are about saving millions of human and non-human lives, and our little waves will only damage property, not lives,' Charles said coolly.

'Mr Langham, you will not do this damnable thing. You will either cease and desist or face the consequences.'

'Mr President, please do not threaten me with your empty words,' Charles stated slowly. 'Let me get one thing clear, Mr President. You do not know what we are capable of. Yes, I will admit that we have disabled your warships that were a distinct and real threat to me and my family and were only neutralised as a last resort whilst preparing to attack and not before.' He paused. 'The tsunamis, well, we can always ramp those up across more United States cities – Los Angeles, Miami, San Francisco, Vancouver and New Orleans. Shall I carry on, or do you want to stop threatening me and get on with the most important issue of the day – saving the world?'

'Mr Langham, you forget that you are talking to the president of the world's most powerful nation.'

'Well, then,' interrupted Charles, 'lead the world on the environmental front and spend some of the hundreds of billions of dollars on that rather than on weapons of mass destruction.'

'And leave my people open to weapons of mass destruction from other countries? You're an idealist, Mr Langham.'

'No, Mr President, a realist. You start, and other countries will follow your lead, or you will lead your people to starvation, death by pollution by your own hand,' Charles stated as a matter of fact.

'If you persist with your acts of aggression against the United States, we will have no option but to retaliate with full force.'

'We only act in self-defence, Mr President. You are fully aware of that. We can send you or the TV networks the video evidence if you wish, plus you have no idea where we are.'

'Why, you are on that fancy super yacht of yours, and we know where that is,' the president said and chuckled.

'Well, Mr President, you are wrong. I am not on board the *Sundancer*. Your call was intercepted by our surveillance system and routed through to me.' Charles looked at the faces in the command centre. 'We will stay on our course of action until we hear that you will do what your people want and need.' He looked at James and ran a finger across his throat in a cutting motion. James leant forward and pressed a button, cutting the call.

Charles looked around the command centre. 'Well, you all heard that call. He's too short-sighted to see what's coming further than his re-election campaign. We stay on track, but tell the surveillance team to keep on it 200 per cent. Make sure we are armed, and go in stealth mode and deploy the nets.'

James got up. 'On to it now, sir.' He went over to a cubicle where three men and two women, who were the armaments, systems, and safety control team, sat wearing headsets, looking at large display screens and keyboards. He lifted a headset from one of the desks, flicked a switch and spoke to them through it. They all turned, looked at him and nodded their heads as they listened to him, their fingers flying over the keyboards.

Through the hooded windows, Charles could see the nets extending into position far above, which would halt any depth charges and add to the camouflage design of the undersea habitat. The nets were carefully designed not to affect any of the local fish.

Keith Pritchard came over. 'Charles, two hours to tsunami initiation,' he said.

'Commence countdown: T-minus two hours.' Charles looked at Keith. 'And let's pray the modelling works just fine.'

'It will. We have done our homework and checked it again and again.' Keith returned to his console and typed into the keyboard set into his desk, put his headset on, and throughout the habitat, his voice could be heard. 'We are now at T-minus two hours to tsunami initialisation and counting.'

Chapter Fourteen

The Presidential Squad

Thomas sat at the head of the conference table, looking at the other seven seated men, all top in their fields and dedicated to serving the United States of America. They were in their compound in Texas that was marked as a military training ground. The compound was surrounded by a high barbed-wire fence with nothing of significance visible from the fence line. At the centre was a two-kilometre runway, aircraft hangar and accommodation block. The only access to the compound was down a rough track to a gate guarded twenty-four hours a day.

'So what's the gig?' asked Jake, the second-in-command, a short, stocky built young man with a serious demeanour. Thomas had chosen him for the squad due to his ruthless but pedantic style when on complex missions, never one to leave anything to chance; he had once re-entered a cleared building when something in his gut told him things were not quite right and taken out a hidden enemy insurgent.

'We are to silence this man Charles Langham on behalf of our commander-in-chief,' replied Thomas.

'What do we know about him?' Jake queried. 'What does he look like?'

'We only have one picture. It's a frame from the United Nations speech video. His face is obscured by dark glasses and a hat pulled down at the front.'

'Do we know his age, height, hair colour?'

'No information.'

'What about his home address?'

'Unknown.'

'I suppose the same is true of his work address?'

'Unknown.'

'His present location?'

'Pacific region.'

'Great, that's just 155 million square kilometres, which narrows the search area down a bit,' Jake laughed. 'We do not know a great deal, do we?'

'I know,' replied Thomas. 'But our starting point will be Nuku'alofa. That's where *Sundancer*, his private yacht, is heading. Our cover will be a game-fishing trip.'

'What is he supposed to have done?'

'He has threatened the United States with two tsunamis,' replied Thomas.

'What is he – God or Poseidon?' Jake said jokingly.

'He made the announcement on a news report,' Thomas replied.

'What size force does he have?'

'Unknown.'

'Have we a rundown on his capabilities?'

'No, we have a lot of research to do,' Thomas said precisely.

'How will we get our gear into Nuku'alofa?' asked Connor.

'We will use a HALO canister drop which we will pick up while we are out fishing. We will need to charter a pretty decent-sized vessel. Alfred, you get hold of our contact and arrange that. We will not need a skipper.' Thomas continued, 'It will need to be blue-water capable boat, say, out to sixty kilometres, and arrange air tickets from Dallas.'

'Okay, sir,' Alfred, an experienced ex-Navy SEAL demobbed for disobeying orders, said, taking notes. 'Do you want to use our usual cover names?'

'Yes, of course, and the earliest flights possible.'

'Jake, I will leave you to sort out our equipment for the canister, handguns, machine pistols, flash bangs, electronics, night vision and scuba gear, but we will need to be flexible,' Thomas said, stretching his arms. 'No one will leave the compound until we leave for the airport. Martin, you can study the area. Look for any islands where this guy could be holed up.' He looked from man to man. 'Any questions?'

'If we get caught, are we on government business, or are we hung out to dry?' asked Jake.

'We will be hung out to dry, but I do have our Get-out-of-Jail-Free card.' He tapped his breast pocket and then asked, 'Anything else?'

Each man shook his head. 'Okay then, you all know what to do, so let's get to it.'

Chapter Fifteen

The Tsunami Arrives

Charles, Anne, Duke, Max, Keith and James sat around the command-centre console, watching the three large display screens. The centre screen showed the countdown, and as the figures rolled over to T-minus ten minutes, James typed commands on his keyboard, bringing both undersea Acoustic Generation Devices slowly up to full power. He watched the gauges as the power for each unit climbed to 100 per cent. On the display screens to the left and right were video feeds from each Acoustic Generation Device. A few more taps on his keyboard and James powered up the laser targeting probes. The display screens showed a very large light-green haze appear in the water, some kilometres across and hundreds of metres high in front of each Acoustic Generation Device. James knew that once the acoustic waves were initiated and hit the light-green haze area of water, the impact would move that section of water forward with such force that it would mimic the effect of an earthquake lifting water to form a tsunami. The display rolled down to T-minus sixty seconds, fifty-nine. 'We are on automatic computer control,' James said. A hush hung over the command centre as everyone stopped what they were doing and stood and watched the display screens. James followed the countdown. 'Five, four, three, two, one: initiating acoustic wave.'

The display screens showed the effect of the acoustic waves on the laser-target area; the pictures grew very hazy as the waves moved through the water with a rapid rippling effect, Then the light-green haze grew in brilliance as bright as burning phosphorous. The brilliant white slowly died away to the colour of the dark ocean depths with a white mass of water rolling in a boiling turmoil. James typed on his keyboard and changed the two outer display screens to show ocean-monitoring information. 'The waves have been initiated and are rolling in towards their designated targets,' he announced. 'Wave heights nominal and growing exactly as projected, and speed 821 kilometres per hour as predicted. We are all in the green.'

'Can you bring up a feed from ABC News, as they were going to have helicopters and reporters with cameras at both locations?' Charles asked James.

'Sure thing,' James replied and typed on his keyboard. The central display screen showed two pictures: one from New York and another from Washington.

'Time to impact?' Anne asked.

'Any minute now we should see the water recede from the coastline. Yes, there it goes,' James pointed to the display screen.

The news reporter sat ready to give a running commentary on the tsunami hitting New York from her position high above Staten Island, in the safety of news helicopter. Even though it was hours to sunrise, the cloudless sky and bright moon gave an eerie light to the scene. The helicopter circled around as the pilot answered the cameraman's requests to move this way and that for the best pictures of the scene. To the reporter's disbelief, in the beam of the helicopter's searchlight, she saw people lining the water's edge, eager to see the tsunami. She saw the blue and red flashing lights of police cars as they raced around, trying to control the growing crowds, and a couple of police helicopters flying around, trying to move people out of harm's way. She could imagine the same things happening in Washington.

She sucked in a deep breath as she imperceptibly saw the water being drawn out to sea. 'Oh my,' she said. 'Ladies and gentlemen, it is starting, it is happening, the water is receding. People are putting their lives on the line by standing at the water's edge to watch this thing. It's unbelievable. Wait, I can see. Yes, I can see in the distance a thin white line. We can just pick it out in the searchlight of our helicopter. Yes, it's the wave. It is coming. It's not high like the Japanese Tsunami of 2012 nor have the waters receded totally like we saw in the Indonesian Tsunami, where vast areas of the seabed became visible. The wave is approaching fast. We will hover here so we can keep it in the beam of our searchlight. Oh my, it has just hit Long Beach and Sandy Hook Bay, but it's more like an exceptionally extra-high king tide. It's rolled to the top of Long Beach and lapped at the base of houses. It has now passed under the Verrazano Narrows Bridge and is heading unabated towards the statue of Liberty and Governors Island, and it's weakening. I can see a lot of debris in the water, a few small boats that have broken free from their moorings, and wooden pallets. Wait, there's even a twenty-foot container. I can still see people standing around who have been soaked through to the skin. The water is still lapping at the quays and very turbulent and very rough.'

The helicopter flew low over the people standing on the quay side and the cameraman took a long panning shot, lit by the searchlight, before the pilot flew past the Statue of Liberty and headed up the Hudson River, following the diminishing wave. 'How someone can control such an event is incredible,' the reporter carried on. 'Material damage and its only slight from what we can see so far. No loss of life reported here or by my colleagues in Washington DC where the other wave has struck simultaneously.' She took a breath. 'Police report no loss of life. That has been confirmed, which is a miracle, but the question now has to be, if Charles Langham can carry out such a threat and cause an event like this and control it to the degree he stated he would, what else is he capable of?' She was warming to her report. 'How much power does he have at his fingertips, and what action will he take next if our governments continue to ignore his demands to stop the damage that is being done to planet earth? Will the next tsunami be much more damaging? Can he, in fact, create a larger tsunami? This is Rebecca Haxter for ABC Network News.'

Charles and the group watched the news reports live, then watched recordings overlaid with the oceanographic data. 'Run that again and overlay with our projected data as well,' Charles asked James. 'The results are pretty well matched. Can you extrapolate the differentials and overlay that on the new report?'

'Yes,' James said as he typed on his keyboard. 'This will show only the non-matching data between projected and actual and should overlay on the new report time synchronised.'

'So the main differential was the breakaway of the water flow from Chesapeake Bay into the Potomac,' Keith said, rubbing his chin. 'Interestingly, the sea floor and tidal flows were correctly input, so why the variation?'

'Well, we need to find out. I would hate to think that no deaths were a result of luck,' Charles said seriously. 'I will not allow any more use of the technology until we know for sure what happened and why.'

'I'll check the topographic data in case there's been a coastal development that's not on the latest images we have.'

'I'll leave you guys to sort that out,' Charles said. 'Duke, Anne, Max, let's get a coffee. James, get one of the data technicians to sort the news feeds, social media, Internet, you know the drill, for any information from political sources about the two events, and loop it on to the internal information screens.'

'Okay, no worries. I will sort that before I check the topography data.'

Keith removed his headset. 'Charles, that was Mike on *Jupiter*, they are forty-eight minutes from docking.'

'They've made good time,' he replied. 'Keep the nets up till the last possible moment.'

'Will do,' said Keith who then turned back to his console as he said, 'I'll get an update from *Mercury*. They should be close to Tonga by now.'

Charles sat with the group in one of the leisure rooms, with deeply cushioned chairs, bean bags, low tables, LED lighting recessed into the ceiling with a rainbow of soothing colours, and an open drink and snack bar. 'So, Duke, how long before we hear the president do you think?'

'He will wait till the first press conference in the morning for maximum exposure,' Duke said. 'He won't want to waste the impact of what he says on an insignificant number.'

'Max, what's your view?'

'Well, boss, I think the level of impact was right – no deaths, no injury and minor material damage only, but one hell of a show of technological strength.'

'And from a political viewpoint?' Charles questioned.

'I think the US will try to retaliate, not sure how, but the US president might use his own private army. Europeans will be worried they have some ports and cities at low levels,' Max said thoughtfully.

'I've heard about this private presidential army. Is it true?' Charles asked Duke.

'Yep, it's true enough. I've even met one of two of them though I'm not supposed to know anything, but being an ex-VP does have some advantages,' Duke said.

'Is Mike Read likely to use them?'

'I'm afraid so. Mike is showing some odd behaviour, which leads me to believe he would use them. It's really bugging me. Something is not quite right, but I'll be damned if I know what it is.'

'I think it will be worthwhile getting Julie to analyse some of the videos of his recent conversations with me and see what she thinks.'

'Who is Julie?' Duke asked.

'Don't worry, Duke, I'll take care of it. Julie is our resident psychologist. I will get her to take a look at the video and also some from a year ago,' Anne said.

'I would think going back a year, she will see a step change in his personality,' Duke agreed.

Chapter Sixteen

Sundancer Security

John Whitcome stood on the bridge of *Sundancer* and deftly closed the distance between the super yacht and the quay, using the small joystick. The cameras showed him the exact position and distance of the super yacht from the quay. 'Cut engines two and three,' he called.

Martin Deeks powered the two inner engines down. 'Two and three offline,' he said.

John saw the bow and stern mooring lines being looped around bollards, large fenders being deployed to protect the side of the super yacht from scratches, and used the side thrusters to bring her to a controlled stop. 'Cut engines one and four,' he said.

'All engines offline,' Martin said. 'Nicely done, Captain.'

'Martin, shut down all power systems the security team won't be using and secure the yacht,' commanded the captain as he picked up his headset. '*Sundancer* to *Mercury*, we are safely moored and will be ready to depart within the hour.'

'Lisa here, Captain, we are stationed 500 metres off your port beam, resting on the bottom. Can be by your side ten minutes after you give the go.'

'Thank you, Lisa. Good to know you're out there,' he said and then turned to the first officer. 'Shut down all electronics except the security and surveillance systems, then clear the yacht from bow to stern, sealing each area as you go.'

'Aye, Captain,' the first officer replied and started typing commands on his central control position. 'I'll extend the gangway so the security team can get on board. I assume they know the entry code?' he asked as he stood up and made his way to the bridge door, picking up one of the electronic clipboards from behind it.

'They have been briefed. It's the team of five who toured *Sundancer* with us just before she was launched,' the captain advised.

The first officer left the bridge and went to the gangway control and opened the door and extended the gangway, then called up the surveillance team. 'Activate gangway security,' he said into the microphone. The surveillance team confirmed activation of gangway security, which involved a security-code entry on a keypad at the start of the gangway and face recognition before entry through the hull door. He then commenced clearing the super yacht of the skeleton crew who had stayed on board to sail the super yacht to Nuku'alofa. He knew that there were only ten crew members on board, including himself. There would be the two deck crew who had just secured the mooring lines and two engine-room crew members who would currently be powering down the systems not required for security or the comfort of the security team and, lastly, the three systems crew who would be running through the security and surveillance systems which comprised the closed-circuit TV, underwater cameras, motion detection, and keypad entry on all bulkhead doors. He did not expect to find anyone anywhere except in the engine room, surveillance room and on the main deck. He made his way down deck by deck, sealing doors as he finished checking each area, which meant contacting the surveillance team as he closed and locked each door. By the time he reached the engine room, the crew had finished their powering down and system checks and were ready to leave. The first officer led them to the surveillance crew's room to find one of the security team already there and taking over from the three leaving members.

'Hi, Franklin, long time no see,' said Ralph Cohen, the security member who was taking over from the surveillance team.

'Seems like a lifetime,' Franklin agreed. 'You guys ready?' Franklin, the first officer, asked.

'They are ready. I am fully briefed on what they have set up, how it works and the possible threat from the president's private army,' Cohen replied for the three surveillance-team members.

'Okay, well, have a good time, Ralph,' Franklin said. 'The boat is secured, and I have done a complete sweep and locked everywhere down, but you know that already.'

The first officer led the five crew members down the central gangway that was similar to what you would find in a five-star luxury hotel, deep-pile wool carpets, solid cherrywood doors leading to other cabins, polished handrails, pictures, mirrors, and recessed lighting in the ceiling and above the skirting board. The gangway opened up when they reached the central atrium; rather than using the stairs, they got into the lift and went straight up to the bridge level to report to the captain.

'Search complete, Captain. All areas now sealed. Engine room and surveillance teams are with me. One of the new security-team members is now stationed in the surveillance room,' the first officer, Franklin, reported to the captain. The engine-room chief went to Martin Deeks, and both commenced a deep conversation, ignoring all others on the bridge, until they were joined by the senior surveillance-team member and the conversation moved to the subject of security. Martin looked at some display screens and scrolled through menus. 'All looking good, Captain. The teams have done an excellent job. The security team have everything they need at their fingertips, controllable from these displays here. With everything else secure, they have access to the galley and their cabins in the crew area. If they need access to the surveillance room or engine room, they can with the correct access codes.'

'Weapons control?' the captain asked.

'From here as well, Captain, deck guns, torpedoes, Tasers and underwater flash bangs, all available and can be aimed from here,' Martin advised. 'Hand weapons are locked in the bridge locker as usual, and all have been cleaned on route here.'

'Thank you, Martin,' the captain said and nodded to the technical officer as he unusually acknowledged him by his first name. He looked at the chief security officer. 'Well, *Sundancer* is now your responsibility. You have food and fresh water aboard for two months. She is refuelled and fully armed. Good luck.' He saluted the chief security officer.

Miles Channing saluted. 'Thank you, Captain. I accept *Sundancer* and will take good care of her as Mr Langham has ordered. Have a good trip to the HQ.'

The captain called Lisa on *Mercury*. 'Lisa, we are ready for pick-up. Come alongside the port forward door.'

'Be there in seven minutes,' Lisa replied.

Miles Channing went to the control board and raised and stowed the gangway, closing the access hatch at the same time, isolating *Sundancer* from the quay.

The captain led his team from the bridge to the lift and went down to deck two and walked the gangway to the forward hatch. He pressed four numbers on the keypad, and the hatch lowered downwards to form a large boarding deck. From his position, standing on the hatch deck, he watched as the submarine *Mercury* rose slowly from the depths. Lisa appeared standing in the conning tower, in full uniform of white blouse and blue slacks, directing the submarine to align with the deck hatch. Once in position, two submariners threw mooring lines to the *Sundancer* team who looped them over two bollards and threw them back. The *Sundancer* crew quickly jumped aboard the *Mercury* and went below.

The captain went over to the hatch keypad, pressed a four-button code, and hit the thirty-second delay button, giving him enough time to release the mooring lines and jump aboard *Mercury*. As soon as Lisa looked down and saw the captain on board, she gave directions for *Mercury* to move forward and slightly to port before giving the order to dive. John Whitcome climbed down the hatch into *Mercury*, closing it behind him and locking it. One of *Mercury's* crew jumped up the ladder as soon as John had cleared it and checked whether the hatch was sealed. *Mercury* slipped quickly below the waves and headed for Kermadec base HQ at full speed and running deep. Lisa called James on the submarine's radio. 'James, we have the crew from *Sundancer* on board and heading home now at full speed. We will be running deep. Do we have any United States naval assets in the area?' she asked.

'No, you have a clear run all the way. We will keep surveillance for you,' James replied.

'Well, Captain, you might as well make yourselves at home. You have nothing to do now but relax with your crew. The galley is open 24´7, and we have a great selection of DVDs in the lounge area,' Lisa said.

'Thanks, I will get my crew settled in their quarters, then take advantage of the hospitality *Mercury* has to offer,' John Whitcome replied. 'By the way, if you need the talents of my crew or myself, don't hesitate. We are all on the same team.'

'Thanks, I'll remember that,' Lisa replied as John left to round up his crew, and Lisa got back to captaining the submarine.

In the Oval Office, all hell had broken loose. The president paced around the Oval Office like a bulldog on heat, ready to snarl and snap at anyone who spoke out of turn. His team sat in silence around the Oval Office rug that held the crest of the president of the United States, quietly looking at one another.

'So he did it,' he snapped. 'He attacked the United States of America with two tsunamis, so will somebody tell me how the hell he could do that?' Before waiting for an answer, he carried on his rant. 'How could he attack our borders without our defence systems activating? He gave the time and locations, and we were powerless to stop him or the tsunami. Well, are you all going to just sit there and stay silent?' he asked in a raised voice whilst continuing to pace around the office.

'Without knowing how or what technology he could have used, it's impossible to counter any attack,' Ryan responded quietly. 'Our scientific team is incapable of advising us on the mechanism that could have been used to create a tsunami, let alone control the timing or scale as he has done.'

'So you're telling me that a private individual has greater technological ability than our top scientific brains.' The president slammed the palm of his hand on the desk and continued his pacing around the Oval Office like a marauding wolf.

'Eh, basically, yes, that is correct, Mr President,' Ryan replied, looking at the others seated opposite him.

National security advisor, Helen Stark, spoke clearly and carefully, 'Besides the televised notification, we had no intelligence to confirm any attack would take place.'

'Intelligence! At the moment ... that is a joke,' the president retorted. 'We had over twenty-four hour's notification and still no intelligence reports to clarify the data or find the equipment or technology that was used.'

The president raised both his arms. 'That is just unbelievable with the billions we spend on defence and intelligence agencies.' He sat at his desk and glared at those seated. 'I want answers, gentlemen. I want to know where this guy is, how he did this and how open we are to further attacks.' He paused for effect. 'If that's not asking too much? We are talking about national security. This is serious. You have the biggest and most expensive intelligence agencies in the world, so find out.'

'With respect, Mr President,' William Paige, his military advisor, spoke. 'The man is totally off the grid. Not one intelligence service around the world has a clue where he is located.'

'Oh come on, we know he was on that fancy boat of his,' the president said sarcastically, losing his cool. 'And we know where it was going and where it is docked.'

'That's quite right, Mr President,' Clive Harris, the defence chief, agreed. 'But he was not on board when the yacht docked in Nuku'alofa. In fact, I can tell you here and now that the team on board at this very moment were not the crew who sailed her to Nuku'alofa. That crew were not seen departing from the yacht, but we know for sure they are no longer on board, and that is a mystery. The crew on board now just turned up and boarded.'

'Oh, for goodness' sake, you're now telling me that people disappear and others just appear out of thin air,' the president said with contempt.

'Mr President, we do not know how or when the crew disembarked, and we do not know where the current crew came from,' Helen Stark commented, shifting uncomfortably and avoiding the president's glare. 'We only have one agent in Nuku'alofa and need to get more agents there who have more experience.'

'Well, do it and get me some answers. I suggest, you all get back to your agencies and start getting those answers,' the president said, picking up some papers and ignoring the four as they got up and left.

Thomas led his group through Fua'amotu International Airport and grabbed the courtesy shuttle bus to the nearby Scenic Hotel, which they planned to use as their base of operations for two nights only before taking over the charter vessel. Thomas was pleased that the nearest United States embassy was in Suva, far enough away not to interfere with them or their activities. He knew that the CIA had an intelligence officer on the island and knew who he was and where he was based. He was a relative novice, so it would be easy to keep well out of his way, and until they were ready to board *Sundancer*, they would keep well below his radar. Alfred had done a good job for the team and hired a forty-three-foot catamaran for one month as a bareboat charter. The boat was equipped with sounder, GPS, binoculars and flash lights, so that had lightened the canister load which meant they could load other specialist gear. Thomas had made sure that each team member carried game-fishing gear in their luggage to help legitimate their tourist persona.

Thomas could not wait to get on board the catamaran and get to work, but first, they had two nights booked at the Scenic Hotel, which Thomas wanted to use to get the team acquainted with the island and particularly the layout of the port where *Sundancer* was moored. In the meantime, they would act like typical game-fishing tourists. They arrived at the hotel and carried their luggage and rods to the check-in desk and received their electronic room keycards and went off to find their rooms. Thomas directed everyone to meet in the bar by the hotel lobby in an hour and to dress for the weather which was twenty-eight degrees centigrade with 80 per cent humidity. He would be there first and get a tour organised by the reception staff. In the meantime, he went into the bathroom, plugged in his shaver and had a good clean shave, then he undressed and took a long cooling shower. Feeling refreshed, he dried himself off, combed his hair, dressed in shorts and T-shirt and picked up his wallet, room card, camera and sunglasses. With one glance around his room, he found the air-conditioning control and adjusted the temperature and fan setting. Satisfied, he opened the door and made his way to the reception desk.

As he approached the reception area, he took in the eight clocks on the wall behind the reception desk which covered different time zones. Glancing at his own watch, he made a mental note of the different times. He spoke to the reception clerk who showed him a few tour leaflets. Thomas chose a tour that would concentrate on the Nuku'alofa region and pass by the port and government building. The tour coach would pick them up in just under an hour which suited his plans for the day. He received a detailed tourist map of the island and checked with reception clerk where the charter-boat office was located on the map. After the tour, they would meet by the pool and review the maps he had just received and refine the plans for the next few days.

Once on board the catamaran, they would arrange the canister drop and then plan the assault on *Sundancer* to grab Charles Langham if he was on board or find out where he was holed up by analysing the data on board. But for now, he could relax with a drink at the bar while he waited for the others to arrive, then relax and act the typical tourist on the tour bus whilst taking important strategic high-resolution photographs. He took a seat at one of the bar stools and ordered a double Jameson Irish whiskey with no ice. He decided to stay at the bar stool and picked at the bowl of salted peanuts and potato crisps while he savoured his Jameson. He took in the ambience of the hotel which had undergone a renovation. The cool marble floors and light décor with picture windows gave the hotel a light and airy atmosphere. The long pool would come in useful each morning and evening as a good form of exercise.

He saw Jake and Alfred both wander into the lobby and head towards him. 'Drinking a bit early, Governor,' said Jake.

'Help yourself, and put it on my tab,' Thomas said. 'As soon as the others arrive, we have some work to do.'

Jake ordered himself and Alfred double Jack Daniels, their favourite tipple, and took up bar stools next to Thomas.

'So what's the plan for today?' asked Jake.

'We are taking a tour. The coach arrives in half an hour. It will take us around the Nuku'alofa region past the port and government building and major tourist attractions,' Thomas replied. He took a sip of his Jameson and saw the other five members of his team walk into the lobby and head towards them, all dressed in T-shirts and either shorts or slacks. A few had cameras on straps around their necks, but all had sunglasses pushed up on their foreheads. 'Order your drinks on my tab, and be ready to leave in twenty minutes,' Thomas said, checking his watch.

'It will be interesting if we can see *Sundancer* as we pass the port,' Jake said.

'With her size, I doubt if we could miss her,' Thomas said. 'She's 185 metres long and has eight decks, so she's quite tall. She has four decks above her main deck and three below the main deck. On deck seven is the helicopter, and that's a huge bird.'

'We will need a lot more information than that to plan the assault with precision,' Alfred commented. 'I have done a very rough plan, but it needs to be massively refined, and for that, I need to know access points, heights, number of souls on board. Where they are?'

'I know all that,' Thomas retorted. 'We have no access to any plans for the yacht. None exist. All we have at this time is one photograph, so we take our own shots and then we can calculate dimensions.' He downed his Jameson. 'Surveillance from the charter boat during the day and infrared at night will tell us how many crew members are on and their movements.' He saw the tour coach arrive. 'We only move on the yacht when you have your plan refined, Alfred. That's your call, but for now, we are tourists. Let's move.'

Thomas got up, picked up his camera and maps, and led the group into the lobby and out on to the covered courtyard where the coach stood waiting. He gave his name to the tour guide and was ushered aboard followed by the rest of his team and settled into a window seat near the front. The rest of the team spread themselves down the length of the coach, each taking a window seat. The coach moved off for the twenty-one-kilometre journey to the Nuku'alofa area of Tonga. The coach was air-conditioned which made the journey pleasant. From the Tuku'aho road, they quickly joined the main Taufa'ahau road from where the tour took them on a circuitous route around the lagoon past the hospital and Free Church of Tonga, along the waterfront to the Royal Palace.

As they passed the port, Alfred took some long-range high-resolution camcorder footage, while Jake took high-resolution digital still photographs. The other team members took lots of normal tourist-site photographs. The tour continued until they stopped at the Waterfront Bar opposite the Queen Salote Wharf for refreshments. Jake and Alfred took a walk, while Thomas and the others walked up to the colonial-style building and took seats at small tables on the veranda and ordered some cooling drinks.

'Let's see if we can get some close-up shots,' Jake said to Alfred as they crossed the main road to the port. The air was heavy and humid, and Alfred was sweating heavily by the time they got within sight of the large white super yacht which was moored at the outermost point of the port. 'Well, we're not going to get very close until we have the charter boat, are we?' Alfred said, looking through the viewfinder of his camcorder.

'Doesn't look like it. Wait a minute,' Jake said, straining his eyes whilst increasing the zoom on his camera. 'That yacht is called *Cresenda*, not *Sundancer*!' he exclaimed.

'What, that cannot be right,' Alfred said. 'There is only one super yacht in Tonga according to the intelligence report, and it is *Sundancer*.' He lifted his camcorder to his eye and zoomed in quickly. 'You're right. It is called *Cresenda*.'

'Let me see. Yes, the name on the side is *Cresenda* as well,' Jake said.

'What else do we know from the reports?' Alfred asked as he placed his camcorder back in its shoulder bag and pulled a towel from one of its pockets.

Jake pulled out his notepad and flicked through some pages, while Alfred wiped his forehead and neck with the small towel.

'*Sundancer* has twin slim-angled funnels,' Jake said.

Alfred tucked the towel back in its pocket and grabbed the camcorder. 'Well, this yacht has only one funnel, and it is pretty upright,' Alfred said, looking through his viewfinder and using the zoom control.

'Right, let's get back to Thomas and see what he has to say,' said Jake.

'And get a nice cooling beer,' Alfred agreed, placing his camcorder back in its bag. They crossed the main road and walked quickly back to the Waterfront Bar where Thomas and the group sat at two outside tables with half-finished drinks on the tables, watching the passing traffic and pedestrians. 'Any luck?' asked Thomas.

'She's not there,' said Jake. 'Only a yacht called *Cresenda*.'

'No way!' exclaimed Thomas.

'He's right, Thomas,' confirmed Alfred. 'Name *Cresenda* is on the stern and sides. Besides, this yacht has one straight funnel and not two, which *Sundancer* has.'

'What about number of decks and the helicopter?' queried Thomas.

'Correct number of decks but no helicopter or empty helipad,' advised Alfred.

'We'll check the footage and stills when we get back the hotel,' said Thomas. 'In the meantime, get a drink and relax. Our coach is due to leave in fifteen minutes.'

Alfred and Jake put their gear down and went to the bar to get their drinks, leaving Thomas to ponder on the accuracy or inaccuracy of the intelligence they had been given by the commander-in-chief. *Could it be that far wrong, or had – no, wait a minute*, he thought, *they couldn't alter the shape of the funnel, but if they had, there is still the question of no helipad or helicopter. No, must be a different yacht, so where had* Sundancer *gone, or had she, in fact, ever arrived in Tonga?* They would have to ask around, and as a last resort, they could always see if they could hack into the port authority's computer system.

Jake and Alfred returned with a bottle of beer each, water dripping from the cold bottles. They sat at the same table as Thomas. 'So any thoughts?' asked Jake.

'Before we report back to the chief, there are a few things I want to check out. First, Michael, I want you to wander around the port and marina. Casually talk to a few people, and see if you can find out whether *Sundancer* docked here recently.'

Michael stood up. 'Yes, sir. I'll take John with me, and we'll take a cab back to the hotel.'

Thomas looked back at Jake. 'Can you hack into the port authority's computer?'

'Should be able to. Depends on what firewalls they have and who put the system in,' Jake replied, taking a slug from his beer bottle.

'Alfred, how much zoom did you use when you filmed the yacht?' asked Thomas. Alfred put his bottle down and pulled the camcorder from the bag. 'Full zoom, so that's fifty times,' he said, reading from the label on the side. 'So it should be good enough to see individual screws.'

Thomas drained his beer. 'Jake, when we get back to the hotel, I want you to try hacking into the port's computer system and see if *Sundancer* ever docked here, and if she did, when she left and if she logged a planned route. Alfred, we will run the video recording on the laptop and have a good detailed look at that yacht.'

'Don't forget the high-definition digital stills,' said Jake.

The tour guide up came to Thomas and ushered him and his group back to the coach. The journey back was quiet, with a few of the team taking a few tourist stills. Jake made his way to his room and took Connor with him for his additional computer skills. They sat at the desk and plugged the laptop into the computer port by the power socket. Jake looked at Connor. 'First, we'll try the easy way and see if there is anything on the port's website,' he said as he googled the port name for its website address. 'Nothing on the website,' said Jake. 'So over to you, mate, see what you can do.' He pushed the laptop over to Connor.

'No worries. Give me half an hour,' Connor said, his fingers flying over the laptop keypad.

'While you're doing that, I'm going to have a cooling shower,' Jake said.

Alfred followed Thomas to his room, powered up the laptop on the desk and connected the camcorder to the laptop and transferred the file. Thomas grabbed the other chair and pulled it up to the desk so he could see the laptop screen as Alfred tracked slowly through the footage frame by frame. 'So what are we looking for?' Alfred asked.

'During World War II, the German naval commanders changed the name and silhouettes of their vessels to fool allied naval forces into thinking they were allied or neutral merchant ships,' explained Thomas said. 'Hold it there and zoom in on that image.' Thomas said, pointing to the fourth deck. Alfred tapped the mouse pad and froze the frame, then zoomed in slowly while Thomas concentrated on the image. 'No, nothing there. Let's take a look at the funnel.' Alfred moved through more frames until he came to the funnel and shuffled back and forwards until Thomas chose a frame. 'Hold that one. Now let's zoom in and take a closer look at the finish compared to the rest of the superstructure.' Again, Alfred methodically chose the frame and slowly zoomed in until Thomas said, 'Okay, hold there. No, I cannot make out any distinct differences, so this looks like original build.' He hit his fist into the desk. 'Bugger, I thought this was a disguised *Sundancer*,' he said, upset.

'Let me load up the digital stills,' said Alfred as he took the micro SD card from the camera, pushed it into the slot on the laptop and opened the camera software. After a few seconds, thumbnails of the pictures taken by Jake came on the screen.

'Go straight to the ones of the funnel,' said Thomas. Alfred scrolled through the thumbnails until he came to one showing the funnel and clicked on it so it filled the screen. 'Okay, good. Now zoom in on that section there,' said Thomas, pointing to a section of the photograph. Alfred used the mouse pad to zoom in on the area requested by Thomas.

'No, it looks original in this picture as well,' said Thomas, sitting back and thumbing his forehead. He picked up the telephone and dialled Jake's room. 'We have nothing. The pictures are not of *Sundancer*. How are you getting along?' he asked as Jake answered. He listened thoughtfully to Jake's reply. 'Well, that leaves us somewhat in the doldrums. I'll have to contact the commander-in-chief by secure email and see what he says. Dinner at 6.30 pm. Pass it on to everyone.' He replaced the handset. 'Send this to the commander-in-chief on the secure email. *Sundancer* is not in port and has no record of arrival. Please advise location,' he said to Alfred. Alfred opened up an encrypted email system and started typing.

James sat at his console in the circular command centre on the uppermost floor of the deep-sea headquarters, when an area of the display he was looking at went red. 'I have a red alert,' he called over his shoulder to Keith and Charles who were sitting in the next console. 'It's an email originating in Tonga on an encrypted system and says, '*Sundancer* not in port, please advise location.''

'Warn Miles on *Sundancer* that the president's private army is on Tonga. The disguise Max implemented may help for a short while, but they may be able to work it out,' said Charles. During her construction, Max had the idea of commissioning special panels made to fit around the funnels and to enclose the helipad, thus providing a different silhouette. 'Miles must have all the security systems running above and below water,' continued Charles.

'They will be safer moored at the port than anchored at sea. Either way, a magnetic mine could be planted on the hull,' said Keith.

'Not with the motion-activated electric pulse that will kill anyone in the water near the hull,' said James. 'It's a nasty way to die but protects the yacht 100 per cent. Not forgetting the depth flash bangs that are activated by motion as well.'

'Get Miles to activate all systems, and see if they can identify the president's people,' Charles said.

James typed on his keypad. 'The email originated from the Scenic Hotel. I can't get a closer fix than that.' He continued typing. 'I'm emailing Miles now with the security advice and about the email from the Scenic Hotel.' He looked at the display. 'Huh, that was quick. Miles says all security systems have been running at full extent since he took over, and they have noticed two men taking a very active interest in *Cresenda*, taking lots of pictures. They are ready for any eventuality. Message ends.'

'We can leave *Sundancer* in the capable hands of Miles. Send the same message to *Launch One* and the aircraft teams, please,' said Charles. 'Also send a note to the Tonga port authority and Tonga police force about a credible threat to port security.'

Chapter Seventeen

The Davidson Seamount

Charles wandered around the circular command centre, looking out of the hooded windows and the people working at the consoles. *That was quick*, he thought, *the president's team already in Tonga, tracking down Sundancer. They obviously think I am still on board, which is good, and Max's disguise is playing its part for a while. If the president's team try to get on board Sundancer, they will not survive the security offensive.* The security teams on *Sundancer, Launch One*, and those looking after the aircraft were ex-SAS, extremely well paid and deadly. Charles found Duke in front of a large display screen and sat beside him. 'What's the feedback on the two events from around the world?' asked Charles.

Duke leaned back in his seat and had a good stretch with his arms above his head. 'Two schools of thought are coming across,' Duke stated. 'Those who are still puzzled as to how the events were manifested, and those who now understand that the events were controlled, and worse is still to come from nature herself.'

'So is opinion with us or against us, Duke?'

'Generally speaking, with us, except the president of the United States who is wholly against us, and that is the big concern for other governments. They are worried that the president's actions could precipitate a heavier response from him or us that could affect them, such as the low-lying nations like the Maldives,' said Duke. 'I have promised them that no action will be taken on our part that could have an effect on them, but I cannot vouch for the United States, of course.'

'You have heard about Tonga,' said Charles.

'Yes, I have. So what's our next move?' asked Duke.

'Nothing yet. We will take twenty-four hours out for the video we made to take effect and check on world opinion then. Give everyone time to consider what happened and what will happen to the world if nothing changes. We will meet and discuss options based on that feedback,' said Charles, leaning forward, elbows resting on his knees.

'Good idea,' replied Duke. 'And in the meantime?'

'In the meantime, I will work on some options with Keith and James based on the variables that we already know,' replied Charles. 'We have a generic computer-model that we can input many variables into and predict outcomes.'

'And your current thinking?' asked Duke.

'If you really want to know, and I am sure you can already guess, the American president is foremost in my mind, and the outcome of the psychological analysis by Julie will have a major input into my thinking.'

Charles walked back across the control room to James's desk. 'Run a diagnostics check on all the acoustic devices, will you?' he said.

'Sure thing, will take a few hours to do all of them,' said James, turning away from his console. 'I will get the team on to it now.' James got up. 'Do you want the ocean sensors testing as well?'

'That's a good thought, might as well. Tell me, can we still tap into Scripps Institution of Oceanography and Woods Hole Oceanographic Institution systems?'

'Yes, we share heaps of data. Our teams have almost daily contact with their teams. With Woods Hole, it's mainly with their ocean life and deep-ocean teams who Chris and Cathy have already been in video conference with, sharing their Niue information. With Scripps, we interface with two teams, biodiversity and conservation and their global environmental monitoring teams. Our ocean sensor system provides data to Scripps through an uplink we put in place for them. They, in turn, did the same for us from their sensor system.'

'I need to spend some time with each of our teams getting up to date,' Charles said, running his fingers through his hair. *I have got a bit out of sync with what's going on down here,* he thought. 'Schedule me time with each team, please.'

'Ah,' said James a bit sheepishly, 'Anne is ahead of the game. She is already organising that, and I think you'll find her, along with Chris, with the deep-ocean team, looking at seamounts and their ecosystems.'

'Okay, cheers. I think I will go and join her. Buzz me if any news comes in.'

Charles walked away, leaving James, to walk over to his armaments, systems and safety control team main-console and spoke to them via a headset. They looked at him, and a discussion started over the headsets which, to any outsider, would have looked surreal.

Marge, the team leader, removed her headset and typed a command on the keypad, and an array appeared on the display screen in front of her. She looked at it carefully, split the window and pulled up some graphs in a new window. She turned and looked at James. 'This is what I have been trying to explain for a while. Three of our sensors off the West Coast are sending us data that does not match with data from the Scripps' sensors. All the rest are okay. It's just those three. We have run full diagnostics three times over the past ten days, which always confirms clear. Scripps has done the same and confirms clear diagnostics on their sensors.'

'Enlarge the map of the area,' said James.

Marge typed a command, and the map filled full screen. 'There you are,' said Marge.

'Send the map to one of the large screens in the conference room and the data to the other. I'll get the *Deep Sea* and sensor teams to meet us there in thirty minutes,' James said. 'We need to get to the bottom of this.' He went back to his console and dialled the *Deep Sea* team. Chris answered his call, 'Chris, get the team to meet me in the command-centre conference room in thirty minutes, please.' He disconnected the call and dialled up the sensor team. Anne answered, which surprised him. 'Anne, I am getting the *Deep Sea* team to meet in the command-centre conference room in thirty minutes. I need the sensor team there as well.' When she confirmed that the team and Charles would be there, he disconnected the call and stood up and stretched and made his way to the conference room where he poured himself a chilled glass of water and walked over to the data screen and examined the numbers.

He turned one of the seats and sat down, the data running through his mind. There was only one explanation, but a few pieces of information were missing: temperature and acidity readings at varying depths, plus sea floor and seamount height over the past few months. The teams started to file in and take their seats, the sensor team on one side and the *Deep Sea* team on the other. Marge was the last to arrive with Charles and Anne.

'So, James,' asked Charles, 'what's the reason for this urgent meeting?' Charles turned as Keith came in and went over to the water cooler.

'James, what's the buzz?' asked Keith.

James turned to Marge. 'Best Marge explains. She knows more in-depth than I do.'

Marge took her place at the end of the conference table between the two large display screens. Her curly auburn hair matched her dark-tanned complexion. She was a highly respected and liked member amongst the permanent *Deep Sea* staff, with a quiet demeanour. 'Well, I have noticed over the past few days – six, to be precise – that our sensors have not matched the data coming from the Scripps' sensors in this area here,' she explained, walking over to the large display screen and pointing to a group of three sensors. 'They are monitoring the area around the Davidson Seamount.'

'For the uninitiated what is that?' asked Charles.

'It's like an underwater mountain ridge, height is 2,200 metres and it sits 1,200 metres below sea level. It's huge at forty-two kilometres long and thirteen wide and only eighty clicks from California,' said Marge.

'Thank you,' said Charles. 'So what have the sensors been saying, and what's worrying you enough to call this meeting?'

'Sir, I have reason to believe that there is growing activity along the seamount which could result in a tsunami from earth slides.' She went over to the data screen, and all eyes followed her.

'This data shows increase in noise levels and short-wave deep-sea current, but it does not match Scripps' sensor data which are primarily to the west of the seamount, whereas ours are positioned to the east. So I am speculating that the activity of the seamount is only on the side where our sensors can pick up the signals.'

'What about temperature and height changes?' asked Chris, getting up and looking closer at the data on the display screens.

'We do not have that data or chemical information either,' Marge said with a sigh.

'So what do we need to do to confirm or placate your concerns, Marge?'

'We need present height to compare to that on record, acidity data and temperature data, video would be brilliant,' said Marge.

'We can test the new variable-depth sensors,' said Keith with some excitement in his voice. He turned to Charles. 'It's a new sensor that can be programmed to rise or fall in the water column over a set time frame. The sensor is equipped with video, on-board chemical analysis and temperature recording. All data is transferred when the sensor rises to the surface at a preset time and sends remotely by satellite.'

'Okay, how do we get this sensor out there?' asked Charles.

'I would like to send five, if possible. We have twelve built and ready. They are designed to be released by either a submarine or surface vessel.'

Marge looked at Charles. 'I know you are putting a lot of faith in my feelings towards the data, and I greatly appreciate that.'

'Marge, we have no reason to doubt you. We have *Jupiter* docked below. Is she set up to launch these sensors?' asked Charles.

'Yes, she is configured to launch them. I will need to work with the *Deep Sea* team to determine the best release locations and the sensor team to ensure the sensors are set up on the right frequency.'

'There are some rare marine species around the base of the seamount that we recorded on a survey trip with Wood Hole. I would like the opportunity of recording the effect that any activity has had on them,' Jane, the leader of the *Deep Sea* group, said. Jane was a slim blonde with a plethora of degrees in marine science and many publications; to some people, she came across as blunt, and to those who knew her, it was just her passion for marine creatures coming across.

'How do we accomplish that?' asked Charles.

'We use the ROV and the new ultra-deep sensor,' replied Jane.

'That sensor has not been fully tested to those depths,' said Marge.

'How many do we have?' asked Anne.

'Two finished and one in build,' answered Marge. 'They work the same way as the variable-depth sensors. They just go a hell of a lot deeper.'

'Well, we'll use one of them, and if we don't get it back, we have another one, so I am sure we can sacrifice one of them,' said Anne, looking at Charles.

'I agree, Keith, James. I think we back Marge fully on this. Direct both teams to work with her and get *Jupiter* ready to launch,' said Charles. 'Marge, you pull whoever and whatever you want.'

Charles stood up. 'Okay, let's get to it, folks.' As people filed out of the room, he looked around. 'Anne, Keith, James, I would like a word, please,' he said and refilled his glass from the water cooler, walked to the conference table and hit the Tannoy button. 'Mike Holdsworth to the command-centre conference room now, please.' He released the button and sat down.

'James, we will need a complete and thorough update on United States naval operations between here and the seamount and any that can enter the operational area whilst we are there.'

'No issue there. We have been monitoring their activities continuously for the past few days,' said James.

Mike Holdsworth entered the conference room and took a seat. He looked relaxed and very much at home. 'I hear we have an operation about to launch?' he said.

'How long will it take to get the *Jupiter* from here to the Davidson Seamount?' Charles asked.

Mike thought for a moment, rubbing his eyebrow, a trademark habit that everyone knew meant he was deep in thought. 'At least seven days at flank speed.'

'We will need to reduce that. It is way too long,' Charles advised.

'Easy,' said Max as he sauntered into the conference room. 'We use *Sundancer*, the Bell 525 and *Mercury*.' He pulled a chair next to the table and sat, resting his right elbow on the table.

Charles looked at Max and smiled. 'And how exactly do we do this?'

Max walked over to the large world map fixed to the wall. '*Mercury* changes course now and heads to the Davidson Seamount. *Sundancer* heads this way at full speed. Once *Sundancer* is 600 kilometres away, the Bell 525 takes off and heads here. We release the refuelling platform, she lands, refuels, takes the sensors with her and returns to *Sundancer*, refuels, and meets up with *Mercury* and then drops the sensors for *Mercury* to pick up. Easy, takes two days for the whole exercise.'

'I can go on the Bell 525 and drop to *Mercury* with Marge,' Mike Holdsworth said.

'Max, it's your plan. You can be the orchestra leader. Liaise with James on US naval movement. Mike, you had better brief Marge on the winch down to *Mercury*. I doubt she has ever done that before. Keith, order *Sundancer* to leave port and route her here. Change *Mercury's* course and calculate the rendezvous points with Max as he knows the Bell's range and speeds better than anyone else.'

Keith got up. 'I'm on it now,' he said and left the conference room and went to his console. He sat down, pulled on his headset and dialled up *Sundancer*. 'Miles, how are things in Tonga?'

Miles Channing was sitting in the captain's chair on the bridge of *Sundancer* when the call came through from Keith. 'Quiet. A few people have been taking stills and video of *Sundancer*, but otherwise quiet, very quiet.'

'Well, things are going to get busy for you now. You are to leave port immediately and head to Kermadec at full speed. I assume you have refuelled the tanks,' said Keith.

'Yes, we are full to the brim. I will leave now if you can send a course for us to follow,' Miles Channing said.

'Course will be on your screen in a few minutes. They will be fully pre-programmed, so all you will need to do is put her on autopilot. I need to contact *Mercury*, so bye for now.' Keith signed off and called Lisa on *Mercury*. 'Hi, Lisa, change course and head for Davidson Seamount at the fastest possible speed. Will give you more information later. Bye.'

Miles Channing called Ralph Cohen to the bridge. 'We are leaving and heading for Kermadec, so start all engines and turn on the navigation lights,' he said.

Ralph sat in the first officer's chair and pressed the four green buttons and instantly felt the low vibration of the engines and watched as the tachometer needles rose.

Miles picked up a handheld radio and pressed the talk button. 'Dave, Mitch, let go all lines, and advise when done. Over.' He sat back in the deep captain's chair and looked at the array of display screens in front of him and saw one refresh with a course plotted on it sent directly from Keith. A voice sounded over the handheld radio. 'All lines released and being stowed.' Miles pressed the talk button. 'Thank you. Once we are clear of port, stow the disguised names and stow the silhouette panels.' He carefully held the joystick and, with gentler movements, eased *Sundancer* slowly away from the quay. 'Ralph, you had better call the port and advise that we are leaving,' he said whilst maintaining a focused mind on cameras that showed him where *Sundancer* was in relation to the quay. He flicked a switch, and the searchlight's mounted flush on either side of the bow came on. He adjusted their angle to give him the best view. 'Ralph, increase power to ten knots,' said Miles Channing as he checked the display map. 'We will be heading east through the Piha passage before turning south. Increase power to twenty knots.'

Miles carefully followed the course charted by Keith that led them from the port to the Piha passage, always maintaining a good depth of water. Miles was impressed by what the guys at the Kermadec HQ could do. Even though he had never been there or met any of them, he felt very much a part of them. 'Okay, give me all she has got,' he said to Ralph and turned off the bow searchlights. He felt the surge of power as *Sundancer* smoothly powered up to full speed. 'Balance the revolutions across all four engines,' he said to Ralph and picked up the handheld and pressed the talk button. 'Remove the disguised nameplates now, please.' He replaced the handset on the console in front of him. 'It seems weird steering this huge yacht using this tiny little joystick,' he said, looking at Ralph. 'It's just not right. There should be a nice steering wheel just here. Better engage the stabilisers for a smoother ride.'

Ralph looked across, having taken time to balance the revolutions of all four engines. 'Put her on autopilot. If you look at the navigation screen you've been following, in the right-hand bottom corner is a touchscreen button which says "engage autopilot". I think Keith has set it all up for us.'

Miles leaned forward and pressed the touchscreen button and instantly felt *Sundancer* change course slightly.

'I'll be damned. That guy is clever.' An alarm sounded. Miles and Ralph both looked around until Miles saw the warning on the screen. 'Turn the radar on,' he said to himself and turned the radar system on. 'Sonar is on, I assume,' he said to Ralph.

'Yes, I have a mirror image of all the surveillance screens here,' Ralph said. 'So nothing to do but sit back and relax.'

'Help the guys remove and stow those silhouette panels, will you?'

'Sure, no problem,' Ralph said and got up and left the bridge, leaving Miles Channing to look at the systems around him, where everything gave the impression that *Sundancer* was controlling herself. He loved technology, but this was something else – a super yacht this size that can, in many ways, be controlled by someone thousands of miles away. He went into the library, poured himself a coffee and returned to the bridge. He sat down in the deep captain's chair and relaxed. *Nothing to do except drink a nice coffee and enjoy the view.*

Keith turned his attention back to *Mercury*, satisfied that he had sent all the navigation and autopilot codes to *Sundancer*. He plotted the course he wanted *Mercury* to follow and sent the data to their system and then called up Lisa, 'You should have received the course and speed data we want you to follow,' he said to Lisa over his desk microphone, having had enough of the headset for the day.

'Yep, got it, and the navy officer is loading it now,' Lisa said. 'What's the op?'

'You are meeting up with the Bell 525 which will winch down Marge and Mike with some sonar gear.'

'Okay, that's a first for me. I've never performed any winch retrievals.' She looked around the control room. 'Anyone done a winch retrieval before?' she asked of the crew in the control room. She breathed a sigh of relief. 'Two crew members have done winch retrievals before,' she said into the microphone to Keith.

'Mike has experience as well, so you'll be okay,' said Keith. 'So relax and stay on the course plan till I contact you again. Talk soon.' He ended the call, got up and walked into the conference room where Charles and Anne were still seated, deep in conversation. It never came as a surprise to him that, after all their years of marriage, they still acted like a newly married couple. He had grown close to them over the years, helping them change the company to the conservation-oriented business it now was – the fights they had had with government officials and other industry giants who thought they were mad – but they remained stoic in their attitude, and every adversity brought them closer together. Then the bombshell when Charles, at just forty-seven years of age, was diagnosed with multiple sclerosis. They learnt about the disease and invested heavily in research. Charles was slowed down considerably by the disease, and Anne made sure he rested frequently between his bouts of high activity. In many ways, the diagnosis had drawn them closer than they were before, if that were possible.

'*Sundancer* has left Tonga, and *Mercury* has changed course,' he reported. 'Why don't you take some time out – its 2 am and you look shattered, Charles? There's nothing to do for a while now except wait.'

'Do we have an acoustic device near the seamount?' Charles asked.

'The closest one is just off the California coast. Why?'

'Marge thinks there is an imminent danger of a major landslide which she believes could cause a huge tsunami. Records show it has happened before with devastating results.' He took a few breaths, and Anne put her arms around his shoulders. 'I was thinking, can we aim the device towards the seamount and fire it if there is a tsunami and counter any wave generated by a landslide?' Charles asked, rubbing his eyes.

'I will have to run some computer simulations, but at this moment, I cannot say,' said Keith. 'While James and I do that, you take a rest, or I'll get Max in here!'

Charles got up and, with Anne's help, went to his stateroom to lie down.

Chapter Eighteen

Tonga

Thomas woke up early and, after helping himself to an orange juice from the minibar, turned on his laptop and checked the secure email. He read the email from the commander-in-chief. 'Bullshit,' he said under his breath, closed the laptop lid, went into the bathroom and took a shower. After drying himself off, he had a shave and got dressed, packed his bags which he left by the door and made his way to the restaurant for breakfast. He was not surprised to see all his team already there.

'Any news from the chief?' asked Jake as Thomas sat down and poured a cup of coffee and ordered breakfast from the waiter who was at hand.

'The reply email stated that as *Sundancer* was the only super yacht in the region, it has to be her. It also stated that there is no super yacht by the name of *Cresenda* on record,' he said to Jake, as he buttered some toast. 'So we get on board our charter boat and take a much closer look at this mysterious yacht.'

'That will prove difficult,' said Jake cautiously. 'I checked the port's records again this morning, and the boat we know and saw as *Cresenda* left in the early hours of this morning.'

'That's quite a drop on us!' said Thomas after the waiter served his cooked English breakfast. 'By the time we get on the charter boat, that's another two hours. Do we know where it's heading?'

'All I can ascertain at this moment is that it left through the Piha passage,' replied Jake.

'Are there any satellites you can access to pinpoint her current location?'

'Eh, well, yes, but not through official channels,' replied Jake.

'Okay, let's all finish here, check out and get on the charter boat so Jake can get to Work,' said Thomas, cutting into a piece of bacon. *What have I got us into?* He thought. *A yacht that does not appear to be the yacht they want but is so according to so-called intelligence channels. Now it's left port late at night, and they cannot even go through official channels to locate its position.* Thomas disagreed with the commander-in-chief's decision and wondered about his motives. He had seen the TV reports and the video by Charles Langham and Duke Warren and personally agreed with their findings and the scientific basis for them, which made the president's actions all the more strange. All his life he had followed orders, first from his parents until he was sent to a remand home, where he spent two years for stealing and crashing a car. Then there was a stint in prison for three years for causing death by dangerous driving. After leaving prison, he could not get a job as no one would employ him with his record, so he enlisted with the army which seemed to fit with his psyche. He excelled and was given the opportunity of trialling for the elite Navy SEALs; he excelled throughout the training and tests. Years later, he was seconded to the commander-in-chief's private army. Maybe now was the time to do what he thought was right rather than take orders from others. He looked around the table and wondered whether the team would follow him if he disregarded their orders from the commander-in-chief.

Thomas finished his breakfast, poured one last coffee, which was only just warm, and stood up. 'Right, come on, check-out time. Let's get moving. You've sauntered over breakfast long enough,' he said and pushed his chair back towards the table. After checking out, they used the hotel minibus to get to the charter boat where a European sales assistant went through the paperwork with Thomas and operation of the forty-three foot catamaran with Connor who was the most experienced of the team with sailing boats, which was his hobby and life outside work. Once alone, they unpacked their gear, while Jake went below to set up his laptop and concentrate on trying to get a satellite fix.

'Get this thing on the move,' ordered Thomas to Connor who nodded and started to give orders and, in some cases, instructions to the rest of crew while he turned battery isolators on, fuel cut-off valves on and started the engine. 'Alfred, contact the HALO drop aircraft. Get the drop coordinates from Jake.' Thomas stood at the stern and watched the receding landscape as they left their mooring. He wished he could have stayed in Tonga a bit longer and rested; it looked like a wonderful place to chill out, but he had work to do. He was deeply divided about what to do and had never been in such a predicament before. He had time until they sighted the super yacht before he had to make a final decision.

Jake appeared at the hatch to the cabin. 'I think I have her. She's about 400 kilometres south of Tonga,' he said.

'Right, Connor, plot an intercept course. We will pick up the HALO drop on route. Let's get this thing going as fast as we can.'

'Jake, I want a word with you,' Thomas said and went through the hatch and sat in the dining area where Jake had been working. He rested his arms on the table and rubbed his face. He suddenly realised how tired he was. 'You know I'm not sure about this job. In reality, we are chasing a guy who wants to do good and save people and wildlife – the world, in fact,' he said quietly, looking Jake directly in the eyes.

'Sure thing, but he attacked our homeland with not one but two tsunamis,' replied Jake. 'You're not going to disobey the orders of our commander-in-chief, are you?'

'No, but we need to keep our options open and keep a close eye on what's happening out there and the opinion of other world leaders.'

'Guess you're right. Okay, we need to review the operations status before taking any direct action. I'll talk to the others and brief them up,' replied Jake.

Thomas patted Jake on the arm. 'Okay, thanks.'

Arnold came to the dining area. 'HALO drop in six hours,' he said.

'Get the team to practise retrieval, and get them used to working around the rigging,' replied Thomas.

Arnold went back on deck to round up the other team members. The weather was clouding over, and the sea state becoming choppy. 'Weather is deteriorating, and we are in for a rough ride,' said Jake. 'The HALO drop time will be worse, I would say, thirty gusting forty knots with two to three metres seas.'

'Let Connor know so he can prepare the boat for the bad weather,' Thomas said. 'I'm going to sit outside under the canopy and enjoy the scenery for a while.'

Chapter Nineteen

Events South of Tonga

Miles Channing brought *Sundancer* to a halt with her bow into the wind. Ralph Cohen sat in the Bell 525, closed the door and turned on the helm displays. He could see why this was Max's baby. He waited until the two crew members unlocked the landing gear from the helipad. He transferred the course he was to follow from the micro SD card to the GPS Navigation display. Keith had left nothing to chance and had sent the course to Miles's laptop. Ralph fired up the engine, scanned the display, and once he was happy that everything was okay, increased speed and lifted the big Bell 525 off the helipad and crabbed sideways to port. Increasing speed and height, he cleared the super yacht and followed the course on the screen. Miles had nothing now to do except keep on station and await Ralph's return. He sat in the captain's chair and set the computer to hold station, using the bow and stern thrusters and the two outer engines. He shut down the two inner engines. He had five to six hours to wait before the helicopter returned; also, the weather was deteriorating, which could delay the helicopter's return.

'HALO drop position,' called Alfred. 'Should see the chute any minute. Get ready for retrieval.' The boat pitched and heaved with spray soaking most of the crew. Jake stayed below, checking the radar and satellite imaging, which was intermittent due to the squally weather. Connor was the first to see the parachute, 200 metres off their starboard quarter. He altered course, whilst other members of the crew grabbed boat hooks to try and snag the canister. Connor turned the boat towards the canister and carefully backed towards the two-metre-long canister. Two crew members struggled to hook the canister with the pitching of the boat until Alfred joined in and managed to get a loop of rope around the nose of the canister, which enabled the two crew members to finally get their hooks into cleats on the canister and ease it into the stern between the two pontoons. Alfred quickly tied the canister to the boat's cleats. 'Okay, let's get on board,' he said, and it took four of the crew to haul the heavy and slippery canister on board the pitching catamaran. With the canister securely on board, Jake came on deck and punched in the code which opened the canister. Jake passed automatic rifles to one of the crew. 'Let's get this stuff below,' he said, passing flash bangs, hardened cases containing electronic equipment, bulletproof vests and scuba gear. 'You chose to bring a drone?' asked Thomas, looking at the drone which was the last item in the canister, its wings and fin laid carefully at its side.

'It can take off from this catamaran, and I can control it with the electronics in that grey case,' he said, pointing to a large grey metal case. 'We can see live video feeds and release air-to-ground missiles,' he said, grinning. 'Gives us an edge, don't you think?' He lifted the drone body out of the case and took it down below, returning to collect the tail, wings and mounting bolts and tools. 'I'll put it together down below if Connor can keep this thing steady,' Jake said.

'Boys and their toys,' said Thomas. He turned to Connor. 'Let's get going. I'm feeling rather sick sitting here with the way this thing is rolling around.'

Connor fired up the two large outboard motors and pushed the throttles forward as he swung the boat back on to course, heading into the oncoming sea swell. The two four-stroke outboard motors pushed the boat forward as the bows punched through the waves.

Mike Read walked down the staircase from Air Force One at Enniskillen Airport with his entourage, which included William Paige, his military advisor, Ryan O'Hare, his chief of staff, and Clive Harris, the defence chief. They climbed into the fleet of armoured limousines and made their way to the G8 meeting at the Lough Erne Resort. The exit to the airport and all the roads leading to the resort were lined with protestors shouting and waving banners, putting pressure on police cordons. The president could well see this meeting being hijacked by the Langham affair, certainly in his mind those attending, Canada, Japan, Russia, and the European group of France, Germany, Italy and the United Kingdom, along with the presence of the president of the European Union would not leave it unspoken about. After a short quiet drive, they arrived at the resort, and the president introduced himself to the other leaders and then took his place around the conference table with still and sparkling mineral water bottles in front of him. He poured a glass and took another look at the papers his aides had provided him although he had been fully briefed on the flight over.

'Gentlemen, welcome to the thirty-eighth G8 Summit.' The British prime minister stood. 'The Agenda and first item have been changed in light of recent events, and it is of utmost importance that we address these even at the expense of other agenda items.' He sat and continued, 'Our countries have suffered from riots and protests throughout the past weeks, aimed specifically at our governments and their perceived inaction politically at the issues that have been raised and brought to the general population's view by Mr Langham, following his address at the United Nations.' There were nods of consensus from around the table, especially from the French prime minister who spoke up.

'Protests have brought our ports to a close, our farmers are on strike and we have been, how you say, bombarded with emails and phone calls from our low-lying islands around the globe, in addition to our scientists and conservationists! It is unbelievable, but this one man has almost taken control of France!' He stood up. 'I am being told that what he says is true and should not be, eh, brushed under the carpet – I think it is the English term. New Caledonia and our Polynesia Islands are threatened by sea-level rise and that will affect their tourist dollar, not to mention endemic species.'

The British prime minister stood. 'With respect to my French colleague, we have seen the papers submitted from his country as we have seen the papers submitted from all attendees plus many from concerned leaders from around the globe.' He sat. 'May I suggest that we take a first quick vote on the question of do we support or do we not support the issues raised by Mr Langham, followed by a secondary vote on whether or not we work with Mr Langham on achieving progress to the issues he has raised.'

With consent from around the room, Andrew Chalmers, the British prime minister, was about to take the vote, when Mike Read protested. 'Are we seriously talking about taking a vote possibly in favour of a non-elected individual who is, in reality, attempting to take control of the world, potentially to his own ends?' he asked with a raised voice.

'Mr President, if you have read the reports that is certainly not the analysis that our specialists, which includes your own team of scientists, have come to. We vote.' The British prime minister continued, 'The first vote is on the question of do we support or do we not support the issues raised by Mr Langham.'

All except the American president voted affirmative. Andrew Chalmers looked around the room. 'The secondary vote then, which is whether or not we work with Mr Langham on the issues he has raised.' Again, all except the American president voted affirmative. 'It is, thereby, voted by this group, the G8, in the majority to support and work with Mr Langham on the climate and environmental issues he has raised. I will endeavour to contact Mr Langham and open the appropriate dialogue at the closure of this meeting. In the meantime, no harm will befall him, and I will take it as agreed, Mr President, that the US will recall its fleet in the Pacific that is undeniably trying to trace his whereabouts which can only be to cause him harm,' Mr Chalmers said whilst looking at the United States president.

'I will recall our fleet if that is the wish of the G8,' Mike Read said and indicated to William Paige to come to his side and spoke quietly in his ear. 'Send an aircraft or drone and destroy the charter boat that Thomas and his team are on. There may be collateral damage which, unfortunately, cannot be helped,' he said without emotion. 'When actioned, the fleet is to return to Pearl,' he continued.

William Paige retired to his chair at the side of the room and spoke to Ryan O'Hare. 'The president has his private army in the Pacific, tracking down the super yacht *Sundancer*,' he said quietly.

'Really? What the hell was he hoping to accomplish?' asked Ryan.

'Obviously hoping to take him out.'

'So what's the plan?' Ryan asked.

'He wants the charter boat that Thomas is on taken out,' explained Paige.

'And what happens to Thomas and his group?' asked Ryan.

'Collateral damage is to be expected, apparently,' said Paige. 'I had better make the call.' He left the room quietly and showed his pass to the guards as he exited the building and walked across the gravelled car park and stood next to one of the limousines. He took his phone from his inside jacket pocket and dialled a pre-programmed number. 'This is Pegasus. Remove scorpion. I repeat, this is Pegasus. Scorpion is to be retired. Confirm code three six four one nine.' He listened to the voice on the other end of the phone. 'This is Pegasus. I can confirm initiate immediately.' He disconnected the call, then leaned back against the car and sighed. He looked at the phone, deep in thought, and wandered around for a while before re-entering the building, showing his pass as he entered the G8 meeting room and sat next to Ryan and said quietly, 'Well, the calls have been made. May God be with them.'

'Did you warn Thomas?' Ryan asked.

'No, God help me I thought about it, but no, I didn't.'

Ryan sat thinking, ignoring the talk amongst the G8 leaders that was becoming animated. Should he call Thomas whom he had known for many, many years? It would breach his oath to the office of the president, but Thomas was a friend, and you had to draw the line somewhere. The president had known Thomas for many years, and Ryan knew that Mike Read had helped Thomas when his wife and eight-month-old daughter were killed in a hit-and-run car crash. The president, a Senior Senator at the time, had taken him under his wing, bringing him into the service of the senator security team. How could he callously order his execution? Ryan began to believe the rumours that the president was losing his grip on reality.

'Excuse me,' Ryan said to Paige and quietly left the room and headed for the front of the building, looking around so as to avoid being picked up by security cameras that could read his lips or pick up the keys he pressed on his phone.

He dialled the satellite phone that he knew Thomas had. When Thomas answered in code, Ryan responded the same way. 'Your vessel and its activities have been retired with immediate effect. Suggest take appropriate action to eliminate any collateral damage.'

Ryan listened to the reply from Thomas before replying, 'I can say no more except good luck.' He disconnected the call and turned his phone off and took a walk around the perimeter of the lodge, trying to clear his mind.

Thomas put the satellite phone in his pocket and shouted down to Jake. 'Hey, Jake, can you pick up any incoming aircraft or drones?'

'I may be able to see aircraft but not drones if they are riding the waves. Why?'

'Well, for heaven's sake, check now. We have just been terminated!' Thomas shouted. 'Everyone get ready to bail on my word,' Thomas shouted to his team. 'Get that dinghy launched, and throw the life raft over the side, but do not pull the inflation cord until I say so.'

'No incoming aircraft that I can see, but they may be moving too fast for me to see,' Jake replied just before he was instantly blown to pieces as a missile hit the side of the boat, exploding on impact. The flash of flames soon engulfed the cabin with a heat intensity that caused materials to instantly combust. Thomas dived over the side and dived deep and away from the boat just as the stern splintered into pieces with the whoosh of an explosion and became engulfed in flames as a second missile hit the boat. The dinghy was blown into pieces of jagged rubber and human body parts. The mast fell in a tangle of splinters of wood and ropes, killing another crew member instantly. Of the team on the stern, only Connor made it over the side in time and swam towards Thomas and the white shell of the life raft housing. 'Wait. We need the plane or planes who fired those missiles to confirm no survivors before we inflate the raft,' Thomas said between taking breaths as water lapped at his mouth. They heard the screams of the two F16s as they flew at low altitude and buzzed the floating debris before hitting their afterburners and climbing straight up in a deafening roar, their delta swing wings closing, before pulling into a High-G turn, heading back to their aircraft-carrier base. Thomas pulled the line, and the life raft opened up, and they climbed on board.

'What the hell is going on?' shouted Connor, wiping his wet hair out of his eyes.

'The president has obviously decided that we are no longer needed, so I think we should change sides and team up with Charles Langham, if he will have us.' Thomas looked at his watch. 'His yacht should be no more than sixty kilometres from us.' He took the satellite phone from his pocket and dialled a number from the memory. 'Mr Langham, please, my name is Thomas. I used to work for the president of the United States until a few minutes ago. I have information that will be very useful to you if you could pick us up.' He listened to the reply and smiled at Connor. 'We are about sixty minutes by fast boat from you. I'll pass you over to Connor who will give you our exact location. Thank you.' Thomas passed the phone to Connor who read out their longitude and latitude.

Paige took his phone from his pocket when it began to vibrate and read the message. He stood up and walked quietly over to the president and bent down to whisper in his ear. 'The operation was a success, but collateral damage was 100 per cent. The aircraft are returning to their carrier, and then the fleet will withdraw.'

'Thank you,' said the president, covering his mouth with his hand. 'Shame about the collateral damage, but that's war.'

Paige returned to his chair and looked at the agenda to see what was currently under discussion as Ryan walked back in. 'The mission has been completed,' he said to Ryan.

'Any survivors?' asked Ryan.

'None seen by the aircraft. president seemed quite happy, and the fleet is now returning to Pearl, which should calm down this meeting,' Paige replied.

Charles, having been woken from his sleep by Anne, sat by James and called up *Sundancer*. 'Mike, this is Charles. I have a pick-up for you, so launch the RIB. James is sending you the exact coordinates as I speak. Keep the two persons under tight security until they arrive here, but look after them with all the home comforts, if you get my drift.'

'I understand clearly, Charles. No problem. The Bell 525 is due to land in five minutes, so will work out well,' Miles Channing replied. 'Coordinates have arrived. I'll get off the radio now and get things moving. Talk later.' Miles ended the call. Miles called two of his security team to the bridge and passed them the coordinates. 'Launch the RIB, and pick up two people from these coordinates. Bring them straight to the bridge and ensure they see nothing on route. When Ralph returns, we will head in your direction. Off you go,' Miles said, dismissing them. He picked up a microphone and pressed a preset frequency button. 'Ralph, your ETA please?' he said into the microphone.

'I have you in sight. The weather is rotten, with gusty winds. So keep her as steady as you can at ten knots. I have precious cargo on board. Touchdown in a few minutes,' Ralph's voice came over a speaker.

'Very good. Nick will be on the pad, ready to secure the Bell as soon as you land. I will get under way at around ten knots and actuate the stabilisers. Give me the nod as soon as you secure,' Miles replied.

'Understood. Coming alongside now,' replied Ralph.

Miles opened the bridge door slightly so he could clearly hear the sound of the helicopter increasing as it came nearer to landing and got a face full of water for his efforts. He watched as the RIB crossed his bow and could see the row of green lights on the left helm panel that signalled that all the garage doors were closed. He keyed the coordinates into the navigation system and sat back in the captain's chair and powered up the two inner engines and brought the super yacht up to ten knots and extended the stabilisers, shutting down the bow and stern thrusters, when Ryan's voice came over the speaker. 'Down and locked,' he said.

Miles put his hand over the four throttles and eased them slowly forward to the full notch, then eased them back, balancing the revolutions. He felt the power of the engines beneath his feet as the bow rose slightly and the huge craft picked up speed. He was always astounded by just how fast the super yacht accelerated. Ralph, Marge and Mike Holdsworth came through the library and sea-view dining room on to the bridge. 'What's the buzz?' Ralph asked as he took off his jacket. 'I saw the RIB leave at high speed.'

'Hi, Mike, hi, Marge, I'll be with you in a minute. Ralph, Charles wants us to pick up two people in a life raft and keep them secure until we can get them to Kermadec. That's all I know at the moment,' Miles explained to Ralph as he carefully made a course change.

'So we don't know who they are?' queried Ralph.

'Nope, not a clue. Once they are on board, we should be able to find out more. The impression clearly was to pick them up post-haste so to speak,' Miles said.

'I'll organise a secure room for them,' said Ralph as he turned to leave the bridge.

'Hold on a moment. Charles said they are also to be afforded all comforts,' said Miles, recalling the brief conversation he had had with Charles.

'Must be pretty important people, but then what the hell are they doing in a life raft in the middle of the Pacific in this weather?' Ralph said with a concerned voice.

'I do not have a clue. Let's get them on board and find out then,' Miles said, keeping one eye on the huge navigation display.

'Well, if you will excuse us, we'll get out of your way as we have work to do on the gear we brought along,' said Marge and looped her arm around Mike Holdsworth and led him off the bridge.

The radio speaker buzzed. 'We have them in sight, getting ready for the transfer, but, boy, it's going to be tricky in these swells!'

'If they have to get in the water, and so be it, they must be soaked through anyway,' Miles said and clipped the microphone back in place. He glanced over at Ralph. 'Get the secure room organised and then get to the garage with Nick and help recover the RIB.'

Ralph left the bridge and went to the helipad where Nick was completing a refuel.

'How long before you are finished?' he asked.

'Not long. Just a quick wipe to mop up any drips and she's finished,' said Nick.

'Good, we need to get to the garage and prepare for the RIB recovery,' said Ralph.

'Should be fun in this weather, but from what I hear, the recovery gear is designed to cater for bad weather,' Nick said.

'Well, we are about to find out. Come on,' said Ralph, leading the way to the lift. After choosing a room and adjusting the communication options and locking out the keypad entry, Ralph led Nick down one flight of stairs, along a plush corridor until they entered the garage. Ralph walked past the large luxurious tender to a console where he picked up a microphone and called Miles on the bridge. 'We are ready. How long till retrieval?' he asked.

'They have recovered the two people and should be coming alongside in a few minutes. I am slowing down so you can open the garage door,' replied Mike over the speaker. Ralph could feel the speed dropping away and switched on the panel's safety switch and pressed one button. A large section of the hull folded upwards. He pressed another button, and the RIB's sled moved out of the hanger and angled till it was just above the waves. Ralph used a joystick and angled the sled rearwards as the RIB came from behind the super yacht and carefully lined itself up with the sled. Ralph used the joy stock, and the rear of the sled disappeared beneath the water. The RIB helmsman made careful adjustments to his speed and altitude and deftly powered the RIB up the sled until it attached to the automatic retrieval device. Ralph swung the sled back to its retrieval position and drew the sled into the hull and closed the garage door, locking out the wind and rain in the process. Ralph picked up a microphone and called the bridge. 'RIB and four persons recovered.' He put the microphone back into its bracket and switched the panel off. 'You two wash and refuel the RIB, then back to you normal duties,' he said to the two RIB crew. 'You two gentlemen can come with me. We have a dry change of clothes for you, and you're wanted on the bridge. Nick if you please,' he said, indicating Nick to follow from behind.

Ralph and Nick arrived on the bridge with Thomas and Connor between them in a change of clothes. 'Good day, gentlemen. My name is Miles Channing. I am the current captain of the super yacht, *Sundancer*. I welcome you on board. We have been advised to offer you all the comforts that we can, but you will not have free-run of the yacht.'

Thomas walked towards Miles. 'Thank you, Captain. My name is Thomas, and this is my colleague, Connor.'

'What were you doing out there?' Miles asked.

'We were attacked by two F16s from the US *Pacific Fleet*. We lost six friends when they fired on us,' Thomas explained calmly.

Miles sat in the captain's seat and pushed the throttles to their max. 'We have one drop off to do before we return to base.' He took a few minutes to correct their course before asking, 'Why were you attacked?'

'The United States president decided to end our contract which was to eliminate Charles Langham whom we thought was on board this ship,' Thomas explained honestly. 'I have spoken with Charles Langham and have evidence that he will find useful.'

'Well, you will eat with us and relax with us, but unfortunately, when two of my men are not available, you will be confined to your quarters, which, you will find, are more luxurious than a five-star hotel. There is an entertainment console with hundreds of videos and music tracks online, tea and coffee facilities plus the Internet, which we have set to receive data, not send. At the press of a button, you can contact our chef who will provide you with anything you desire,' said Miles.

'Well, it's a lot better than what the Americans had in store for us, so I thank you,' said Thomas graciously.

'Ralph, please escort Thomas and Connor to their quarters,' Miles said. 'Then come back with Nick and relieve me for a spell.' After the four men left, Miles picked up the microphone and called Kermadec base to advise that the two survivors had been retrieved successfully and that they were now steaming at full speed to meet up with Lisa on *Mercury*.

Chapter Twenty

Seamount Arrival

Miles Channing returned to the bridge after taking a few hours rest in his cabin and sat in the captain's chair, looking out over the bow, pleased that the weather had finally improved. Ryan sat at the technical station and Nick in the first officer's chair. The inter-company radio sounded, and Miles leant forward and pressed the pick-up button. 'Miles here,' he said.

'Miles, this is Keith. You are now in range to launch the helicopter. I will send the location coordinates directly to the Bell 525's system. By the time the helicopter reaches the location, Lisa will have *Mercury* on the surface, ready for the transfer. I estimate that they will have fifteen minutes hover time before the helicopter has to return to *Sundancer*.'

'Thanks, Keith. I will get Ralph to take off now. I will call as soon as I know that the helicopter is on its return,' said Miles, pressing the disconnect button. 'Ralph, you'll find Mike and Marge in the library, finishing packing. I will slow *Sundancer* to ten knots.'

'On my way,' said Ralph and left the bridge and walked through the sea-view dining room to the library where Mike and

Marge, now dressed in immersion suits, were loading everything back into the helicopter. 'You guys ready?' he asked. 'We need to leave immediately.'

'Everything is loaded,' said Marge, picking up her helmet and following Ralph and Mike through the glass door to the Bell 525 and climbed on board. Mike and Marge strapped themselves in and connected their communication leads, while Ralph turned the electronics on and powered up the engine. Nick unlatched the helicopter from the deck and withdrew to the library where he stood behind the glass wall and watched as the Bell 525 slowly lifted off the deck, gained some height and crabbed to port, clearing *Sundancer*, before the nose dipped, and it headed off at speed.

Lisa, her long hair clipped up in a bun, watched as the depth gauge changed from 250 metres to 200 metres, as the submarine slowly rose to the surface. 'Retrieval team to the control room now,' she said to her second-in-command who put the call out on the intercom. The submarine slowly broke the surface, and the retrieval-team leader climbed the ladder and opened the hatch with a spattering of water falling down the tube. The other two members of his team followed him up the conning-tower ladder with Lisa not far behind. She looked through her binoculars in the direction from which the helicopter would arrive. One member of the retrieval team climbed down the ladder on the outside of the conning tower and positioned himself with a tether on the deck; should anything go wrong, he was the backup.

'Here they come!' Lisa shouted as she sighted the helicopter to their stern. *It is an impressive sight*, she thought. The burgundy colour scheme suited the machine which looked extremely sleek with its undercarriage retracted. It was coming in fast; she could see that and quite low. She watched intently as the helicopter came closer and slowed down to a near hover. Ralph used on-board cameras to bring the helicopter to a hover exactly above the conning tower. Lisa watched as two large bags were lowered by the winch and waved at Mike Holdsworth as he waited for the bags to be unhooked. Four more sets of bags were winched down before Lisa saw Marge being fitted into the winch harness and lowered down. The retrieval team carefully grabbed Marge as Ralph manoeuvred the helicopter to match the movement of the submarine and the effect of the wind on the winch operation. Lisa could see that Marge was happy to be down. Mike Holdsworth winched down, and Ralph retracted the winch using the cockpit controls and electrically closed the sliding door. With three minutes to spare, he dipped the nose twice to say goodbye and accelerated away back to *Sundancer*. The retrieval team stowed the numerous bags below, while Lisa welcomed Marge and Mike.

'Hi, Marge, long time since we last met,' said Lisa as Marge reached the top of the conning tower.

'At least six months,' Marge replied, kissing Lisa on both cheeks.

'Permission to come on board, Captain?' Mike said to Lisa, joining them in the conning tower.

'Of course, Mike. It's good to have you back. Do you want to relieve me as captain?' Lisa asked respectfully of her superior.

'No, Lisa, you're the captain. I am here to assist Marge.'

'In that case, below we go. I need to dive and keep to the schedule. After you, Marge,' said Lisa.

'Dive Officer, make depth 250. Navigator, check course and speed to destination,' Lisa snapped the orders out. 'Retrieval team, get these bags to the launch pods.' Lisa led Marge and Mike to the officer's quarters so they could change out of their full immersion suits into more suitable attire before getting to work with the sensors and launch pods.

'Captain to sonar control. Captain to sonar control.' The voice came clearly over the Tannoy system.

'Excuse me,' Lisa said to Mike. 'Looks like I am needed.'

In the sonar room were the operator and dive master. 'Captain, we are picking up some pretty heavy sonar returns, at least two that we can pinpoint,' said the sonar operator, removing one of his earpieces.

'Could they be our acoustic devices?' asked Lisa.

'Wrong location for them. These returns are coming from 500 metres subsurface, so they must be on the side of the seamount,' he explained.

'Distance?' asked Lisa.

'About 7,000 metres. They should pass to our port side if we maintain our planned course,' said the sonar operator.

'As we get closer and get a visual sighting, call me again,' Lisa said and left to return to Mike and Marge.

'What's up?' asked Mike.

'Inconclusive heavy sonar readings. When we get closer, we can get some visuals,' she said. 'Are you guys ready to launch?'

'All five variable-depth sensors and the ultra-deep sensor units are in their launch pods, ready to go,' Marge replied. 'Your ROV driver is ready.'

'Good. We are not far away. Anyone for a coffee?' Lisa asked.

'I thought you'd never ask,' Mike replied.

'Love one,' said Marge.

Relaxing in the mess, Lisa asked, 'What do you hope to find out with the sensors?'

Marge smiled broadly. She liked talking about her favourite subject, especially this one with its current intrigue. 'We have been getting different readings from our sensors than the Scripps' sensors, which indicate a higher level of noise than normal plus a higher shortwave sea current at depth. The variable-depth sensors will provide the missing data such as temperature, height, current and chemical analysis. The ultra-deep sensor will do the same, but additionally, check seismic activity and the deep-seabed current.' She took a bite from her sandwich.

'And the ROV?' questioned Lisa.

'I'll answer that one, or we will have little pieces of bread everywhere,' replied Mike. 'The ROV we have with us can go to increased depths and has a high-definition camera with expansive optical zoom. It's never been tested in action like the ultra-deep sensor.'

'It also has an infrared camera on board,' said Marge, wiping her mouth with a napkin.

The Tannoy speaker rang out, 'Captain, we are on station and holding position.'

Lisa went over to the communications panel on the bulkhead by the door and pressed a button and leaned towards the built-in microphone. 'Thank you. All crew to sensor launch positions.'

Lisa left the mess, followed by Mike and Marge, and stopped at the sonar room. 'Are we in camera range?' asked Lisa.

'Yes, and what we can see does not really make sense. The two objects look like shipping containers stacked on top of each other, but much bigger with what I would say were drill derricks sprouting from the top.' The sonar operator pulled up the video on a large display screen for Lisa to view. 'There are small portholes with very dim lighting coming from them, but no bulkhead doors or signs of activity, but one thing's for sure – they have both been precisely placed and built to fit the ledges that they sit on,' he explained, pointing his finger at the objects on the screen.

'Send this to Kermadec. They need to see this.' She turned to face Marge. 'Could these things be causing your anomalies?' she asked.

'Depends on what they are and what they are doing, but it's possible,' Marge replied. 'Let's launch the sensors as programmed and see what data we get. After the sensors are launched, we can come back and take some high-definition video and infrared video with the new ROV.'

'Right, I agree. Come on,' said Lisa and led the way to the control centre. 'Start sensor launch sequence,' she ordered the navigator who started giving commands to the helm.

'Sensor one launched,' he said. After the sixth launch, he gave the helm a course change that would return the submarine to the position of the anomalies. Marge and Mike sat in front of their computers, checking the readings from the sensors and ensuring the automatic depth control systems were working.

'All looks good to me,' Marge said, stretching her arms above her head. 'After sitting here cramped up, I need to stretch my legs.'

Mike looked up from his laptop. 'I agree that all the sensors are working, but some of the data looks really odd,' said Mike standing up. 'All the data will be transmitted back to Kermadec, what daily?' he asked Marge.

'Yes, once a day at night, of course, they will each surface, send their data, and then return to the depths.'

'Good. Now let's find Lisa and take a look at those objects.' They left the cramped quarters and made their way aft to the stairs and went up one level and forward to the control room. Lisa was with the navigator at a large glass table, looking at the chart on the flat electronic display screen. The control-room lighting was dim and the atmosphere dank, tense and quiet.

Lisa looked up as Marge and Mike approached. 'This shows the position of your sensors, and we have added the location of the Scripps' sensors to give a fuller picture.' She pointed to two marks on the display. 'These two marks here are those structures or objects, whatever they are.'

'Which makes sense as they are on the same side of the mount where our sensors have always been and sending the questionable data,' said Marge, leaning over and resting her elbows on the glass, her chin in her hands. 'We need to find out what they are and what they are doing here.'

'Any luck with the ROV?' asked Mike.

'We have the close-up high-definition video which we have already sent to James and Keith. We are now taking infrared video of the two structures,' explained Lisa, looking rather tired.

'When that's complete, I would like some infrared imaging done on the seamount below and around the objects,' said Marge.

'Jimmy over there is controlling the ROV; might be easier if you work directly with him while he's flying the ROV,' Lisa said, motioning to a figure behind her, hunched over a joystick in front of a small display screen.

'Thanks,' said Marge and walked the few steps and sat beside

Jimmy, introducing herself with a broad smile at the young submariner that almost made him blush. After half an hour, she called Mike and Lisa over and explained that she would like to use the ROV and take images of the seamount that required the submarine to change course and depth at various points. When Mike asked why, she explained. 'It will provide a fuller picture of the activity inside the seamount. From what I've seen so far, I am concerned with what is happening to the seamount and really worried about what those structures are doing to it.' From the look on her face, Mike saw that Marge was getting more concerned, and Lisa agreed to the manoeuvring. Mike discussed with Marge exactly where she wanted to take the ROV and went over to the electronic-chart table to go through the detail with Lisa and the navigator who started to give the helm orders and get the three hours of activity under way.

At the end of the three-hour run, that actually lasted four hours due to Marge sighting something and wanting to go deeper, Lisa gave the order to recover and stow the ROV, whilst Mike started transmitting the data back to James and Keith at Kermadec. Lisa received confirmation that the ROV was recovered and gave the order to the navigator to plot a course for Kermadec. The submarine rose to 200 metres and increased speed on a course for home.

Chapter Twenty-One

Seamount Secrets Uncovered

'*Sundancer* has recovered the two survivors and the Bell is back on board. They are heading back to Tonga. Marge and Mike are on board *Mercury* and have completed their sensor launch and sent us a heap of data which we are uploading now,' Keith said to the group around the conference table as he sat down.

'How are we going to relocate the survivors here?' asked Charles.

'Divert *Sundancer* here before she heads for Tonga. It's the only way to do it under the radar,' said Max, lounging in his chair with his coffee mug firmly grasped between both his hands.

'Okay, do that. When will we have the data in a usable form?' Charles asked, looking directly across the table to Keith and James, while Max left the conference room to redirect *Sundancer*.

'Give me around four hours. We can then analyse the sensor data and overlay it on the high-definition video and infrared on a true-time basis,' said James, looking at Keith. 'You agree?'

'I believe so. I would like to video conference with Marge when we run the results. She's the expert after all,' Keith said, looking at Charles and Anne.

'Set it up in here and get the *Deep Sea* and sensor teams up here now to analyse a copy of the raw data you have,' said Charles. 'It gives them a heads-up before they see your overlay version.'

'Right away,' James said as he pushed his chair back from the table.

'Okay, then everyone else reconvenes here in four hours, and those of you who can, I suggest you get some rest,' Charles said.

'I'll spell James in two hours. He's been at this all night,' Keith proffered.

'Thanks, I could do with some shut-eye,' replied James as he left the room.

Charles and Anne went to the restaurant and had a hearty meal of lamb shanks and red wine with Duke and Max before retiring to their stateroom for a rest. Charles put his feet up and closed his eyes, while Anne sat beside him and read a book. Charles had trouble relaxing. His gut told him that those structures were not supposed to be there, but who besides the American Government had the resources to install them so close to the United States and power them, let alone keep them operational which would require either a submersible or submarine? *The United States government has to be involved, but why, and what are they doing?* His thoughts were interrupted by a knock on the door. Anne put her book down and opened the door to find Chris and Cathy who had Abbey at her feet.

'James and Keith are ready to run the data, and everyone's in the conference room,' Chris said smiling, as Abbey had jumped up onto the bed beside Charles.

'Okay, let's go then.' Charles swung his legs off the bed and ruffled Abbey's hair. 'You can come too if you behave,' he said to Abbey. Anne held his arm as he stood up and led the way to the conference room. Marge and Mike were already talking to the group in the conference room by video link when Charles and Anne entered and took their seats next to Max.

'Coffee is on its way, boss, and some cognac as well,' Max said.

'A thoughtful addition, Max, thank you.' He looked at the video screen. 'So, Marge, Mike, I hope everyone on board *Mercury* is okay?' he asked.

'Yes, everyone is fine, and they have all been extremely helpful,' Marge said, and Mike nodded his agreement.

'That's good to hear. Now before we run the combined data that James and Keith have completed, what's your take on what you have seen out there?' Charles asked casually.

'We do not know who it is. There are no markings of any kind on the structures. I would say that they are mining for a very specific and rare ore,' Marge replied. 'But what they are doing, if I am right of course, is very dangerous. I believe one of the shafts may have ruptured a minor lava plume, and when they cut the two ledges, they have also destabilised the seamount face.' She paused for a second to gather her thoughts. 'Let me explain. You see the Davison Seamount is an underwater volcano. It is populated by over twenty different corals and well over 200 different species of marine life. So ecology is vitally important and is part of a designated marine sanctuary. It is covered in lava flows and some pillow lava, and any eruptions are mildly explosive, and the gas-rich lava covers the summit caused by ash and pyroclastic material.'

'So are you saying it is still active?' Chris asked.

'It has not erupted for many, many hundreds of years, but by altering the pressures in a lava tube, yes, it could. But my main concern is movement on the face which could initiate a landslide, destroying corals and marine life,' Marge replied which caused an undercurrent of conversation around the table.

'What size landslip?' Cathy asked.

'There is no way of knowing. Bear in mind, though, it is 2,000 metres high and twenty-six kilometres long,' explained Marge.

'Before we start a debate, let's see the data that Keith and James have come up with. James, run the data, please,' Charles said, bringing all discussion around the table to a halt.

James leaned over his laptop and typed on the keypads. The image of Marge and Mike moved to the smaller screen, and a video film showing an underwater scene appeared on the main screen. 'Can you guys see this?' asked James.

'Yes, it's coming through here,' said Mike aboard *Mercury*.

'First, I will run the normal video with the sensor data showing in time sync along the bottom of the screen, then I'll run the infrared version,' James said, still tapping keys on his laptop.

Suddenly, there was a commotion on the display screen, showing images from the submarine. Everyone heard the sound of Lisa loudly shouting commands in a clipped and controlled voice, coming clearly came over the speaker. 'Dive! Dive! Port eighty, silent running, silent running!'

'James, connect to their systems and see what's happening,' Charles said calmly.

After a few taps on his keyboard, James said, 'There has been some pinging, in a very pinpoint manner, the same way we search for lost items on the seabed using sonar when they cannot be seen visually.'

'Can you tell if *Mercury* has been targeted itself?' asked Charles, his elbows resting on the table with his fingers interlaced.

'No, they haven't. Lisa is just being careful and avoiding taking action and heading away from the vessel that is doing the search,' James replied, without looking up from his laptop screen.

Lisa appeared on the display screen. 'Apologies for that, but we had a large vessel close by that was actively pinging. It has now stopped right on top of where those two structures are and has ceased pinging. We are deep, running silent and heading in for a closer look,' she said, looking quite calm on the screen.

'What's your aim, Lisa?' Keith asked with a touch of concern to his voice.

'I want to get close enough to launch the ROV and also go to periscope depth and take a look at the vessel to see if we can identify it,' she explained.

'Okay, but proceed with extreme caution,' Keith said. 'Use Mike. He has a lot of experience in submarine warfare situations.'

'Thanks. Mike has his hands full, helping me plot our course and actions.'

Lisa kept the submarine deep until they were within 200 metres of the face of the seamount and aligned below the first structure. She then gave the order to take the submarine up to the same depth as the two structures. 'Mike, when we get to the structures, how quietly can we launch the ROV?' Lisa asked across the control centre to Mike who was on the other side, next to the navigator.

'As quietly as a mouse, but to be safe, I will launch it now and fly it beside us,' replied Mike with a sly grin.

'You can do that?' she asked.

'You bet,' Mike replied. 'Haven't done it for a while, so it should be fun.'

Mercury rose silently beneath the waves, with the sonar operator passing information to Lisa who had told him to keep her informed of what the vessel above them was doing. She knew from his information that there were the sounds of a chain and winch being used, with the propellers silent and side thrusters being used; they were obviously keeping the vessel on station.

'We are at the designated depth,' said the dive officer to Lisa and Mike.

'Well, here goes nothing,' Mike said and used the joystick and screen on the desk in front of him to guide the ROV. 'Searchlights are on now.' He concentrated on the display screen's image. 'Take us up twenty metres,' he said to the dive officer. He stared at the screen. 'What the hell! Make sure we're recording this,' he said to the rating beside him. 'Lisa, are they getting this back at base?' he called over his shoulder to her.

'Yes, it's being sent directly to them. But am I seeing what you're seeing?' she asked as she watched a large cylindrical pod being lowered down and into the structure of the left. She joined Mike as they watched the clamps on top of the pod released and the cable moved inextricably a few metres to the side and clamped onto and lifted an identical cylindrical pod out of the structure and up through the depths to the vessel above.

'Mike, retrieve the ROV, and Dive Officer, make periscope depth,' commanded Lisa in a tone and volume that everyone in the control room could hear.

'Aye, Captain,' said Mike as he started to fly the ROV back to its launch bay.

Mercury slowly rose through the depths until the dive officer advised that periscope depth had been reached. Lisa pulled the two handles down and lowered the periscope to eye level and scanned through the lens. 'It looks like a standard coastal container freighter. No outward signs of any ocean-survey capability. She is flying the US flag, and registered port is New Jersey. The name is very badly faded. I cannot make it out.' She stepped back from the periscope. 'Mike, you try.'

Mike looked through the periscope. 'Nope, the name has been defaced to make it hard to read.' He snapped the handles up and pressed a button on the side which stowed the periscope.

'Captain, sonar here. The vessel has started her engines, high revolutions, and she's heading in our direction.'

'Dive Officer, make depth 200, and let's head for home. There's nothing else we can do here.'

'Captain, I think I just heard depth charges being launched,' the sonar operator reported, causing Mike to get up and head for the sonar operator's station.

'Crash dive,' ordered Lisa, 'and brace for depth charges. Go to red.'

The attitude of *Mercury* became nose down as she dived deeper into the darkness of the crushing depths. The interior lighting went to a red glow, the crew's training and experience overtaking nerves as they readied the submarine for any depth-charge damage and braced themselves against the bouncing around that would inevitably occur, which it did with four large explosions on the starboard side of the submarine, which were too high and distant to cause anything other than a deafening noise. 'Port thirty, and keep diving, Lisa. We have thousands of metres clear below,' Mike urged when he came back into the control room.

'Do it,' Lisa said to the dive officer. Then, turning to Mike, she said, 'Mike, you have the con. This is way above my level of experience and where we really need yours.' There were more explosions but this time further away.

In the conference room, they could only watch the display and listen. Only James ignored what was going on, as he was too busy looking at the video that had come in and cleaning and optimising the pictures taken through *Mercury's* periscope.

Mercury kept diving deeper until she was just clear of her maximum operating depth of 450 metres. 'Level the dive planes, increase speed to thirty-two knots,' Mike advised the dive officer. 'Navigator, set course for home, please. Lisa, you have the con.'

'Is everyone okay, and has *Mercury* suffered any damage?' Charles questioned when Mike and Lisa appeared on the display screen.

'*Mercury* is undamaged, and no one even got a scratch,' Mike reported, looking at Lisa.

Charles looked over at James. 'Are you ready, and is Marge still okay to review the data?'

'I'm fine,' Marge said who appeared beside Mike as Lisa left to take up her Captain's duties again. 'A bit shaken, but I'm fine.' She shook her head. 'What have we got?'

James started to run the data. 'Well, for a start, we have heat signatures of at least four people in both those cylinders. On the one going up, there were people on the top and containers in the base. On the one going down, there were people on the top but empty below.' He looked up from his laptop. 'As you can see from this data, there are heat sources in the structures which extend below, but more worrying is the heat sources picked up by the infrared much further down and to the left. That's a lava tube on the move, and the lava is slowly rising. I need to calculate the speed. It's the same for the other structure.'

Marge took up the talk through. 'The normal video shows movement in the seamount face and fissures starting to appear. These are relatively new, which we can easily determine by looking at the coral. This one particular fissure is deep, around the 900-metre mark, and as can be seen from the sensor-data soundtrack, it's newly formed. Now, if that were to break away, it would cause a huge tsunami that would reach the United States coastline and cause significant damage and loss of life.' She watched closely as the video and data continued. 'There is a heat gradient which is rising faster than the surrounding region, which must be due to the activity of those structures and of the increase in recent lava activity.'

Charles looked on with concern. 'What do you think they are after?'

'I would think they would be after some rare heavy metals such as molybdenum, manganese, vanadium or even plutonium.' Marge looked worried. 'But the way they are going about it is extremely dangerous and must be stopped.'

Charles looked at Max, then back at Marge on the screen. 'Without knowing who the hell it is, we don't have many options on that front.' He thought for a moment. 'Keith, can we reposition the acoustic device of the San Francisco coast so that it is facing west?'

'Eh, well, yes, we can, but may I ask why?'

'I wonder if we could use it to neutralise a tsunami wave if we matched its frequency?'

'Yes, I would say it could be done. I did run a few scenarios after you mentioned it before. So let me get this straight in my mind. You want us to target the device towards the seamount and be ready to calculate and match the frequency of a tsunami if a landslide generates one, correct?' Keith looked at Charles and then at James.

'You got it. Well?'

'We will need *Launch One* on route, but the main team needed to do the work of repositioning and aligning are here,' Keith countered.

'Get them on the way into *Jupiter* now, and they can meet *Launch One* on route. Max, I want the two guys in *Sundancer* recovered here. Now we have a job for them to do. James, the pictures of the vessel taken by *Mercury*, can you get a name?'

'Afraid not, it's been professionally masked. All I can do is track her to her next port of call.'

'Okay, do that. Mike, Marge, tell Lisa I want you all home in one piece.' Charles stood up. 'Okay, folks, let's get to work.' As Charles left the conference room, he held Anne's hand and said, 'I think we need to sit and work out what we should do ethically and ecologically and then formulate a plan with the team. I have a feeling that the United States government is behind the Davidson Seamount activity.'

Anne looked at him as they walked through the circular hallway to the main control centre. 'Which agency though?'

'That's the six-million-dollar question. Maybe our friends on *Sundancer* know the answer to that one, being close to the president.'

Max walked towards them and fell in step. 'The two survivors will be here in eighteen hours, the fastest I could do, boss.'

'That's fine, Max, thanks. Come with us for lunch. I have some things to discuss with you,' Charles said and smiled. 'Some of your more illustrious talents may be of use.'

They sat in a corner of the restaurant, away from the hustle and bustle. After the waiter took their order for lunch, Charles opened the conversation. 'Our environmental fight has just got larger and more complex. We have a request from our friends in the Brazilian government to help take down the drug barons, and we need to find out who the hell that vessel above the seamount belongs to.'

'Well, boss, I guess the two survivors from the president's assassination squad and our own security forces with their helicopters could destroy the drug baron's homes at night and obliterate their fields and factories. I have some mercenary friends who, for the right amount, will come on board. I've been putting feelers out over the past months after the subject first came up.'

'Okay, you can pull a plan together. The Brazilians have sent a map through, showing all the locations that need to be wiped clean.' Charles paused while the waiter served their lunch of toasted sandwiches and fresh salad with a pot of Earl Grey tea. 'Now the vessel is obviously American and must have the financial backing of a state service, defence, Homeland Security, or some CIA, FBI undercover operation.'

'I will put some questions out there, but I think you're right with your summation. I would certainly focus on some CIA or FBI operation with enough of a devious trail to allow total deniability.' Max bit into his toasted sandwich. 'Wow, that's hot.' He put the sandwich down. 'I'll let that cool off a bit. The president is involved, and I say that based on his behaviour of late.'

'There's Duke and Julie. I wonder if she has finished her review.' Anne waved her hand. 'Duke, Julie, join us, will you?' They came over, and each took a seat, and Duke called the waiter to let him know where they would be seated. 'Julie, we were wondering if you have finished your review of the president.'

'Yes, I have just finished my report,' Julie hesitated. 'In a nutshell, he is a paranoid schizophrenic with narcissistic personality disorder.'

'That's what experts say Adolf Hitler suffered from,' mentioned Max.

'Max, you are, as always, very well informed, and yes, you are right. The president is showing all the classical signs that Hitler did, but that does not mean he will follow exactly the same path,' Julie countered. 'But his recent actions are of concern.'

Duke spoke, 'I think he is a very dangerous person. He has assassinated his own assassination squad to cover his tracks. At recent meetings, he has totally lost it and shouted at his own advisors and ignored their advice in totality. I know he has a few pet projects which are off the record and off the books. One of them which will interest us is his nuclear disarmament stance. I always had the feeling that what he said on the public stage and in congressional meetings never reflected his true feelings and was said almost too easily. It is my belief and that of Ryan O'Hare and Clive Harris that he was truly against disarmament and had a hidden agenda – this could be it.'

'You are heading down the road of implying that he has a secret nuclear development programme.' Charles alluded after some thought and finishing his sandwich. 'He must have the backing and, by implication, the support of the CIA.'

Duke looked at the lunch placed before him. 'Ryan was pretty convinced. He saw many comings and goings from the Oval

Office and Camp David to which no records were kept. His research identified some top nuclear scientists as visitors.'

'But that means he could have a nuclear arsenal at his fingertips.' Anne took a sip of calming tea. 'Hence the huge budget deficit that Congress could not account for.'

Duke looked at Charles. 'So where do we go now, my old mate?'

Charles sat deep in thought and with a troubled mind. He wondered what else Thomas knew about Mike Read, the president. Ironically, if the president was behind the Davidson Seamount operation, he could inadvertently cause a major disaster on his own watch. 'All I can think of at the moment is to carry on with what we are doing until we can access more information. This Thomas guy may provide more useful information, and I would like to give Max a chance with his contacts.' Charles drained his cup of tea and refilled it from the pot. *Who else would back the president on an illicit nuclear armament programme, and where could they house the assembly facility? Without launch missiles, they must be small enough to carry in a vehicle or airplane or on that mysterious vessel.*

James approached the table. 'I thought you'd want to know right away. The vessel is registered to a Hawaiian company based in Honolulu called Research USA Inc. The company's website says it carries out marine surveys for American government agencies and foreign companies. Research area is primarily hydrothermal vents, aka black smokers, and manganese nodules. Two vessels in its fleet one based in the Atlantic, the other in the Pacific plus two submersible. It provides no names or vessel specifications except photographs taken from a distance.' He sat down at the end of the table. 'The company does not exist in the register of companies in

Hawaii or the USA and lists no contact people or numbers on the website except for an office address.'

'So how did you track it down?' Duke queried.

With a slight bow, James replied, 'I uploaded the photograph from *Mercury* into one of my many sophisticated search programs.'

'Kids these days!' Duke laughed. 'Give them a computer and they can do things I would never ever have dreamt of.' He slapped James on the back. 'Well done, my lad. What you just described has all the hallmarks of a presidential CIA covert operation.'

Chapter Twenty-Two

The President's Role

The presidential plane, Air Force One, left Enniskillen Airport after what the president summed up as an absolute waste of his valuable time. With him on board the giant Boeing 747-400, besides his normal entourage of aids and security team, were his military advisor William Paige, Chief of Staff Ryan O'Hare, Defence Chief Clive Harris and CIA Director Glenn Haines who had flown in the night before. The president was sitting in his private office with Paige and Haines. 'Thomas and his team are now no longer,' President Read said, leaning back in his comfortable light-beige leather armchair.

'Yes, Mr President, but we have had an incursion into our mining programme,' Haines said from an identical armchair, whilst remaining relaxed in the deep comfort of the upholstery. Glenn Haines was a large and imposing man in his late fifties with a spattering of grey in his fair hair. He had a knack of remaining cool when all around him others would be gravely concerned. 'Which is why I have flown out here.'

Before he could continue, Mike Read cut in, 'What do you mean an incursion?'

'Just that, a submarine was spotted by the service vessel on a routine crew changeover and commodity extraction. Depth charges were launched with no direct hit heard, which leads us to believe that the submarine dived deep and escaped unharmed,' Haines replied as a matter of fact, with no emotion in his voice. 'The changeover was completed, and we have another full load of the commodity on route to the processing facility.'

'A submarine you say,' Paige entered the conversation. 'Who besides national military forces own submarines?'

'Except for tourist-style equipment, only Charles Langham is known to have a submarine capable of the depth and distance that would have been required to undergo an incursion of this nature. Certainly from what the captain advised and the description of the submarine's depth and speed capabilities, it was no tourist or research submarine.'

'Does this compromise our operation in any manner?' the president asked as his thoughts returned to the day seven years ago when he was a senator and started on his road to not only becoming the next president of the United States, but one who would secure the nation's national security by implementing his plan for a secret nuclear arsenal known only to a few who shared his objection to the disarmament, advocates in the senate, house of representative and the office of the president. It had been a long hard road, fraught with danger, until he sided with the then deputy head of the CIA, Glenn Haines, who had the clandestine operations portfolio. Together, they were able to filter the huge sums of money required and install the security teams necessary to keep others out of the facilities based in the Nevada desert hills. The two facilities were separate, and only the people in the nuclear facility were aware of the initial processing facilities' presence. Haines set up the Hawaiian office to filter the money and expertise required for the construction of the mining pods and purchase and commission of the modifications to the vessel to complete the installation and ongoing servicing of the pods. To those who operated the facilities and initial processing plant, it was purely research into marine tectonics and black smokers. The people who operated the Nevada nuclear facility were recruited for their allegiance to the cause championed by the then senator. To date, they had built eight nuclear bombs, each with a yield of thirty megatons of TNT. Haines and Read wanted to build the arsenal to at least fifty bombs. Initial technical difficulties with operating at the depths required on the Davidson Seamount had caused delays, totalling two and a half years. Haines had taken the setback in his stride and altered his planning to suit. Read had taken the delays and setbacks badly, and for a while, Haines thought the senator might have a breakdown and put in place contingency plans. Read had taken to drinking heavily when out of the public gaze, much to the concern of his wife Janice. Janice had confided in Haines, whom she saw as her husband greatest supporter and friend. Together, they brought him back from the brink, but all through this, Janice never knew his biggest secret, his burgeoning nuclear arsenal.

Haines looked serious and crossed his leg and wiped the knee with his hand, as if clearing some dust. 'It shouldn't, Mr President. If they are persistent and attempt to find out what is occurring at the seamount, all they will find out is that it's a marine research organisation. We are, however, attempting to track the submarine, but that's a very difficult task, given that we do not know the exact direction it took, just a general heading before contact was lost.'

Paige looked at Haines. 'But they were depth-charged, hardly the action of an innocent marine research organisation!'

'True enough, which is why we are working actively at finding out their identity.' Haines leant forward and looked at both Read and Paige. 'Mr President, we remain on track and should not be shaken from our commitment by this.'

'I agree. How many weapons exist now?' Read asked, his index finger running along his lower lip.

'We have eight complete and four awaiting the next delivery of material from the seamount.' Haines pulled out his tablet PC and looked at the screen as he scrolled through the menu and located the file he wanted. 'Plus another six in initial production phase, which will need a further two loads from the seamount at the current extraction levels.' He put the tablet PC away and leant back and relaxed.

'Thomas and his team would have been useful at a time like this.' Regret filled the president's face. 'We should not have eliminated them. We should have waited.'

Paige looked at Haines with a withered look. 'Mr President, the right action was taken, and we have our own teams that are more than capable of resolving this. It will not take long for us or the CIA to locate the owners of submarines of this kind. They must, when you think about it, be very few and far between.'

'I agree, Mr President. I will have some of our own CIA members track it down, and I guarantee to you now that we will find it's Mr Langham.' Haines smiled. 'So forget about it.'

'Forget about it!' the president exclaimed. 'Everywhere I turn, this Langham guy is there. We need to get rid of him and rid of him now.'

He's losing it again, thought Haines. *Paige and I will have to do something about this before he finally cracks up.* 'Mr President, he is just a thorn in our side and does not have the power or resources such as we have, so do not worry.' Haines looked across at William Paige. 'We will take care of him. You concentrate your energies on carrying on with our agreed policies and agenda.' He stood up and chuckled. 'And it's about time we showed our faces around the plane before conspiracy theorists rise up amongst our own staff.'

William Paige and Glenn Haines sat in one of the forward lounges and discussed the way they should move forward. It was agreed that Glenn would use the tame members of his CIA team to track down the rouge submarine and attempt to locate Charles Langham. William would visit the Nevada facilities to fast-track the nuclear programme. 'What about him?' William asked, nodding his head towards the president's office.

'Yes, that's a bit harder. If he looks like cracking apart, we will have to force his hand to stand down,' Glenn mused.

'That's a lot easier said than done. So tell me, how much does the vice-president know about the operation, and can we trust him?'

'He knows nothing about our activities, but he does know about the president's past problems, which means I should be able to manipulate him and use him to oust the president from office,' Glenn said as quietly as one could on an airplane.

'And if he does not play ball, then our game is up and so are our careers,' Paige scowled as he spoke.

'Not necessarily,' Haines remarked with a look that Paige had seen many times before when Haines was planning a coup de grâce. 'We have the nukes and the full details of the president's plans up our sleeve. That would be the tipping point. I know what you are thinking. You are thinking it will sink us, but no, not if we can prove that we only uncovered it during one of his drunken or drug-induced episodes just before we went public and decided it was in the country's best interest to advise the vice-president.' Haines sat back and sighed. 'Until we need to make a move, we carry on with the plan.'

'You're cunning...' Paige said and grinned. 'How about a brandy? I think I need one.' He stood and went over to the drinks bar and poured two large brandies and handed one to Haines. 'To our future,' he toasted and settled back in his seat for the rest of the long flight back to Washington.

Chapter Twenty-Three

The Discovery

'I have some good news. The official press release from the G8 conference has come through. It's a bit late, considering the conference finished a week ago, but the unofficial word is that it took a long time to negotiate the final wording to the satisfaction of the Americans. But the nuts and bolts of it are that the G8 has voted to support our aims,' Duke said with a beaming smile on his face as he walked over to Anne and Charles, who were seated in the restaurant with Cathy, Chris and Max, looking at the dinner menu.

'That's about the best news we've had for a long while,' Charles said and motioned for Duke to sit. 'Join us for dinner, and we can discuss the seamount situation.' The restaurant was not dissimilar to that on board *Sundancer*, if one ignored the extra tables, seating and the underwater view from the windows. Charles believed that those working here for extended periods deserved some of the luxury that they would have topside.

'Yeah, what's been happening?' Duke took a seat beside Max.

'Chris, you've been working closely with Keith and James and the *Deep Sea* team, so you explain,' said Anne.

'Okay, well. *Launch One* met up with *Jupiter* and transferred the crew. *Jupiter* is shadowing every move *Launch One* makes. The submersible on board *Launch One* has repositioned the acoustic device and turned it to the seamount. It's all been tested, and computer simulations show it should – and I emphasise the word *should* – work if there is a landslip. The crew are back on *Jupiter* and heading here, and *Launch One* is on her way back to Tonga.'

'Where is *Sundancer* now?' Duke asked. 'I thought she would have been here by now.'

'She is just fifty kilometres away. We slowed her down so we could top up our fuel tanks, ready to fill her up for the run back to Tonga,' Charles explained.

'And I suppose *Mercury* is at her side. It seems to be the way you guys work with security,' Duke commented.

'You're right. *Mercury* has shadowed her since she's been in range. She will be docking below us pretty soon,' Charles said and paused while the waiter took their orders. 'So let's discuss the seamount issue. Everything is leading towards the extraction of minerals for nuclear weapons use. Now we know the US has extraction sites on its own soil, so why the clandestine operation on the seamount? Unless it's nothing to do directly with the United States government and, as Max and James are suggesting from the information they have gathered, that it's a Mike Read and CIA covert operation. But it would need more than just the CIA. The US Army or Navy will have to be involved simply to cover the logistical side. I reckon one of the defence chiefs is involved or, yes, of course.' Charles's eyes gleaned at the sudden memory recall. 'His military advisor, what's his name, eh, Paige. Yes, that's it, Paige. He used to work at the Los Alamos National Laboratory.'

Duke looked excited. 'Why the hell didn't I make the connection? He was associate director of national security weapons science, which means he had access to all the information and knowledge he would require to develop a nuclear-weapons programme! He would know who to recruit, especially with their background information from the CIA.'

Two waiters served their main courses as Charles tasted the wine. 'So we can join all the dots, but without evidential proof, there is nothing we can do legally and above board. So do we turn to covert operations? How soon can *Jupiter* catch up or be within EMP range of the mining vessel, Max?'

Max looked at his watch and checked his tablet PC; after some thought, he said, 'I guess within maximum range for an EMP shot, five to six hours. The *Deep Sea* team decided to hang around and do a few more tests before heading home.'

'Right then. I suggest you send *Jupiter* on a new mission: to EMP the vessel with a hard burst. If we can disable it, then we can stop or at least slow the material getting to its destination.' Charles looked at Anne and Duke. 'Everyone agree?'

Max picked up a handset and spoke to James, telling him the new orders that needed to be relayed to the interim captain of *Jupiter*, Brent Mitchell, as Mike Holdsworth was on board *Mercury* with Lisa.

'Now look, we are really getting sidetracked from our main activities with all this and must not lose sight of the famine, rainforest destruction and damage to marine habitats.' Charles was tired and needed rest, but his motivation and drive kept him wanting to go on although he knew he would suffer with massive fatigue later.

'Darling, take it easy. The Amazon and Indonesian rainforests are now thankfully protected not just by us and the indigenous tribes, but by their own governments as well, so we have succeeded far beyond our own expectations.' Anne looked deep into his eyes. 'We have three teams on the ground in Asia, helping famine-stricken areas, and from what Cathy tells me, John Houston of Sea Sheppard is causing havoc with the Japanese Whaling fleet with those new boats of yours. So wind down and take stock for a moment.'

Cathy put a hand on Charles's arm. 'Mum's right, Dad. There is only so much we can do. *Jupiter* will stop that vessel, the acoustic device is in position, and once this Thomas guy is here, we can find out more.'

Keith came to the table. 'Sorry to interrupt, *Sundancer* has just docked to the refuelling platform, and Thomas and the other survivor have just transferred to *Mercury* which is now diving to the docking pod. *Sundancer* has commenced refuelling. Thought you'd like to know.'

Anne replied for Charles, who would normally reply in these situations, 'Thank you, Keith. Please bring Thomas and his friend here as soon as they are docked.'

'Will do, Mrs Langham,' Keith said, then turned smartly and left.

'Now, hopefully, we can find some answers and confirmations to our deductions,' Duke said.

'You think so?' said Max questioningly. 'This Thomas character, to whom does his allegiance lie? We don't know. Maybe his allegiance to the United States is stronger than to its president, or maybe he's with the CIA.'

'Max, you may be right, but don't forget he contacted us and asked us for assistance. Until he is seated here and answers questions, we won't know,' Charles stated. He picked up his crystal wine glass and sipped his wine. 'And here are our two guests, I believe.' Charles watched as the two men, clean-shaven and smartly dressed and looking relaxed and intrigued, walked towards the table. Both men were taking in everything they could see, and from the look on their faces, they were surprised and amazed. Charles stood up as Mike Holdsworth escorted them to the table. Charles held out his hand and shook the hands of both men. 'Welcome to our HQ. My name is Charles Langham, and this is Anne, my wife, and here we have Max, my son Chris, my daughter, Cathy, and Duke,' he said, introducing all those at the table.

'My name is Thomas, and this is Connor. I would prefer to stay on just first names until we get to know each other a bit more, and I assume you are not going to tell me where we are?' Thomas took the seat offered and gestured for Connor to follow suit. 'And I assume these two guards will be our shadows whilst we are here.'

'You are, of course, correct. You are now off-grid, if you like,' Charles remarked, placing his knife and fork on his empty plate. 'No one outside our organisation knows where you are, and no one here will tell you where you are. Have you had dinner, by the way?'

'Yes, we ate on *Cresenda*, or *Sundancer* as she should be and is now called – very clever disguise. And this set-up, well, from what I have seen which isn't much, it's phenomenal,' replied Thomas. 'A coffee and some cake would be nice though,' he continued, seeing the cake trolley being wheeled over to the table.

'Thomas, Connor, you may help yourselves. You will be treated with respect while you stay with us, and I think it would be good to straighten out a few things so that we can assess whether or not we are truly on the same side and can trust one another fully to the safety of all.'

'Well, Charles, you come straight to the point which is exactly what I learned to expect. The president of the United States is on the verge of a breakdown and has ordered your execution, and I should know because it was my team that was sent to carry it out until he had my team exterminated. I have information which I will let you hear, and if after that we can shake hands, I will pass more information over, which will prove why we must work together.'

'Thomas, after coffee, we will adjourn to our main conference room and see if we have a mutual meeting of minds,' said Charles. 'In the meantime, may I ask, what did you think of *Sundancer* and why did you call me?'

Thomas relaxed considerably. 'Nice coffee by the way, better than that served in the Oval Office. *Sundancer* was some machine.' He laughed quietly. 'Of course, I was not allowed to see the technology or engines, but she was capable of outstanding acceleration and speed, which was highly impressive. Luxury, well, that goes without saying. Even our so-called safe room was better than a five-star-plus hotel room. No, Charles, you have a wonderful ship, and I would expect it has an impressive array of defensive systems.' Thomas picked up his coffee cup and looked around. 'This looks pretty much the same, so we should be quite safe and comfortable here.'

'I can assure you of that,' replied Charles. 'Shall we adjourn?' He stood up and led the way to the main conference room near the command centre and smiled when he heard Thomas whistle under his breath and say, 'What the hell, this is incredible!'

Charles gestured to everyone to be seated. 'So, Thomas, let me start by telling you what we are truly about. If you need proof of what we say, then we can show you. But let me say this: only after we have your sworn word that you are working with us, and no one else, will we divulge our location to you. There are over 150 people working here, and I will not endanger their lives.'

'I think you have made yourself perfectly clear, and we both accept fully what you say,' Thomas replied.

'We are fundamentally an environmental organisation. We replant and reinvigorate rainforests, especially in Indonesia and the Amazon. We send teams to famine-stricken areas, not with plane loads of supplies, but with the knowledge and equipment to educate the population on how to look after themselves and how to irrigate the land and grow crops sustainably for the long-term. We push hard, using lobbyists, for a reduction in the use of fossil fuels. We do *not* use force or terrorist activity, which is why the latest activity from Sea Sheppard is not using their usual tactics. They are using boats we supplied, and part of the deal was no aggressive action. We do a lot of marine and environmental research which is what the majority of the staff here does.' He motioned to Max. 'Virtual tour on the large screen, please.' He looked back at Thomas and Connor. 'If you watch this live virtual tour, you will see some of the research we do.' He sat back and closed his eyes, while Max performed the virtual tour. At the end of the virtual tour, he opened his eyes and looked at Max once again. 'Run the presentation video that Duke and I produced – the recent one we sent to all the news networks.'

Max looked at Charles and said, 'You mean the one where I was cameraman, boss?'

'That's the one.' Charles closed his eyes and relaxed as the presentation played. When it ended, Thomas rested his arms on the table and spoke to the group.

'I can see what this is all about,' he said, 'and you have gone to some extreme lengths to ensure your security. I can say this, and I know I speak for Connor as well, when I say this. There are things that you do not know about or you do not have the full story of. I can help fill in the blanks. I was close to Mike Read who, I now believe, is on the verge of insanity, not just because he tried to kill me but because of his insatiable desire to terminate you for what can only be described as unreasonable grounds – unless of course you know what I know.' Thomas sat back in his chair and looked at Connor who nodded his head. 'The president is building his own private nuclear-armament stockpile which he intends to covertly deploy in all the major oilfields outside the United States. The intent is to not only destroy the oil wells, but also to leave the land irradiated, barren and unworkable for many years to come which, in turn, will neatly leave the United States as the only oil producer.' He gestured with both hands open. 'I can tell you where he is extracting the materials and also where he is processing them.'

'Davidson Seamount,' Max said.

Thomas looked up in surprise. 'Well, you are obviously much better informed than I gave you credit for. But, please, tell me how in hell you found out what has to be the world's greatest secret?'

'Our ocean sensors were picking up anomalies that did not concur with the data from the Scripps' sensors. Marge, one of our top researchers, was concerned about the readings, so we went to investigate what was causing the sensor-data anomalies and happened to be there when a vessel arrived. We watched as it dropped a pod down into one of the structures and picked up a pod,' Anne said, sitting upright in her chair with both elbows rested on the table and her hands cupped around a warm mug of coffee. 'We picked out human figures and mineral signatures. What they are doing on the seamount could cause a landslip with a resultant tsunami large enough to inundate the Californian coastline. The loss of marine coral and creatures is unimaginable. But even worse, they may have severed a lava tube which needs careful monitoring as a volcanic eruption could result.'

'A major environmental disaster, which is why you investigated and are so passionate about ceasing the activities. I get that.' Thomas rubbed his eyes. 'Along with the environmental disaster, deaths and economic fallout from the nuclear blasts, we together have a lot of work to do to stop this madman and his allies who are highly thought of leaders in their own rights.' He looked intently at Charles and then around the room. 'You are up against his military advisor William Paige and CIA Director Glenn Haines. They have a tight band of trusted men around them who also fanatically support what the president is doing. But we will have allies in his Chief of Staff Ryan O'Hare and the Defence Chief Clive Harris who are not part of the inner circle.'

Charles looked at Thomas carefully, weighing up the man before him. 'It's good to have you on our side. Duke will be able to fill us in on the president's staff and, I hope, be a line into the good guys. Tell me, do you know where they are processing the material?'

'That's easy. Two facilities situated close together in Nevada. One does the initial processing, which I know little about, and the other facility produces the weapons. Both facilities are heavy with covert armed guards.' Again, Thomas looked around the room at the people and got a sense of real concern from them and realised that he could work and trust these people. They were open and honest and passionate in their beliefs. 'Look,' he said, 'we are going to have to do three things, and I do not want to tell you how to suck eggs, but you need me, and I, well, we, need to try and develop a plan to do those three things.'

Charles stood up and walked over to Thomas. 'In that case, welcome to our organisation – you as well, Connor.' He held out his hand. Thomas stood and shook hands with Charles, followed by Connor. Charles returned to his seat. 'We have or are soon to take care of the vessel we saw at the seamount. She will soon become becalmed on the high seas with no power at all. She will not be able to radio for assistance either – a little trick we have up our sleeves. We would use the same trick on the seamount structures, but it could mean loss of life.' Charles turned his attention to Duke. 'What can you tell us of this Ryan O'Hare and Clive Harris?'

Duke did not hesitate in his response. 'Ryan is an all-American boy and will do anything for his country that is above board and lawful. I have seen him fight hard against the president when he disagreed with an order. We have both been dismissed from the Oval Office together a few times, and although we have disagreed on some environmental issues, yes, I can contact him and bring him up to speed and enlist his help. He has Clive Harris on his side for sure, who will, I assure you, be shocked and deeply concerned about what's going on.'

'I'm thinking out loud here. I think our first move will be for me to contact the president and innocently tell him what we have found off the Californian coast in relation to a potential landslip and see what he says.' He let his thoughts run free. 'But after we have neutralised the ship, and I can, at the same time, advise him that we can assist against any possible tsunami.' Looking directly at Thomas, he asked, 'Excuse the reference, but you are some sort of a black-ops guy, with only one team member left. How many others can you rustle up for an assault on the Nevada installations?'

Thomas put his hand in his pocket and pulled out a USB stick. 'Play this first, then I'll tell you as it may change your mind on how to proceed.'

Max took the USB stick and plugged it into his laptop, and the video commenced playing on the large display screen. It clearly showed Mike Read, the United States president, in the Oval Office of the White House, with very clear audio of his conversation with Thomas concerning the elimination of Charles Langham.

Charles was taken aback, and Anne was shocked and sat rigid with her hand over her mouth. Cathy and Chris look at each other in disbelief, and the atmosphere in the room could be cut with a knife. Thomas broke the deathly silence. 'Charles, you can use that as you see fit. It could be put to very good use as a lever against him.'

'I agree,' replied Charles. 'You said earlier we had three things to do. Can you expand on the three things?'

'One,' Thomas counted on his fingers, 'elimination of the nuclear threat. Two, elimination of the potential landslip. Three, expose the president for what he is and replace him with the vice-president.'

'Well, the landslip is under our control. As far as it occurs, we can eliminate the tsunami risk. The nuclear threat will, in a few hours, reduce by the becalming of the ship, so that's a start. I think I should contact the president, as I said before, but by video-call, and discuss the seamount situation and slip this video on to a display behind me so he will be able to see it,' Charles pondered out loud. 'His reaction to both will enable us to gauge what action we can take. At the same time, Duke, you call this Ryan and talk to him. If need be, let him see the videos of the seamount and the president's discussion with Thomas. Have Thomas join in your call. He can advise on the Nevada facilities, and if Harris is available for the call, all the better. Keith, get the Jumbo and Learjet to Auckland airport, please, and keep *Sundancer* on station here, and get her and the Bell 525 fully refuelled. I want *Mercury* on her way to the seamount, and *Jupiter*, when she has finished her current mission, to return to and standby off the seamount. Max, set up my video call. Also Thomas, Duke, we will follow up with a call to the vice-president if Ryan and Harris can oblige us.'

Duke took Thomas into the smaller conference room to make their call, while Max and Charles went into the media room to set up Charles's call to Mike Read. Charles positioned a chair in front of the large display screen, while Max moved a screen in front of the chair for Charles to see and positioned the camera. 'Can you sit in the chair, please, so I can align the camera?' asked Max of Charles, while he swung the HD camera around. 'A little to your left and bring the chair forward so more of the rear screen can be seen,' Charles obliged. 'Great, that's it,' Max said. 'We are all set. Shall I dial the number?'

'Yes, let's get this moving,' Charles replied and sat back in the chair's deep upholstery, while Max dialled the number and spoke to someone, waited, and then said to Charles, 'Putting you through now. I have the president on the line.'

The face of Mike Read appeared on the screen, looking tired and haggard. 'Mr President, good evening. I have some information for you on a natural disaster facing the Californian coastline,' Charles began.

'Really, Mr Langham, is this one of those tsunamis that you can produce?' The president's voice was full of sarcasm, and his face stayed grim, confident and unchanging.

'No, Mr President, what I am talking about is a potential underwater landslide from the Davidson Seamount,' Charles stated calmly and motioned for Max to start the rear video.

'Mr Langham, do not play games with me...' the president's voice tailed off as he saw the video in the background of the meeting between him and Thomas, ordering Charles's elimination. His face became ashen and changed to one of shock, and his mouth hung open with no words forthcoming.

'Mr President, you see I know a lot more than you think. Besides trying to eliminate me, what else are you up to your neck in? The potential landslip is due to work that is being undertaken on the east side of the seamount. Are you aware of any United States operation on the seamount?' Charles asked, pushing the already shocked president.

'I've heard enough' was all the president could manage before he ended the call.

'That went well,' Max said, coming from around the back of the media console.

Duke and Thomas entered the media room. 'This gets more incredible. As each door opens, it's like *Alice in Wonderland*,'

Thomas said, gazing around the room at all the equipment.

'So how did you two get on with Ryan O'Hare?' Charles asked.

'He's waiting for us to call back, wants to see the videos of the meeting between Thomas and the president and the seamount, which is fair enough. We can't ask him to stick his neck out on just our word,' Duke said, passing a piece of paper to Max. 'That's the number we can call him on, if you would oblige.'

'I'll dial him up now,' Max said, disappearing behind the console and tapping numbers into the keyboard, while Charles, Duke and Thomas arranged themselves to sit facing the camera with the display screen behind them to show the videos that Ryan O'Hare wanted to see. 'Mr O'Hare, good day to you. My name is Charles Langham. You have just spoken to these two gentlemen,' Charles said, introducing himself.

'Hello, Mr Langham. I am alarmed and a trite sceptical by what Duke Warren has told me and will need to see any video evidence you have.'

Charles signalled to Max to run the videos and said to Ryan O'Hare, 'We will show the videos, back to back.'

Ryan O'Hare watched the videos. The first was the meeting between the president and Thomas, which he watched in silence, and was visibly taken aback when the seamount video with the time-sync data was shown. Charles could see someone else moving in the background and watching the videos. 'Mr Langham, what I have seen comes as a great shock. It is very evident that we must, without delay, take some action to evaluate and develop a proactive response. I have Clive Harris with me, by the way, who was, like me, totally unaware of the president's actions on both counts. That is, of course, if he is involved in whatever is happening on the seamount.'

'Mr O'Hare, may I ask if you intend to advise the vice-president?' asked Charles.

'Yes, I believe that with the evidence you have, regardless of who is involved, we need to take the appropriate action. Are you willing to be part of that conversation?' O'Hare replied.

'Yes, we will be of any assistance that is needed to cease the ecological and human disasters that may result,' replied Charles.

'Let me see if we can find him. He should be in his office in the West Wing. Clive, can you get the vice-president on the phone?'

Charles could see Clive Harris pick up a phone and tap out a number. He could see him speak, but could not hear what was said until Harris replaced the handset and spoke to Ryan O'Hare. 'He's on his way,' Harris said.

O'Hare turned to the camera and spoke to Charles. 'Mr Langham, the vice-president in on his way. He will be four minutes at most.'

Charles muted the microphone. 'Duke, what do you know about the vice-president?'

'He is a purist, quite religious, and unusually for a politician, who has got as high in office as he has, honest. My advice to you is to tell it as it is and tell him what you intend to do, and give me an opportunity to advise him on what I think he should do,' replied Duke. 'Ah, here he is now,' Duke said and pointed to the screen.

Charles turned the microphone back on and watched the screen as the three men sat down, and the vice-president, resplendent in a tailored double-breasted dark-blue suit, started to speak. 'Mr Langham, ah, I see you have Mr Warren with you. How are you, Duke?' he asked.

'I am very well, Mr Vice-president, but wish we were speaking under better circumstances,' replied Duke.

'Yes, yes, I understand from Mr O'Hare that we need to discuss some highly sensitive and potentially damaging issues which could well affect the United States and the Office of the president,' the vice-president answered.

'And implicate the CIA and your defence forces,' Duke explained.

'Thank you. Now, Mr Langham, would you please explain, as I understand from these two gentlemen', he motioned towards O'Hare and Harris, 'that you hold the evidence.' The vice-president shifted in his chair and unbuttoned his double-breasted suit jacket.

'Mr Vice-president, what you will see are two videos. The first will show the president instructing one of his staff to assassinate me. The second is by far more concerning, showing deep-sea mining of the Californian coast, which could have two effects. The first is a tsunami with massive ecological damage, and the second, a link to nuclear-warhead manufacture. Max, run the videos, please.' Charles sat quietly as the videos were played, watching the face of the vice-president slowly become more serious and concerned, his right hand rubbing his chin. 'Mr Langham, first, I will apologise on behalf of the people of the United States for the actions of the president. May I ask how you linked the mining on the seamount to a tsunami and nuclear weapons?'

'If I may, Mr Vice-president, I will ask James here to explain the link to nuclear weapons, and I will ask Cathy to join us to explain the tsunami and ecological disaster,' Charles said. 'Our marine scientist who first uncovered the anomalies on the seamount is on board one of our other vessels, but Cathy is well versed on the issue. Furthermore, Duke here can provide more information and evidence implicating the president.'

'I am well aware of Duke's credentials and his knowledge of what goes on within the administration that is unknown to most,' the vice-president said smoothly. 'Let me hear what James has to say and what he has to back up his claims.'

James, never one to bow to authority figures, sat down, looked at the camera and without deferring or acknowledging the vice-president, started to speak and explain the research he had done and exactly what he had found out about the vessel and the link to Hawaii and a non-existent company. When James finished, Cathy took her turn in front of the camera and, in contrast to James, acknowledged the vice-president and carefully explained in layman's terms the data anomalies. She asked Max to upload photographs which clearly showed fracture lines beneath the two structures and explained why this was a major tsunami risk. She looked at the slightly stunned-looking vice-president and advised him that there was more. Max loaded up an infrared photograph, and Cathy explained what the images meant in terms of the lava heat signature. When she finished, she stood up and excused herself and left the room. Duke took up the dialogue and brought the vice-president up to date on the two Nevada facilities.

All through Duke's talk, the vice-president remained quiet, with a look of intense concentration on his face. At the end, the vice-president looked at Harris and O'Hare and asked, 'Did you know about any of this at all?'

'Mr Vice-president, I can assure you that this is as big a shock to us as it obviously is to you,' O'Hare said. 'We had no reason to believe that anything was awry.'

'So, gentlemen,' the vice-president said, speaking to both those in his office and those on camera, 'we have a major crisis on our hands, and I don't think I have to tell you how serious and sensitive this situation is.' He took a breath. 'Duke, I am sure you have some suggestions on how to handle this situation?'

'Mr Vice-president, we have a few things to worry about which I believe is best done by separate specialist teams. First, Charles has a team taking care of the vessel in question, which will soon become becalmed at sea. We will advise its exact location so the *Pacific Fleet* or coastguard can intercept it. The two seamount structures can be neutralised, but this would require a coordinated strike on the Nevada facilities to avoid alerting the people involved to the fact that their operation has been uncovered, and thus the president finding out. One thing we must do is to prove that the president is deeply implicated in this. The only way we can do this is to either get him or those working with him on video admitting it. I would suggest that at the next Oval Office meeting, a presentation be done on what has been uncovered, and I would strongly recommend that you three are present, along with William Paige and Glenn Haines, as it is my belief they are in this up to their necks.' Duke paused and added, 'Although I have no proof at this time.'

'Wait a minute. Come to think of it,' O'Hare said, recalling some earlier event. 'The three of them did spend quite a bit of time incommunicado in the president's private office on Air Force One.' He looked at the vice-president. 'Thought nothing of it at the time.'

'Still does not prove anything. Duke, this meeting, how do you propose that we get an admission of guilt?' the vice-president asked.

'I still have some detailed work to do on that. But to start with, I will need an official invitation from you for both myself and Charles to present to the Oval Office team on matters of the utmost environmental importance.'

'I can arrange that. What are you thinking, Duke? I know that mind of yours, and you already have the start of an idea?'

'As I said, I still have a lot of detailed work to do to bring it together, but my thoughts so far are for Charles to do the presentation focused on the seamount, but leaving out any mention of the two structures. We will need a way of tripping up the president on the two structures and their purpose. We may get some information from the people on the ship and those that evacuate the structures, when we hit them. I am hoping that James may come up with some link to the Hawaiian office. It's frustrating, but we have a lot of loose ends to tie up to make it work.' Duke looked at the face of the vice-president on the screen, then across at Charles. 'I hope to bring it all together.'

'Don't forget, Max, that he has some very good underground contacts and already has many feelers out there,' Charles reminded the group, then facing directly at the camera, said, 'Arrange the invitation, and leave the rest to us.'

'We will start lobbying for support in the senate for the invitation and talk to some of our political allies on what we have uncovered. Talk soon, gentlemen,' the vice-president said and ended the call.

Charles stood up and stretched. 'Max, Duke, Anne, we will transfer to *Sundancer* in the morning. In the meantime, let's see what more we can detect.' He left the media room and made his way across the vast control centre to the console manned by James and put a hand on his shoulder. 'James, keep up your research on the Hawaii connection, and while you are at it, see what you can find out about the Nevada facilities.'

James looked up. 'Sure thing. I have found a tentative connection, but it will take time to get enough detail that will stand up to scrutiny,' James pointed at the screen in front of him. '*Mercury* is shadowing the vessel and waiting further instructions, and *Jupiter* is 251 kilometres off the seamount.'

'Have *Mercury* disable the vessel, then set course for the seamount,' Charles instructed. 'When *Jupiter* arrives at the seamount, let's take some action that causes an immediate evacuation. Give that some thought, and let's talk when you have a plan of action.'

'Sure. I'll instruct *Mercury*, then talk it over with the skipper and Keith,' James said, and Keith patted him on the shoulder and left.

Chapter Twenty-Four

The Warning

Charles stood on the aft deck of *Sundancer*, his hands grasping the polished wood railing, staring at the wake left behind as the four engines powered the vast super yacht through the pacific waters. After five days at sea, he was never tired of the view and feeling the power of the engines at full bore through the deck. Charles enjoyed the sea breeze which made the cloudless sky and brilliantly bright and hot sun quite bearable. No other vessels were in sight as far as his eye could see. With no one else on deck, it was quiet and gave him time to reflect on the news that had come in overnight from James and Keith. He needed time to digest what he had learned and develop a plan in his mind on the way forward. Something still bothered him although he could not quite put his finger on what it was. He had a feeling in his gut that there was more to this saga than even they had uncovered to date. He needed this quiet time to carefully think things through before he got the team together to further develop the plan he had in his mind. *Boy, I could do with a coffee*, he thought as his mind went over the call from James. Overnight word had come in that *Mercury* had successfully disabled the vessel using its on-board electromagnetic pulse generator and was now heading at full steam to the seamount. Keith had relayed the coordinates to the United States Coast Guard who had immediately sent a rescue crew and salvage tug.

James had called to discuss his findings. He had managed to link the Hawaiian operation through various bank accounts, bills of lading and truck manifests. He explained to a puzzled group how he had tracked the Hawaiian company's bank account through to the Cayman Islands. By infiltrating the banks computer – he would not explain how, and Charles made it very clear that he did not want to know anyway – he had tracked vast sums of United States dollars appearing in the company's account which were then distributed to only two accounts. James explained that the incoming monies were impossible to track further than the Swiss numbered account they came from. The distribution of the money was easier to trace. One recipient was the skipper of the vessel and the other a Nevada-based bank. The name of the Nevada-based account was States Investments Inc. The only shareholder of States Investments was the Hawaiian-based company called Research USA Inc. He had come full circle, and the trace ended back where it began. James's findings made Duke even more convinced than ever that the CIA was involved.

Charles walked along the vast deck into the main salon where Max and Duke were sitting on the curved couch, both typing into laptops. He walked over to the coffee machine and poured himself a freshly brewed Columbian coffee. 'Well, have you found any more answers to our ever-increasing questions?' he asked, as he sat down in front of them in one of the sumptuous armchairs.

Max looked up from his laptop and replied, 'I have managed

to follow James's money trail from the Swiss numbered account back to Brazil. One of my contacts there followed up the trace and found millions of dollars from the same account going to the president's closest aides, William Paige and Glenn Haines, and it would appear it has been going on for quite some time.'

'Not the president himself then?' asked Charles, placing his empty coffee mug on the table beside him.

'No, the only creditors from the Brazilian account were the Swiss account, the two aides and cash-and-card withdrawals. But, and this is very interesting, there are tens of millions in the account, and money goes out, but none comes in.' Max put his laptop down. 'We're trying to track back to when the account was opened, but I don't hold out much hope as our contact's contact in the bank holds a very low position and does not have the access required.'

Charles turned to Duke. 'Do you think Paige or Haines could have some sort of hold over the president?' asked Charles, trying to see if the president could be the victim of blackmail.

'It's possible and not an angle I have explored, and I agree it could well be an avenue worth looking at. He does have a chequered past that is known only to a few of his very closest of friends and aides,' Duke explained.

'What was the problem?' Max asked, sitting back with one arm resting across the back of the settee.

'For a while, he had a big drink-and-drugs problem, and it landed him in rehab for three months, and the cover story was that he was on an exploration trip to the world's remotest regions.'

'So he would still be classed as a recovering alcoholic or drug addict, wouldn't he? In his high office, he would be for the right group that has the money, power and contacts targeted for blackmail or coercion,' Max said, confirming his own thoughts.

'So, guys, how do we find out if he is being controlled, and if so, by whom?' Charles asked, bringing the conversation back to focus on the problem.

'Well, I am not sure, to be honest.' Duke leaned forward and rested his elbows on his knees. 'If we tried to find out, it would have to be done in such a way as to not arouse any suspicion from both those doing the controlling, which in my opinion, is the CIA or the president himself.' He looked up to the ceiling. 'Not an easy task. But I think that if we concentrated on the presentation to the Oval Office, as we agreed with the vice-president, the pressure that would put on Mike Read may be enough to drive him to drink and allow us to uncover the controllers.'

'I'll go with that,' agreed Charles. 'Why don't you and Max work on the presentation whilst keeping your feelers out, and I'll see what more James can come up with on the Brazilian connection?' Charles added, as he stood up and picked up his empty coffee mug and went over to the coffee machine and refilled his coffee. 'In the meantime, I will see John and find out how long it would be before we dock in San Francisco and make sure Keith and Marge are keeping an eye on the seamount.'

On the bridge, the captain, John Whitcome, advised Charles that they had around one and a half days' sailing before reaching port, although Max would be in helicopter range earlier. Weather forecast was good, so they could steam at full speed until they reached land. Charles decided to head to the library behind the bridge and aft of the sea-view dining room where he found Anne talking to Cathy by video link. Anne sat facing the screen with a stern look on her face and a rigid posture. 'So what you are saying is that it could go at any minute. You do realise that we are heading straight into its path?' Charles wandered over to her and sat beside her on the arm of the chair.

'Hi, Cathy, what could go at any minute? The seamount?' he asked.

'Yes, Daddy. Marge has been monitoring it constantly for seismic activity and is getting very concerned that there have been many minor slips that could weaken the main side below the two structures,' Cathy said with a worried look on her face. 'Chris has been monitoring the sensors from here and has been talking non-stop to Marge on *Mercury* all day.'

'Okay, honey, don't worry. We're in the safest place to take on a tsunami. In this depth of water, we will hardly feel it. In fact, if it wasn't for our on-board sensors, I doubt we would know it went under us. When you see James, tell him I have sent him a file and need him to join the dots and add some more. He will know what I mean when he looks at the file.'

'Okay, Daddy, but you two take care.'

'We will, Cathy, don't worry. Love you, and give our love to Keith. Bye for now,' Anne said, ending the call.

'We should let the United States Coast Guard know about the dangers. I'll pop forward and let the captain know so he can be ready to swing this thing around if necessary and radio the coastguard,' Charles said. He kissed Anne on the cheek and left the library.

Chapter Twenty-Five

The Connection

Haines put the phone down and was not surprised to find he was sweating even though his office was air-conditioned. It had been a very hard phone call where he found he was on the receiving end of a tirade of abuse and received some very exacting orders. For one accustomed to giving orders, not receiving them, he had had to bite his tongue and take it. Not surprisingly, he was left with a bad taste in his mouth, sweating, and when he held up his hand, he was surprised to find it shaking. Now he had to face Paige and give him the news and, together, work out how to get the president to toe the line. His paymasters expected to get exactly what they ordered and had advised Haines that the ship that carried the ores from the Davidson Seamount to port had become becalmed. It was news to Haines, which infuriated his paymasters even more. They had expected him to know and to have taken action to secure the vessel. They now threatened to send in their own people. Haines had managed to forestall this on his promise of recovering the situation. At the end of the call, he was taken aback and totally off balance when they gave orders to speed up the operation by doubling the output. He had argued that it was impossible due to the speed of mining on the seamount and that another rig would be required, but they did not care. 'Just do it' were the orders as they cut the call. He sighed deeply and picked up his mobile and called up Paige. When Paige answered, all he said was 'William, he has just called, and we need to talk now in our usual place and time tonight.'

Glenn Haines parked his car and walked around the corner of the building and entered the bar. The lights were low, and the bar was not busy for the time of night, which was exactly why he chose the early evening. He went to the bar and asked for Bourbon, double and straight. He chose a small table in the corner at the back, far enough away from the window so as not to be seen, checked his phone for messages and sat waiting for William Paige to arrive. He kept an eye on the door as he sipped his Bourbon. How the hell had he got into this mess? A messy divorce that had cost him dearly, a mortgage way above his pay grade and an insatiable appetite for the good things in life, like his beloved Chris Craft Catalina and personal Jaguar motor car. The side-line started easily when he was approached to oversee some offshore financing which they needed to keep away from the IRS. He had the right contacts, and the financial recompense for the work helped clear his mortgage. But then there was no going back, and he needed more help to accomplish the ever-increasing demands backed up by the threat of exposure. He was left with no choice but to talk to William Paige, who was happy to come on board with the money that was on offer. More difficult was dealing with the president, and they tackled that by leading him gently along the path of a greater America without letting on who was really the brains and money behind the plans. Now they had gone way too far and were way beyond the point of no return. He saw Paige come through the door and waved him over to his table. Paige stopped at the bar, got himself a Bushmills and a Bourbon for Haines before joining him at the table.

'So what's the buzz? You sounded worried and, I must say, look it as well,' Paige said, unbuttoning his jacket.

'They want the output doubled with immediate effect. I tried to tell them that it was impossible, but they then threatened to send in their own people, and that would mean goodbye to you and me,' Haines explained, looking into the depths of his tumbler.

'Oh shit! What can we do?' Paige asked, fidgeting with his drink.

'I need you to go to the seamount and talk to the guys there and speed up their work, while I go to Nevada and talk to the guys there,' Haines said, and took a large swig of his Bourbon. 'Sorry, but the alternative is not worth thinking about. You know how ruthless these guys are.'

'Yeah, I know, but never thought it would get to this.'

'There is one other problem.' Haines put his tumbler on the table. 'The ship is becalmed at sea, and she's your only way of getting to the seamount facilities. You'll need to get on board, sort out what's wrong, then head for the seamount.'

'What do you mean becalmed?' Paige asked quizzically.

'They were bloody angry when they found out that I did not know anything about it,' Haines paused. 'They could not tell me what's wrong, just that she's becalmed. The coastguard are on their way to her, so get in contact with them, and get a lift out to her,' Haines said. 'We have no choice.'

'And what happens when they find out we can't double production?' Haines made a slitting action across his throat.

'Okay, I get the message,' Paige said. 'I'll get going and see what I can do.' He drained his tumbler and patted Haines on the shoulder as he left.

Haines watched him leave, then stood, went to the bar, ordered another Bourbon, drank it in one go and left. He turned on to the main highway and headed for the aerodrome where his plane was waiting to fly him across the country to Nevada. His in-car phone rang, and he accepted the call. It was the head physicist of the Nevada facility, confirming the hotel booking for one night the next day and checking on Haines's estimated time of arrival. Haines gave him a brief on why he was coming and got the gist of the physicist's negative reply amongst a lot of technical information. Haines's terse reply was, in essence, to leave the discussion till he arrived, and he ended the call with a press of a button on his steering wheel. At the airport, he drove straight to the private-jet hanger and stepped aboard the *Gulf Stream* and settled back in the leather seat for the flight to Nevada. The air force jet was at his beck and call and would wait in Nevada till he was ready for the next step of his journey, whatever that may be, depending on the outcome of both his meeting with the chief physicist and a call from William Paige. The five-hour flight was smooth and uneventful and gave him time to think and plan an exit strategy if it became necessary. A government limousine was waiting for him in Nevada to take him to his hotel. He had already decided to have a late dinner, and it would be a late dinner in his room.

William Paige had managed to board a flight to San Francisco and, on arrival, made his way to the coastguard headquarters to be advised by the rear admiral that he could not get to the

Coast Guard Cutter that was on her way to the stricken vessel. The cutter was too far offshore to be caught by another boat and the Coast Guard Cutter was not equipped for a helicopter landing. He was out of luck. He asked to use the phone and be connected to the commander of the naval base, San Diego. After a brief discussion, it was arranged for a helicopter to pick him up and fly him to the destroyer which was on its way to rendezvous with the stricken vessel on the direct orders of the vice-president who deemed the stricken vessel as a direct threat to the safety and security of the United States. That worried Paige. Did the vice-president know something? If so, how did he find out, and how much did he know? He had better call Glenn Haines; he should be able to find out as, after all, he was the director of the CIA. He would wait until he was on the vessel and find out what was wrong and whether or not he could get to the seamount before he called. He could feel himself sweating a little, and the sound of the arriving helicopter took his mind off the current train of thought. He climbed aboard the *Seahawk*, put on his life-vest headphone and crash helmet with a practised hand, without having to be reminded by the copilot who said, 'Welcome on board, sir. We have the coordinates of the *Arleigh Burke*, sir, and should be with her in a few hours.'

'Can you land on her, or do I winch down?' Paige asked through the headset.

'Yes, sir, we land on the afterdeck. Now sit back and enjoy the ride. There are refreshments, flask of coffee and sandwiches under your seat.'

Paige realised it was some time since he ate, so he tucked into the sandwiches and a mug of coffee, and the helicopter flew over the ocean with a sky getting darker and darker the further they went. Looking through the cockpit window, he could clearly see the sun going down over the horizon and the lights of a ship that was obviously steaming at some speed through the gently rolling waters. 'That's our ship, sir,' said the copilot, pointing to the warship. 'We will be touching down in around eight minutes.'

'Thank you' was all Paige could say, his mind casting back to his concern over the vice-president labelling the vessel a danger to the United States, and here he was on his way to it. *I must come up with a reason for wanting to see the vessel.* His mind lit up with an idea. On hearing the vessel was a danger to the United States and becalmed gave him the perfect reason to join the team on board the USS *Arleigh Burke* to see for himself the crew in an operational mode. Yes, that should suffice. He felt the landing gear extend and the helicopter flair as it came over the stern of the USS *Arleigh Burke*, then the gentle settling as it touched down on the deck. The engine whine decreased as the pilot switched the engines off, and the rotors began to slow their circular speed.

Three crewmen ducked as they came over other to the *Seahawk*; one opened the rear door and saluted William Paige, while the other two chocked the wheels. 'Welcome to the USS *Arleigh Burke*, sir. The captain is waiting to see you on the bridge.'

Paige grabbed his attaché case and followed the crewman to the bridge. 'Captain,' acknowledged Paige, as he noticed two ratings arrive behind him and stand to attention.

'Mr Paige, I regret to inform you that I have received orders from the vice-president's office that you are to be put under arrest on your arrival on board the USS *Arleigh Burke*. You are to have no contact with anyone until you are handed over to the designated parties,' the captain said, whilst still seated in his helm chair. One of the ratings moved forward and took the attaché case from Paige, whilst another appeared and patted him down, removing his mobile phone and wallet. Paige remained speechless, unable to think of anything to say. 'Take him to the brig,' the captain ordered, turning to the two masters-at-arms.

Paige found his voice as the two masters-at-arms grabbed his arms and started to escort him off the bridge. 'You cannot do this. I am the military advisor to the president of the United States and only answer to him,' he said, as he struggled without effect against the grip of the two masters-at-arms. 'Let me go!' he shouted. 'The president himself will hear about this,' he continued.

The captain sighed and stood up and walked over to face Paige just inches from his face. 'Give my crew any trouble whilst you are on board and you will regret it. I have my orders and enough detail behind them to carry out the order without any reservation. You will be secured in the brig on full rations, but, and hear me well, cause any trouble for any member of my crew and you will be put on short rations and forced to wear brig clothing.' He looked at each of the masters-at-arms. 'Now take him away and get that attaché case, phone and wallet to the intelligence officer.' The captain walked back to his helm seat as Paige was hustled out of the bridge.

Glenn Haines walked over to the government limousine and saw the chauffeur standing by the rear door. As he neared the limousine, the chauffeur bent slightly and opened the door. Haines ducked his head into the rear and was startled to see two men sitting in the rear facing seats, one holding a small handgun.

He felt the chauffeur close in behind him and the pressure of a pistol muzzle in the centre of his back. 'Get in, Haines. Don't make a scene,' said one of the men, a serious and clean-shaven man in a crisp black suit and gold tie. Haines sat in the rear left-hand seat and saw that both men were similarly dressed except for their ties. The chauffeur closed the door and made his way to the driver's seat where, at the touch of a button, the rear doors, to the surprise of Haines, locked. 'So who the hell do you think you are? I am the head of the CIA and on the personal business of the president,' Haines demanded in his most officious manner.

'To be honest, it makes no odds to you who we are. And while we are at it, it makes no odds to us who you are. You are under arrest on the direct orders of the vice-president,' said the man with the gold tie and flashed his badge too quickly for Haines to read or recognise it.

'This is crazy. On what grounds have I been placed under arrest?' Haines asked tersely as the limousine moved away, picking up speed. Haines noted the four motorcycle outriders, two out front and two to the rear, all with lights flashing. 'Where are we going?' he demanded.

'You will find out the answer to both of your questions at the appropriate time and place. In the meantime, just sit back, relax and shut up.'

Chapter Twenty-Six

The Plan

Charles walked into the library, followed by a steward carrying a tray. The library was his favourite quiet sanctuary on *Sundancer* and conveniently placed behind the sea-view dining room behind the bridge. The views through the expansive windows were always relaxing. He was surprised to find Duke sitting there, using one of the computer terminals. 'So, Duke, a change of plan I hear, and it's already in play,' Charles said as *Sundancer* closed in on San Francisco. Charles sat down, and the steward came over and placed a crystal glass containing Islay Malt on the small table beside Charles. 'Duke, you want anything?'

'I'll have the same, please,' Duke said. 'Paige is on board the USS *Arleigh Burke* which has changed course to intercept with us, and Haines has been picked up and is on route to Nellis Air Force Base. Later, he will be picked up by Max as soon as we are in range.'

'When did you think all this up, if I may ask?' Charles took his Islay malt and luxuriated in its peaty flavour.

'Last night, Max came to see me. He has a very devious mind, you know. His idea was to alienate the president before the meeting. He will be without his left and right hands and therefore totally without his life support. We can interrogate them both on board *Sundancer*, using Thomas and his man, Connor, who is well versed, I hear, on the latest interrogation techniques. The president will be unnerved at the meeting, not knowing what has happened to his two most trusted aides, which will give us an edge,' Duke explained and took his glass from the steward's tray and toasted Charles. 'Cheers.'

'Cheers. I like the thinking. We have our security detail on board, so they can enjoy the comforts of our secure room and be guarded at all times,' Charles said. 'What's next, there's bound to be a part two?'

'Yes, there is, and I wanted to talk to you about that.' Duke turned to the steward. 'Can you get Max here, please, Steward?'

The steward picked up a handset and spoke for a few minutes. 'He is on his way, sir.'

When Max arrived, he carried the inevitable coffee mug that he was never seen without. 'So what's part two of your plan developed by that devious mind of yours, now that we have Paige and Haines in custody?' Charles quipped.

'We hit the two mining structures with EMP bursts. The people working in them will evacuate using the escape pods we have picked out on the high-resolution images. The USS *Arleigh Burke* will pick them up after it has taken into custody all the crew of the ore-carrying vessel.' Max motioned to the waiter. 'If that's the twelve-year-old Ardbeg Islay Malt I can smell, I will have one of those myself.' He turned back to Charles. 'Whilst you and Duke are presenting to the White House team, the Secret Service supported by the army will raid the two Nevada facilities on the orders of the vice-president.' Max took his glass and savoured the taste. 'Really nice' was all he could say.

'But how do we get the truth from the president?' Charles asked Max.

'Leave that to Thomas. I reckon he can get Haines or Paige to squeal and implicate him. One of them is bound to have a Get-out-of-Jail-Free card that implicates the president beyond all doubt.'

'It should also flush out the financier behind their operation, I hope,' said Duke.

Captain John Whitcome put his head through the door. 'Sir, we have a US destroyer of our port bow. They are hailing us and want us to stop so they can send a RIB over to us.'

'That's fine. They have a guest on board for us. Open the port aft door and have the security team bring our guest to me,' Charles said.

'Okay, sir, I understand,' the captain said and left for the bridge where he gave the orders to bring *Sundancer* to a stop.

Anne came into the library. 'We're slowing down,' she said. 'What's happening?'

'Duke and Max have changed the plan. This is the first chapter. We will have a guest for a while, the president's military advisor, William Paige, who will be later joined by CIA Director Glenn Haines,' Charles explained, as Anne sat on the arm of his chair.

'This should get quite interesting then,' Anne replied.

'We intend to alienate the president and flush out the people who are financing their operation,' Max explained, as *Sundancer* picked up speed very quickly and tracked back on to her original course. 'In fact, I think I know who the financiers are already. The money comes from Brazil, we know that. And we have a request from the president of Brazil to help eliminate the drug cartels and their growing fields, so there's a whole lot of money available, and don't forget the SS and senior Nazi officers who used the clandestine network called Odessa to get out of Europe to the safe haven of South America funded by looted art treasures and gold.'

'But Odessa is just a story, a fantasy that cannot be confirmed,' Anne retorted.

'Either way, between 1,500 and 2,000 fled to Brazil. Simon Wiesenthal found Josef Mengele there and brought him to justice,' Duke said.

'Okay, this could get very dangerous, so you will need the input of Miles Channing and Ralph Cohen,' Charles said, looking at Max.

'Excuse me, who are they?' asked Duke.

'Miles is our security chief, and Ralph, his second-in-command. They are very well versed with undercover operations and are both ex-SAS officers,' Charles explained.

'Max, if the ex-Nazis are funding the drug cartels, how does this change your plan?' Charles asked.

'It doesn't. It only brings two separate operations into one. How we wipe the drug cartels off the map does not change at all, and if by doing so, we damage the financial arm that is feeding Haines and Paige and therefore the United States president, then brilliant,' Max explained with a glint in his eye.

Channing and Cohen entered the library with a rather unhappy and bewildered William Paige between them. 'Mr Langham, your guest, Mr William Paige,' said Channing, gesturing to Paige.

'Thank you, Miles. Would you and Ralph stay and keep him under guard, please?' Charles asked.

Channing released Paige and motioned him to enter the room and for Ralph to stand outside the door.

Paige walked across to Charles, stumbling as *Sundancer* lurched slightly as she rapidly accelerated to top speed and returned to her original course. 'So, you are Charles Langham. Well, maybe you will explain to me why I am on this floating ego palace,' he said with venom in his voice.

'Please, take a seat and make yourself comfortable,' Charles said pleasantly, ignoring the testy remark.

'Not until I know why the hell I am here!' Paige shouted, standing still, with his legs slightly apart to maintain his balance.

'Thomas, take this guy away, and do what you need to do. Miles, you and Ralph maintain a guard at all times. I don't want him loose on *Sundancer*,' Charles said.

Thomas and Miles ushered Paige out of the library, with Connor and Ralph falling in behind.

'Max, the Brazilian operation, exactly how will that work?' Anne asked when Paige was finally ushered from the library.

'The plan is to use our security teams and the elite squad from the Brazilian Armed Forces, their version of the SAS Navy SEALs, for night attacks on the homes of the drug cartel and incendiary missiles on the fields launched from our own helicopters and Brazilian attack helicopters,' Max explained. 'We have done some simulations and practice runs, and we're all happy with the results.'

Duke leant forward and asked, 'Talk me through the attack scenario?'

'The helicopters are all at one point. On the words "get ready" they will move to their defined holding positions. On the word "go" each of the helicopter pairings will hover at a predetermined height, light up its two designated targets with lasers and then launch their AGM Maverick missile, which will follow the laser targets right to the point of impact. The explosion will be the cue for the helicopter to move forward to take down anyone trying to flee whilst ensuring the fields are totally incinerated before turning back to ensure total destruction. It's pretty much an all-or-nothing approach. The buildings will be totally erased and anyone in them killed instantly. The growing field will be turned to dust. It's the only way, I'm afraid.'

'Max, set the action in motion. Let's cut off the funding and eliminate one of the largest drug-supply regions,' Charles said.

Anne looked horrified and spoke quietly. 'There could be young children, babies even in those houses.'

Max spoke before Charles or Duke had a chance to. 'Mrs Langham, I know it's not pleasant, but if we send in ground troops, then more people will die, innocent members of the armed forces, our guys even. I'm focusing on the hundreds, thousands, millions who are addicted and the babies born already addicted to drugs.' He stood up. 'I'll set things in motion now. I will need Keith, James, and the surveillance room and its team for quite some time.'

'You take whoever and whatever resources you need, but leave the Nevada facilities till later,' Charles agreed.

'And what about the seamount?' Max asked.

'EMP those facilities, and have our submarines recover survivors.'

'Yes, sir. Duke, if you will, I could use you,' Max said and led Duke out of the library.

'Steward, a refill, please, and some fresh coffee. Make it Kenyan. Anne, will you join me?' Charles asked.

'Yes, why not?' Anne replied. 'And now that we are alone, we need to talk.'

Chapter Twenty-Seven

The Attack Begins

Max entered *Sundancer's* darkened surveillance room with Duke and sat down on one of the free stools. The two surveillance-team members quietly acknowledged Max and Duke and carried on with their work. 'Take a seat, Duke, and put on a headset.' Max put his headset on and spoke into the microphone. 'Well, gentlemen, it's time to put our plan into operation. Link in Keith, James at Kermadec, and Jo and Mark in Brazil. They should be near Tabatinga by now.'

One of the members of the surveillance team started typing away, and the other tapped quickly through menus on a touchscreen built into the desk, while the display in front of him quickly changed to show a map with red and green dots with text beside each, identifying the target. Another sixty-inch screen divided into eight segments, showing live views from cameras which were obviously showing a night scene. Jo and Mark appeared on another display screen which then divided into two segments, and Keith and James appeared in the other segment. 'Gentlemen, we are authorised to proceed. Keith, James, initiate the EMP attack on the two seamount structures, and make sure we pick up all the evacuees. Jo, Mark, we have been through the plan a number of times, and you have practised the attacks. Now is the time to put that all into action,' Max said, looking at the faces on the screen. 'We will go at 1 am our time, that's in forty-five minutes.'

'All equipment and personnel are in their ready positions. All targets are identified and accounted for,' Jo replied.

Eight pairs of helicopters were standing by and hidden five kilometres from their targets. The operation had been carefully orchestrated to ensure total obliteration of the targets. Each pair consisted of one helicopter and crew from Charles Langham's rainforest protection force and the other from the Brazilian Special Forces. One helicopter in each pair would target the home of a top drug-cartel family and either a production or storage facility. The other helicopter would target the growing field and people trying to escape the attack. Max had insisted on a zero survival rate and manned each helicopter with four people: the pilot, the machine gunner, the missile target painter and launch controller, and the copilot navigator.

The atmosphere in the surveillance room could be cut with a knife. The tension built as the clock ticked away the seconds. Max pressed a key on a communication console. 'Coffee for four people, and keep it coming,' he said into his microphone. The silence was broken by Keith who had turned around to look back into the camera. '*Mercury* and *Jupiter* are on station and ready to initiate EMP burst.'

'Proceed,' was all Max said in response, as he looked over at Duke who just nodded.

Deep below the calm of the Pacific Ocean, two dark shapes

moved in tandem through the depths. Brent Mitchell, acting captain of *Jupiter*, was commanding the attack, with Lisa as captain of *Mercury*, following his every move. 'Prime EMP systems, ready for initiation on my command,' he said aloud in the control room. Ratings moved into position and started pressing buttons, turning dials and reading instruments. 'System initiated and waiting for your command, Captain,' the firing sequence officer said.

'All systems ready,' Lisa's voice came over the speaker loud and clear.

'On my mark,' said Brent Mitchell as he started the countdown. 'Five, four, three, two, one, initiate.'

'EMP initiated,' confirmed the firing sequence officer.

'EMP initiated, Mike,' Lisa's voice again came over the speaker. 'Sorry, EMP initiated, Captain,' she corrected.

'Sonar, keep an ear open for the escape pods and report immediately and lock onto them. Dive Officer, surface,' Brent Mitchell said. 'Officer of the Watch, once on the surface, locate the escape pods.' Brent knew that Lisa would be following every word and copying every command.

'Escape pods, two of them, heading for the surface,' the sonar operator advised the captain, as the submarine broke the surface and held station.

'Captain, we are on the surface, charging propulsion systems and replenishing air supply. Opening the hatch,' the dive office said, scrambling up the ladder and opening the hatch with the usual downpour of water. The Officer of the Watch followed him up the ladder and scanned the horizon to locate the escape pods. He watched as *Mercury* broke the surface with just a small ripple in the glass-like sea, 200 metres to their starboard. Brent joined the Officer of the Watch in the conning tower and used his own binoculars to scan the sea.

'Eleven o'clock, 600 metres, two distinct yellow shapes with red flashing beacon on top,' the Officer of the Watch reported.

Brent swung round to the same direction as the Officer of the Watch was and spoke into this throat microphone, 'Port five, slow ahead 500 metres, then stop.'

Both *Jupiter* and *Mercury* closed in on the yellow pods until their crews could attach lines and bring one each to the side of a submarine and tie them off before opening the hatches. Brent stood on deck, while his crew opened the hatch to the first submarine. Looking over at *Mercury*, he could see that Lisa and Mike were doing the same. A fair-haired man, clean-shaven in a chequered shirt and beige slacks, whose age Brent judged to be mid-fifties, clambered out, followed by a much younger man in his twenties.

'How many of you are there?' asked Brent of the first man, giving him a hand to cross over to the submarine.

'Eight in each pod, but we have to move quickly away from this area!' he exclaimed, as he steadied himself on the deck of the submarine.

'Are there any others still down there?' Brent asked.

'No, but both facilities are rigged to explode when the pods are emergency-released by manual means,' the man persisted.

'What do you mean?' Brent asked, as he watched his crew assist the other people from the pod.

'The facilities are rigged so that if the pods are released manually and not electronically, as they are when hoisted from the recovery vessel, they will explode. We have thirty minutes to get clear.'

Brent spoke into his throat microphone, 'Lisa, can you get one of your survivors to confirm if the facilities are rigged to explode?'

'Brent, I have already been advised. We have less than half an hour,' Lisa replied instantly. 'And Mike is coming over to you.'

'Officer of the Watch!' Brent shouted to the officer. 'Get everyone below, cast off the pod, get ready to recover the captain, stow the inflatable, and get ready to crash dive and flank speed!' He looked over and saw that Lisa was ahead of the game and had already cast the pod adrift and had only a few of her crew left on deck, heading for the inner sanctum of the submarine. He watched as his crew deflated the boat and stowed it below and ushered the last of his crew into the submarine and closed and latched the hatch. 'Dive, dive, flank speed, make 200 metres.' He walked over to Mike Holdsworth and said, 'Captain, I hand *Jupiter* back to your command. You have the con, sir.'

Mike Holdsworth walked over the electronic-chart table. 'Thank you, Brent. Navigator, I suggest we head here. Set course and advise *Mercury* to do the same,' he said, pointing along the ridge line to a depression where they could safely traverse the seamount and sit behind a ridge, clear of the explosions. He could feel the submarine diving into the depths and turning at high speed, all the crew hanging on to anything in reach; it felt good to be back on *Jupiter*, his own boat.

'Radio Officer, patch me through to Mr Langham on *Sundancer*. It's an emergency transmission, conference call, linking in Keith and James at Kermadec and Marge on *Mercury*. Patch it through to my cabin. Brent, you have the con.' He left the control room and went to the privacy of his cabin, one unit back from the control room. Settling at his desk, he turned on his LCD screen and waited for the call to be put through. *Bloody idiots*, he thought, *didn't they know what they could start by their actions?*

'I'm putting the call through to you now, Captain.'

Charles's face appeared on the screen. 'Hi, Mike, what's the emergency?' At that moment, Keith and James appeared in another window on the screen.

'We have recovered sixteen personnel from the pods, and they have advised that the facilities are due to explode in' – he looked at his watch – 'twenty-four minutes from now.' He saw Marge appear in a new window on the screen.

'It could well precipitate a landslide. Do you know the size of the bombs that have been placed?' Marge asked.

'No, they have no clue, never saw them, and don't know where they were placed. All they know is that they are set to go off if an emergency evacuation takes place,' Mike said.

'Let's work on a worst-case scenario and plot the potential outcome and see if we can use the acoustic wave to counter any possible tsunami,' Charles said.

'Okay, I will run the scenario of the landslide and send it to Keith and James,' Marge said. 'I can update it quickly if a tsunami actually occurs.'

'Marge, will your sensors pick up the explosion and data on current and speed, or will they be knocked out?' questioned Charles.

'No, they will be fine. They were built to withstand a substantial shock force such as an undersea volcanic eruption.' She smiled. 'Not just a pretty face, you know.'

'Mike, where are you heading?' Charles asked, smiling at Marge's remark.

'We are currently heading south to a depression in the seamount where there is a ridge we can hide behind and safely ride out the explosions. After the explosion we will head back and get Marge closer to assess the damage. By then, any tsunami will be well on its way.'

'Okay, keep me advised. Keith, James, will you have time to assess the data Marge sends you and calculate the acoustic-power requirement and any angle adjustments?' Charles asked.

'We are ready to run the program in a couple of minutes at most, and if Marge updates, it will take us seconds to recalculate when to fire and what power level.'

'Okay, guys, how is the operation Max is carrying out interfering with you on this?'

'We are fine, boss. James is concentrating on the seamount, while I'm taking care of Max, if that's humanly possible,' Keith replied with a grin.

'I know what you mean. How is the operation going, by the way?' he asked.

'Max has given the go, and we are counting down – twenty-two minutes to go. Everything is in place and looking good.'

'Keep me posted,' Charles said and turned to Anne, who had been listening and watching from their chairs in the library.

'Ask Duke to call the vice-president about the potential explosion and resulting possible tsunami.'

Anne picked up a handset. 'True enough,' she said and spoke to Duke.

'You need some rest, darling. Put your feet up for a few

minutes and listen to some music and have a cognac,' Anne said to Charles and motioned for the steward. 'Be a dear and get Charles a Cognac,' she said to the steward.

Charles put his feet on a stool and stretched out and closed his eyes, while Anne put on some quiet orchestral music.

Jo spoke into his helmet microphone. 'Max, we are at zero time, initiating attack. Eagle leader to Falcon group, commence the attack.' Jo pushed the stick forward and adjusted the collective and throttle and lifted the helicopter vertically out of the clearing in the rainforest hills, then accelerated forward towards their target. Beside him, Mark kept an eye on the infrared high-vision camera, radar and navigation target-acquisition system. He calculated twelve minutes before he could paint the targets with the laser guidance system. Looking around, he could see the other helicopter of his pair right on their tail, the gunners leaning through the side door and manning the machine guns, while in front, the copilot mirroring his actions to laser-paint the field of drugs for the incendiary missiles to home in on. Jo used his night-vision helmet with head-up display to allow him to fly fast and low, safely at treetop level, down deep valleys and over hills. Even then he could feel the sweat and drain of utter concentration. He was used to fast flying at treetop level in the daytime. At night, even with the best technical equipment, it was at a totally different affair. He recalled his SAS days and now more than ever appreciated the skills of the pilots who flew him behind enemy lines at night.

'I'm lighting up first two targets,' Mark said.

'Eagle leader to Falcons, confirm target acquisitions by the number,' Jo said into his helmet microphone. One by one, Jo and Mark counted off the affirmations.

'Eagle to Falcons, fire, fire,' Jo commanded.

Mark pressed the two fire buttons and saw the AGM Mavericks drop from their pods under the stubby winglets, light up their engines and accelerate rapidly towards their targets. He felt the helicopter increase speed with a dip of its nose, as Jo pushed hard to reach the point of designated impact. Mark saw the two incendiary laser-guided missiles light up and leave the pods of their paired helicopter and head off at an incredible speed to their designated field of drugs. As he watched their tail flames disappear into the night, he saw two huge balls of flames shoot high into the night sky, lighting up the area around. Their two AGM Maverick missiles had found their targets. As they got nearer, they could see two buildings in total ruin amongst the flickering backdrop of the rainforest, with intense fires still burning. Much of the surrounding bush was ablaze. The remains of cars that had been parked on what would have been the driveway were reduced to mangled pieces of burning twisted steel. The buildings were all but foundations, with only the ragged remains of destroyed internal and external walls. Craters in the middle confirmed the missiles had tracked the laser target to the exact dead centre. No survivors were seen, and the helicopter's infrared vision picked up no body-shaped heat signatures in the surrounding bush, but a land search would be required due to the fires. A cacophony of explosions ruptured the air as the paired helicopters' incendiary missiles dropped their payloads and sent a blaze of flames rolling across the glowing fields, lighting the sky up for miles around.

Jo landed the helicopter a safe distance from the flames and then shut down the engine. The four occupants wandered around the devastation. First, they checked through the remains of the main house, counting bodies and photographing the scene, and where possible, taking face shots or fingerprints and DNA for identification. Few bodies were found intact. Most were dismembered, badly disfigured or burnt beyond recognition, the initial blast killing all instantly. Then they searched the secondary building; there were no bodies, just a mass of wrecked laboratory equipment and machinery. Anne would never be advised on the number of children killed, and she would never ask, but it made Jo and Mark, although hardened by life in the SAS, sick when they saw the dead children and babies in the main house in what would have been, according to the plans, bedrooms. Their paired helicopter had flown on to the blazing growing fields, and the staccato sound of machine gunfire could be heard, and two more explosions shook the air which the pilot reported as two smaller outbuildings, hidden in the rainforest surrounding the fields, being destroyed. These outbuildings had only been located when lights appeared at the windows and doors opened by workers startled by the incendiary missiles.

Sitting back in the helicopter, Jo and Mark called each Falcon pair and carefully listened to each report, asking questions and taking notes. One by one, they signed off on the missions and advised the pairings to return to their bases. After lifting off, Mark called Max and reported the mission a complete success with no fatalities or injuries on their side.

Max listened to the report, taking copious notes and questioning some of the data, number of adults killed, type of equipment found and then asked for the photography and video taken by each lead helicopter to be transmitted to the *Sundancer* surveillance team for examination. From the report, Max was happy that the required outcome agreed with the Brazilian authorities and within the constraints that Charles had dictated had been fulfilled. He now had to wait for his informants on the ground and information from the forensics that would be carried out by the Brazilian authorities to confirm that the major cartel bosses had been eliminated. He was more than confident based on the pre-attack intelligence. 'Gentlemen, examine carefully the video and stills when they come in, and let me have your thoughts.' He took his headset off and motioned for Duke to do the same and stood up in the darkened room. He led Duke from the room and closed the door behind him. The luxurious corridor seemed extremely bright after the dimly lit surveillance room.

'Let's go to the library via the afterdeck. I could do with some fresh air,' Max said and led Duke up the rear staircase. By the time they reached the deck, Duke was slightly out of breath and leant on the polished wood railing, taking in the sea air. Max stood beside him. 'Look at that, not another vessel to be seen, and a beautiful calm sea all the way to the horizon. This is the part of this job I like the most. It's a great perk being able to be aboard this yacht – the peace and quiet, the luxury, the food, the company and all the best toys for me to play with.'

Duke looked at him carefully. 'But we have just orchestrated death and destruction on a massive scale. How does that sit with you?'

'Yes, I know. But they were murderers on a grand scale. How many had they killed with their drugs around the globe? How many innocents killed as a result of their drug wars with Peru? My conscience is clear. I know children have died. I am more than aware of that fact. But how many children, babies even, have we saved!' Max turned around and leant with his back to the railing. 'That's the bit Anne cannot understand or equate – the death of babies, children during the raids versus those that have been saved.'

'Max, you're a darn complicated character, you know, and I can fully understand Charles's total faith in you. Your conscientious and have a conscience. You have a clear view of right and wrong unlike most politicians that I know,' Duke said, his hands grasping the railing as he looked down to the moon-lit wake being created by *Sundancer* as it powered its way through the ocean.

'Yeah, yeah, well, let's hope we destroyed both the drug bosses and the money factory for Haines and Paige,' Max said. 'Let's go to the library. Charles is bound to be there. I want to find out if Thomas has gained any information from his interrogation of Paige.'

Duke leaned forward off the railing. 'And any tsunami activity?'

'True enough,' said Max, patting the railing before walking the length of the huge deck towards the main deck lounge. 'The pool looks so inviting in the moonlight,' he commented as they rounded the pool and stepped up towards the glass partition doors. In the main lounge, they walked across the deep-carpeted floor and took the curved staircase up past the cinema and onwards up to the sea-view deck and the library. They found Charles lounging in a recliner armchair, talking to Keith and James by video, with Anne beside him in an armchair. They saw that Keith was speaking and so walked behind Charles and pulled two armchairs closer and sat down.

'...have inputted the data from Marge and preset the devices, so we are ready,' Keith was saying. '*Jupiter* and *Mercury* are both heading back to take some video and high-resolution stills. Marge is pretty sure that the explosions have destabilised the area and caused a large fissure in the face of the seamount. The acoustic signatures are clear and defined from that standpoint.' Keith sighed deeply and rubbed his eyes. 'There's nothing else to report except to say we're ready to roll if we get more data.'

'Thanks, Keith. You and James get some rest and put the duty squad on. They can call you as soon as any more news comes in,' Charles said, ending the call and turning to face Duke and Max. 'Congratulations on a successful mission, gentlemen.'

'Not yet, boss, I want the evidence in my hands first,' Max said.

'Okay, I'll go with that. Thomas has had some success in his interrogation of William Paige. The guy's a pawn run by Glenn Haines, who has scandalous information of the president and uses it to exert some control, but Paige believes it's Haines who wields the real power in the White House. Paige does not know where the money comes from except to say that Haines is in serious trouble with the money men who have demanded a doubling of output from the seamount and Nevada facilities. They are ruthless individuals, according to what Haines told him. Glenn Haines will be with us as soon as we are in flying range of Nellis Air Force Base, which will be in about' – he looked at his watch – 'twenty-three minutes, so you get to fly your favourite toy again soon.'

Chapter Twenty-Eight

The President Gets a Scare

The president was enjoying a round of golf at one of his favourite golf courses, Andrews Air Force Base, with his trip director and chief security guard, when his mobile rang. It came as a shock as very few people – his closest aides and family – had the number to the highly secure and encrypted phone. Normally, all calls were routed through an aide who would answer; only in matters of national security would the aide interrupt the president's game. 'Excuse me,' he said, handing his club to his caddy and answering the incessantly ringing phone.

A deeply accented and slow-speaking voice came over the speaker. 'Mr President, I am sorry to interrupt your game of golf, especially as I know that Andrews is your favourite course. But we have a...'

'Who is this?' interrupted the president.

'Do not interrupt me again, Mister Read, it will be very dangerous of you to do so and very certainly not in your best interest. We have a lot of business to discuss, now that Glenn Haines and William Paige are no longer contactable and unable to carry out their duties which now fall to you. So be quiet and listen very carefully.'

'You are not talking to some everyday person. You are talking to the president of the United States of America,' Read said with venom in his voice.

'Interrupt me one more time and you will deeply regret it. I have warned you once, and I will not do so again. You will double output from the seamount and the Nevada facilities, and tell me when we will reach sixteen units. I will call you back in two days, and you had better have good news for me, Mister Read, or you and your family will suffer immeasurable pain.'

The president stood and looked at the phone, stunned and speechless, and dialled up Haines from the contact list. When there was no answer, he tried Paige and got the same result. He walked back on to the green. 'I need to get back to the White House now,' he said and started to walk to his limousine. He dialled up Ryan O'Hare and, for some reason, was surprised when he answered. 'Ryan, is Glenn or William there?'

'No, Mr President, neither have been seen since last night, and we have been unable to establish contact with them. I have the Secret Service on to it.'

'Well, find them, and get them to call me as soon as you do.' The president disconnected the call and stepped into the limousine. Who was it that called him, and how did he get the number, and why were Haines and Paige missing? How did he know about the seamount or Nevada facilities, and for that matter, what was his business with Paige and Haines? How did he know about a top-secret project? It then came as a shock to him that he had no contacts at either facility he could call to discuss the project. Besides Haines and Paige, who else knew about the project? He was cornered; there were too many questions but not enough answers. As he walked into the Oval Office, Ryan O'Hare was right on his tail. 'Mr President, we still cannot find Haines or Paige, and now we have a potential national disaster looming off the West Coast,' O'Hare said as the president sat down and leant on the Oval Office desk.

The president looked up in a daze. 'What did you say? Please sit down, Ryan.'

Ryan sat and said, 'There is the potential for a tsunami being generated just eighty kilometres off the West coast. Charles Langham is on his way with Duke to discuss the danger in more detail. I have arranged a meeting of the chiefs of staff.'

'How is that big-headed oaf involved?' asked the president.

'One of his teams found the issue, and they have sensors monitoring the area along with the Scripps Institute,' Ryan said, puzzled by the offhanded remark.

'I see. Well, forget that load of hype for the moment, and get me the head of the FBI and the White House security chief. I want Paige and Haines found.'

'Neither is in the building, but I will get them here shortly.' Ryan returned to his own office and made the calls. Before returning to the Oval Office, he called the vice-president and told him in detail of the situation. The vice-president agreed to call Charles Langham.

Max came in low over Nellis Air Force Base and saw a limousine with four motorcycle outriders heading towards the landing area that the control tower had designated. He slowed the Bell 525 to a hover, extended the landing gear and slowly touched down, and saw the limousine and outriders pull up beside him. The rear doors of the limousine immediately opened, and three people emerged and headed directly towards the rear of the helicopter. A man handcuffed, with his arms behind him, wearing ankle shackles and a black hood, was bundled into the back of the helicopter and strapped in. 'He's all yours now' was all one of the men said before closing the door and climbing back into the limousine and driving off at high speed. Max said nothing as he increased the engine speed and lifted off the pad, retracted the landing gear and swiftly headed back to *Sundancer* which was still 190 kilometres offshore and south of the seamount. He called up the captain and inputted the rendezvous point into his on-board navigation system. 'Sit tight, buddy, we have a quick twenty-five-minute ride before we land and can lap up absolute luxury.' Max saw *Sundancer* twenty minutes later and came in low around the stern of the yacht, flying down the port side. He called *Sundancer's* captain to arrange for the deck crew required to secure the Bell 525 to the deck and Thomas to take care of the guest. He came level with the sea-view-deck helipad and slowed to match *Sundancer's* speed. He deftly crabbed sideways, extended the landing gear, and lowered the helicopter gently onto the pad. He cut the engine, turned off the displays and shut down all the systems. He watched as two crew members secured the landing gear to the helipad as he removed his helmet and headset. He snapped off his quick-release seat belt just as Thomas and Connor appeared to take Haines away for questioning. Max stepped out of the cockpit and closed the door. 'Make sure she's refuelled, clean the windscreen and cover her up, please,' he said to the deck crew. He watched as Thomas and Connor helped the hooded Haines down from the rear cabin.

Haines was vociferous from under the hood. 'Be quiet. You will have ample time to talk when we are ready,' Thomas said, as he and Connor hustled Haines through the glass-wall door into the sea-view dining room and into the library where they sat him down. Miles and Ralph entered with William Paige between them and, at a signal from Thomas, sat him opposite the still-hooded Glen Haines.

'Remove his hood,' Charles said. 'They might as well see each other.' He noticed Max enter the library. 'Good flight, Max?' he asked.

'Hardly had time to touch down before they bundled this guy in the back,' he explained. 'They obviously wanted him out of their hair darn quick.' He walked over to the steward who unusually, but at the request of Charles, had been on duty in the library for the past two days. 'Cognac, please, and a coffee,' he requested. 'Boss, Mrs Langham, would you like to join me?' he asked.

'Yes, Max, I think we will,' replied Anne.

Charles was looking at the large display screen which showed their position and the positions of both submarines *Jupiter* and *Mercury*. He ignored the voices behind him as both Haines and Paige verbally kicked off. 'Mike, bring *Jupiter* to shadow us, please.' He pressed a keypad and connected to Marge on *Mercury*. 'Marge, any update?'

'We can see some of the fissures from where we are and have an excellent side-scan image as well. We have taken a new measurement, and the fissure has opened eighteen millimetres since the explosion and elongated by well over 112 metres,' Marge explained. 'When will it go? No way of saying, but we are picking up continuous seismic activity which were not before, so the whole area is substantially unstable and will definitely go sooner rather than later.'

'Ensure Lisa keeps *Mercury* a safe distance from the seamount and parallel to any tsunami path. We don't need to take any undue risks,' Charles said. 'Now, looking at the current fissure and area affected, how large would any resultant tsunami be?'

'Huge. We have estimated the area to be a mass of a one-cubic-kilometre of rock, which would be, let me think, around three billion tonnes falling into two kilometres of water. To project the wave height, I would need to run the computer simulation but would hazard a guess at not less than 100 feet and a velocity of 800 kilometres an hour. I'll run the program now and see what the result is.'

'Thanks, Marge, that's just six minutes from the get-go to impact,' Charles said, looking over at Anne. 'I don't think Keith and James can adjust the acoustic wave that fast, so send them everything you have, and tell them to program the acoustic-wave response to that. It will be better than no response.'

'Will do,' Marge replied. 'I'll send it now and get Lisa to move us out of the firing range and use the ROV to monitor the fissure.' The screen blinked off, and Charles cut the link and swung his chair around to face Haines and Paige on the other side of the library who were being guarded by Thomas, Connor, Miles and Ralph. 'Well, gentlemen, your little exploit with the president could cost the West Coast dearly, and please do not denigrate things further by denials. We have enough to place you on death row and impeach the president, and lower America's standing on the world stage lower than the Pacific Ocean Gyre that we are cleaning up.' He stood up and walked over to them. 'The only questions we have for you two are simple ones. One simple question each, if you like – the name of the financier in Brazil and your intentions with the weapons.'

He sat down in front of them and raised his glass of Cognac to his lips. 'Provide that name and the intention, and we will pass you into the safe custody of the CIA.' He looked at Haines. 'That's rather fitting, is it not? Refuse to provide the name and/or the intention and Thomas here will take you back downstairs with Connor and, one way or another, get it out of you. The choice is yours.' He sipped his Cognac and looked at the two quiet sullen faces. 'Oh, I almost forgot, no one knows you are on board this yacht, so there will be no rescue and also no repercussions if you disappear or, should I say, rendition you into nowhere.' Charles stood up and looked from Anne to Thomas to Max to Duke and back to Anne. He spun around to look back at Paige. 'Was it you who ordered the murder of Thomas and his squad of men? I would have a lot to fear if I were you. He has sworn to get retribution for those dead souls. I would not rate your chances if you were left in a room alone with him.'

Charles could plainly see that both men were more comfortable dishing out orders than taking them. They were certainly more used to sending men off to risk their lives than putting their own on the line.

'All right,' said Paige. 'I do not know the name of the man behind the money except that Haines feared him greatly. The build-up of weapons was for the president to build an arsenal on the quiet to replenish those lost to weapons treaties that have left the Unites States open to attack.'

'Oh come on,' Duke interrupted. 'No person in Brazil is going to help the United States president to rebuild his nuclear arsenal.'

'You may be right,' Haines said in a quiet, defeated voice, his eyes focused on the carpet. 'I do not know his name, but he had a thick Germanic accent, an old voice, but still very strong.'

'So what or how much does the president know about this?' Duke asked savagely.

'Only that we had access to money to rebuild the nuclear arsenal to protect the people of the United States,' Haines replied, his eyes still focused on the carpet.

'With you two out of the way, what will happen?' Max asked. 'You two were on your way to inspect the facilities.'

'I would imagine the Brazilian will contact the president directly,' Haines said.

Paige came more vocal. 'You don't even know who the guy is? Not even his name?' He looked at Haines with incredulous eyes.

'No, I never met him. He was always a voice on the phone. He always made the call,' Haines said. 'God, I was so stupid.' He started to break down. 'I needed the money. It all started so simply, and before I knew it, I was in way too deep and could not get out. Even with all the resources at my fingertips, there was nothing I could do.'

'So how do we find him?' Charles asked Max.

'How does he contact you?' Max asked Haines with cold eyes.

'Always on my cellular telephone,' he replied.

Thomas passed a black cellular telephone to Max. Max took it and looked at Haines. 'Is this it?' he asked, thrusting the phone under Haines's nose.

Haines lifted his head and looked at the handset and just nodded. Max stood up. 'I'll get a trace on the call log.'

Haines spoke. 'With all the resources of the CIA, don't you think I've tried that?'

'Maybe so, but you have no idea of the technological resources we have at our disposal,' Max spat.

Charles stood up and drained his Cognac and looked at Miles Channing. 'You guys take them away and lock them up in the secure room. Make sure they see nothing on route and cut power to the room.' He grinned at Max. 'See what you and the team can do with that thing.'

When the guards had left with Haines and Paige, Charles sat down with Duke and Anne. 'We need to put a call through to the vice-president. Steward, my coffee and my Cognac glass is empty, refresh all round.'

Duke put the call through and spoke to Ryan O'Hare who immediately found the vice-president.

'We have to be careful, Duke. The president must sense something is up. He's on edge and stalking the place like a hunter,' the vice-president said. 'I need to know what's happening with the seamount and the Nevada facilities.'

'Mr Vice-president, the seamount fissure has grown and is continuing to enlarge. We are continuing to monitor the situation on a second-by-second basis. We also do have a method by which we can reduce the impact on the Californian coastline. From your perspective, the more important issue is the use of those nuclear weapons. Both Paige and Haines have implicated the president by his agreement to enlarge the United States nuclear arsenal against all the world treaties.' Charles looked at Duke.

'I think the financier had something else in mind, not the defence of the United States,' Duke added.

'Especially if he's an ex-Nazi,' Anne said quietly.

Max returned and grabbed a coffee from the steward. 'Hi, VP,' he said, looking at the screen, 'I do believe that we may have a hit on who the financier is. We can link the phone that calls Haines to the record of calls made to the leaders of the Brazilian Drug Cartels. So that gives us a tangible link. Going one further, we have linked the calls from the drug cartels to the phone that calls Haines. A nice three-sixty, then taking the calls, times, satellite and surveillance imagery, we pulled up a picture of the guy. He is Gustav Axmann, was a leading member of the Nazi party, top Hitler aide who fled using the Odessa in – 1945. He has been linked to many terrorist groups, including Black September, The IRA, Al-Qaeda to name but a few. I think we can guess pretty accurately where those weapons would land up.'

'Gentleman, I must insist that the fewer people who know about this the better. We have a big clean-up to do,' the vice-president said. 'The president is obviously not in a fit state to lead the nation, and I need to bring the leader of the House of Representatives, Dennis Jarret, the White House counsel, the director of the White House Military Office, John Easton, and Clive Harris, the defence chief, into this conversation.' He looked over at Ryan. 'Get on to that straight away, will you? And Ryan, I know you're the president's chief of staff, and this must be at odds with your loyalties, but you are doing the right thing.'

'I know, sir, but thank you for saying so,' Ryan said, picking up the phone and starting to make calls, gathering all the people for an urgent immediate meeting that the vice-president had the power to convene.

Within twenty minutes, everyone was in the vice-president's office behind closed doors with a 'no interruption' order to the two guards standing outside. The vice-president opened the meeting by introducing everyone to Charles and Anne Langham and Max. They all knew Duke, so he just said hello to everyone. Without any preamble, the vice-president had Charles run through everything he had told him earlier and the images. After thirty minutes, the room fell very quiet.

'Well,' the vice-president said, 'now you know what we are up against. We need to remove the president from office and shut down the Nevada facilities and destroy those weapons without the truth coming out.'

'We can surround the Nevada facilities and put them in lock-down in an instant,' Clive Harris said. 'It should not draw attention as they are rather remote.'

'We can assist in that. We can sling a portable EMP unit beneath our Bell 525 and disable all power and communications just before you arrive,' Max said, smiling.

'You have that capability?' Harris asked.

'Don't ask,' cut in Charles. 'But yes, we can do that.'

'We have the power in this office to impeach the president and can write a press release that he has stepped down quietly for health reasons. We can keep him out of the way for quite a while on mental health grounds,' Jeannette Rouse, the legal counsel, advised; she was a trim, older woman with the aura of a bench judge and a stark face from many years of fighting in the law courts.

'He is currently in the Oval Office, trying to find Paige and Haines,' Ryan said.

'And where are they?' the vice-president asked Ryan.

'No one knows,' Ryan replied, crossing his fingers and not looking at the vice-president.

'I see and I think I understand.' The vice-president looked

questioningly at Ryan. 'Victor, John and Clive, I will need you to come with me to the Oval Office. Jeannette, I need you to complete the transfer of power and press release. John, we will need some of your guys and an enclosed vehicle at the side door to remove the president from the White House.'

'Where will the president go?' Jeannette asked.

'The Walter Reed Medical Centre, of course. I will talk to the Commander,' advised Clive. 'I know the guy very well, and after I explain things, he will understand. He is, of course, aware of the president's past problems.'

'Okay, let's get to it.' The vice-president placed his hands on the arms of the chair and heaved himself up.

The vice-president entered the Oval Office unannounced, with the others following closely behind to be confronted by a ragged-looking president whose tie was three quarters of the way down his shirt. His suit jacket was hanging off the side of the desk. His hair was a mess, and his eyes and mouth drawn. He carried on pacing the Oval Office. 'And what do you want?' he said, coming to a stop just inches from the vice-president's face.

'Mr President, it is with the deepest regret that I must carry out one of the hardest duties ever required by a vice-president. Sir, you are removed from office and will be taken under guard to the Walter Reed Medical Centre where you will be handed into the care of the Commanding Officer until further notice.'

The vice-president stepped to one side as John Easton and two of his armed White House Military officers came forward, each officer taking the president by an arm; John picked up the president's jacket and held it for him to put on as each military officer let go of an arm in turn. Ryan O'Hare came forward and tidied up the president's tie. 'There you are, sir, you look better now. This is for the best, sir. You have been under a lot of strain and have been led deeply astray,' Ryan said and stepped aside as the president was led out of the Oval Office.

Jeannette came in and walked over to the Oval Office desk, placing a piece of paper on the desk. 'I need you, Mr Vice-president, Victor and Ryan to sign where I have signed. This is the official transfer of power from the president to the vice-president.' In turn, they each signed, after which Jeannette took the signed paper and added the president's seal. 'I will now lodge this. Mr Christopher Johnson, you are now president.' She bowed and left the office.

A mobile phone rang. Ryan went to the Oval Office desk and picked up the handset. 'Hello, this is the president's phone, how can I help you?' he said.

'Where is the president? I must talk to him,' said a Germanic voice.

'Sir, I have a Germanic person on the president's personal mobile phone.'

'Okay, let me take it,' the new president said and took the handset from Ryan.

'To whom am I talking?' he asked, taking a seat behind the desk.

'You are not the president. I want to talk to the president. Put him on now.'

'I am the president of the United States. The previous president has stepped down,' Christopher Johnson, the ex-vice-president, said and then covered the microphone with his hand. 'Ryan, transfer the video call to Charles to this screen and get that Max chap to trace this call.' Ryan went to the console and transferred the connection through to the Oval Office.

'Well, well, I have a new pawn. You will listen and not interrupt me. I have an arrangement with the United States president, which is now you, for the supply of sixteen nuclear weapons. They are being manufactured in Nevada, and it is taking too long, and I want their manufacture speeded up. I will call you back in two days for the supply date.' The line went dead.

Max and Charles could be seen on the screen, staring into a laptop, when Max said, 'There he is. We have been tracing his phone every time he made a call since we targeted the drug cartel. We can take him out with our Brazilian friend. One thing at a time. Clive, when can you have your troops ready to hit both Nevada facilities?'

'Three hours, sir,' Clive Harris replied.

'Charles, how soon can you be ready with the helicopter device?'

Charles spoke quickly to Max before replying, 'We can fire the device in two hours and forty-five minutes from now.'

James looked over at Clive Harris. 'Well, let's do that now and disable any bombs and take all the personnel into custody for questioning, no exceptions.'

'Yes, sir. Max, call me as soon as you are ready to fire the device. I want to be fifty kilometre away when you do.'

'No worries, mate. I will configure for a narrow beam, and you should be safe at a kilometre's distance.'

'Bloody hell that's accurate. All right then, we will be closer in, less than fifty clicks, then ready for a fast entry as soon as you give the word that you have used the EMP. If you don't mind, Mr President, I will take my leave and get things moving,' Clive said as he started to leave the Oval Office.

The newly instated president said, 'Yes, please, the sooner we get control over those weapons the better. Now Mr Langham, let's turn our attention to this tsunami potential. What more can you tell me?'

'Mr President, it's a true and present threat to the West Coast. In layman's terms, eighty kilometres off the California coast lies the Davidson Seamount which is a mountain ridge 2,200 metres high, and its peak is 1,200 metres below sea level. A very large fissure has opened on the east side of the ridge and is slowly increasing in size due to the pair of explosions in the mining structures. If the fissure gives way, then the resultant landslide will cause a tsunami, and you will have only six minutes warning,' Charles said.

'How big will the wave be?'

'At this stage, we can estimate 100 feet. We are running a more accurate simulation now, but the thing is that the landslide could occur either now or tonight or tomorrow. I would suggest an orderly move back from the coast and all ships to leave port and move to deeper waters where the wave will ride underneath them.'

'Yes, yes. I will call an immediate emergency meeting of Homeland Security and set things in motion. Please keep me informed of any further developments.'

'Of course, I will, Mr President,' Charles said. 'Now what do you want us to do with Paige and Haines?'

'Well, legally, we cannot lose them overboard, although I must admit that would be my first choice,' the president said. 'Ryan, your thoughts? I know you've been working with Charles on these issues.'

Ryan looked at the president. 'The USS *Arleigh Burke* is currently embarking the people from the two submarines.

I would dump them on board her and then ship the lot off to Guantanamo Bay, awaiting trial for terrorism.'

'Charles, can you hold on to them until we can get the USS *Arleigh Burke* to you?'

'Sure thing. We will coordinate directly with the captain. Talk soon,' Charles said and ended the call. 'Okay, Max, you are on. Take Martin Deeks with you. Fire the shot, then get back here and take those two scumbags to the USS *Arleigh Burke*.'

'Okay, boss,' Max said and left the library and went forward to the bridge. 'Captain, I need Martin for an hour or two. We have a mission to undertake for Mr Langham and the United States president,' Max said, deferring to the captain rather than advising Martin directly even though he had the authority to do so.

The captain, John Whitcome, looked over at Martin and said, 'Martin, you heard the man. Off you go. Franklin, you can look after the technical duties for a while.' Martin got up and followed Max to the helipad. Franklin got down from his first officer's chair and walked across to the technical officer's area and scanned the screens to bring himself up to speed on all the instrument readings before settling back in the deep plush leather seat. 'Franklin, bring her slowly back to ten knots, please, ready for helicopter take-off, and send two deck crew to the helipad and keep them on standby on the helipad for her return,' the captain ordered.

Franklin lifted a handset and connected with the deck crew and sent them to the helipad. He then placed his right hand on the four throttle levers and eased them slowly back whilst keeping his eye on the digital speedometer. At fifteen knots, he released his grip from the two outer levers and eased the two inner throttles to the neutral position which gently slowed *Sundancer* to ten knots.

The captain touched one of the touchscreens and switched the view to show the helipad so he could monitor the helicopter's take-off. He watched the screen as the two deck crew released the landing gear and stepped back, while Max and Martin finished configuring the EMP device.

Max and Martin jumped into the cockpit and put on their helmets and headsets. The captain saw the rotors start spinning and rotating faster and faster until Max lifted the Bell 525 off the deck and crabbed sideways to port. Once clear of the yacht, he moved forward, passing the bridge where he turned and waved to the captain and first officer. 'Let's speed her up again,' the captain said to the first officer who once again grabbed the two middle throttles and eased them forward till their revolutions matched the two outer engines. He them gripped all four throttles and eased them forward till *Sundancer* was once again cruising at thirty-five knots.

Max looked at the coastline and, pointing to the ships moving below, said, 'Looks like everyone is heeding the warning and heading for deeper waters.'

'Quite a flotilla,' Martin replied as he watched a whole line of ships of all types leaving the port for deeper waters offshore. Luxury cruise liners, freighters and trawlers who were either moored in port or lying at anchor were leaving, escorted by navy and coastguard vessels. Lines of cars and trucks crowded the freeways from the coast heading inland; blue and red flashing lights lit up every junction. 'They are evacuating the immediate coastline,' Martin said into his headset.

Max looked across the cockpit. 'Let's hope they have enough time to get to higher ground. I heard Mr Langham say any tsunami will only take six minutes to arrive.' He banked the helicopter to starboard and increased speed towards the Nevada desert. They watched the lines of traffic snaking below them, and Max pulled more height to keep the news and police helicopters that were buzzing around far below them. Max leaned above his head and adjusted the radio frequency. 'Mr Harris, this is Max aboard *Bella*. We are ten minutes out and commencing arming of the device now.'

They watched as the ground below changed from a bustling metropolis to the barren landscape of desert with just the line of the blacktop snaking its way to the horizon.

Martin lifted a laptop on his lap and starting running through the sequence to start the EMP device, while Max concentrated on bringing the helicopter to the altitude required for optimum firing of the EMP. 'Mr Harris, we are five minutes to firing.'

Martin concentrated on the laptop's screen. He could hear the exchanges between Max and Clive Harris, but saw no need to engage in the conversation. Looking out of the cockpit window, he could see that they had just flown over a host of army vehicles and some helicopters.

'I'm commencing countdown in two minutes,' Max said, as he slowed the helicopter down and aimed for a point exactly equidistant between both targeted facilities where he would hover while the EMP device was fired. He could see plenty of cars, vans and trucks parked outside. The facilities were in the middle of nowhere. A couple of security guards came out of the guard house and looked up.

Martin said, 'Max, increase altitude by 200 metres.'

Max gently increased the altitude and watched as one of the

guards pressed his shoulder microphone. Max looked across at Martin and said, 'Firing in ten, nine, eight, seven, six, five.' Martin nodded. Max continued the countdown, 'Four, three, two, one, fire.' He watched as Martin hit the enter button. The only sign that anything had occurred was the information on the laptop screen, Martin confirming the shot and the guard repeatedly pressing his microphone in a frantic attempt to talk to someone. 'All good. Our job is done. You guys can go in,' Martin said to Max and Harris.

'Thank you, gentlemen,' Harris replied. Max increased the Bell 525's speed and banked sharply, heading for *Sundancer* without waiting to see Harris and his military force close in and raid both facilities.

Chapter Twenty-Nine

The Brazilian Connection

The elderly gentleman paced the room, his hands clasped behind his back. His black double-breasted suit was unbuttoned, showing a fancy waistcoat with a gold pocket-watch chain. The two younger, late-middle-aged men, sitting around the large heavy mahogany conference room table that matched the heavy chairs upholstered with dark-red cracked leather, looked pale and worried as they sat in the air-conditioned office. Both wore well-cut expensive dark-blue suits and tailored shirts, one a crisp white and the other a pale yellow. They had been called into this extraordinary meeting as news of the attacks had surfaced. They had seen him like this a few times before in their long association and rise to the top in his organisation and knew that whatever happened, many heads would roll – not that many were left after the raids in the early hours of the morning when all the major drug lords, their lieutenants and their families were killed along with their cannabis and opium fields.

They both knew that the deep-sea mining facilities had been lost, and worse still, the ore vessel and their contacts high up in the United States government and the president had disappeared.

Now their leader was about to call the newly installed president again but was not expecting him to play ball after the result of the last conversation. So they watched anxiously as he paced the floor, planning the call. He stopped and looked out of the penthouse window across the city that lay spread out before him. 'I think we should call our man in the Nevada weapons facility and see if he can round up enough of his contacts to take over the guards and take control of the facility.' His voice was strong and deeply accented.

He turned slowly and looked at his two lieutenants. 'You two are quiet, too quiet. Why did we not know about the attacks? We have moles in all the government agencies and armed forces, so someone somewhere must have known,' he said, his voice rising just shy of a shout. 'So why did they not tell us, warn us?'

'They did not hear anything. They say it was not carried out by any of their agencies. Word is that it was carried out by external agencies and contractors and was not even planned by Brazilian agencies. They have not had time to converse and agree stories which backs up what they are saying,' the lieutenant in the yellow shirt spoke first.

'Humbug. Someone knows who these people are,' the old man said, pulling a chair back and sitting down, resting his arms on the table and clasping his hands.

'The attacks were so fast that no one had time to call. Were they missiles from offshore warships or aircraft, we don't know?' the white-shirted man said.

'Lassen sie es sein. Leave it be,' he corrected himself and picked up his mobile phone. 'I will call the president. One of you can call our Nevada facility contact, and the other can find out the state of our organisation.' He dismissed them with a wave of the hand. 'Auf wiedersehen, bis spatter,' he said and pulled up the contact list on his phone and hit the dial button, placing the phone to his ear. He stood up and walked to the heavy wooden bar and poured himself a large schnapps and downed it in one go. The two lieutenants opened the door and left, but not before seeing their boss down the schnapps. 'It's not even ten in the morning, and he's downing the hard stuff. Things are real bad. Might be an idea to leave town!' The man in the yellow shirt said.

'Leave the country more like,' said the other man as he closed the door quietly behind them.

'Mr President, why have you not called me as I asked?' the old man said in a brisk Teutonic voice.

'I don't know who you think the hell you are. I do not answer to you, neither do I, for that matter, need to talk to you about anything.' The president looked at Ryan who, by twirling his hand, indicated to the president to continue talking before turning back to the laptop that was tracing the call.

'You will do as I say, Mr President. I have a lot of powerful friends and can tell you now that I hold your country to ransom with weapons that will cause great destruction.'

The president laughed quietly. 'Oh, I don't think so. You have lost your links into my government agencies, your drug cartel is in shatters and the weapons have now been returned to my direct control. You have nothing.' He looked at Ryan who gave the thumbs up. 'You are just a broken old man without any power. So, as I have said to you before, I have no need to talk to you.' The president ended the call, and as he turned to Ryan, he could hear him talking to someone on his mobile.

'So that confirms your location target. Great. When will the Brazilian authorities be apprehending him? That soon? Great, I will tell the president. Cheers, Keith,' Ryan said and then turned to the president. 'That was Keith, one of Charles Langham's team. The Brazilian security services have the building surrounded and are entering as we speak. That old fox Max had the location dead on.'

'I want him extradited and bumped off to Guantanamo Bay to stand trial for terrorism. Speak to the chief justice and arrange the extradition. So now we have just that darn tsunami left to contend with.' The president sat down. 'Get the Cabinet together in the Situation Room immediately, and I'll want an update from Homeland Security on the evacuation.'

'Right away, sir.' Ryan picked up his laptop and left the Oval Office for his own room to arrange the meeting.

The president stretched his arms above his head and yawned. *Been a long day*, he thought. He swung his arms down and pressed the intercom button. 'Get me Charles Langham,' he said and released the button.

The phone rang, and the president picked it up and heard the voice of Charles Langham. 'Mr President, I hear that the German escaped custody, but the Nevada operation went well.'

'Oh, I was not aware of that Mr Langham...' the president said but was interrupted before he could continue.

'Call me Charles, please. It's less formal,' Charles said.

'Okay, Charles it is then. Yes, the Nevada facilities were secured without a shot being fired, and only a couple of security guards had any advance warning that something was about to happen, and that was only because they saw the helicopter.'

'So just two battles remain – the potential tsunami and capturing the German,' Charles said.

'Tell me, Charles, have the two US citizens at the centre of this affair been transferred to the USS *Arleigh Burke*?'

'Not yet. Max and his team are removing the EMP system and then will refuel. We have made sure the USS *Arleigh Burke* is out of the dual-impact zone which will be worse than a rogue wave. We are about to head out of the path ourselves.'

'How are you monitoring the fissure then?' asked the president.

'I have an ROV operated by one of our submarines which is lying south of the fissure, out of harm's way, plus we have sensors in the water that we are monitoring.'

Ryan stuck his head into the Oval Office and said, 'Everyone is in the Situation Room, sir.'

'Okay, I am on my way,' he said to Ryan before speaking back into the phone. 'Charles, I have a meeting about the tsunami in the Situation Room. I will call you from there.'

'Right' was all Charles said and ended the phone call.

The president left the Oval Office with Ryan and made his way to the Situation Room. 'You know I reckon Charles used the EMP on our fleet, don't you?' the president asked Ryan.

Ryan laughed. 'More than likely, but the previous president did send the fleet to attack him and his secret army to assassinate him, so he had good cause.'

'We could do with that technology within our armed forces. I will have to discuss it with him.' They walked the rest of the way in silence. Ryan thought to himself that Charles would never give the EMP system to anyone who planned to use it as a weapon of war. He thought of how the fortunes of America had changed with the impeaching of the president and the loss of Glenn Haines and William Paige, neither of which had been made public and his timely change of allegiance from the president to the vice-president who was now the president. How will the Nevada operation be covered up and the disabling of US warships? All these issues will be discussed and covered up one way or another over the next few weeks. He would be part of those meetings and part of the lies developed for the public good, democracy at work. No wonder Duke left politics. His thoughts came back to the moment as they entered the Situation Room, and all those around the table stood and applauded as the newly appointed president entered the room. Ryan closed the door behind them and took his place at the table beside the president. 'Please be seated. Ryan, get Charles Langham back on the line,' the president said. 'Ladies and gentlemen, we have been through a major crisis and now face another.' He looked at Steve Rosenberg, the director of Homeland Security. 'Steve, please give us an update.'

'Mr President, the immediate coastline identified by Mr Langham's organisation has been cleared back to one and a half miles inland. We are still evacuating people beyond that point. All ships capable of leaving for deeper water have left and are mostly out of the direct line of the tsunami.'

Chapter Thirty

The Tsunami

Marge sat at the same seat aboard *Mercury* in the confines of the command centre, staring at the same two screens at the same scene and same figures, looking for any change that would indicate the rock wall would give way. She looked carefully at the figures on the screen. 'Lisa, if *Sundancer* is still where I think it is, tell them to get the hell out of there now!' she shouted across the command centre without taking her eyes off the screen.

Lisa called up Charles Langham who was sitting in the library with Duke, Anne, Max and *Sundancer's* captain, John Whitcome. Charles answered the call by splitting the screen that was showing the president's meeting in the Situation Room. 'Charles, Marge says you are to get out of the area now,' she said.

'Thanks, Lisa. Tell Marge we are on our way,' he replied, then said, 'Captain, get us moving now to the fail-safe point, full power pull no punches.'

The captain was already leaving his chair after hearing Lisa. 'I'm on to it.'

'Max, prep the helicopter ready to launch so we can get a bird's-eye view of this thing,' Charles said.

On the bridge, the captain sat in his chair. 'Gentlemen,' he said to the first officer, Franklin, and Martin Deeks, the technical officer, 'we are heading to the fail-safe point. Martin, keep a close eye on the engine readings and stabiliser positions. Franklin, full power all engines.' The captain held the joystick and guided the super yacht into a tight turn as Franklin held all four throttles and eased them smoothly to the stops. *Sundancer* leaned into the turn, the bow lifting as it pushed a wave of white water out of its way and left a long turmoil of white froth behind her, as the water was ejected at high speed by the water jet propulsion systems. The lean could be felt through the yacht and left no one on board under anything other than the indication that this was an urgent high-speed turn.

Max, walking to the glass door that led to the helipad, kept his balance with consummate skill whilst speaking into a handset, rounding up two deck crew. He climbed into the Bell 525 and sat in the pilot seat. At the touch of a few switches, the dash screens came to life. He touched the screens and configured the helicopter for take-off and turned on the video cameras. He jumped down and spoke to the two deck crew. 'I will be required to do an immediate take-off at any time, so I need you guys constantly available. While we wait, give the windscreen a clean and rig the landing clamps for quick release,' he said, his voice slightly raised to counter the noise from the helicopter engine and *Sundancer's* power plants.

'I think we will wait until we are running straight,' said one of the deck crew, grabbing a handrail as *Sundancer* rose, then fell sideways as she encountered the rolling sea that she was churning up as she turned around.

'Okay, but get to it as soon as you can,' Max said and returned to the library that was a haven of quiet electric energy, walked over to the steward and got himself a Cognac. As he turned, he could see and hear Charles in conversation with the president and his team through the large display screen, while on a smaller screen he could see Marge still staring at two screens; although he could not see her face, he knew her hairstyle. He stood behind Charles, Anne and Duke, bracing himself against the movement of *Sundancer*. Suddenly, the sound of Marge shouting cut through every other conversation. 'Keith, track and activate the auto response on the acoustic device now!' she shouted. 'Charles, I hope you're getting the hell out of there because when the two waves hit, well, you've seen the simulation! The rock face is going to go any minute. The fissure is opening, and we have lots of rock fall. It's about to go!' she continued, turning to face the screen.

'Poised and ready, system is active and at critical mass and ready to fire as soon as the computer picks up the tsunami,' Keith confirmed calmly from the Kermadec underwater base.

'Mr President, I assume you heard that. If our device works, we should counter the tsunami and negate its effect on the West Coast,' Charles said. 'Max, get airborne.'

Max drained his Cognac. 'Sure thing, boss,' he said and made his way to the helipad.

Anne got up. 'I think I'll check our position with the captain.' But she could not get to the door as she heard both Marge and Keith raise the alarm. Marge broke through first. 'It's started! The whole side is crashing into the depths! We have lost all vision from the ROV due to sediment in the water. Set the ROV to station-keeping hover.'

'We are on a seventy-eight-second countdown to initiation. We are at full power and ready for the shot. Fifty seconds, all boards are green. Simulation still running, and all looks good for negation of tsunami. Twenty seconds, and all still green.' Keith pressed some button and flicked some switches. 'We have initiated video feed from the device. Ten seconds. Countdown finalising and last diagnostics run, all in the green. Firing now. We have initiation and firing sequence completion.' Keith sat back in his seat and sighed. 'Well, we will know in one minute and twenty-three seconds if it has worked. We are tracking; both waves and wavelengths look equal.'

Anne came back into the library and stood and looked at Charles. 'We will not be totally clear, according to the captain. We will be at the very edge of the impact zone.' Her voice was cut off by a siren sounding throughout the yacht.

'This is the captain. All crew to emergency stations, and secure all bulkhead doors. Would all passengers please put on life vests and hold on tight. All exterior doors and open windows will be closed automatically. Thank you.'

The library went quiet as the steward handed everyone an inflatable life vest. Charles stood up. 'I think we should all go up to the star deck. We'll be safe there and get a good view of what's going on, hopefully in the distance.' Turning to the screens that showed the president and Marge, he said, 'I will transfer your calls to there, and we should also be able to send you a feed from the helicopter.' He headed for the circular staircase, pressed a button that opened the sealed hatch at the top of the staircase and started up, followed by Anne, Duke, Thomas and Connor. Charles stood on the star deck just in time to see the Bell 525 slip sideways from the helipad to run alongside *Sundancer* before accelerating and pulling away. The others joined him on the star deck and looked around. Charles sat in one of the chairs and pressed a few buttons to bring up the president and Marge on to the large display screen. Pressing another button, he spoke to the captain on the bridge. 'John, are we at the fail-safe point?'

'Keith has given us the fail-safe coordinates which we won't quite get to. I will be doing a high-speed 180-turn to starboard any second.'

'Thank you, Captain. Did everyone hear that? Make sure you are holding on. We may be 180 metres long, but we have 75,000 horsepower, and this turn will be more dramatic than the last,' Charles said to everyone on the star deck.

Sirens once again sounded around the yacht. 'High-speed turn. Please ensure that you are seated or holding on to a handrail,' the captain's voice sounded through the yacht as once again *Sundancer* entered a high-power turn, leaning over to starboard as the bow sliced a new path through the waves. There was no change to the engine noise as the bow rose and the huge yacht forced her way to starboard, churning up water into waves of foaming white. *Sundancer's* decks flattened out, and she completed the turn and slowed down, the bow easing down and creating a large bow wave. Everyone on the star deck faced forward, looking for the confluence of the two waves. Miles Channing and Ralph Cohen came out through the hatch and joined the group looking forward over the bow.

Charles looked at the panoramic view that the star deck provided. The blue sky with just a few wispy clouds and the odd vapour trail contrasted with the blue-green ocean. The waters around *Sundancer* were calming down from their white water and lapping waves as the captain slowed the forward progress. 'Everyone stay behind the glass windscreen. I'm going down to the bridge.' On his way, he had a sudden thought. 'Miles, where are Haines and Paige?'

'They are locked in their cabin,' Miles answered. 'They don't have good sea legs.'

The bridge was quiet as the captain, first mate and technical officer concentrated on the expansive view and clusters of display screens. 'How are things, John?' Charles asked as he looked out of the windscreens.

'Any second now we should see two large vertical cliffs of water appear as the tsunami and our generated wave impact each other. We estimate about four kilometres to our port side. The three of us have looked and studied the simulations carried out by Keith and Marge, so we know roughly what to expect and how to handle it, given that we cannot get far enough out of the impact zone,' he said, his eyes switching back and forth from Charles to the windscreen.

'Can *Sundancer* handle it?'

'Yes, of course, she can. It's how we handle her that matters. We need to accelerate fast at the right time in the right direction, and that's what we are waiting for. Currently, we are idling along at five knots. We are keeping the stabilisers deployed at the angle estimated from Keith's data,' the captain explained.

'Sir, look, it is starting,' the first officer, Franklin, said quietly. In the distance, around three kilometres away, Franklin could see through his binoculars the ocean begin to rise inextricably. A bulge topped with white foaming waters, as far as the eye could see. Franklin estimated the bulge to be 250 metres high; he watched, transfixed, as the wave reached its peak and started to collapse in a broil of frothing white foam. The water rushing down both sides of the huge bulge, like the wave a surfer would love to come across and get a thrill riding down. Franklin felt nervous and unsure for the first time in his life. That he knew they would be deliberately turning into this maelstrom made his stomach churn over even though he knew that it was the safest and best approach. He placed his binoculars back into their holder and sat back in his seat. He heard Charles Langham talking calmly to the captain, and from the looks of it, neither seemed overly worried about *Sundancer's* capabilities.

'Time to get going,' the captain said. He touched the joystick and slowly turned *Sundancer* towards the approaching wave. 'Fifty per cent power, if you please, Franklin. Martin, confirm that we are watertight and go on all systems,' he said. He could feel the power coming on as *Sundancer* moved to line up the quickly oncoming wave. He heard Martin confirm all green, but his mind was calculating angles and speeds.

'How high do you think that wave is?' he asked Charles, glancing sideways.

'By the time it reaches us, I reckon it will be down to thirty, maybe twenty plus metres,' Charles replied. 'A little less than the simulation, I think, which is good.'

'Sounding the alarm,' the captain said just as *Sundancer's* bow pierced the wave and reared up. 'Full power on all engines, if you please,' he said to Franklin. Instantly, *Sundancer* pushed herself forwards and up the wave. Charles hung on to the grab rail as torrents of water exploded over the bow and across the decks, washing the bridge windscreens with tons of water initiating the automatic wipers and obscuring all vision. The star deck was inundated with torrents of water like one would expect in a tropical thunderstorm. Everyone was soaked through to the skin. As the water cascaded down the decks, the view from the bridge windscreen, which was still sparkling with water that was being wiped away by the wipers, was that of a blue sky. The bow hung for a second before finally cresting the wave.

'Quarter power, please,' the captain called as he deftly operated the joystick, controlling *Sundancer's* movements. 'Sounding alarm,' he called as once again *Sundancer* pitched downwards and rode to the bottom of the wave, forcing water once again over her bows and down the decks. 'Adjust stabilisers, Martin,' he called as *Sundancer* tried to heave herself up under the enormous weight of water on her decks. 'Increase power to half-throttle,' he said, looking at Franklin. *Sundancer's* bow finally lifted as the four engines drove her forward. 'Full power, if you please,' the captain called, and *Sundancer*, under the full power of all four engines, broke free and levelled out of the surface, water cascading down her sides from all four decks.

'Bet the swimming pool will need emptying and refilling,' Charles quipped to break the tense atmosphere that filled the bridge.

'Reduce speed to ten knots,' the captain said and then pressed two buttons on his console. 'Max, you are free to land. What's the view like from up there?'

'That was pretty amazing. The confluence of the two waves was spectacular beyond belief. *Sundancer* was quite a sight as she dug in and then broke free. Charles should rename her *Wavedancer*,' Max said over the speaker system.

'No way, Max,' Charles said. 'What are the waves doing now?'

'Petering out. The coastline was hit, but nothing different from a typical pacific storm. Coming in to land now.'

'Captain, once Max has landed, take us into San Francisco Bay and set anchor. I'd better see how they are on the star deck,' Charles said as he left the bridge, breathing a deep sigh of relief that the technology worked and that Keith and Marge got their figures right. His thoughts ran through the period of time that had got him to this point and how he was going to fully square things away with not only the new United States president but also Kim Lee Hoon, Secretary General of the United Nations. Well, time would tell. He reached the star deck, having got a bit wet as a trickle of water ran down the stairs as he opened the hatch. Everyone was soaked through to the skin but all were in very good humour.

'Boy, what a rush!' said Duke. 'I might be soaked through, but when those waves hit, it was an incredible sight, and *Sundancer* performed amazingly well. At one time, I thought you guys had bitten off more than you could chew.'

'Well, you might have thought it was a rush. I just want to get changed and have a gin and tonic, a large one,' Anne said, moving over and holding on to Charles. 'I really thought we had pushed our luck too far.'

Charles held Anne tight. 'Well, it's just a nice cruise to San Francisco, then a quick flight to Washington.' He kissed her on the forehead. 'Go and get changed, and I'll bring you the G and T.'

Half an hour later, Charles and Anne sat in the quiet of the library with the door closed and called the president of the United States. When Christopher Johnson, the president, came on the screen, Charles could see Ryan O'Hare beside him. 'Well, Charles, Anne, you did it. You neutralised the tsunami. We have a lot to thank you for,' Johnson said with a broad grin on his face.

'Mr President, we have quite a bit of cleaning up to do. May I suggest that Anne, Max, Duke, Thomas and I come to Washington to discuss these issues behind closed doors? I'm talking about stabilisation of the seamount, your disabled warships, Thomas and Connor and their status, the acoustic device and the cartel tie-up, to name a few,' Charles suggested as he watched Ryan nodding and whispering in the president's ear.

'Good idea. Air Force One is at Nellis Air Force Base and is at your disposal to bring you to Washington. You can safely leave your Bell 525 there.' He looked over at Ryan and said, 'See to it, please.' Then he looked back at Charles and said, 'I look forward to meeting you all and welcoming you to the Oval Office.'

'We will land at Nellis at ten tomorrow morning,' Charles said.

'Great. Air Force One will be ready for you. Oh, have you still got those two United States citizens with you?'

'No, after the wave, Max took them to the *Arleigh Burke*. They were suffering badly from sea sickness.'

'Well, that's their hard luck. See you tomorrow. Goodbye until then,' the president said as the screen reverted back to its screensaver which showed the view from the bow camera.

'I think it's time for a swim before dinner,' Charles said and stood up. 'You coming?' he said to Anne.

'You bet I am.'

Chapter Thirty-One

The Oval Office and Off Again

Sitting in the Oval Office, Anne admired the cream carpet and parquet flooring. The group was sitting on settees either side of the large coffee table, with the president sitting in his armchair atop the seal of the president of the United States. Anne, Charles and Max occupied one settee, and Duke, Thomas and Connor on the other. Ryan O'Hare also joined the group but sat opposite the president.

'Not many private individuals get to fly on Air Force One. I hope you enjoyed the flight?' President Johnson asked, as a member of his staff served coffee.

'I would have thought you would have the latest 747-8i, not the outdated 747-200b,' said Max, again showing his cavalier attitude to authority and status. Charles and Anne both nearly spilt their coffee.

'Max, Air Force One was a wonderful aircraft,' Charles said, attempting to tone down Max's comments.

'That may be so, but the electronics were outdated, and it was not as luxurious as our 747-8i,' Max continued.

'Charles, it's okay; Max is right, of course. But we have federal budgets to contend with, Max, and Air Force One is not due to retire for a few years yet. I have heard the rumours about the 747-8i and A380 you guys have, and I would love to see them one day, not to mention *Sundancer*. I heard directly from Alex Boyed, who is the commanding officer of the USS *Eisenhower* which became becalmed at sea, when I directed him to explain to me personally what happened to one of our most advanced aircraft carriers, and he said his XO could not stop talking about *Sundancer*.'

'Mr President, you are welcome aboard *Sundancer*, with the First Lady, of course, for a long weekend any time you wish,' Anne said as she patted Charles on the leg. 'Charles and I would look forward to that.'

'Thank you. I might just take you up on that.'

'If we may turn to business, Mr President? We need to stabilise the seamount, and my team believes two detonations will be sufficient if placed at the right points. The danger, of course, is another tsunami, but we can counter that once again. This folder provides your naval engineers with the size and exact location for each explosive device and contact details to coordinate the explosions with our team to counter any tsunami and minimize damage to wildlife,' Charles said, handing a folder to the president.

'Thank you, Charles,' the president said and, holding the folder in his hands, leant forward with this elbows resting on his knees. 'Tell me, Charles, honestly, did you disable the USS *Eisenhower* and the *Pacific Fleet*?'

Charles sat back in his chair. 'Mr President, the USS *Eisenhower* was sent with specific instructions to attack my yacht. The *Pacific Fleet* was also sent for the same purpose. As a matter of self-defence, we disabled those vessels without harming anyone on board. The technology we used was the same as that used to disable the seamount mining operations and the ore-carrying vessel, but different to that used to counter the tsunami,' Charles explained. 'You see, we are a passive organisation who will only use force passively. Regrettably, as you are no doubt aware, in Brazil, all the drug-cartel families and their associates were killed. There was no other way. Max spent months working covertly with the Brazilian government on the best tactics to use to minimise collateral damages, and the results show he did a sterling job.'

'Yes, I have seen the reports. I understand that the profits from those drug cartels went to the German who, in turn, used it to bribe Haines and Paige?' the president asked.

That is correct." Duke said. "Haines had money issues from an expensive divorce and, in the end, became reliant on the money for his increasingly extravagant lifestyle. He later hooked Paige in when he realised he could not go it alone in achieving the more ambitious demands of Axmann and then they together manipulated President Read into building a secret nuclear arsenal to defend the Unites States, not knowing that Read planned to use them to destroy foreign oilfields and that the intent of Gustav Axmann and his cohorts was to destroy the United States and, at the same time, take out all the heads of states or their ambassadors to the United Nations."

'That means there are more of Axmann operatives right here in the United States,' President Johnson said.

'Yes, and we have identified most of them,' Max said, smiling. 'He had a long list of American phone numbers on his mobile phone, both landlines and cellphones, and Haines had just as many.'

'Do I want to know how you got those numbers?' Johnson asked.

'Nope, you don't. Needless to say, we traced the numbers to their addresses and the cellular to their locations through GPS. All the data was supplied to your FBI and Homeland Security, who are rounding up the suspects,' Max said.

'Max, I wish I knew how you manage to do everything so quickly, faster than my own security teams can do with all their high-tech equipment,' Johnson said, looking first at Max, then at Charles.

'I wish we could show you, but the safety and security of our organisation comes first. When you visit *Sundancer*, we can give you a tantalising taste,' said Charles.

'Believe me, it's darn impressive and way beyond anything we have, eh, had,' said Duke, correcting himself, having remembered that he had left the United States government.

'Duke, you are welcome back into the heart of the government. We would love to have you back. As for you, Thomas and Connor, you were just following orders and are totally exonerated of any responsibility for actions taken under orders of the previous administration and president,' Johnson said, his face full of sincerity. 'You are free to leave and take up you prior positions as the president's private army, although I fear that you will have to rebuild your team.'

'Thank you, Mr President. If you will excuse us, we have a lot of work to do if we are to rebuild the team for your protection,' Thomas said, standing up. He walked over to Charles and shook his hand. 'Sir, it was an honour serving with you and working with your team, and I hope we get to work together sometime in the future. Anne, it was a pleasure meeting you.' He kissed her on both cheeks. He turned to Max. 'Max, boy, you know some tricks, and I only wish I had more time to spend with you. I could learn a lot,' he said, slapping Max on the back. With that, he and Connor saluted the president and left the Oval Office. Thomas was proud that the new president wanted him to lead his secret army. He was happy that Connor was with him, but sad at the loss of such great men who had made up his team.

'Mr President, I will be staying with Charles and his organisation. There is a lot more that I can achieve working outside of the government bureaucracies than within them. But thank you for the vote of confidence,' said Duke, interlocking his fingers and resting his chin on his hands.

'Duke, you will be sorely missed, but I must respect your decision and look forward to your input into the environmental working party as my independent advisor, if that's okay with you and Charles.'

'Sure, Mr President, it will be an honour,' Duke said, his demeanour becoming increasingly happy as the meeting progressed.

'Mr President, do I take that to mean that the Unites States will take a serious lead in environmental issues from now on?' Charles asked, placing his coffee cup on the table.

'Yes, we will, and I believe that your organisation has a lot to offer not only the United States but also the United Nations and the world. You have technologies that will help us all to understand more fully the impact we humans are having on the environment and how we can offset those effects and, more importantly, avoid causing them in the first place.'

'That is great news. We have ongoing work in both the Amazon and Indonesia to cease the destruction of the rainforest and build on our reforestation work, plus many famine-sustainable relief efforts and a full programme on marine research. Having the United States on board with us will be very welcomed. You are aware, of course, that we work very closely with Scripps Institution of Oceanography and Woods Hole Oceanographic Institution, right?'

'No, I was not aware of that. I will give them my full approval and support to continue to do,' Johnson said.

'We also have some mopping up to do from this last operation. The Hawaiian office that was used to transfer the funds from the Swiss bank accounts and provide a legitimate face to the ore vessel needs pursuing. There is another vessel and two submersibles unaccounted for, plus Gustav Axmann and his cohorts still at large. I wonder what their next target for attack will be,' Max said, joining in the conversation again. 'From the pictures I saw, the two vessels had almost identical super structures, which means they can carry out similar activities, and with two submersibles on the loose, what are they doing?'

'I agree we have grave cause for concern until we round up the missing vessels and this Axmann and his men. I will have Homeland Security distribute his picture to all ports and Interpol and get a team into the Hawaiian office,' Johnson said.

'Can you guys help us with the ore vessel and submersibles?' Ryan O'Hare asked Charles.

'We will keep a watch out. That's all we can do,' Charles answered. 'Max will keep you updated on anything we come across, Ryan, and thanks for believing in us during this operation. Without that, who knows how many people could have died.'

'Thanks, I had no choice with all the evidence you guys had,' Ryan said gratefully.

'Well, I think we ought to be heading home to *Sundancer*. We have a lot to do,' said Charles, standing up and walking over to the president who stood as Charles held out his hand. 'It's been good to see you and have this opportunity to talk,' he said. 'Clear Thomas and Connor's names and Duke's, of course,' Charles continued.

'The thanks are from the people of the United States,' Johnson said.

Ryan O'Hare led the way from the Oval Office to the waiting helicopter to ferry the group back to Air Force One for the trip to San Francisco.

Back on board *Sundancer*, the captain greeted them as they disembarked from the Bell 525. 'Weigh anchor, and let's head for the Kermadec base, a nice gentle cruise as the weather forecast is clear all the way,' Charles said. 'Where are *Jupiter* and *Mercury* and the other assets?'

'They are heading south for Kermadec. *Launch One* has left port and is heading for Auckland. Both the Lear and 747 are about to take off and head for Auckland as well. The A380 is still unloading famine relief and will return to Auckland once she's unloaded,' explained the captain, John Whitcome.

'*Sundancer* looked clean as we came in for the landing,' Anne commented.

'Yes, the crew have scrubbed her from top to bottom while you were away. Dinner is ready by the pool. The chef thought a pool-side barbecue was in order.'

After getting changed, Charles and Anne made their way to

the main deck. Charles was aware that *Sundancer* was under way on just the two outer engines for the gentle cruise home. The sky was a dark blue with stars just starting to become visible. The external LED deck lights were aimed in such a way that the light lit the deck and fittings without upsetting the view of the sky. Charles turned on one of the main external screens and left the communications channel open. Duke and Max arrived. 'So, a nice cold Tiger beer for me, I think. What does everyone else want?' Max asked and made his way over to the outside galley and bar area and asked the steward for a Tiger beer.

'I'll have one of those,' Duke replied, and Anne decided on a nice cool Pinot Gris and Charles joined the men in a Tiger beer.

As they sat around the teak table, two stewards started to serve the first course. The display chimed, Charles pressed a few keys, and Marge appeared on the display. 'Charles, we have a problem...'

The end till the next installment called *The Atlantic Affair*.

About the Author

Gary Paul Stephenson

Born in London, England to a New Zealand father and English mother, Gary thoroughly enjoyed weekends away on his father's boat on the river Thames and South of France. He moved out of London to the Bedfordshire country side, preferring the quiet of the country to the hustle and bustle of the city. Becoming a member of the RSPB, owning a border collie and foraging for Marabella plums, Elderflowers and Blackberries all meant many long country walks. Later a move to Cumbria and the Lake District then south to Cheshire where membership of Chester Zoo was a given. A holiday to see the land of his father resulted in a move to New Zealand where favourite pastimes include wine making, gardening, propagating shrubs, growing vegetables and looking after two house rabbits. Gary is married has 3 children, two moved to New Zealand and one remains in England. With a career starting in sales, Gary crossed the desk taking a role in Purchasing, he rose through the ranks of Supply Chain Management in many international companies, becoming a frequent traveller through Europe, Mexico, America and the Far East where he still has many friends.

With the diagnosis of Multiple Sclerosis in 2008 life started to change and in 2012 Gary sold his business and took to writing as a way of keeping his mind active. Writing and Multiple Sclerosis are a good match, you can work at a pace that fits with the cognitive fatigue. Writing is enjoyable and the books take on a life of their own.

CPSIA information can be obtained at www.ICGtesting.com
Printed in the USA
LVOW10s0103190716

496851LV00041B/465/P